GENERAL MEADE

GENERAL MEADE

— A NOVEL OF THE CIVIL WAR —

ROBERT KOFMAN

LION VALLEY
PUBLISHING

This is a work of historical fiction.

Published by Lion Valley Publishing, a Florida LLC
Miami, Florida

Edited and Designed by Girl Friday Productions
www.girlfridayproductions.com
Editorial: Alexander Rigby, Clete Smith,
Michelle Horn, Sharon Turner Mulvihill
Design: Paul Barrett
Image Credits: Cover art painting by Violet Oakley, "General Meade and the Pennsylvania Troops in Camp Before Gettysburg," with permission from the Pennsylvania Capitol Preservation Committee.

ISBN (Paperback): 978-1-7329910-0-2
e-ISBN: 978-1-7329910-1-9

First Edition

Printed in the United States of America

*This novel is dedicated to my wonderful, supportive,
and understanding wife, Rosa; to our beautiful
daughters Jenny, Abby, Miriam, and Becca; and to our
grandchildren Jordie, Spencer, Jacob, and Aaron.*

TABLE OF CONTENTS

LIST OF MAPS

ALL MAPS ARE NORTH FACING

AUTHOR'S NOTE

This novel covers many significant events of the last three years of the American Civil War from the perspective of Major General George Gordon Meade, who is best known for defeating Robert E. Lee at Gettysburg. The characters in this novel are historical figures. The thoughts and characterizations of individuals are fictional. Some of the dialogue is taken from historical documents, but most of it is fictional. All the military and political events occurred, but the descriptions and interpretations of these actions are the author's. Part of the story is told in Meade's own words in letters written to the person he most trusted: his wife, Margaret.

PROLOGUE

In 1860 Abraham Lincoln becomes the first Republican President, winning a four-candidate race with less than 40 percent of the vote. Southern states start seceding from the Union before Lincoln takes office. Eventually eleven states declare their independence from the United States, forming the Confederate States of America (CSA).

The CSA demands all Federal forts in the South be turned over to Confederate forces. Lincoln refuses, and in April 1861, the CSA attacks Fort Sumter in Charleston Harbor, beginning the Civil War.

The twenty-three states that remain loyal to the Union have a population of twenty-one million, of which five million are recent immigrants. The Confederacy has a population of nine million, of which three and a half million are slaves.

The Union has a vast advantage in industrial resources over the Confederacy, which has a largely agricultural economy.

In the spring of 1862, the Civil War is entering its second year. Only one major battle has been fought in the Eastern Theater: Bull Run in July 1861, a Rebel victory where Confederate general Thomas Jackson earns the nickname "Stonewall" for being immovable on the battlefield.

In the Western Theater, in February 1862, Ulysses S. Grant captures Fort Henry on the Tennessee River and Fort Donelson on the Cumberland River. In April 1862, Grant wins a bloody victory over the Rebels in Tennessee at the Battle of Shiloh.

After Bull Run, President Lincoln makes George McClellan his senior general. Based in Washington, McClellan creates the Union's largest fighting force, the Army of the Potomac. McClellan is slow to launch an offensive. After much prodding by Lincoln, in April 1862, McClellan transports his army by water to Fortress Monroe on the Virginia Peninsula and begins a campaign to capture the Rebel capital of Richmond.

THE SEVEN DAYS BATTLES

CHAPTER 1

The general strode past the manor house and down the hill. Six feet tall and very thin with alert blue eyes, he stopped and took in the panoramic vista. Below him flowed the blue waters of the Rappahannock. Across the river was the colonial town of Fredericksburg, with its stately church spires. He took off his spectacles and absentmindedly rubbed the bridge of his prominent Romanesque nose. His quiet reverie was interrupted by a familiar voice.

"George Meade, what are you in such deep thought about?"

Meade turned and saw the handsome face of his friend and fellow brigadier general, John Reynolds. "Hullo, Reynolds. Isn't this a beautiful spot?"

The two men warmly clasped hands.

"Meade, it's so tranquil here. It's hard to believe the people of Virginia view us as invaders."

"Did you know this was George Washington's boyhood home? He grew up on a farm right across the Rappahannock from Fredericksburg. I wonder what Washington would have done if he lived during these times. While he was a Virginian and a slaveholder, he was also the father of our country. Would Washington have remained loyal to the Union he was so instrumental in creating? *Qu'aurait-il fait?*"

"Only a cosmopolitan Philadelphian like you would think of a question like that in French." Reynolds looked across the river. "As the military governor of Fredericksburg, I've had a fair degree of contact with its citizens. And let me tell you, in that town, they're very pro *secesh*. They claim they are following in Washington's footsteps, rebelling against the tyranny of greedy, despicable Yankees." Reynolds laughed. "Their stereotypical views are kind of comical."

"That hateful caricature is the product of decades of venomous speeches by Southern politicians and hateful articles in Southern newspapers that paint Northerners as unsavory swindlers," Meade said angrily. "They have poisoned the minds of their citizens to view anyone living above the Mason-Dixon Line as evil incarnate!" Meade's face muscles tightened. "I have two sisters and a brother-in-law living in the South. Before the war, they talked about damn Yankees all the time."

"When I was the commandant of cadets at West Point, I saw first-hand the antagonism, the hostility, the deep-seated anger between the cadets from the South and the North." Reynolds's dark eyes shone with intensity. "I did my best to educate those young men that we're one country and that the army is a unifying national institution. I wasn't very convincing, because all my Southern cadets are now serving in the Confederate army."

"I told my Southern relatives that their arrogant political leaders' insistence on spreading slavery to new territories was going to tear the country apart. Their response was that without new slave states, the South would lose power in Congress and the Northern states would abolish slavery." Meade shook his head. "They would rather have their own country than stay in the Union. My sisters living in the South are secessionists; my nephews are fighting in Joe Johnston's Confederate army."

"I had similar discussions with Southern cadets. Some made the ludicrous argument that slavery is actually good for blacks. Sadly, they have more allegiance to their state and region than to the Union."

Meade took a watch out of his pocket. His beloved Margaret had given it to him. "Reynolds, it is time to meet the President."

They walked up the hill toward the stately redbrick Chatham Manor House. As they stepped into the large entry foyer, Meade saw President Lincoln towering over his Secretary of War, Edwin Stanton. On the other side of the President was General Irvin McDowell, who had commanded the Union army that had lost the Battle of Bull Run. McDowell now commanded the Army of the Potomac's First Corps.

Meade studied Lincoln's face. He looked shockingly older than the photos taken at the time of his election. The relatively smooth, angular face that graced the photographs was gone, replaced with one full of furrows and wrinkles. There was a softness and warmth to the President's smile that offset his look of sadness. Lincoln's voice was pleasant but surprisingly high-pitched. He seemed indifferent to how he dressed, wearing a creased and soiled black dress coat with sleeves that should have been longer.

After McDowell introduced Meade, Lincoln said, "General Meade, it is a pleasure to meet you. I hear you have some politicians in your family. John Sergeant was your father-in-law?"

"Yes, he was, Mr. President. I learned much from him before his passing."

"I met Sergeant once in Springfield. I was a young Whig politician. At first, I felt a little awkward in the presence of such a prominent member of our party. He had just become our vice presidential nominee. Sergeant treated me very kindly and put me at ease."

Lincoln had a faraway look in his eyes, as if he were thinking of how he had risen from a frontiersman to the highest office in the land. "And Henry Wise, that fire-breathing secessionist governor of Virginia, is your brother-in-law?"

"Yes. Wise married my wife's older sister."

"Talking about politicians reminds me of a story. When I was running for a seat in the Illinois legislature, a woman said to me, 'Lincoln, you're nothing but a two-faced politician.' I replied, 'Madame, if I had two faces, would I choose to wear this one?'"

Lincoln's melancholic eyes sparkled with humor, and his long, ungainly body shook with laughter. The look of sadness had temporarily disappeared from his face.

Meade laughed heartily. The President patted his shoulder and then welcomed the next officer in line.

Meade and Reynolds walked over to chat with George McCall, the general in charge of their division, the Pennsylvania Reserves. McCall was a sixty-year-old West Pointer who had come out of a comfortable retirement to fight for the Union.

"Reynolds was making fun of our beloved Philadelphia," Meade said.

"I was only teasing Meade about acting so intellectual," laughed Reynolds.

McCall smiled. "George is a little bit more worldly than us, John, though we do share a love for the great city of Philadelphia."

Meade chuckled. "Reynolds, you're not an unsophisticated country boy, even though you are from Lancaster. Why, you have been a foreign traveler. Remember, Uncle Sam had the three of us tour the beautiful country of Mexico."

"Some tour! The Mexicans welcomed us with bullets and bombshells. Although, you're right. Mexico was stunningly picturesque."

"I formed so many friendships during the Mexican War." McCall shook his head wistfully. "Now, most of those friends are officers in the Rebel army: Robert E. Lee, Stonewall Jackson, Pete Longstreet, George Pickett . . . it would take a long time to compile a full list."

Reynolds asked, "General McCall, why are we not with McClellan in front of Richmond?"

McCall appeared lost in thought. "Stonewall Jackson keeps routing Federal troops in the Shenandoah Valley. My guess is Lincoln is afraid Jackson will get out of the valley and attack Washington. I can think of no other explanation for his withholding McDowell's First Corps of forty thousand men from McClellan's army."

Meade interjected. "Jackson can't have more than ten thousand men. He is no threat to Washington. The Rebels are using Jackson to distract Lincoln from sending reinforcements that McClellan needs to capture Richmond."

The President joined them. "I love how the Reserves became Federal soldiers." Meade knew the story well. Pennsylvania had raised an entire division in excess of its quota for volunteers; armed, equipped, and trained it with state money; and then gave it to the Federal army. Lincoln continued, saying, "It is very gratifying that so many men answered my request for volunteers to fight for their country."

Meade addressed Lincoln. "I congratulate you, Mr. President, for rescinding General Hunter's order. I don't think army officers should be making civilian policy decisions."

"I appreciate the acknowledgment that the military is subservient to civilian leadership. General Hunter did not have authority under martial law to free the slaves in the small area he controls. His declaration of emancipation caused unrest in the four border states where slavery is legal. I feel tremendous pressure to keep those border states in the Union."

Meade thought the President was smart to do everything he could to keep Missouri, Kentucky, Maryland, and Delaware from joining the Confederacy. If those states seceded, the Rebels' odds of gaining their independence would be greatly enhanced.

Lincoln arched his back, stretching his long frame. "I have been studying the War Powers Clause of the Constitution to determine whether the President can emancipate the slaves in rebellious states."

"Have you considered how emancipation would impact the troops?" McCall asked. "Everyone in our division is a Pennsylvanian, and I think they all are opposed to slavery, but they didn't volunteer to fight and die to abolish slavery. They volunteered to suppress the rebellion and restore the Union."

"I have given it a great deal of thought. Many, including me, hoped this would be a short war. The great effusion of blood on the Bull Run and Shiloh battlefields has proven that to be a false hope."

Lincoln paused. "If the South had lost at Bull Run and petitioned to rejoin the Union, I do not believe there would have been public support to continue the war if its only goal was the abolishment of slavery. Circumstances have changed. We are engaged in a long and very sanguinary conflict. I believe the words of our glorious Declaration of Independence, that all men have the right to liberty; as such, the eradication of slavery in the rebellious states could be a legitimate second aim of the war."

The President looked intently at the men, seeming to appraise them. "You are professional soldiers. If I emancipated the slaves, would our troops lose their fervor to defeat the rebellion?"

Reynolds answered. "Some might object to the additional goal of abolishing slavery, but I think virtually all would continue to fight to restore the Union."

Meade nodded. "I agree with Reynolds."

McCall shrugged. "I suppose Reynolds and Meade are right."

"Speaking of patriotism reminds me of a story. When I got here today, I was told that George Washington visited this very house on a number of occasions."

Stanton joined their group with the air of a man who has important business to conduct. He was portly, with a long, dark beard; a large head; and behind his glasses, sharp, piercing eyes.

"Mr. President, we have pressing war issues that must be addressed. I need you to come with me immediately."

"Stanton, I was just about to tell one of my favorite stories."

"Mr. President, we don't have time for one of your stories."

"A man needs a little humor every day to keep his sanity. I certainly need a daily dose of humor to keep my equilibrium. The war business can wait a moment. Now, I am sure you all know of the famous Ethan Allen and his Green Mountain Boys and their contributions to the Revolutionary War. After the war, Allen returned to England, and some of the British liked to make fun of him. One day, they put a picture of George Washington in an outhouse, where Allen would be sure to see it. Allen used the outhouse for several days without mentioning the picture. Finally he was asked about the picture. Allen said he thought an outhouse was a very appropriate place for Englishmen to hang that picture because nothing will make an Englishman shit so quick as the sight of General Washington!"

Everybody but Stanton burst into boisterous laughter.

"Stanton, I am going to have you laugh at one of my stories before the war is over."

———————◡

That night, Meade sat at his camp desk and composed a letter to his wife.

Camp opposite Fredericksburg, May 23, 1862

My Dearest Margaret,

We are now encamped on the bank of the Rappahannock, directly opposite the town of

Fredericksburg. The people living around here are all pretty strongly tinctured with "Secesh." The men are away, and the women are as rude as their fears will permit them to be.

War is a game of chance, and besides the chance of service, the accidents, and luck of the field, in our army, an officer has to run the chances of having his political friends in power or able to work for him. A poor devil like myself, with little merit and no friends, has to stand aside and see others go ahead. On the whole, however, I have done pretty well and ought not to complain.

Today we had a visit from the President and the Secretary of War in anticipation of an immediate forward movement. Previous to the review, I had been at General McDowell's Headquarters and there saw the President. I took the liberty of saying to him that I believed the army was much gratified to see his recent proclamation in regard to Hunter's order. He expressed himself gratified for the good opinion of the army, and said: "I am trying to do my duty, but no one can imagine what influences are brought to bear upon me."

Your Loving Husband George

CHAPTER 2

Meade was riding his favorite horse, Old Baldy, on the heights above the Rappahannock. It was ironic; his horse had seen more action in the war than he had. During the Battle of Bull Run, Old Baldy had been hit in the nose by a piece of shell fragment.

Meade had found the warhorse at the Cavalry Depot in Washington. He was brown, with four white feet and a white blaze on his face, so Meade named him Old Baldy. He paid the army's Quartermaster Department one hundred and fifty dollars for the horse. Handsomer horses were available, but Meade couldn't afford the asking price.

He thought about his brigade of volunteers. Meade had worked hard to turn them into soldiers. He had been an intense and stern leader. He sometimes pitched into people when they made mistakes. His men nicknamed him the Old Snapping Turtle.

His darling Margaret would scold him when she saw his temper flare. He had promised to control it, a pledge he knew he would have difficulty keeping.

When Meade returned to camp, he saw Reynolds. His friend looked distraught.

"What's wrong?"

"Just three days ago, Lincoln and Stanton were here and finally agreed to McClellan's repeated requests that McDowell be ordered to rejoin the Army of the Potomac. Now, because Stonewall Jackson has pushed General Banks to the north end of the Shenandoah Valley, they have panicked and reversed themselves. Keeping reinforcements from getting to McClellan is unpardonable."

"I liked Lincoln. He has a folksy, Western-frontier charm about him. But he is struggling with the Commander-in-Chief role. His fixation with protecting Washington is crippling McClellan's offensive."

"I liked Lincoln too, but he has appointed a dozen incompetent political generals! Take Nathaniel Banks. He had no military experience, yet Lincoln made him a major general in charge of the Union army in the Shenandoah Valley. It is a travesty that brave soldiers are commanded by someone like Banks."

Meade shared Reynolds's sentiments. Banks had been the Democratic governor of Massachusetts and had voiced abolitionist sentiments. By making him a general, Lincoln gained support from the War Democrats and the Radical Republicans in Congress who favored abolitionist generals.

"I don't know how we are going to win the war when Lincoln ignores the requests of professional military men like McClellan"— Meade shook his head—"and infects the army with political generals who have no military training or experience."

Camp opposite Fredericksburg, May 30, 1862

My Dearest Margaret,

I am very glad you saw Mrs. McClellan and were pleased with her. Although I don't think General McClellan thought much of me after I was appointed, I am quite sure my appointment was due to him, and almost entirely to him. At that time, his will was omnipotent, and he had only to ask and it was given. He told me himself that he had simply presented my name to the President, to which I replied that I considered that the same as appointing me. I am prouder of such an appointment than if all the politicians in the country had backed me. We, who are in the midst of the troubles and dangers, are greatly amused to see terrible excitement produced in Philadelphia, New York, and Boston by the inglorious retreat of Banks before a force little larger than his own. McDowell has gone to Manassas and has taken everyone with him except our division, who now have the honor of holding Fredericksburg and the railroad from thence to Aquia Creek. The truth is, we must expect a disaster, so long as the armies are not under one mastermind. In nothing is the old adage so fully verified as in matters military that "too many cooks spoil the broth."

Your Loving Husband George

CHAPTER 3

A week later, Lincoln ordered the Reserves to join the Army of the Potomac. Meade had left Fredericksburg and sailed down the Rappahannock to Chesapeake Bay and then up the York River to the Pamunkey River. He had been held up by transport issues, and most of the Reserves, including his brigade, were already with McClellan's army.

A stately plantation house came into view, sitting regally on a hill above the river. Meade looked around in amazement at the huge supply base McClellan had created. It contained food, cannons, guns, tents, horses, baled forage, and everything else an army could need. Ships of every description floated in the river, including a large vessel loaded with locomotives and railcars.

After disembarking, Meade asked a sergeant, "Whose plantation is this?"

"This here is White House Plantation, a very historic place. It was the home of Martha Custis, who married George Washington, and is now owned by her great-great grandson, Fitzhugh Lee, the nephew of General Lee. Old Bobby Lee's wife was here when us Federals arrived. She's a high-spirited and bossy lady who didn't like us bluecoats being around her. She's angry as hell that the Federal government took her Arlington plantation to use as an army campsite. McClellan sent her through the lines to Richmond."

He found his brigade camped along the north side of the swampy Chickahominy River. The air was hot and humid and buzzed with swarms of mosquitoes. The Reserves were attached to Fitz John Porter's Fifth Corps on the army's right flank.

After settling in, Meade visited Reynolds. "We're finally on the front lines of the war."

"Yes, our division is here, but the rest of McDowell's corps, close to thirty thousand men, is still being withheld from McClellan. They have McDowell chasing Stonewall Jackson, who is too wily to be caught."

"Lincoln and Stanton are ignoring the military maxim of concentration of force."

"They certainly are." Reynolds rubbed his beard. "You really have to give McClellan credit. Even without McDowell, he has maneuvered his army to within five miles of Richmond."

Camp Near "New Bridge," Va, June 18, 1862

My Dearest Margaret,

The "New Bridge" is the bridge by which one of the main roads into Richmond crosses the Chickahominy. We hold the approaches on this side, the enemy the other. The New Bridge is only five miles from Richmond, and from the high ground near our camp we can plainly discern the spires of the Sacred City.

I can hardly tell you how I felt this afternoon, when the old familiar sound of heavy firing commenced. I thought of you and the dear children—how much more I have to make me cling to life than during the Mexican War; I thought too, of how I was preserved then and since in many perilous times through God's mercy and will, and prayed He would continue His gracious protection to me and in His own good time, restore me to you. Or if this was not His will, and if it was decreed that I was to be summoned, that He would forgive me, for His Son's sake, the infinite number of sins I have all my life been committing. You see, I do not shut my eyes to the contingencies of the future, but I look upon them with a hopeful eye and a firm reliance on the mercy of my Heavenly Father. It is now ten o'clock at night, dark and rainy. All is quiet in both camps, and the immense hosts arrayed against each other are, doubtless, peacefully sleeping, unless someone with thoughts like those I have expressed has a disturbing conscience.

Your Loving Husband George

CHAPTER 4

A few days after arriving at the battlefront, Meade received an invitation to visit McClellan. They both came from socially prominent Philadelphia families, had entered West Point at fifteen, and fought as engineers in the Mexican War.

The commanding general of the Army of the Potomac was short and powerfully built, with intelligent, dark eyes. The troops adored him, affectionately calling him Little Mac. McClellan was only thirty-six, and newspapers had named him "Young Napoleon."

He had chosen a substantial redbrick farmhouse for his headquarters. As Meade was ushered into McClellan's office, a man wearing civilian clothes was leaving.

"General Meade, this is Allan Pinkerton. I used his detective service when I was in Chicago running the Illinois Central Railroad. When the Army of the Potomac was formed, I had Pinkerton create an intelligence operation. Please tell the general about the strength of the Rebel force we're facing."

"Based on our best estimates gathered from various sources, including spies we have behind Rebel lines, the Confederates have one hundred and eighty thousand troops in front of Richmond," Pinkerton said.

McClellan said, "Thank you, Pinkerton. You may leave."

When the door closed, McClellan slammed his fist into the palm of his hand. "We are outnumbered by at least fifty thousand men. Lincoln took away McDowell because he and Stanton are paranoid about the Rebels attacking Washington and believe I didn't leave enough troops behind for its protection." McClellan stood and began pacing. "I supervised building forty-eight forts around Washington. Our capital is one of the most fortified cities in the world! It would take a huge Confederate force to overpower Washington's defenses, which can be augmented by Union troops in the Shenandoah Valley. Men from this army can quickly sail up the Potomac to aid in its defense."

"Doesn't Lincoln understand that Washington is safe from a Rebel attack?"

"He can't comprehend the military realities."

"I met Lincoln. He struck me as being intelligent."

"Lincoln's not dumb. The problem is, he fancies himself a military strategist because he borrowed some books on warfare from the Library of Congress." McClellan's jaw tightened. "Take his strategy for fighting an overland campaign from Washington to Richmond. He wants the Army of the Potomac to stay between Washington and the Rebel army to ensure our capital is not attacked."

Meade said, "An overland approach would require a railroad for supplies; a lot of men would be needed to guard the line from Rebel cavalry raids."

McClellan stopped pacing. "That's an excellent insight. I explained to Lincoln, in the simplest fashion possible, the problems with his strategy. Staying in front of the Confederate army would severely limit my ability to maneuver and necessitate taking thousands of troops out of combat operations to protect the Goddamn railroad. Fighting our way across the many rivers and streams of Virginia would be costly, both in time and the blood of our gallant troops."

McClellan pointed to a map on the wall. "Look at Chesapeake Bay, with all its lovely tributary rivers. Any fool can see that using a water route is the best and most efficient way to get the Union army close to Richmond!"

Meade knew the Union navy dominated the Confederate navy. "There are advantages to using navigable rivers to supply the army, speed and security being two."

"Correct. Transporting troops and supplies from Washington, down the Potomac, and up the York or James Rivers to this area before

CHESAPEAKE BAY

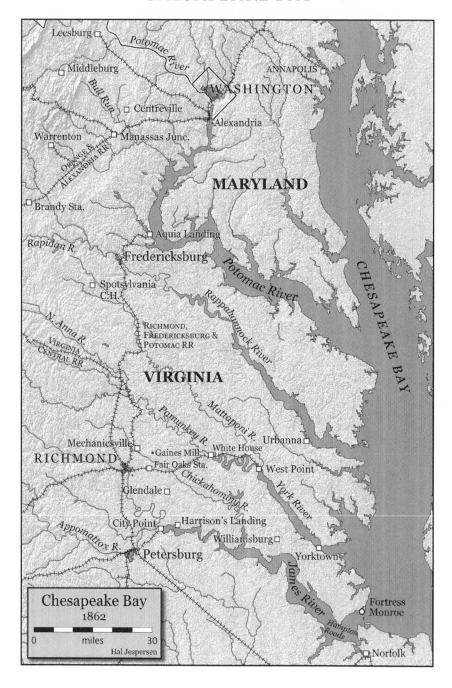

Richmond has been easy. We are almost to Richmond and have suffered light casualties. Clearly the water route I chose is superior to the overland approach favored by the President."

"Do you think that McDowell will ever join us?"

McClellan's face darkened. "We are about to fight the greatest battle in American history, and I am being stabbed in the back by the Secretary of War! Lincoln is under the influence of Stanton, who is the devil himself. He is the vilest man I have ever known! Stanton is allied with the Radical Republicans in Congress. They want to transform this conflict from a war to restore the Union to a campaign to abolish slavery. The Radical Republicans hate me because I'm neither an abolitionist nor a Republican."

"Why would Stanton want to hurt you?"

"Stanton thinks I have political ambitions as a Democrat. He wants to destroy my reputation by sabotaging this army! He has manipulated Lincoln by playing on his fears that Washington will be captured and kept the President from sending desperately needed reinforcements. If I had McDowell's corps, I would have already captured Richmond!"

"Washington politicians should let the military professionals manage the war," Meade said.

McClellan shook his head. "The destiny of the Union rests on my shoulders, and Lincoln and Stanton are not supporting me! The pressures on me commanding the greatest army this country has ever fielded are enormous. If the Army of the Potomac is defeated in the great battle ahead, it will be their fault and not mine!"

McClellan took a deep breath and composed himself. "Ranting about Washington will do me no good." He reached for a pitcher and poured a cup of water. "I understand that my wife, Ellen, had a chance to meet your Margaret, and they got on well."

"Margaret saw Ellen in Philadelphia, and they spent a lovely time together."

McClellan's aide appeared. "Sir, Generals Franklin and Smith are here."

"Please bring them in."

Franklin, the commander of the Sixth Corps, and Smith, a division commander, entered the room.

"Gentlemen, thank you for coming. I was about to explain to General Meade my plan to lay siege to Richmond." McClellan walked to the map on the wall. "Laying siege to an enemy city is the best way to capture it with minimal casualties for the attacking force. We have five army corps, four of which are south of the Chickahominy." He pointed to the Rebel capital. "The corps south of the river are going to advance and push the Rebels back toward Richmond until we get close enough to begin the siege. Then we will transport our large siege weapons by railroad from White House Plantation. I want to avoid as much as possible making frontal assaults on entrenched positions. I intend to use maneuvering and engineering to minimize our losses."

The men nodded to indicate their understanding.

Smith asked, "General McClellan, what is your opinion of Robert E. Lee replacing the wounded Joe Johnston as the Rebel commander?"

"I know both men well from the Mexican War. General Meade, wasn't Johnston a topographical engineer with you in Mexico?"

"Yes, Joe Johnston was a captain, and I was a second lieutenant. Both Lee and Johnston impressed me as first-rate soldiers."

"I agree that both men performed well in Mexico," replied McClellan. "I would rather face Lee as the Rebel commander. In Mexico, Lee was clever in finding ways to flank the Mexican army. However, exhibiting creativity as an individual soldier does not mean he will be a good commanding general. I believe that Lee, when pressed by heavy responsibility, is likely to be timid and irresolute in action."

Meade was shocked at McClellan's appraisal of Lee, who had earned widespread admiration for his bold and daring adventures during the Mexican War. Contradicting McClellan would accomplish nothing, so he kept his opinion to himself. Instead, he asked, "General McClellan, do you have any concerns with the army being divided by the Chickahominy River? Porter's Fifth Corps is isolated on the north bank."

"I do have concerns. In normal circumstances, I wouldn't allow my army to be divided by a river. There are good reasons to keep Porter north of the Chickahominy. I pray for McDowell to join us. He would march from Fredericksburg, arrive north of the Chickahominy, and link up with Porter. A second reason is to have troops available to defend our White House Plantation supply base. I have had my engineers build bridges over the Chickahominy so that we can rush reinforcements to the north side of the river if that should become necessary."

———————

Camp Near New Bridge, June 22, 1862

My Dearest Margaret,

Yesterday I rode over to headquarters and saw McClellan. While with him, Franklin and Baldy Smith came in, and I had a very pleasant visit. He talked very freely of the way he had been treated and said positively that had not McDowell's corps been withdrawn, he would long before now have been in Richmond.

Your Loving Husband George

CHAPTER 5

Perspiration dripped from Meade's brow. The Virginia summer heat and humidity were suffocating. He swatted away a mosquito as he entered McCall's headquarters tent.

McCall's expressive face looked grim as he addressed Seymour, Reynolds, and Meade, his three brigadier generals. "We have intelligence that says Stonewall Jackson is marching toward our right flank."

Reynolds exclaimed, "How can that be? McDowell is supposed to be cornering Jackson in the Shenandoah Valley."

McCall replied, "I guess he slipped around McDowell. Remember how intense and determined Jackson was in Mexico? Nothing Jackson does surprises me."

Meade's blue eyes flashed with anger at the unprofessional management of the war. "Unbelievable! Jackson is here to help Lee while McDowell is in the middle of Virginia with no Rebels to fight!"

"We are to prepare defensive positions at Beaver Dam Creek. Reynolds, I want you to deploy your brigade opposite the bridge from Mechanicsville. Seymour, deploy your brigade south of Reynolds by Ellerson's Mill. Meade, your brigade will be in reserve. Prepare rifle pits ascending the slope of the creek. Place your artillery on the high ground."

Meade was finally going to see combat again. In Mexico, he had worried about his reaction to hostile fire. Would he be courageous? Would he do his duty? He thanked God that when he faced the elephant in Mexico, he had proven brave. How would his young volunteers fare in the coming battle? He had done his best to prepare them, and he prayed they would be equal to the challenge.

A day passed without a Confederate attack. The Reserves were in a strong defensive position. An attacking force would have to cross open ground, exposing themselves to heavy and destructive artillery fire. Trees had been felled to create clear fields of fire. Any man who got to the edge of the creek would have to plunge down a sixty-foot bank and cross the water, which in many places was swampy and difficult to ford, all the while exposed to musket and artillery fire. The timber had been shaped with axes into sharp points and placed at the bottom of the slope they were defending to form an abatis.

The left of the defensive line rested on the Chickahominy River, and the right was in a dense woods and swamp north of the road coming from Mechanicsville. The Bucktails, rugged outdoorsmen from the mountainous regions of Pennsylvania who sewed white deer tails to their hats, were assigned picket duty across the bridges. If attacked, the Bucktails were to fall back, destroying the bridges after crossing them.

The divisions of Generals Morrell and Sykes bolstered the Reserves. In total twenty-six thousand Federal troops were under Fifth Corps Commander Fitz John Porter.

The day had dawned bright and beautiful. The Reserves had done everything they could to prepare for an attack. Meade thought it was a good time to write a letter to Margaret.

Camp Near New Bridge, Va, June 26, 1862

My Dearest Margaret,

There is a report that the great "Stonewall" Jackson is coming to Richmond with his army to turn our right flank. This report, in connection with the fact that they keep up a great drumming and bugling in front of us to make us believe they're in great force, leads me to doubt whether their army is as strong as represented and whether they actually outnumber us.

*The health of the army, at least of our divi-
sion, is very fair—some little bilious attacks and
diarrhea, but nothing serious. We have an abun-
dance of good food; no army in the world was
ever better supplied and cared for than ours is,
all reports to the contrary notwithstanding.*

Your Loving Husband George

Meade heard the distinctive crack of musket fire at midafternoon. The Bucktail pickets were driven in by advancing Confederate infantry. Rebel cannons opened fire, the thunderous sound booming across the land. Federal artillery responded, and the air was filled with bursting shells and falling cannonballs.

The cannonading increased into a continuous, deafening roar. Confederate cannons fell silent as their infantry advanced across the open plain. Union artillery fired both fused shells, which exploded above the enemy, dispersing deadly iron fragments and killing and maiming men, and solid shot that knocked soldiers over like bowling pins. Direct hits dismembered men, and body parts littered the advance. Ignoring the death around them, the Confederates continued to advance.

When the Rebels got within musket range, the Federal rifle pits erupted with sheets of flame and lead, and Confederate casualties rose dramatically. The firing of thousands of muskets, the thunderous roar of cannons, and the shrieking of the shells formed a discordant symphony. The Rebels got close enough for the artillerists to change to canister rounds, which were tin cans filled with iron balls that acted like giant shotguns. The unending fire from the Reserves had a horrific effect on the Rebels, whose advancing column withered and fell back, leaving the field filled with dead and dying men.

The Rebels regrouped and charged again. The result was the same. The combined artillery and musket fire from the Reserves wreaked an awful carnage on the attackers.

BEAVER DAM CREEK

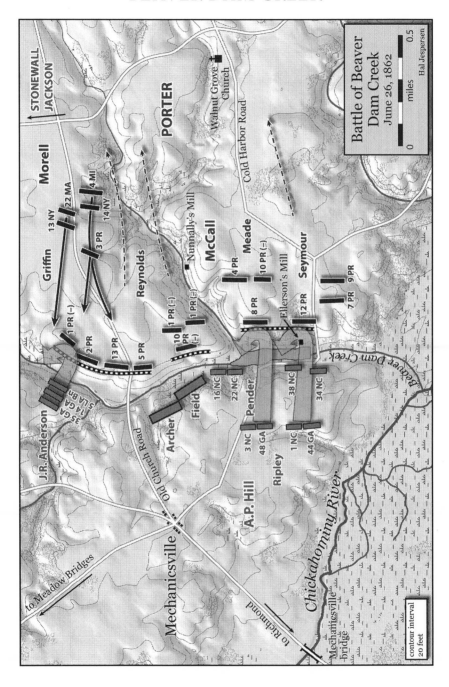

Battle of Beaver Dam Creek
June 26, 1862
Hal Jespersen

General McCall rode up to Meade, shouting to be heard above the roar of the artillery. "Meade, the Rebels are pressuring Reynolds's right flank. Select a regiment and a battery from your brigade and take them to Reynolds."

Meade found Reynolds in the woods, looking magnificent on his horse and exhorting his men to cut down the attacking Confederates. While the Reserves were taking casualties, the Rebels were getting the worst of it.

"Reynolds, you're in a hot place here."

"Lee is trying to flank us, but my boys are holding their own."

Meade felt the whiz of minié balls slicing through the air close to his head but didn't flinch. God would determine when it was his time to be called. After placing his men where Reynolds directed, Meade returned to his Reserve position.

The Rebels launched an assault at Ellerson's Mill. Meade was dispatched to place one of his regiments in support of Seymour. A few Confederates got to the Federal side of the creek, where they became entangled on the abatis and were easy targets for infantry fire.

As afternoon turned into evening, the Confederates continued to make assaults. Every attack failed. Night came, and the fighting ended. The ghastly groans and cries of the wounded and dying could be heard in the darkness.

It had been a great day for the Reserves, who had relatively light casualties—only thirty-eight men were killed. It was a terrible day for the Confederates and Robert E. Lee, whose attack had been bloodily repulsed. Meade was exhilarated by the victory.

———————⚔

Meade was on his cot, deep asleep. At 3:15 a.m., an aide shook him awake.

"Sorry to disturb your sleep, sir. You are to report immediately to General McCall's headquarters."

Meade thanked the man and quickly dressed. Reynolds and Seymour were with McCall when he arrived.

McCall looked sullen. "McClellan has decided to retreat. He learned from interrogating prisoners that Stonewall Jackson was not involved in today's battle. The intelligence McClellan received says Jackson will attack our right flank in the morning. I don't want to retreat, but in the army, we follow orders."

McCall paused. "McClellan is calling it a change of base and not a retreat. He is giving up his base at White House Plantation and establishing a new base across the peninsula on the James River. We need to get the troops up and on the move."

Reynolds asked, "Is McClellan going to send reinforcements, or are we expected to fight off the Rebel attacks with only one-fifth of the Army of the Potomac? While we licked the *secesh* today, they clearly had more troops in the battle than we did. It was only because of our extremely strong defensive position that we were able to win the battle."

"I don't know if we're getting reinforcements. General Porter is establishing a new defensive position four miles from here"—McCall looked at the map he was holding—"near a place called Gaines Mill." McCall folded his map and handed it to the men packing his trunk. "Let's get moving. We need to be out of here before the sun comes up."

CHAPTER 6

The Reserves had fallen back to their current location, Turkey Hill, marching past nearby Gaines Mill. Meade was pacing back and forth on the hill, an open plateau above Boatswain's Swamp, waiting for Reynolds to return from a call of nature. When Reynolds returned, Meade said, "I don't understand McClellan's thinking. By retreating without being beaten in battle, he abandoned his Richmond offensive. Without control of White House Plantation and the railroad to transport his huge guns to Richmond, he can't execute his grand strategy of besieging Richmond."

"I'm as baffled as you are," Reynolds said. "McClellan should have sent us reinforcements. We could have successfully defended Beaver Dam Creek against both Lee and Jackson."

As they talked, ninety Union cannons were being maneuvered into position on Turkey Hill. They watched as men from Morrell's and Sykes's divisions entered the woods bordering the steep banks of the swamp to form a defensive line.

Because the Reserves had done most of the fighting at Beaver Dam Creek, Fitz John Porter was holding them in reserve behind the newly formed battle line.

Meade and Reynolds separated to place their troops. Meade positioned his men below the crest of the hill on the far left of the line, behind Morrell.

Meade placed Captain Mark Kerns's battery of six 12-pound howitzers below the crest of the hill to the east of his men. "Kerns, do you like this position for your guns?"

"I have good elevation to shoot over Morrell's men into the Confederates when they advance across the farmland that leads to the swamp. If the *secesh* manage to breach Morrell's line, we'll be in a position to repulse any enemy charge up this hill."

Meade nodded. They had a strong defensive position.

———————⚬

Midday brought summer heat. Meade sat up straighter on Old Baldy and squinted into the distance. Clouds of dust. The Rebels were advancing.

When the Confederates formed battle lines, Federal batteries on the hill opened up, and the ground trembled. *McClellan must be rethinking his evaluation of Robert E. Lee as timid and not aggressive,* Meade thought.

The battle had been raging for two hours when McCall approached. "Meade, take one of your regiments to the aid of Colonel Gouverneur Warren's New York Zouaves regiment. They're being heavily pressed by the Confederates."

Meade mounted Old Baldy and led his men down the hill into the heat of battle. The army had many Zouave regiments with uniforms patterned after French soldiers fighting in Algeria. The Zouaves were renowned for their military skill and courage in combat.

When Meade entered the woods, the screams of men who caught minié balls with their flesh and bones surrounded him. The musket fire was continuous; it sounded like the roar of a waterfall. The air was dark and smoky, the heat intense and suffocating.

The baggy red pantaloons made the Zouaves easy to spot. Their heads were covered with red fezzes with yellow tassels. Meade quickly found the commander.

"Colonel Warren, I have brought reinforcements."

"Thank God! My men have been fighting for hours, and we're taking terrible casualties."

GAINES MILL

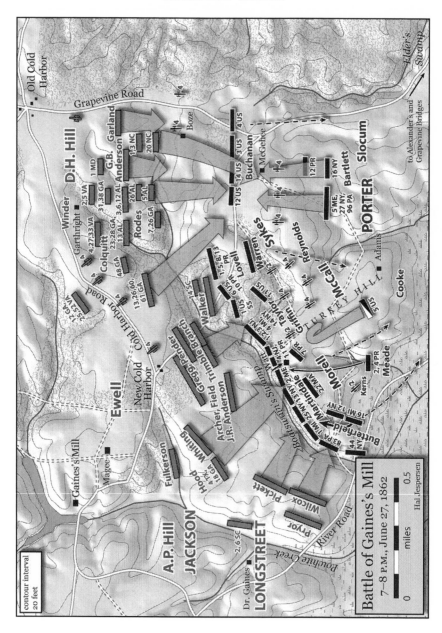

Battle of Gaines's Mill
7–8 P.M., June 27, 1862

Hal Jespersen

contour interval
20 feet

Meade assessed the situation. The Zouaves were at the edge of the swamp, standing shoulder-to-shoulder in a battle line as they exchanged fire with the Rebels, who were fighting up the steep embankment. The ground was littered with the mangled bodies of dead and dying men.

Meade pressed his lips together in a tight line. The Rebels are determined men. *They will not be easily defeated*, he thought.

By 4:00 p.m. Meade had placed, in a piecemeal fashion, all his regiments into the line of battle. Reynolds and Seymour had done the same with their regiments. The battle was raging, hot and furious. The only soldiers left on Turkey Hill were the artillerists.

McCall approached him. "McClellan has sent us Slocum's division as reinforcements. Help me place his regiments into the line of battle."

Meade tried to control his anger over the lack of reinforcements they had received. McClellan had a hundred thousand men south of the Chickahominy that weren't in the fight. Lee must have sixty thousand men attacking Porter's twenty-six thousand.

"Sir, we need more reinforcements than a single division!" Meade said. "We need at least two corps to come across those Chickahominy bridges. We desperately need fresh troops to keep the Confederates from breaking our line!"

McCall appeared stressed. Today he looked older than sixty. "I don't know what in the hell McClellan is thinking."

The situation was getting desperate. Lee had been attacking in successive waves all day, seemingly oblivious to the thousands of dead and wounded Confederates on the slopes of Boatswain's Swamp. He showed no sign of stopping the attacks.

Adjutant Robert McCoy of the Eleventh Regiment brought his horse to a sudden stop next to Meade. "General Meade, we're in a precarious position. We're taking fire from both flanks. We have been fighting in dense woods. Colonel Gallagher didn't realize that the friendly forces on both of our flanks have withdrawn. We need reinforcements immediately."

Meade heard the desperation in McCoy's voice. "We don't have any reinforcements left. Tell Colonel Gallagher that he'll have to fight his way out."

By the time the sun was setting, no more reinforcements had appeared. The sound of battle intensified, and the ravine at the bottom of the slope disappeared in smoke created by the increased musketry fire. Meade thought Lee must be making an all-out attack before darkness descended on the battlefield.

Sudden, furious movement caught Meade's attention. The Union line had broken! Troops from Morrell's Division were running up the hill. They were followed by Confederates, who were screaming their wild, eerie rebel yell like possessed men. Meade grasped the reins and spurred Old Baldy forward, galloping to Kerns's battery.

"As soon as our troops pass your guns, pour canister into those Rebels. Hell, give them double canister!"

After Morrell's routed men ran past them, Kerns's guns opened up. Whole swaths of Confederates were cut down. Still, the Confederates advanced up the hill. Kerns urged on his gunners, screaming, "Come on, boys. Deliver death to these Rebels! We need to sweep them off the hill!"

His artillerists responded with urgency and destructive effect on the charging enemy.

Kerns yelled, "General Meade, they're retreating back down the hill!"

"Those men are not going to give up. They will regroup and charge again. They need to silence your cannons to take this hill."

The Rebel charge had affected Kerns's battery. A number of the horses had been killed, and others were severely injured. A dozen of his artillerists laid around their guns dead or wounded.

Again Meade heard the defiant Rebel yell, and Confederates appeared out of the haze, storming up the hill.

Kerns screamed, "I've been hit!" Blood was pouring from his leg. He tore a cloth and used it as a tourniquet, tying it tightly. Through gritted teeth, he said, "I will not abandon my guns."

The artillerists kept up their savage fire, and more and more dead Confederates covered the hill. Kerns tightened the tourniquet around his leg and yelled, "We have repulsed them! They're retreating down the hill!"

Meade watched the battery to Kerns's right fall back, exposing his flank. Rebel troops were coming out of the swamp and advancing everywhere up the hill. The Federal position was collapsing. It was time to pull back and save the guns.

Meade told Kerns, "Captain, move one of your cannons to cover your right flank and fire on the Rebels one more time. Then limber up your guns and move back over the crest of the hill and form a new line of battle."

Kerns's six cannons roared simultaneously, and the canister rounds cut down dozens of charging Confederates.

All the dissonant battlefield sounds had almost become routine, but then Meade felt and heard something new. The ground shook from the hooves of rushing horses. He looked back and saw the Fifth US Cavalry charging down the hill, their sabers drawn. The Confederate troops held their ground, and their fire emptied the saddles of a quarter of the Union cavalry.

Riderless horses and fleeing cavalry troops retreated through the Union batteries. Chaos ensued. The Rebels overran many guns and captured many Federal soldiers, who were cut off and surrounded in the confusion. Kerns managed to limber up four of his six guns and disappeared over the crest of the hill.

Meade grabbed an American flag from its color-bearer. He waved it over his head and screamed, "Rally to the flag, boys! Form a new battle line around me!"

A few men answered his call, but the majority had seen enough fighting for one day and continued to flee the battlefield. Meade gave the flag back to the color-bearer and pulled out his sword. He had to instill courage and discipline in these fleeing troops. He raised the sword and started to bring it down on a man running past him when he was distracted by the sight of a green flag. Reinforcements were coming across a Chickahominy bridge: the Irish brigade. Its presence steadied the retreating men, and Meade sheathed his sword.

Darkness fell, and the Confederate attack ended. Porter's battered Fifth Corps retreated across the Chickahominy.

CHAPTER 7

Meade felt the heat from the scorching Virginia sun as he surveyed the sad scene at Savage's Station. The wounded survivors of the Gaines Mill battle had been delivered by ambulance and train. The area around the station had been turned into a huge field hospital. Surgeons were busy amputating limbs on outdoor operating tables.

What a turn of events, Meade thought grimly. After the stirring victory at Beaver Dam Creek, Gaines Mill had been a disaster. Lee's relentless attacks had worn down the beleaguered Union forces. Why hadn't McClellan sent in reinforcements? While McClellan had belittled Lee's odds of being a successful commanding general, he seemed paralyzed when it came to reacting to the Rebel commander's daring aggressiveness.

Meade dismounted from Old Baldy and stretched his weary limbs. McClellan had assigned McCall to escort General Henry Hunt's Artillery Reserve batteries to Savage's Station. It had been an excruciatingly slow all-night march before they had arrived midmorning at the train station.

McCall's men hadn't eaten for two days, and they took advantage of the opportunity to feast on the huge amount of food passing through from the White House Plantation supply base to the new base being established at Harrison's Landing on the James. Meade had received the distressing news that Reynolds and many men of the Eleventh Regiment had been captured during the chaotic ending to the Gaines

Mill battle. Meade knelt, bent his head, and prayed to the Almighty God to have mercy on the wounded Union soldiers who surrounded him and for the safe return of the captured Federals.

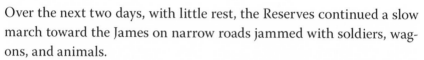

Over the next two days, with little rest, the Reserves continued a slow march toward the James on narrow roads jammed with soldiers, wagons, and animals.

McCall had his troops take a break while he attended a meeting with McClellan. When he returned, he briefed his commanders. "During last night's march, we were separated from the rest of the Fifth Corps. We are near Glendale, a crossroads hamlet. Behind us is the road being used to move supplies to the new base at Harrison's Landing. McClellan has placed the divisions of Kearney and Slocum on our right flank. On our left flank are the divisions of Sedgwick and Hooker. We have been assigned to hold the center of the Union line on Long Bridge Road."

McCall took a swig of water from his canteen. "I expect old Bobby Lee to launch a vigorous attack right where we have been placed. If Lee breaks our line, he would cut McClellan's army in half. We've been ordered to hold the Glendale crossroads at all hazards.

"Meade, your brigade has been sharply reduced with the losses suffered at Gaines Mill. I don't have additional troops to give you. General Hunt has given us a battery from the Artillery Reserve, Lieutenant Alanson Randol's Battery E First United States Regulars. He will be attached to your brigade."

Meade asked, "Are our flanks going to be in the air?"

"McClellan didn't appoint anyone to be in charge in Glendale. He left for a meeting with the navy. Every division is under independent command. I don't have authority to order Hooker or Kearney to extend their lines to our flanks."

Meade thought it was crazy having five divisions fighting with no one coordinating their actions.

McCall issued instructions for the placement of the troops. Meade placed Randol's guns in front of his decimated brigade. It was a fine

GLENDALE

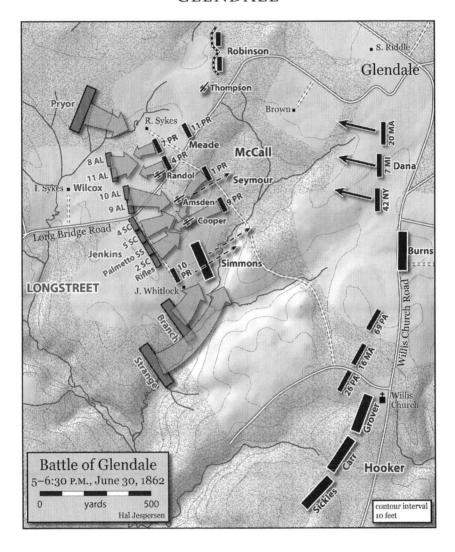

Robinson

S. Riddle

Glendale

Thompson

Pryor

Brown

R. Sykes

11-PR

20 MA

7 PR

Meade

McCall

8 AL

4 PR

7 MI   Dana

11 AL

1 PR

42 NY

I. Sykes   Wilcox

Randol

Seymour

10 AL

Amsden

9 PR

9 AL

Cooper

Long Bridge Road

4 SC

Burns

5 SC

Jenkins

Palmetto SS

2 SC

10

Simmons

LONGSTREET

Rifles

PR

J. Whitlock

69 PA

Branch

16 MA

Strange

26 PA

Willis
Church

Grover

Willis Church Road

Battle of Glendale
5–6:30 P.M., June 30, 1862

Hooker

0   yards   500

Carr

Hal Jespersen

Sickles

contour interval
10 feet

battery consisting of six 12-pound Napoleons. The wide-mouthed Napoleon was the best cannon in the Union arsenal for firing canister.

The day wore on, and the heat and humidity increased. Nobody had changed their clothes in four days. Meade ignored the odors.

He checked his watch. It was past 4:00 p.m. His pickets had reported the woods to the west were filled with Rebel soldiers.

Meade approached Randol, who looked too young to have ever used a razor.

"Lieutenant, how old are you?"

"Twenty-five, sir."

"You're in the regular army. Are you a West Pointer?"

"Yes. Class of 1860. Are you also a West Pointer?"

"Yes. A couple of decades before you, the class of 1835. Have your cannons loaded with double canister. If the Confederates use the same tactics they did at Gaines Mill, we can expect a frontal assault on your guns."

Meade then went to Colonel Magilton, who commanded the Fourth Regiment.

"Place your regiment in front and to the left of Randol's battery," he told him. "Have your men lie down in that high grass. When the Rebels charge, wait till they are a hundred yards away, then jump up and pour musket fire into their flank."

Meade rode out to his picket line. He could see the sunlight flashing off bayonets in the woods and quickly rode back to Randol. "They're coming any minute. Are your guns loaded with double canister?"

"Only single canister, sir."

"Randol, open your ears! I told you double canister!"

Meade looked to the battlefield. The Rebels had advanced out of the woods and immediately dipped into a gully. All Meade could see was the tips of their battle flags. He felt adrenaline surging through his body.

"Open fire when the Confederates come out of that gully!"

A few minutes later, Randol's guns exploded, and the ground shook. The cannons had a monstrous effect. Men fell in droves, yet still the Rebels advanced. They raised the rebel yell and surged forward. The Seventh and Eleventh Regiments opened fire with their muskets, and more Confederates were cut down.

Randol's gunners were firing as fast as they could load. The Rebel ranks were thinning as more men fell. Red blood and human gore spread across the field.

The Confederates periodically stopped and fired at Randol's battery and the infantry protecting it. A dozen of Randol's men and half his horses were down.

When the attackers got within a hundred yards, Colonel Magilton's men leaped to their feet and fired a volley into the Confederates' flank. The attack faltered, and the Rebels retreated across the field, past the bodies of their dead and wounded comrades.

From their battle flags, Meade knew they were fighting Alabama men.

The Federal troops cheered the successful repulse of the attack.

Meade went to Randol. "Good job, son. I'm sure they're going to regroup and make another charge, so have your men and guns ready."

Half an hour later, the Rebels again charged into the teeth of cannon and musket fire. More Southern soldiers found their maker on that bloody ground, yet they continued to advance. The attackers got within fifty yards of Randol's battery before retreating.

Meade rode among the troops, observing that the raw volunteers were becoming soldiers. "I'm proud of you men! You're fighting with valor! Your families will be proud of your heroics on this battlefield! Get prepared for another assault. Those Rebels are not going to give up. They're sure to come again."

Meade looked across the field, which was covered with bodies. *What brave men to make such deadly frontal assaults. They were fighting for the wrong cause, but they were also Americans. What a tragedy,* he thought, *for gallant and courageous Americans to be killing each other.*

Meade went to Colonel Harvey of the Seventh Regiment. "Those Confederates are going to charge again. This time, if they retreat, I want you to lead a counterattack. Remember, if the Rebels make a stand and drive your men back, don't mask Randol's guns by running in front of them."

"My men will be ready."

Forty minutes later, the Rebels were again advancing across that gruesome field. Randol's cannons roared, and more men fell. Meade was becoming numb to the violence. The Confederates got within thirty yards of the muzzles of the cannons before retreating. The Seventh Regiment charged with loud hurrahs and fired a volley into the enemy.

The Rebels kept retreating, and the Union men pursued them. Confederate reinforcements came out of the woods and mounted a countercharge. The Federals recoiled from the force of the Rebel attack and retreated. Contrary to their instructions, they ran in front of Randol's guns, blocking their line of fire. Rebel soldiers, screaming their devilish yell, followed on the heels of the retreating Reserves, reached Randol's cannons, and attacked the artillerists.

Meade knew those guns were critical to protecting the Union line, and they could not be captured by the Confederates. Mounted on Old Baldy, he gathered his soldiers around him.

"We cannot let the Rebels drive us off this field! Our comrades who have fallen defending this position cannot have died in vain. We must counterattack and force them to retreat. Now is the time to do your duty for your country! Fix bayonets."

Meade raised his sword above his head and screamed, "Follow me, Pennsylvanians! We must save the guns!"

His cheering troops followed him, racing to the guns. Vicious hand-to-hand combat ensued. Men used muskets as clubs, smashing them on the heads of their enemy. Gunners used their ramrods as weapons. Officer sabers slashed and cut. Blood and brain matter splattered the combatants. A Rebel flag-bearer climbed atop one of the Napoleons and waved his colors. Seconds later, his bullet-ridden, lifeless body fell to the ground.

Randol tried to remove his guns but couldn't because so many of his horses had been killed. The attacking Confederate force outnumbered the Federal defenders. Gradually, they wore the Pennsylvanians down and drove them off the guns and into the nearby woods. The Rebels had captured Randol's battery.

Meade rallied his battered troops in the woods. He looked into their eyes. Some showed steely resolve; others looked like they had seen enough death. They needed leadership.

"You have fought bravely today and inflicted severe casualties on the Confederates, but our work is not done! We must retake those guns! Our duty—our honor—requires it. Follow me!"

His men raised a lusty cheer; they still had some fight left in them. Meade led them out of the woods on Old Baldy and back into the frenzy of battle.

Before he reached the cannons, Meade felt a sharp sting in his forearm and then a searing pain above his hip. He looked down and saw he was bleeding. But he ignored it. He was determined to continue to lead his men in battle.

His men ran past him and slammed into the Rebels, who were trying to turn the guns around to fire at the Federals. The hand-to-hand fighting was brutally intense.

Meade blinked hard. His eyes were having a hard time focusing. It wasn't just the smoke, the haze of a furious battle. Everything looked blurry, and he felt dizzy, disoriented.

Meade used his good arm to feel his wounds. He was drenched in blood, and more was draining out of him every minute. The sun was setting, and the battle would likely end when darkness came. Meade was having a hard time staying on Old Baldy and feared that if he stayed on the battlefield, he would die from the loss of blood.

He turned over command to Magilton.

As he rode toward the rear, holding on to Old Baldy with all his remaining strength, he saw the division surgeon and called out. "Dr. Stocker, I need help."

Dr. Stocker helped him dismount and examined his wounds.

"You're a lucky man. Both minié balls passed through your body without hitting any bones or arteries. You should live."

City Point, Headquarters Army of the Potomac, July 1, 1862

My Dearest Margaret,

After four days fighting, last evening, about 7:00 p.m., I received a wound in the arm and back. Fortunately I met Dr. Stocker and got a hold of a little cart I had, in which I was brought here.

Dr. Stocker says my wounds are not dangerous, though they require immediate and constant medical attendance. I am to leave in the first boat for Old Point, and from thence home.

Your Loving Husband George

CHAPTER 8

Meade awoke, disoriented. His bed was rocking. Some sort of engine noise was roaring in his ears. He reflexively reached for his spectacles, but they were not perched on his nose. Everything looked hazy. He squinted at his surroundings and discovered he was in a large room filled with men in hospital beds. Gradually the darkness in his mind retreated, and his sense of being returned. He realized he was on a hospital ship with other soldiers. The events from the past few days flooded his mind: the victory at Beaver Dam Creek, the devastating loss at Gaines Mill, and the heroic stand at Glendale. He thought of the gallant men who had given their lives for the Union cause, the otherworldly rebel yell, and the incredible fierceness and bravery of the Confederate troops.

What had happened after he had been shot? His hospital nurse had told him the Rebels had been stopped at Glendale, and McClellan's army made it to the James. There had been another vicious battle the next day at Malvern Hill, and the Confederates had been defeated. McClellan's army was now safely ensconced on the James and protected by navy gunboats.

The ship docked. They were in Baltimore.

A faint voice called his name. He shifted his head from the lumpy hospital pillow to see who it was. He lifted his unbandaged arm to wipe the sleep from his eyes. Without his glasses, all he could see was a female shape approaching him. Could that be? It was. "Margaret!"

She rushed to his bedside with tears cascading down her cheeks. She clutched the hand of his unbandaged arm and bent down so her face was mere inches from his.

"My darling, I have been so worried. I have prayed to the merciful God that your life be spared!" She touched his good arm and his shoulders, as if she wanted reassurance that he was really alive.

"Our Heavenly Father has spared me."

Meade embraced her with his good arm, ignoring the pain that the sudden movement caused him. They held each other fiercely while Margaret quietly sobbed. Finally, she composed herself and sat on the edge of the bed.

Meade studied his wife's face after their long separation. She was just as beautiful as the day they married. "I'm surprised but so delighted that you came to meet me."

"I got a telegram from McClellan's adjunct general, giving the details of your hospital transport. I immediately left Philadelphia so I could be here to greet you in Baltimore. But I'm not the only one who came." She turned and waved to someone across the room.

Meade could see a figure moving; then a face came into focus. His eldest son. "Sergeant! How wonderful to see you!"

"Father, it's wonderful to see you, even if you're in a hospital bed. You're quite the hero in Philadelphia. Your quartermaster, Sam Ringwalt, wrote a letter that was published describing your heroics at the Battle of Glendale."

"I don't see myself as a hero. I've done my duty as a brigadier general and led my men into battle."

Sergeant started coughing so hard that his body shook.

"Son, are you OK?"

"Yes, Father. Just a little coughing spell."

Margaret gave Sergeant a reassuring hug and turned to her husband. "You're going to be transferred to a boat making passage to Philadelphia. Sergeant and I will accompany you back home."

CHAPTER 9

Meade looked out the window at Pine Street. It was the Fourth of July. People were passing on their way to Independence Hall for the annual fireworks celebration.

Being in the military, he had moved often. At the beginning of the war, his family was with him in Detroit, where he was supervising a hydrographical survey of the Great Lakes. Presently, his wife and seven children lived with his mother-in-law in a stately and spacious four-story redbrick townhome near fashionable Rittenhouse Square.

He started reading the paper but couldn't concentrate. General McCall had been captured by the Confederates at Glendale. Both Reynolds and McCall were in Richmond's Libby Prison. How terrible that these brave warriors—his close friends—were locked away in what the papers depicted as a dark, dismal, and forbidding place.

Margaret brought him a steaming cup of coffee. He took a sip, sighed, and smiled.

She smiled back. "You're looking so much better. You were ghastly pale when I saw you in Baltimore. That hospital ship was depressing. So many fine men were missing arms and legs. I thank God that He returned you to me and that you're recovering so well."

"There's nothing like being nursed by a beautiful lady to speedily restore your health. Speaking of ladies, it seems like you got along well with Ellen McClellan."

Margaret nodded. "She was raised in a military family and understands the army. Did you know that she turned down General McClellan's first marriage proposal? And then, later, she accepted a proposal from Ambrose Powell Hill, but her father forbade her from entering into the marriage."

"She was going to marry A. P. Hill, the Confederate general?"

"Yes. That was before the war."

"Did she tell you why her father forbade the marriage?"

"It had something to do with an illness that Hill had, that it would be dangerous for her to be his wife."

"Dangerous? Did he tell her why it would be dangerous?"

"Her father refused to tell her the nature of the illness. McClellan continued to pursue her and eventually won her affection. She seems very happy in her marriage. He has written her a letter every single day since they became engaged. Isn't that romantic?"

"I write you letters every chance I get."

"I know, darling. I adore your letters. They help bridge the loneliness I feel when we are apart. I love that you confide in me your deepest feelings."

Margaret sat down beside Meade on the couch, and they kissed with a passion that had sustained their marriage through their long periods of separation.

Sergeant entered the room, coughing. "I'm leaving to see the fireworks with some friends."

"Enjoy the festivities. When I was a young man, I enjoyed going to Independence Hall and celebrating the birth of our great nation."

After Sergeant left, Meade said, "Sargie is still sickly. He has had that persistent cough for a long time. What is the latest prognosis from his doctors?"

Margaret started crying. "They think he has tuberculosis."

Meade felt a pain far sharper than the bullets that had pierced his body. Sargie had lit up their life from the moment of his birth. "Tuberculosis? My God! We need to pray that God looks with favor upon him."

She sat beside Meade, and he held her as tightly as he could. After she composed herself, he said, "We need to be strong for Sargie. We'll get him the best care possible."

The news about McCall, Reynolds, and Sergeant deeply troubled him. "Margaret, could you bring me one of those fine Cuban cigars?"

"I don't think it is a good idea for you to be smoking while you're recuperating from gunshot wounds."

"You're probably right, but I have a craving for one."

"I'm your nurse. It's my responsibility to help restore your health. I'm not going to bring you a cigar."

Meade barked at her, "What? If I want to smoke a cigar, I am going to do it!"

Margaret stood. "George Gordon Meade, you will not use that tone with me! You will control your temper in this house!"

Meade looked at his wife. She had her hands on her hips, and her eyes were boring into his. Margaret was a strong woman. She had raised their seven children on her own for long periods while he was away on duty. He knew from years of marriage that when she took that pose and had that look in her eyes, he was going to lose the argument. He took several deep breaths.

"Margaret, I apologize for losing my temper. I know you only have my best interest at heart."

The next day, Meade was excited to have all his children with him. They amused themselves playing parlor games. Margaret was a fine pianist and entertained the family with a selection of Mozart's music.

He was worried about Sergeant, whose health was deteriorating. The boy wanted to be a lawyer like his grandfather, whom he had been named for. Meade remembered the kind words President Lincoln had expressed about John Sergeant.

Meade looked at his son George. In 1860 he had earned admission to West Point but had been dismissed for accumulating too many demerits. He had volunteered for the army and was serving in an infantry unit.

He looked at his other two sons, six-year-old William, and twelve-year-old Spencer. Both were so lively and energetic. Next, his three beautiful daughters, Margaret, Henrietta, and Sarah. There was a silver lining to being shot at Glendale: in the middle of the horrors of war, he had been given a respite to be home with his loving family.

SECOND BULL RUN

CHAPTER 10

Meade stood on the deck of the ship and looked at the approaching gray stone walls of Fortress Monroe, the Gibraltar of Chesapeake Bay, the only fort in the Confederacy controlled by Union forces. He had spent forty days convalescing in Philadelphia. Leaving Margaret and his children was heartbreaking, but duty called.

Reynolds had written to relate that he and McCall had been released in a prisoner exchange. McCall had suffered physical ailments during his confinement and had gone on leave. Reynolds had been promoted to command the Reserves. Meade wondered whether, if not for his Glendale wounds, he would have received the promotion rather than his friend. He chided himself for feeling a twinge of jealousy.

When he got to the Reserves camp at Harrison's Landing, he found Reynolds. "Hullo, Reynolds!"

The two men warmly embraced.

"How did they treat you in Libby Prison?" Meade asked.

"Miserably. The prison is crowded and unsanitary. The food is atrocious, and the guards are mean and nasty."

"The papers are filled with rumors that McClellan's days are numbered."

"It is beginning to look that way. Have you read about the new army Lincoln has created?"

"Yes, but the paper didn't have much detail about it."

"Lincoln formed the Army of Virginia, cobbling together the failed commands of Banks and Fremont. He added in McDowell's troops, who never joined McClellan. John Pope has been brought from the West and given command."

"I know Pope well. We both served as topographical engineers in Mexico. He was full of himself and a braggart."

"The Reserves have been assigned to Pope's Army of Virginia as part of McDowell's corps."

Meade was stunned. "We're leaving the Army of the Potomac?"

"Yes, and Lincoln is removing McClellan's army from the Virginia Peninsula."

"That makes no sense. We have a huge army, with a secure supply base, threatening the Rebel capital. We should launch a new offensive from here."

"I agree. I'm frustrated with Henry Halleck, who Lincoln brought from the Western Theater and made general-in-chief of all Union armies. As a professional soldier, he should see the strategic value of keeping the army here."

A navy ship on the James loudly sounded its horn. Reynolds waited for the sound to fade away before continuing, "Pope has wasted little time in alienating the entire Army of the Potomac. He issued a proclamation that was distributed to all the troops." He rummaged in a pocket and pulled out a crumpled piece of paper. As he unfolded it, he said, "I will read you a few choice lines."

> I have come to you from the West, where we have always seen the backs of our enemies; from an army whose business it has been to seek the adversary and to beat him when he was found; whose policy has been attack and not defense. I desire you to dismiss from your minds certain phrases, which I am sorry to find so much in vogue amongst you. I hear constantly of 'taking strong positions and holding them,' of 'lines of retreat,' and of 'bases for supplies.' Let us discard such ideas. Success and glory are in the advance, disaster and shame lurk in the rear.

"What an attack on McClellan!"

"McClellan and his inner circle despise Pope. Fitz John Porter called Pope an ass."

Meade took off his glasses and used a cloth to clean the lenses. "At times Pope acted like an ass in Mexico." He hated the thought of serving in an army commanded by the arrogant and conceited Pope.

"I'm leaving today by boat for Aquia Creek to organize our movement to join Pope," Reynolds said. "You need to arrange transportation to Aquia Creek as soon as you can."

Fredericksburg, August 16, 1862

My Dearest Margaret,

I cannot tell you how miserable and sad I was and am at parting from you and the dear children. As the boat pushed off and I saw those three fine boys standing on the dock, I thought my heart would break. But it cannot be helped and must be endured. We must try and bear our trials as cheerfully as we possibly can.

I found Reynolds, who received me very warmly. I see the papers have got hold of the movement. Still, you must not repeat what I write. McClellan's army is to be withdrawn entirely from the James and be posted at Fredericksburg and in front of Washington. This is a virtual condemnation of all McClellan's movements. It must be a most bitter pill for him to swallow.

I have been informed that Burnside has been twice urged to take the command of the Army of the Potomac but always refuses to supersede McClellan, but I believe the thing will soon be done without consulting either of them, for the more I see, the more I am satisfied that McClellan is irretrievably gone and has lost the greatest chance any man ever had on this continent.

Reynolds looks very well but complains bitterly of the want of courtesy shown him in Richmond.

Your Loving Husband George

CHAPTER 11

Meade was staying in Fredericksburg, waiting for his official command orders to come through. He decided to visit the nearby Reserves encampment. His groom saddled Old Baldy. The warhorse looked happy to see him.

As Meade rode toward the camp, he felt a wave of homesickness. This always happened when he left his family for a duty assignment. How he missed the small pleasures of home life, like the meals Margaret prepared and playing games with the children.

When he entered camp, his heart swelled with happiness as the troops lustily cheered his return. Men shouted, "Hurrah for Meade!"

What gratification. There was no better reward for an officer than to receive the cheers of his men. He enjoyed the few hours he spent visiting the troops.

On his return to Fredericksburg, he saw an old acquaintance, General Ambrose Burnside. He was an amicable man, and just about everybody who knew Burnside liked him. He was balding and had enormous side whiskers.

"Burn, is it true that Lincoln offered you command of the Army of the Potomac?"

"It's true. Lincoln, Stanton, and Halleck met with me and asked that I take command. I refused, telling them I didn't think I could command such a large army. It's one thing to command a division or even a corps. It's something entirely different to command an army of over a hundred thousand men."

"Do you think Lincoln will sack McClellan?"

Burnside shook his head. "Lincoln would be foolish to get rid of McClellan. He has done an extraordinary job in creating the Army of the Potomac. The troops love him, and he is an able general. Morale would plummet if he were relieved."

"Are you and McClellan close?"

"We are friends. I left the army in 1853 and started my own company manufacturing a rifle I designed. But I wasn't a good businessman and lost everything. McClellan befriended me and gave me a job working for him at the Illinois Central Railroad. I owe that man a great deal."

Camp opposite Fredericksburg, August 19, 1862

My Dearest Margaret,

I have not yet assumed command of my old brigade. Yesterday I went amongst them, riding to the camps, and was much gratified at their turning out by companies and cheering me. They all seemed right glad to see me, both officers and men, and I do believe they were sincere. This is very gratifying, for they had more opportunity of knowing what I did and what I am than my superior officers.

Burnside returned this morning and received me very cordially. He is quite different from McClellan in his manners, having great affability and a winning way that attracts instead of repelling strangers. Burnside is devotedly attached to McClellan and would not think of taking his place when he was offered it.

I have been talking over the battles with different officers, and I am coming to the conclusion that the Pennsylvania Reserves did save the army in the great strategic change of base—that is to say, had it not been for the Reserves holding the enemy in check on June 30, and thus enabling the different corps to retreat and unite on that night, they (the enemy) would undoubtedly have broken our center and divided our forces into two, which could have been destroyed in detail. Hence, the sturdy resistance made by the Reserves in not permitting the enemy to advance beyond the line of battle gave our forces time during the night to retire and concentrate so that the next morning, the enemy found an unbroken line in front of them.

It appears that General Pope has been obliged to show his back to the enemy and to select a line of retreat, as Jackson, having advanced with a large force, has compelled him to retire from the line of the Rapidan and across the Rappahannock.

Your Loving Husband George

CHAPTER 12

The hot sun beat down on the Reserves who were camped in the heat and humidity on both sides of the Warrenton Turnpike, five miles east of Thoroughfare Gap in the Bull Run Mountains.

Lee had taken advantage of the withdrawal of the Army of the Potomac from the James and marched north. He had divided his army, sending Stonewall Jackson and his foot cavalry around Pope's right flank. At Manassas Junction, Jackson had destroyed a huge Union supply depot.

McDowell had told his commanders he believed that Lee and Longstreet were approaching on the other side of the Bull Run Mountains and were likely to march through Thoroughfare Gap in an effort to link up with Jackson. McDowell had moved his men to their current location to block Lee and Longstreet from uniting with Jackson.

Reynolds approached Meade. "I don't like General Pope one bit! He told me that he didn't know if he could trust any officer who had served under McClellan."

"That's outrageous!"

"Pope thinks he can capture or destroy Stonewall Jackson because he is isolated from the rest of the Rebel army." Reynolds pulled out a handkerchief and wiped the sweat from his face. "Pope, in his infinite wisdom, has ordered McDowell to march to Manassas Junction and try and catch Jackson in a pincer movement with the rest of the Army of Virginia."

"McDowell must be upset."

"He is hopping mad. He thinks Pope is too focused on Jackson and that *our* army will be in danger if Longstreet and Jackson unite."

"Reynolds, we know Jackson from the Mexican War. He's not stupid. What are the chances he stays at Manassas Junction, waiting for Pope to surround him?"

"You're right. Jackson likely will be gone. Regardless, we have our orders. Let's get the men on the march."

Jackson was not at Manassas Junction when Pope's army converged there. He had moved behind an unfinished railroad cut near the old Bull Run battlefield. There had been two days of serious fighting, but the Reserves had not been in the thick of it.

Meade was now camped near the hamlet of Groveton. The Reserves were out of rations, tired, and hungry.

The sound of hoofbeats caught Meade's attention. Reynolds rode up, looking angry. "I told Pope that Longstreet is in those woods in front of us. He didn't believe me! He claims that Jackson is retreating and that Longstreet is not here. Pope is living in a fantasy world! His plan for today is to have Fitz John Porter's corps attack Jackson's retreating troops. I'm pretty sure Jackson is right where he was yesterday. If Longstreet attacks our exposed left flank, the Army of Virginia could be destroyed. I'm going to take a line of skirmishers and ride out toward those woods to confirm that Longstreet is there."

Meade was startled. "It's not a good idea for you to do your own reconnaissance. On your horse, you will be a juicy target. If those woods are full of Rebels, you could be killed!"

"That's a risk I'm going to take," Reynolds said, looking determined. "By the way, I have some gossip for you. Pope accused Porter of disobeying his order yesterday to attack Jackson's left flank. Porter was shocked. He showed me Pope's order that gave him discretion whether to attack. McDowell told me this morning that after this battle is finished, Pope is going to bring court-martial charges against Porter."

SECOND BULL RUN

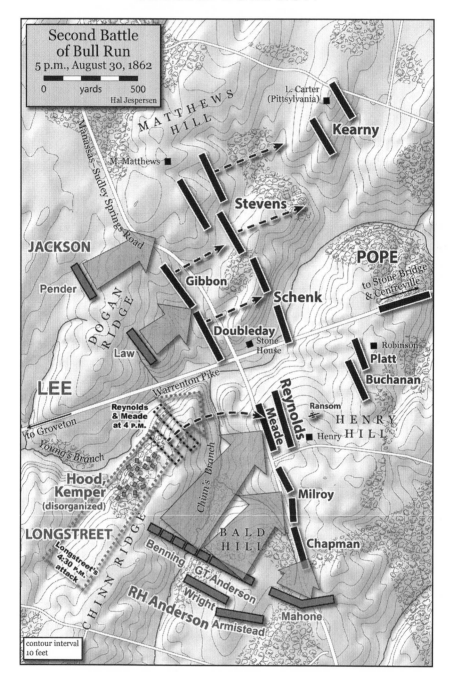

Second Battle
of Bull Run
5 p.m., August 30, 1862

0   yards   500
Hal Jespersen

contour interval
10 feet

Meade was disgusted. The army had too many officers engaged in power struggles and cozied up to politicians to gain advantage in assignments and promotions. He figured this had to be about gaining political favor. Porter was a close friend of McClellan's. The Radical Republicans hated McClellan and every general close to him. Pope would earn support from those politicians if he destroyed Porter's career.

"I am going to confirm that Longstreet is in those far woods," Reynolds said.

Meade rode to the crest of a hill where he had a view of the field Reynolds would ride into. Reynolds was his best friend in the army. *He was dangerously daring fate, and his frustrations with Pope had clouded his judgment.* Meade felt despair.

Meade took out his field glasses and saw a line of Union skirmishers advance across the field toward the woods. Reynolds and an aide rode behind them. Meade heard a spattering of musket fire. As the skirmish line continued forward, men began to fall. Reynolds and his aide continued following the skirmishers. A sharp fight broke out between the skirmishers and the Rebels in the woods. Finally, the skirmish line began to retreat, and Reynolds and his aide turned back and rode toward the Union line. Reynolds made it to safety, but his aide was shot off his horse.

Meade rode down to the headquarters tent and found his friend. "Those woods are full of Rebels," Reynolds said. "It has to be Longstreet. I'm going to see McDowell and report that Longstreet is here in force. I'll let McDowell deal with that fool Pope."

Reynolds returned to Meade an hour later, wearing a tight smile. "McDowell believed me when I reported Longstreet was here. He has ordered us to move back to a more defensible position on Chinn Ridge."

When the Reserves reached Chinn Ridge, they were on higher ground, closer to the main body of Federal troops. Reynolds deployed his men facing west, where a Longstreet attack would likely come from.

The roar of cannons and the rattling of musket fire from Porter's attack on Jackson reverberated along the ridge.

At 4:00 p.m., McDowell appeared on Chinn Ridge, looking frantic. "Porter's attack has failed, and his troops are retreating, scattering everywhere! Reynolds, Meade, move your men over to Henry Hill and establish a battle line that will stabilize Porter's retreating men."

Reynolds protested. "If we abandon this position and Longstreet attacks, there will be nothing to stop him from destroying our left flank."

"Henry Hill needs to be strengthened. There are other troops on Chinn Ridge who could slow down a Longstreet attack." McDowell pointed at Nathaniel McLean's brigade of Ohioans.

Reynolds replied, "Yes sir," and issued orders for the Reserves to move to Henry Hill.

Meade thought that McDowell was making a mistake in removing the seven thousand men of the Reserves from Chinn Ridge. McLean's Ohio brigade could not number more than 1,100 men. There was no way they would be able stop a Longstreet assault by themselves.

As he made his way toward Henry Hill, Meade heard a piercing voice screaming his name. He turned and saw McDowell racing down Chinn Ridge.

"Where is General Reynolds?"

"He's in front of me. He is already on Henry Hill."

"Longstreet is launching an attack. We need to leave part of the Reserves on Chinn Ridge. Go back and place a battery and a regiment next to McLean, then join Reynolds on Henry Hill."

When Meade got on top of Chinn Ridge, he saw Confederate infantry advancing in thick columns. He placed his men to the right of McLean's brigade. The combined firepower of the small number of Reserves and McLean's Brigade was not going to stop Longstreet's assault. The advancing Confederates likely outnumbered the Union defenders ten to one. All they could do was slow down the Rebels to allow time to establish a defensive position on Henry Hill. It was a desperate situation, and Meade realized that McDowell had made a difficult decision: sacrifice a small body of men to buy time. He was sad that many of his brave, stalwart Reserves would likely die defending their country, but he understood the military logic. Longstreet's rolling tide of attacking Rebels had to be slowed down; there was no other choice. They needed time to marshal forces to defend Henry Hill.

After struggling through a throng of dispirited troops retreating from Porter's failed attack, Meade reached Henry Hill and found Reynolds. "How did things look when you went back to Chinn Ridge?"

"Terrible! Those men are being sacrificed to buy time. I hated having to leave our boys up on that ridge. They are going to take frightful casualties."

Soon, the noise of a ferocious fight on Chinn Ridge resonated through the late afternoon air.

Reynolds said, "After Longstreet crushes the defenders on Chinn Ridge, he will come for us. Lee knows that Henry Hill is the key to the battlefield. There is only one way for Pope to retreat, and that is to take the Warrenton Pike east across the stone bridge over Bull Run. If the Rebels capture Henry Hill, their artillery could destroy anything moving on Warrenton Pike. Pope's army would be annihilated."

Reynolds had deployed the troops and Ransom's battery just below the crest of the hill not far from the house where Judith Henry, an eighty-five-year-old widow, had been killed during the previous summer's battle. Pope had found additional troops, and the Federal line extended half a mile on Henry Hill, paralleling Sudley Road.

The sounds of battle continued from Chinn Ridge. *The Union troops were holding Chinn Ridge longer than he thought possible. They must be putting up a hell of a fight,* Meade thought. He looked to his right at the prominent stone house near the intersection of Warrenton Turnpike and Sudley Road. Meade could see ambulances discharging wounded soldiers. He looked to his left and saw Reynolds looking calm and composed on his horse. Suddenly, a stream of movement in blue caught his eye. Union soldiers were retreating off Chinn Ridge.

Someone yelled, "Here come the Rebs!"

The gray-and-butternut colored uniforms of the Confederates were charging over the crest of Chinn Ridge and heading for Henry Hill. Ransom's battery went into action with lethal effect. But the Confederates continued to advance.

Reynolds rode in front of the Second Regiment, grabbing its battle flag. Waving it above his head, he yelled "Reserves, charge!"

Reynolds plunged down the hill, toward Sudley Road.

Meade held his sword over his head and screamed, "Pennsylvanians, charge!" He followed Reynolds on Old Baldy.

With a roar of cheers and hurrahs, the Reserves followed Reynolds and Meade down the hill, past Ransom's battery, toward the attacking Rebels. The Reserves reached the bottom of Henry Hill and formed a battle line on Sudley Road, which through years of use had become sunken and was a natural defensive position.

Reynolds yelled, "Give it to them, boys!"

Sheets of flame erupted from thousands of muskets, and a wave of deadly lead met the advancing Rebels. The Confederate line staggered, then stopped as hundreds of men fell, dead and wounded.

They were fighting Georgians, who regrouped and again charged down the hill toward the determined Reserves. Reynolds's inspiring leadership had electrified the men, and they fought like demons.

Ransom was firing his cannon shots over their heads. Charge after charge was repulsed with a horrifying loss of life. Sudley Road soon filled with Federal casualties as men were felled by Confederate musket and cannon fire.

Reynolds and Meade rode their horses behind the Sudley Road battle line, exhorting their men to give the Rebels their due in lead. They were highly visible targets, and Meade felt the familiar whiz of minié balls.

Old Baldy stumbled. Meade dismounted and saw that the horse had been shot in his left leg and was bleeding. The injury didn't appear too serious. He thought Old Baldy would make it through. He remounted his warhorse and resumed urging his men to hold the line at all hazards.

Despite repeated charges, the Rebels could not pierce the battle line of the Reserves. Darkness fell with Henry Hill still in Union hands.

———————

Centerville, August 31, 1862

My Dearest Margaret,

I write to advise you that after three days' fighting, I am all safe and well. Old Baldy was hit in the leg but was not badly hurt. Willie (your brother) I saw this morning, all safe. All your friends, I believe, are safe. I have had several officers and many men killed and wounded. We have been obliged to fall back from the old Bull Run battlefield, where we fought. The enemy is superior in force and flushed with their success.

Your Loving Husband George

ANTIETAM

CHAPTER 13

Meade looked down on Washington. He could see the Potomac River, the unfinished obelisk being built to honor George Washington, and the enormous dome being constructed on Capitol Hill. He turned around and looked at Arlington House, the prewar home of Robert E. Lee. He admired its graceful Greek Revival columns. The plantation grounds were being used for army campsites.

How quickly fates could change in war. Two days ago, it was a fait accompli that the Army of the Potomac would be given to Pope. Now that Lee had defeated Pope at the Second Battle of Bull Run and was threatening Washington, just the reverse had happened. Lincoln had merged the Army of Virginia into the Army of the Potomac, with McClellan in command.

He found Reynolds. "Can you believe McClellan is back in favor with Lincoln?"

"It does seem incredible. Our Reserves are happy. They despised Pope and are ecstatic to be back under Little Mac."

"Are we going to stay part of McDowell's corps?"

"The rumor is that McDowell is out."

"Any idea who would replace him?"

"Joe Hooker is the leading candidate."

"Reynolds, you know what I find incredible? Nine weeks ago, we were so close to Richmond that we could see the city's church spires. Now Lee is threatening Washington. How in the hell did that happen?"

"You can thank the geniuses in Washington. If they had let McClellan stay on the James River, he could have mounted a new offensive, and Lee would have had to keep his army in front of Richmond. Now Lee may attack Washington, or he could go into Maryland or even Pennsylvania."

Arlington House, Va, September 3, 1862

My Dearest Margaret,

Everything now is changed; McClellan's star is again ascendant, and Pope's has faded away. The whole army has been withdrawn in the face of the enemy, and now we have to defend our capital and perhaps resist an invasion of our soil through Maryland, all from the willful blindness of our rulers.

The principal scene of the conflict was the old battleground of Bull Run. The Pennsylvania Reserves particularly distinguished themselves on the afternoon of the thirtieth, when our attack on the enemy's right flank failed, so they attacked us very vigorously on our left flank. The Reserves came into action and held them in check so that when other troops came up, we were able to save our left flank, which if we had not done, the enemy would have destroyed the whole army. We were compelled to fall back on Washington for its defense and our own safety.

On these recent battlefields, I claim, as before, to have done my duty. My services, then, should, I think, add to those previously performed, that I may now fairly claim the command of a division.

I hardly think the enemy will venture to attack Washington. I believe they will try to get into Maryland, and that will necessitate our moving to meet them.

All my staff and most of the command are completely knocked up, but I am just as well as ever. General Reynolds has been very kind and civil to me.

Your Loving Husband George

CHAPTER 14

Camp Near Leesboro, Md, September 8, 1862

My Dearest Margaret,

On the sixth, I went to Willard's, where I met Willie (your brother) and his wife. I dined with them and returned to camp, where I found orders to march. We marched all night and most of the next day, reaching this point some ten miles north of Washington yesterday afternoon. We have been here one day and are to move again tomorrow. We will, I suppose, be moving now until something decisive is done with the enemy, who has invaded Maryland. Hooker has been placed in command of McDowell's corps, to which we belong.

Your Loving Husband George

———————

Hooker was a tall, clean-shaven man with clear blue eyes and a soldierly bearing. He had summoned his generals to his headquarters for an introductory meeting.

"The Rebels have invaded Northern soil. This corps last fought at Second Bull Run, which was a disastrous defeat. You were then part of the Army of Virginia, which no longer exists. You are now rightfully part of McClellan's Army of the Potomac, the great army of the East! Soon we are going to find Lee's army, and there will be a great battle. I have confidence in this army, in you as leaders, and in your men as fighters. We are going to win a magnificent victory for the Union! Instill confidence in your men that they have the ability and will be given the leadership to win what could be the decisive battle of the war!"

As they left the meeting, Meade asked Reynolds, "What do you think of the changes to the command structure?"

"I'm happy that Pope is gone. I think Hooker could be good. He fought bravely in Mexico. But I'm concerned that McClellan has given Burnside more than he can handle, commanding the Right Wing, combining his old Ninth Corps and Hooker's First Corps. While I like Burnside, he doesn't strike me as the most quick-thinking officer."

"Hooker has complained bitterly to McClellan about being under Burnside."

———————⊃

That night, Reynolds and Meade ate dinner together. Reynolds seemed distracted.

Meade asked, "Is something wrong?"

Reynolds sighed. "I have been harboring a secret. I need to confide in somebody. Of all the men I know, I trust you the most to keep a confidence."

Meade was startled. "A secret?"

"In 1860 I was posted in San Francisco. When I was appointed commandant of cadets at West Point, I took a steamer to New York. On the ship, I met a beautiful young lady. Her name is Kate Hewitt." Reynolds paused, smiling slightly. "She had been teaching at an orphanage in San Francisco. During the journey around the tip of South America, we fell in love. Because we are from different religions—I'm Protestant and she's Catholic—we fear how our families will react when we tell them of our love. At the beginning of the war, we became secretly engaged. When I go into battle, I wear a Catholic medal and a gold ring she gave me. I have given her my West Point ring. We will marry when this awful conflict is over. She has promised, over my protest, that if I do not survive the war, she will enter a convent."

Meade put his hands on his friend's shoulders. "It's wonderful that you have found love."

Reynolds closed his eyes and nodded. "I feel better having confided in you."

"I will not say a word of your secret engagement. I'm so happy for you and for your Kate."

CHAPTER 15

Camp Near Frederick, Md, September 13, 1862

My Dearest Margaret,

Orders came directing General Reynolds to proceed immediately to Harrisburg, which of course placed me in command of the division of Pennsylvania Reserves. Reynolds obeyed the order with alacrity, though very much against his will, and Hooker made an immediate and earnest protest against Reynolds's removal. Today I saw Seth Williams, who had in his hands Hooker's protest. He seemed quite surprised that Reynolds had left so soon. I told Williams very plainly that I saw no occasion for making such an outcry against Reynolds's removal because I considered it a reflection on my competency to command the division.

I am ready to meet the enemy. I feel I am in the position I am entitled to. I should have been delighted to have gone to Harrisburg in Reynolds's place, as I have no doubt he will get a large command there.

Your Loving Husband George

Meade was among a group of officers meeting with McClellan at his Frederick headquarters. A messenger entered the headquarters tent. "I have an urgent communication for the commanding general," he said.

McClellan excused himself and read the message. He came back to the meeting, holding a paper in the air and looking jubilant.

"This, gentlemen, is Lee's Special Order 191. It was found in a field wrapped around three cigars. I now know that Lee is on the other side of South Mountain and has divided his army, sending Stonewall Jackson to capture Harpers Ferry. We are in the position to destroy Lee's army in detail. With God's blessing, we will. We are going to march through the gaps in South Mountain to confront and destroy the Rebel army!"

On September 14, the Reserves marched on the National Road through Frederick and Middletown. They received cheers and words of encouragement as they passed homes displaying the Stars and Stripes. Smiling young maidens handed out bread, cakes, water, and milk. What a difference being on Northern soil made. In western Maryland, they were welcomed as heroic defenders, but in Virginia, they were treated with hostility as foreign invaders.

Last week, Lee had marched his Rebel army through Frederick and received a cold reception. He issued a proclamation claiming that Maryland was a conquered province and that the Confederate army would support Marylanders in throwing off the foreign yoke that was suppressing their freedoms. Lee's appeal had gone unheeded.

Burnside, as the Right Wing commander, planned to attack both flanks of the Rebel position on South Mountain. Jesse Reno's Ninth Corps would attack the southern flank at Fox's Gap, while Hooker's First Corps would attack the northern flank at Turner's Gap.

As they marched, Meade saw McClellan on a knoll. He was sitting on his magnificent black horse, Daniel Webster. When the troops saw McClellan, they broke into frenzied cheers and hurrahs.

McClellan pointed dramatically toward South Mountain. The men's cheers and yells intensified into a roar. The troops loved Little Mac. Their excitement and happiness at seeing McClellan was palpable. Meade was thrilled by the patriotic fervor his men exhibited. *Say what you will about McClellan,* he thought. *He unquestionably inspired the men.*

When they got to the hamlet of Frostown, Meade met with Hooker. They studied South Mountain's rugged terrain: tree-covered, parallel ridges carved by deep ravines. The lower slopes of the mountain had some scattered farms with stone walls separating fields. Pushing the Rebels off South Mountain would be a formidable task.

"George, you will attack on the far right. Place Cooper's battery in a position to safely shoot over your men as you begin your advance. I will have Hatch's Division on your left."

"Joe, my boys' spirits have been lifted being under McClellan again. They are ready to take it to the Rebs."

At 4:00 p.m., Meade launched his attack. The Confederate cannons on the mountain opened fire, and shells rained down as they approached the base of the mountain. Cooper's battery responded to the Rebel artillery.

Meade sent Colonel Hugh McNeil's Bucktails out as skirmishers. The terrain was rough and broken, and it was hard to keep battle lines in formation. Partway up the mountain, they encountered a farmer's stone wall. As the Bucktails advanced, Rebel soldiers who had been concealed behind the wall, unleashed a hail of lead, killing and wounding many men. General Truman Seymour ordered the Eighth Regiment forward in support of the Bucktails. With loud screams and yells, they charged the wall. Many brave men were cut down, but the brigade's charge did not falter. On and on the Eighth charged. When the survivors reached the wall, they leaped over it. The Rebels, startled by their failure to repulse the charge, broke and retreated.

Halfway up the mountain, Meade saw Colonel Gallagher standing on the edge of a ravine. In a curt voice, he asked, "Colonel, why have you stopped the attack?"

"I'm thinking about the best way to attack the Confederates who have taken up a defensive position in the ravine."

SOUTH MOUNTAIN

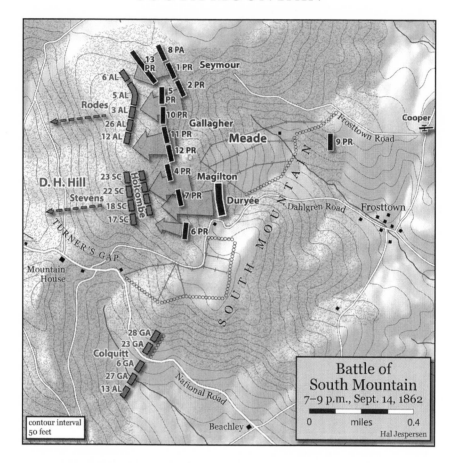

Meade, who was sitting on Old Baldy, peered over the edge. The bottom of the ravine was strewn with boulders. He could see Rebel bayonets poking out from behind the large rocks. He heard a musket fire, and a bullet smacked into a tree behind his head, showering him with splinters.

Neither Meade nor Old Baldy flinched. "Have you come up with a plan?"

"I am going to charge down the slope on both flanks of their position."

Meade nodded. "That's a good plan, Colonel. Good luck with your attack."

As Meade watched the attack unfold, he saw Colonel Gallagher shot as he was halfway down the slope. Seeing their leader go down inflamed Gallagher's men, who quickly drove the Rebels out of the ravine.

They were battling Alabamians and South Carolinians, who fought with toughness and tenacity. The Reserves slowly but steadily pushed the Rebels up the mountain.

The Bucktails were particularly effective. Being mountain men, they used the terrain to their advantage. They took shelter behind the rocks and trees and used their marksmanship to kill Southern soldiers. The Bucktails had the advantage of being armed with breech-loading Sharps rifles, which allowed them to fire two shots for every one fired by the Confederates, who were using front-loading muskets.

Meade followed his troops as they doggedly fought their way up the rugged landscape, routing stubborn Rebels out of their defensive positions. He felt proud as the regimental battle and American flags carried by his men in blue slowly ascended the green mountain.

As Meade crossed a ravine, he came across a wounded Confederate officer. He stopped and offered the man water.

"Thank you, sir. For your kindness. I have never seen Yankees fight like this. Your men have driven my boys right up this rugged mountain. I can hardly believe it!"

"Sir, I admire the courage and tenacity of Confederate soldiers. I will get you medical attention." Meade turned to an aide. "Please get this Southern officer to a field hospital."

As the Reserves got close to the crest, darkness fell. Meade instructed his men to stay where they were until first light.

When dawn came, Meade ordered the Bucktails out as skirmishers. It was cloudy and misty. Visibility was poor. As the Bucktails moved forward, they were met with silence. The Rebels had retreated off South Mountain.

CHAPTER 16

Meade visited Hooker to tell him that the Confederates had abandoned South Mountain. Hooker was in a jovial mood and celebrated by having his orderly bring him a brandy with water. Meade politely declined the offer of a drink.

"George, we should advance immediately and attack Lee while his army is still divided with Stonewall Jackson at Harpers Ferry. I don't know whether McClellan has it in him to move quickly and aggressively."

An hour later, Meade received orders to pursue the retreating Confederates. The Reserves marched through Turner's Gap and down the mountain. When they reached Boonsboro, they were given a triumphant welcome. Spirits were high. The Rebels were on the run.

Meade heard loud hurrahs from the troops behind him and turned to see what caused the noise. McClellan soon passed them on Daniel Webster to tumultuous cheers.

At 3:00 p.m., they were told to stop. Lee was not retreating. He had formed a line of battle by Antietam Creek near Sharpsburg. Meade eagerly awaited orders to continue their advance, but none came, and they camped that night where they had stopped.

There was still no order to advance in the morning. Meade felt that McClellan's advantage over Lee was dissipating quickly. If Lee was prepared to give battle, he surely had ordered Stonewall Jackson to join him and unify his Army of Northern Virginia. Meade worried that McClellan was letting the chance to destroy Lee's army slip through his fingers.

At 1:30 p.m., an order arrived to advance.

Hooker rode up with a huge smile on his face. "George, I'm happy to report that I'm no longer under Burnside! Thank God. I'm a much better general. As commander of the First Corps, I now report directly to McClellan."

"I imagine that Burnside is unhappy."

"I couldn't care less about Burnside's feelings." Hooker pointed up the road. "There are four bridges over the Antietam. Lee has three covered by artillery. We're going to cross the Upper Bridge, which is the northernmost crossing and the one Lee isn't defending."

It was 4:00 p.m. when the Reserves got to the Antietam and began crossing an arched stone bridge.

Once the entire First Corps got to the other side of the creek, Hooker approached Meade. "I'm giving the Reserves the honor of leading the First Corps toward the battlefield."

"Thank you, Joe. The men will be very proud to have been chosen to lead the First Corps."

Meade led the way toward Sharpsburg. They marched past a cultivated landscape of tidy farm fields ready for fall harvest. The divisions of Doubleday and Ricketts followed him.

The Reserves were straddling the Hagerstown Turnpike a few miles from Sharpsburg when Rebel artillery fired on them.

Hooker told Meade to send out a skirmish line toward the woods ahead. Meade ordered McNeil's Bucktails to perform the very dangerous job of scouting out the enemy. Meade told Seymour to take his regiment and support the Bucktails.

The Bucktails advanced across a plowed farm field. One hundred yards from the woods, Rebel musket fire erupted. McNeil had his men lie down in the field and return fire. The Bucktails used their Sharps rifles to pour deadly volleys into the Confederate infantry in the woods. McNeil jumped up and led his Bucktails in a charge toward the woods. Meade watched in dismay as the brave colonel was shot down. Even without their leader, the Bucktails continued their charge into the forest.

Seymour's Eighth Regiment followed the Bucktails into the woods.

Meade rode forward on Old Baldy. Rebel artillery shells exploded around him. He was in a dangerous place, but he had to show the men that he would brave the same risks they did. His nerves were steady. His fate was in God's hands.

An orderly from Seymour reported there was fierce hand-to-hand fighting, but the Reserves were forcing the Rebels back.

Hard fighting continued until darkness fell, with the opposing soldiers mere yards apart in the dark woods.

Meade entered the woods to visit his men. The Rebel pickets were so close, he could hear their voices. Hooker followed him, and after surveying the situation, he asked Meade to step out of the woods for a conference. The men entered the farm field.

"Tomorrow we will rip into Lee's left flank. Leave your troops in the woods, and in the morning, we will launch our offensive from here."

Meade nodded his agreement.

"I will attack directly south. Doubleday will advance on both sides of the Hagerstown Turnpike toward Sharpsburg. Ricketts will move through that cornfield east of the turnpike. Your two regiments not engaged today will be held in reserve. The initial objective will be to secure the high ground behind the cornfield and across the Hagerstown Turnpike around the Dunker Church."

"Have you heard anything from McClellan on reinforcements for tomorrow's attack? We're the only corps that has crossed Antietam Creek."

"McClellan is sending the Twelfth Corps to give us support." Hooker looked upward as rain began to fall. "The fate of our Republic may be decided in tomorrow's battle."

ANTIETAM: OVERVIEW

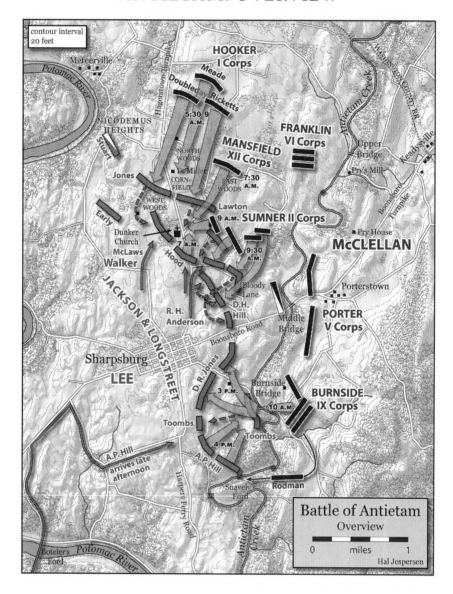

CHAPTER 17

Meade was up before dawn. It was a misty morning, and he was with Colonels Magilton and Anderson. Their regiments had spent the night in the woods north of the cornfield that would be the center of Hooker's battle line.

"The battle will begin at daybreak. Make sure your troops have extra ammunition. I expect that we will be engaged in a fierce conflict."

Meade rode out to examine the terrain. He wanted to understand the topography and any landmarks that he could use when directing troops in battle. He passed the cornfield that Ricketts's men would pass through. It had green cornstalks taller than a man's head.

He heard gunfire from the woods where Seymour had spent the night. He took out his watch. It was 5:30 a.m. The battle had begun.

He placed his regiments at the edge of the woods facing south toward the cornfield. He rode out of the forest and into a plowed field to view the action. To his left, Ricketts's regiments advanced toward the cornfield and the east woods to support Seymour. On his right, Doubleday's troops went forward on both sides of Hagerstown Turnpike.

As Ricketts's colorful, red-legged Zouaves brigade approached the cornfield, Rebel cannons near the Dunker Church started shelling them. Union batteries responded, and the air was filled with screaming and shrieking projectiles. The Zouaves entered the cornfield and disappeared. After a few minutes, Meade heard the roar of musket fire and screams and yells of men engaged in fierce combat. After thirty minutes, Meade watched the Zouaves retreat out of the cornfield. It must have been a terrible fight, because a third of the Zouaves failed to come back.

⸻⚬

The thunder of cannons, bursting of shells, and rattles of muskets melded into a continuous roar, and Meade felt the intensity of the fighting. All of Hooker's corps were engaged except for his two regiments. Meade wondered where the Twelfth Corps was. They were supposed to be providing support. He hoped they would show up soon.

A white horse carrying Hooker came galloping into view. Hooker looked calm and composed, directing troop movements and placing batteries as deadly shells exploded around him. He was living up to his nickname, "Fighting Joe."

The battle had been raging for an hour and fifteen minutes. Most of the stalks in the cornfield had been cut down by the vicious cannon and musket fire. Suddenly Union troops began falling back. Confederates were coming across the turnpike and pushing into the cornfield. The Rebels had mounted a counterattack! Hooker had given him discretion when to enter the battle. Now was the time to act.

He rode to Colonels Magilton and Anderson and told them they were entering the fight. Meade pointed south. "Do you see that fence on the north end of the cornfield? The land dips down on the north side of the fence. Have your men move there at double-quick, take down the fence, and throw some dirt on the rails for breastworks. Have them lie down. It should be a good defensive position. The Rebels are going to be coming through that cornfield!"

He went to Ransom and told him to move forward to support Magilton and Anderson. Meade yelled to be heard over the roar of battle. "Load your guns with double canister."

Magilton and Anderson quickly got their men moving. Meade noticed a solider standing behind a tree. The man refused to move, despite repeated orders. *No man should fail to do his duty,* Meade thought. He unsheathed his sword and rode to the cowering man.

ANTIETAM: 0645–0745

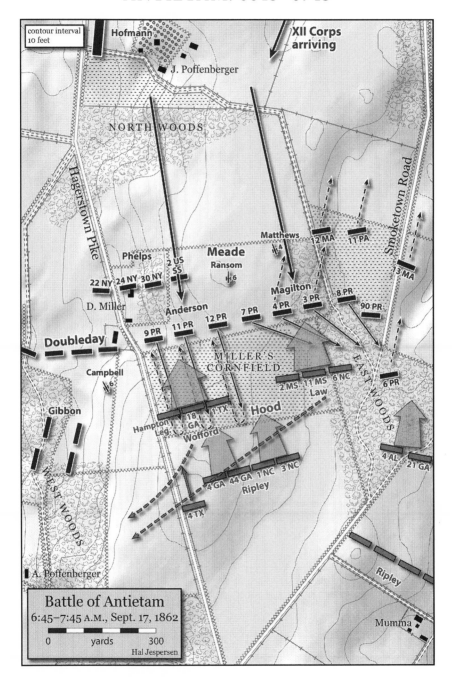

Battle of Antietam
6:45–7:45 A.M., Sept. 17, 1862

0   yards   300

Hal Jespersen

Meade raised his sword and using the flat side, struck the man on the shoulder, knocking him to the ground.

Meade, his face contorted, screamed, "Join your regiment! There are no cowards in the Reserves!"

The soldier rose up, and with fear on his face, ran to catch up with his comrades.

Meade advanced on Old Baldy. He felt a sudden pain in his right thigh. *Have I been shot again?* He saw that his pants were torn, but he didn't see any blood. He reached down and touched his thigh. It throbbed with pain. He was lucky, he had been hit by an object whose force had been spent.

Rebel troops were coming through the cornfield. Ransom's battery opened with canister shells that shredded men who took a direct hit. The infantry, behind the improvised breastwork, poured musket fire into the Southerners. The Confederate line faltered and fell back. The north end of the cornfield was covered with dead and wounded men. Meade noted that he was facing John Bell Hood's division, one of the toughest units in the Rebel army.

Confederate artillery by the Dunker Church started firing on their position. The awful wails and whistles of tumbling shells filled the air and began impacting the Reserves, killing and maiming men.

An aide rode up with a note from Hooker, thrust it into Meade's hands, and rode off, disappearing into the smoky haze that had enveloped the battlefield. Meade read the note. The Federal position in the east woods, where Seymour had been fighting, was collapsing. Meade was directed to send a regiment to support the threatened position. Meade sent Magilton's regiment.

His shortened battle line was dangerously exposed to being flanked by the attacking Confederates. And within minutes, Hood attacked his exposed flank. Meade went to Ransom and pointed to the fast-approaching enemy. "Move your guns and concentrate on that advancing column of Rebels!"

Ransom's cannons blasted deadly canister rounds, which stopped the Confederates and drove them back with great loss. In the pause that followed, Meade grimly surveyed his own casualties. Men were down all over the line, some with holes in their foreheads and some missing limbs. One man had been decapitated.

Down to one regiment and one battery, the Reserves fought with tenacity to hold off the Confederates, who kept regrouping and attacking. During one attack, Meade felt Old Baldy shiver. He looked down and saw blood pouring from the horse's neck. He dismounted, wishing he had time to tend to his trusted warhorse.

Meade's orderly found him a cavalry horse. He mounted and continued urging the Reserves to resist the Confederate counterattack.

One of Doubleday's brigades, which had been fighting in the woods west of the Hagerstown Turnpike, turned east and attacked Hood's left flank. The Rebels began retreating through the cornfield.

When Meade saw the enemy retreating, he went to Colonel Anderson. "Get your men up. Have them follow those retreating Confederates."

Anderson led his men into the bloody cornfield. Meade followed, riding into a nightmarish scene. Dead men in gray and blue everywhere, some in a deadly embrace, others blown apart by artillery shells. Severed arms, legs, and heads littered the ground. The green cornhusks were covered in blood. As they exited the cornfield, Hood's men continued their retreat behind a Rebel battle line across an open field.

Anderson was outnumbered by the Confederates facing him. A sharp fight broke out. Standing less than a hundred yards apart, the Confederates and the Reserves fired into each other's ranks. The Reserves, being outnumbered, were getting the worst of it.

His new horse violently bucked, almost throwing Meade to the ground. He dismounted. A quick examination revealed that the horse had been hit and was badly hurt. *Two horses shot out from under me in a half hour,* he thought. *This is an intense battle.*

More Rebels were joining the fight, but no reinforcements appeared to augment the thinning ranks of the Reserves. His men were used up and couldn't hold their position. Meade gave Anderson the order to retreat, and they moved back across that god-awful, bloodstained cornfield. He was proud of the Reserves. At a terrible cost, they had repulsed Hood's counterattack.

Shortly before 8:00 a.m., the Twelfth Corps arrived on the battlefield and relieved the battered Reserves.

At 8:30 a.m., Meade returned to the woods north of the cornfield.
What a vicious fight. The casualties on both sides had to be astronomical. While Meade was proud of the Union troops and the great valor
they had exhibited in the battle, the unfortunate reality was that Lee's
line had not been broken.

He received a report that Hooker had been shot and carried from
the field. A dispatch arrived from McClellan's headquarters. Meade
read the note, which was written in pencil.

> Headquarters Army of the Potomac, September 17, 1:25
> PM, 1862
>
> Brg. Genl. Geo. Meade
> Genl.
>
> The Commanding Gen'l directs that you temporarily
> assume command of Hooker's Corps, and use every
> effort in your power to reorganize it and make it
> available.
>   It is absolutely necessary that the right should
> be held, and the troops must be got together and into
> position for that purpose as rapidly as possible.
>
> Yours very Respy,
> Coulburn
> A. A. G.

Meade was surprised. He knew Ricketts ranked him. He felt tremendous pride that McClellan had given him a battlefield promotion.

A second note arrived from McClellan's headquarters.

> Headquarters Army of the Potomac,
> 3 hours, 10 min., September 17, 1862
>
> General Meade

General

The Commanding Gen'l directs that you at once take command of the Army Corps, which was under the command of Genl. Hooker this morning. This order is given without regard to rank and all officers of the Corps will obey your orders. The Comdg. General also directs me to say that you will be held responsible for this command as herein assigned to you.

Very Respectfully
R. B. Marcy
Chief of Staff

Meade consulted with Doubleday and Ricketts, whose divisions had also been relieved by the Twelfth Corps. The First Corps had suffered losses in excess of 30 percent. All agreed it was not fit for further offensive action that day.

The Twelfth Corps fought over the same ground—the bloody cornfield, the east woods, the Dunker Church, and the woods west of the turnpike—increasing by thousands the number of dead and wounded Union troops. Lee's defensive line had not been broken, and now the Twelfth Corps was out of the battle.

General Sumner's Second Corps crossed the Antietam, and there had been vicious fighting around the Dunker Church and further south at a sunken road. Then Sumner had been pushed back by a counterattack. Burnside's Ninth Corps was to attack Lee's right flank. Meade heard intermittent sounds of battle from Burnside's sector.

The day's battle had not been smoothly coordinated. On Lee's left flank, three Federal corps had made independent attacks. If they had all attacked at the same time or in support of each other, the chance for success would have been much greater.

At 7:00 p.m., an orderly from McClellan's headquarters brought Meade news of Burnside's fight. He told him that Burnside had fought a bitter, bloody battle and after many frontal assaults captured the Lower Bridge over the Antietam and then drove the Rebels almost to Sharpsburg. Just when it looked like Burnside was going to win a great victory, A. P. Hill arrived from Harpers Ferry and stopped Burnside's advance and drove him back.

The fighting had ended in a stalemate with both armies still on the field. McClellan had chosen not to put the thirty thousand troops of the Fifth and Sixth Corps into the fight.

Meade thanked God for having him live through such a violent struggle.

Field of Battle Near Sharpsburg, September 18, 1862

My Dearest Margaret,

I commanded the division of Pennsylvania Reserves in the action at South Mountain on the fourteenth. Our division turned the enemy's left flank and gained the day. Their movements were the admiration of the whole army, and I gained great credit. I was not touched nor was my horse. Yesterday and the day before, my division commenced the battle and was in the thickest of it. I was hit by a spent grapeshot, giving me a severe contusion on the right thigh but not breaking the skin. Baldy was shot through the neck but will get over it. A cavalry horse I mounted afterward was shot in the flank. When General Hooker was wounded, General McClellan placed me in command of the army corps, over General Ricketts's head, who ranked me. This selection is a great compliment and answers all my wishes in regard to my desire to have my services appreciated. I cannot ask for more and am truly grateful for the merciful manner I have been protected and for the good fortune that has attended me.

Your Loving Husband George

CHAPTER 18

Sharpsburg, Md, September 20, 1862

My Dearest Margaret,

I wrote you a few lines the day before yesterday, on the field of battle, when we expected every moment that the battle would be renewed. The battle had been a very severe one, and our army was a good deal broken and somewhat demoralized—so much so that it was deemed hazardous to risk an offensive movement on our part before reinforcements arriving from Washington should reach the scene of action. Yesterday morning, we moved forward, when lo! the bird had flown. We soon ascertained from the prisoners taken on the field and from the evidences on the field itself that we had hit them much harder than they had us and that in reality our battle was a victory.

    I am afraid I shall not get the credit for these last battles that I did for those near Richmond for two reasons. First, I was not wounded; second, old Sam Ringwalt was not there to write letters about me. I find the papers barely mention the Pennsylvania Reserves and call them McCall's troops, never mentioning my name. I was not only in command, but at South Mountain, I was *on the extreme right flank and had the conduct of the whole operation. I must do Hooker the justice to say that he promptly gave me credit for what I did and have reason to believe it was his urgent appeal to McClellan that I was the right man to take his place when he was wounded which secured my being assigned to command of the corps. I send you two pencil notes received on the field of battle, which I wish preserved as evidence of my having done my duty. A man who under such circumstances is elevated to rank may well be proud of the fact and can hardly have his elevation charged to political or petticoat influence.*

Your Loving Husband George

———————⚔

Meade's time as First Corps commander was short-lived. When Reynolds returned from Harrisburg, McClellan promoted him to First Corps commander and placed Meade in charge of the Reserves.

During breakfast, everybody was talking about the big story from yesterday's papers: Lincoln's preliminary Emancipation Proclamation, which gave the Confederate states notice that if they did not give up their rebellion against the United States by January 1, 1863, the President would use his war powers to free slaves in states still in revolt.

Reynolds asked Meade, "What do you think of Lincoln's preliminary Emancipation Proclamation?"

"Like Lincoln said at Chatham Manor, the war has evolved into such a sanguinary affair that using the army to wipe out the sin of slavery now seems appropriate. Do you know if it's true that McClellan had a fit when he heard that Lincoln was going to emancipate the slaves?"

Reynolds replied, "McClellan wanted to write a protest to Lincoln. He believes emancipation will demoralize the army, that the soldiers don't want to fight for abolition, and the war will be prolonged because the South would never agree to peace if it meant the abolishment of slavery. His senior staff talked him out of it, arguing that a protest would lead to Lincoln sacking him."

After breakfast, Meade and Reynolds mounted their horses and headed toward McClellan's headquarters. When they got there, they saw the familiar figure of the President. He was dressed all in black, and his signature eight-inch stovepipe hat adorned his head.

As they dismounted, Lincoln approached. "I know you two like a good story. The Confederates made a raid in Fairfax County last month, and they captured a brigadier general and several hundred horses. When I heard about it, I told Stanton I was sorry to lose the horses. He threw himself back in his chair in astonishment that I was not concerned with losing a general! I explained that I can make a brigadier general in five minutes, but it is not as easy to replace hundreds of horses."

Reynolds and Meade joined in Lincoln's laughter.

"General Meade, I understand you have relatives fighting for the Confederacy."

"I have two nephews from Mississippi in Lee's army. Henry Wise, the former Virginia governor, is a Confederate general. Wise's son is also in Lee's army."

"It is sad that so many American families are divided by this war. Mrs. Lincoln has four brothers and three brothers-in-law fighting for the Confederates."

McClellan and his staff joined their group. At six feet four, Lincoln was close to a foot taller than the commanding general, and as they stood together, the juxtaposition was striking.

McClellan asked, "Mr. President, are you ready for your battlefield tour?"

Lincoln mounted his horse. "Lead the way, General."

Their first stop was the Dunker Church. The little white battle-scarred building had holes from musket balls and exploding shells. McClellan described how the battle had unfolded. An hour into the tour, when they were on the northern edge of the bloody cornfield, McClellan began praising Meade.

"Mr. President, General Meade's Pennsylvania Reserves played a vital role in the morning's fighting. John Bell Hood's men had launched a vigorous counterattack through the cornfield. The Reserves fought valiantly and stopped Hood from breaking the center of Hooker's line."

Lincoln turned to Meade, obviously impressed. "Well done, General Meade."

McClellan said, "Meade was one of my early appointments as a brigadier general. He is an excellent officer—calm, brave, and intelligent."

After the tour ended, Reynolds approached Meade. "McClellan was really singing your praises to the President. I bet you get promoted to major general."

"It's nice to get some recognition for your service. I don't think the President came out here just to tour the battlefield."

"I think Lincoln is unhappy that three weeks after the battle, McClellan has not crossed the Potomac and gone after Lee. Lincoln wants action, and McClellan wants the army to be in perfect condition before he goes on the offensive. Those two are not a match made in heaven."

Camp Near Sharpsburg, Md, October 5, 1862

My Dearest Margaret,

The President of the United States has visited our camp and reviewed our corps. I had the distinguished honor of accompanying him to the battlefield, where General McClellan pointed out the various phases of the day, saying here it was that Meade did this and there Meade did that. It was all very gratifying to me. He seemed very much interested in all the movements of Hooker's corps. I do not know the purpose of the President's visit. I think it was to urge McClellan on, regardless of his views or the condition of the army.

Your Loving Husband George

CHAPTER 19

A week had passed since the President's visit, and the Union army was still camped near Antietam Creek. The temperature had dropped into the forties. Meade and Reynolds sat before a blazing fire.

"Reynolds, have you seen how the press is lionizing Fighting Joe as he recuperates in Washington from his wound? The President and most of the Cabinet have visited him."

Reynolds looked amused. "Even Kate Chase, the beautiful daughter of the Secretary of Treasury, visited Hooker. He has become a Washington celebrity."

Meade laughed. "I heard that Lincoln joked with Hooker that the Army of the Potomac is McClellan's bodyguard!"

"Jeb Stuart's cavalry raid around the Army of the Potomac is not going to help McClellan's case in Washington. Stuart got all the way to Chambersburg, Pennsylvania, and returned to Virginia with captured horses and supplies. Very embarrassing for McClellan."

Camp Near Sharpsburg, Md, October 12, 1862

My Dearest Margaret,

Hooker and I are old acquaintances. We were at

West Point together, served in Mexico together, and have met from time to time since. He is a very good soldier, capital general for an army corps, but I am not prepared to say as to his abilities for carrying on a campaign and commanding a large army. I should fear his judgment and prudence, as he is apt to think the only thing to be done is to pitch in and fight. Being always intimate with the President, when McDowell was relieved, Hooker got his corps. Now he is made, and his only danger is that he will allow himself to be used by McClellan's enemies to injure him. Hooker is a Democrat and anti-abolitionist—or at least he was. What he will be, when the command of the army is held out to him, is more than anyone can tell, because I fear he is open to temptation and liable to be seduced by flattery.

McClellan does not seem to have made as much out of his operations in Maryland as I had hoped he would and as I think he is entitled to. His failure to immediately pursue Lee (which Hooker would have done) and now this raid of Stuart in our rear will go far toward taking away from him the prestige of his recent victories. I don't wish you to mention it, but I think he errs on the side of prudence and caution, and a little more rashness on his part would improve his generalship.

I am getting very tired of inactivity, and though I am not fond of fighting, if we have to do it, I think the sooner we get at it and have it over, the better.

Your Loving Husband George

CHAPTER 20

Camp Near Warrenton, Va, November 8, 1862

My Dearest Margaret,

Today the order has been received relieving McClellan from duty with this army and placing Burnside in command. I must confess I was surprised at this, as I thought the storm had blown over. If he had been relieved immediately after the Battle of Antietam, or anytime before we moved, I could have seen some show of reason on military grounds. This removal now proves conclusively the cause is political. The date of the order, November 5 (the day after the New York election), confirms this.

The army is filled with gloom and greatly depressed. Burnside, it is said, wept like a child and is the most distressed man in the army. He openly says he is not fit for the position and that McClellan is the only man we have who can handle the large army collected together, one hundred twenty thousand men. We (the generals) are going tomorrow in a body to pay our respects and bid farewell to McClellan.

Your Loving Husband George

The commanding general's headquarters tent was crowded with generals who had come to pay their respects. McClellan had been continuously engaged since Meade had arrived. Reynolds tapped his shoulder. "If we want a private word with McClellan, we should do it before dinner is served."

When they approached McClellan, he separated from the group of officers he was speaking with. "Generals Reynolds and Meade, how good of you to attend this somber party."

Reynolds said, "General McClellan, the army is greatly saddened by your removal."

McClellan was in a reflective mood. "My removal was politically motivated. We just won great victories at South Mountain and Antietam. The army's spirits have soared under my leadership. That devil Stanton hates me and has Lincoln's ear. Lincoln is afraid of me running against him in the 1864 election. He does not want to run against a war hero, so he has taken me off center stage. Lincoln always wanted me to be fighting a battle even if the army wasn't prepared for it or if it was likely to end badly. He and Stanton most certainly will press Burn to quickly launch an attack against Lee. My fear is that Burn will not be able to withstand the pressure that will be placed upon him and that he will engage in a reckless attack with disastrous results."

A dinner bell rang and McClellan took his leave.

At the end of the evening, each general went to McClellan to bid him farewell. Meade was emotional when his turn came.

"You have done so much to advance my career. I have been deeply honored by your trust in me. The men of the Army of the Potomac love and adore you."

McClellan shook Meade's hand. "General Meade, you have served courageously and with great distinction. I'm proud to have been your commanding general."

The next day, the Army of the Potomac assembled to be reviewed by McClellan. McClellan and Burnside rode past the three-mile-long line of troops. Meade could hear loud cheers long before he saw the approaching generals. When McClellan passed in front of the Reserves with his cap in his hand, the men cheered and cheered for their beloved Little Mac. Color-bearers waved their flags in a frenzy. Some men openly wept. It was a glorious send-off. McClellan appeared deeply moved by the outpouring of affection.

It is ironic, Meade thought. *While McClellan had inspired great faith in the soldiers that he was a magnificent military leader, truly a young Napoleon, he had failed to instill a similar belief in his political masters.*

FREDERICKSBURG

CHAPTER 21

Old Baldy hadn't recovered sufficiently from his Antietam wound for campaign duty, though the prognosis was good for Meade's favorite warhorse. He hoped they would be reunited. They made a good team. Meade mounted his new horse and set out to visit Burnside.

He needed to see for himself if Lincoln had given his friend a job that was too big for him to handle.

Burnside had a breezy, good-natured personality. But when Meade entered his tent, he saw that Burnside's normal affability had vanished, replaced by an appearance of depression and exhaustion. He slowly rubbed his hands through his enormous side whiskers.

"Twice before I declined command because I don't feel competent to manage a large army," Burnside said. "This time I wasn't asked but ordered to take command. Lincoln sent General Buckingham to deliver the order in the middle of the night! I was awakened from a sound sleep and received the shock of my life. I vigorously objected to having such a responsibility thrust on me. And then Buckingham said that if I didn't accept command, Lincoln would give it to Joe Hooker. There are few people in this world that I dislike, but Hooker is one of them. He is selfish, a schemer, and full of himself. Worst of all, he incessantly criticizes everyone in the command structure above him. So, I accepted command. But I fear it is a decision I will live to regret."

"The men are upset over how McClellan was treated, but they are true patriots and will respond to your leadership and continue the fight to restore the Union."

"Thank you. Your support is meaningful to me." Burnside wrung his hands. "I will be meeting with Henry Halleck to discuss grand strategy. McClellan had to use a railroad that can't supply the army's needs. The most efficient and safest supply route is by water. McClellan favors the James River, but Lincoln won't approve it. As a compromise, I'm going to argue for a change of base to the railroad that begins at Aquia Creek Landing on the Potomac and runs to Fredericksburg and then Richmond."

"I have always favored a river supply base. Good luck in your dealings with Halleck," Meade said.

Burnside smiled and seemed to relax a bit. "Thank you, George."

Camp Near Rappahannock Station, Va, November 13, 1862

My Dearest Margaret,

Yesterday Generals Halleck and Meigs made their appearance at Warrenton, and it is understood that a grand council of war is to be held today. McClellan has always objected to operating on this line and insisted on the James River as being the proper base for operations. Halleck, under Washington influence, has been trying to force operations on this line—that is, the Orange and Alexandria Railroad. Now, this road has but one track. The known capacity is insufficient by one-third to carry the daily supplies required for this army. This fact, to an ordinarily intelligent mind unbiased by ridiculous fears for the safety of Washington, ought to be conclusive. The next line, and the one Burnside favors as a compromise, is the one from Fredericksburg to Richmond. This is open to the same objection as the other, except it is only seventy-five miles. Still, it will require a larger army to protect these seventy-five miles and keep open our communications than to just attack Richmond itself.

I hear that Hooker is at Warrenton and has been placed in command of Fitz John Porter's corps, Porter having been relieved and ordered to Washington.

What we are coming to I cannot tell, but I must confess this interference by politicians with military men, and the personal intrigues and bickering among military men, make me feel very sad and very doubtful of the future.

Your Loving Husband George

CHAPTER 22

Camp Near Stratford Court House, Va, November 22, 1862

My Dearest Margaret,

It is most trying to read the balderdash in the public journals about being in Richmond in ten days. I question whether we can get in the neighborhood of Richmond this winter on this line. I have no doubt the attempt is to be made and an effort to force us on. All this comes from taking the wrong line of operations, the James River being the true and only practical line to approach Richmond. But I have always maintained Richmond need not—should not—be attacked at all and that the proper mode to reduce it is to take possession of the great lines of railroad leading to it from the south and southwest. Cut these and stop any supplies from going there so their army will be compelled to evacuate and meet us on ground we can select ourselves. The blind infatuation of the authorities at Washington, sustained, I regret to say, by Halleck, who as a soldier ought to know better, will not permit the proper course to be adopted, and we shall have to take the consequences.

I suppose you have seen in the papers the order dividing the army into three grand divisions and giving the command of certain corps to the senior officers on duty with those corps. This places General Butterfield in command of Porter's corps. General Butterfield is my junior, and I am his only senior on duty with the army. I saw Franklin and Baldy Smith today, who referred to this matter. They said that Burnside did not know how to arrange it otherwise, and they thought if I made an application to Burnside and gave him any chance of acting that he would assign me to the corps. This, however, is a very delicate matter, and I have seen several cases ended to the discomfort of the protestant. General Butterfield does not command me, and as his senior, command only of a division, I have a right to complain.

Your Loving Husband George

A cold, wind-driven rain did little to lift Meade's spirits as he rode toward Burnside's headquarters to discuss the injustice of Butterfield's promotion. Once he made a decision, Meade was a man of action. He had no patience to wait for better weather.

He had to pass Hooker's headquarters and decided it would be polite to advise him of his intentions, given that Butterfield was one of Hooker's closest friends.

Hooker gave him a warm welcome. "George Meade, how good to see you. You did commendable work at Antietam. Would you like a little brandy to warm you up on such a cold, miserable day?"

"No, thank you, Joe, but I would love some coffee. Have you recovered from your Antietam wound?"

"Not completely; there are days that the foot is still very painful. The doctors told me I came close to dying from losing so much blood." As Meade was given his coffee, he added, "McClellan acted badly when he took the First Corps away from you when Reynolds returned. You earned your promotion by your deeds on the battlefield."

"I have great respect for Reynolds. I would have loved to have kept command of the First Corps, but I was not surprised or offended by McClellan's decision."

"Can you believe what a mess Burnside has made with the pontoons? We stole the march on Lee and got to Fredericksburg when the town was virtually defenseless. We should be close to Richmond. Instead we are idle, waiting for pontoons to bridge the river. Lee has taken advantage of the delay. There will be a nasty fight to get past Fredericksburg."

An aide handed Hooker a glass of brandy. "You know, there was serious talk of giving me the Army of the Potomac. That Goddamn Halleck must have convinced Lincoln not to give me command."

"Why would Halleck oppose you?"

"We knew each other in California. I had left the army and gone into ranching. I don't know how Halleck did it, but while he was a full-time army officer, he started a law practice specializing in land claims and became wealthy. I had some tough financial times and borrowed money from Halleck. I couldn't repay the loan, and he holds a grudge. Lincoln thinks highly of me though, so we'll see what the future holds."

Meade sipped his coffee. "I wanted to let you know that I'm on my way to see Burnside to advise him that I rank Dan Butterfield and that the Fifth Corps command should have been given to me."

Hooker looked surprised. "I didn't realize you ranked Butterfield. I think it would be very unfair to take the Fifth Corps away from him after he has been promoted."

"I understand your position. But I hope you can see why I am unhappy."

"Of course. We'll let Burnside decide."

Meade finished his coffee and took his leave, going back into the rain.

After a few miles, he reached Burnside's headquarters, the Phillips House, an imposing mansion built in American Gothic style. It had a steeply pitched slate roof; large, soaring chimneys; pointed cross-gables; and gingerbread-trimmed eaves.

Meade gave his horse to an orderly and entered the house.

When Meade found Burnside, he was blunt. "Burn, I rank Butterfield, and the Fifth Corps command should have been given to me."

Burnside looked surprised. "I was unaware of your seniority, George. You're a better general than Butterfield, and I would have preferred you. I think there is a possibility of an officer more senior than you being sent down here. If that doesn't happen, you will have the Fifth Corps."

"Thank you for your support. I know you meant no slight to me."

The men began to talk about the challenges of dealing with Washington. Burnside confided in Meade. "I'm having a problem with Halleck. Not getting the pontoons here on time ruined my plan to get between Lee and Richmond where he would have been forced to attack me. Now I have to attack Lee. At our meeting in Culpeper, Halleck said he would have the pontoon bridging materials at Fredericksburg when the army got there. Now he's blaming me for the mistake."

"I understand your frustration. Halleck is simply a bureaucrat. Being a good bureaucrat, he makes sure mistakes are someone else's fault."

CHAPTER 23

Camp Near Brooks Station, Va, December 6, 1862

My Dearest Margaret,

I have just sent you a telegram announcing that I received notice from Washington by telegraph of my promotion to major general. I am truly glad for your sake as well as my own.

The weather is very cold tonight, with everything freezing hard. But with my stove and buffalo robe, and with the good news today, I bid defiance to the weather.

Your Loving Husband George

———————

Meade bent his body forward against the strong wind as he walked through the frigid air. He was happy to get out of the elements and enter Reynolds's tent.

Reynolds held up a newspaper. "Did you see that Fitz John Porter was arrested and will be court-martialed for allegedly not obeying Pope's order at Second Bull Run? What a travesty of justice! He had discretion not to attack!"

Meade shook his head. "Porter is being treated in a most despicable way." He pulled a chair close to the stove and elevated his frozen feet to soak in the warmth. "You've been spending a lot of time with Burn. How is he holding up?"

"He's haggard and exhausted. Burn has a problem delegating, and his emotions are very transparent. He complains about being forced to take over the Army of the Potomac and doubts his own abilities. He's not generating much confidence in his subordinates."

"Has he finalized a decision to attack?"

"He has decided to cross the river. Engineers are to begin building pontoon bridges over the Rappahannock at three a.m. Franklin's Left Grand Division will cross the river south of Fredericksburg while Sumner's Right Grand Division will cross and take a position north of Fredericksburg. Hooker's Central Grand Division will stay on this side of the river with flexibility to support either flank."

"What is the plan after we cross?"

"Burn was vague. My impression is he will launch attacks both north and south of Fredericksburg."

"Lee's position on the hills behind Fredericksburg looks very strong. There's a rumor that Burn is going to dispatch a force to create a diversion on the James River to force Lee to weaken his forces here."

"That idea was considered but has been dropped."

Camp Near Fredericksburg, Va, December 10, Midnight

My Dearest Margaret,

Tomorrow we shall cross the river and may have an engagement with the enemy. Keep up your spirits, and don't believe any news but what comes in a reliable form. Of course, no man can go into action without running risks, but our Heavenly Father has shown us so much mercy and loving kindness hitherto that we may pray for its continuance and hope for the best.

Your Loving Husband George

CHAPTER 24

During the early morning darkness, Meade heard work begin on the pontoon bridges. As light appeared over the horizon, he heard musket fire, and the men working on the bridges began falling into the water. Confederate pickets hidden in Fredericksburg were shooting defenseless engineers! The survivors ran off the bridges, seeking cover.

As the morning wore on, the Federal infantry shot volleys across the river to drive off the Confederate pickets. When the engineers returned to their work, Rebel fire resumed, killing more men. Union troops couldn't return fire for fear of hitting their compatriots on the bridges.

At midday, Meade heard the roar of Federal artillery and saw buildings on Fredericksburg's waterfront hit by cannonballs. The army of the United States was battering the homes and churches of a historic American city. Rubble filled the streets. Meade didn't see any civilians running from the buildings. The residents must have evacuated their homes, fearing what might happen.

Meade hoped the destruction was worth it and would drive away the Confederate pickets.

When the engineers returned to work, Confederate fire resumed, and more men tumbled into the Rappahannock's freezing waters.

An hour later, Meade saw Union troops rowing pontoon boats across the Rappahannock toward Fredericksburg. When they made it to the shoreline, a sharp fight broke out. After an hour, there was silence. The engineers reemerged and, unmolested, finished building the bridges.

The late-afternoon December sunlight was fading. Meade anticipated receiving an order from Burnside to cross the Rappahannock so they would be positioned for a morning attack. But no order to march came, and darkness fell.

The order came early the next morning. Reynolds led his First Corps through heavy fog and across the pontoon bridges and marched south, forming the army's left flank.

When the fog lifted, Meade examined the terrain. They were on an open plain covered with fields. A mile away was Prospect Hill. It was part of a ridgeline that ran behind Fredericksburg. Here, the ridge was low. On the north side of town, the ridge was called Marye's Heights and was higher and steeper.

An attack would have to cross the Richmond Stage Road; then open farmland; and finally, shortly before Prospect Hill, the Richmond, Fredericksburg, and Potomac Railroad.

The day passed with no order to attack. Around 4:00 p.m., Meade saw Burnside ride across the river and stop at Franklin's headquarters. He heard that Reynolds had been summoned to a meeting with Burnside.

When Reynolds returned, he was smiling. He pulled Meade aside and said, "We persuaded Burn to use the Left Grand Division for an all-out assault tomorrow on Prospect Hill. We will begin advancing the troops before the sun comes up to get close to the Rebel lines so there will be an element of surprise to the attack. Sumner's Right Grand Division will attack Marye's Heights to hold the Confederate troops there from reinforcing the Rebels in front of us. Burn is preparing the orders."

The next morning, Meade was warming his cold hands with a hot mug of coffee when Reynolds entered the tent. His normally calm face was a mask of anger.

"Unbelievable! It's six a.m., and no orders from Burnside. I'm going back to Franklin's headquarters. Come with me."

Meade left his unfinished coffee and went with Reynolds. They found Franklin with Baldy Smith, who got the Sixth Corps command when Franklin was made the Left Wing Grand Division commander.

Franklin was fuming. "That Goddamn Burnside! He left here at six p.m. last night, promising we would shortly have orders. It has been more than twelve hours and still no orders! I stayed up all night waiting for his orders. He can go to hell!"

Meade and Reynolds settled in to wait. At 7:30 a.m., Colonel James Hardie, a Burnside aide, showed up at Franklin's headquarters, wearing a monocle eyeglass like a European aristocrat.

Franklin took out his frustration on Hardie. "Why didn't we receive orders last night as Burnside promised?"

Hardie shook his head. "I don't know. But I have your orders." He handed Franklin the paper he was carrying.

Franklin read it, muttering to himself. "I don't believe it. Burnside has changed the plan we agreed on! It was understood that the entire Left Grand Division, two full corps, would take part in the attack on Prospect Hill with support, if needed, from Hooker's Center Grand Division. Now Burnside says to send a division, at least, to seize the heights, if possible. And we no longer have support from Hooker's two corps. We only have Birney's division for support."

Reynolds held out his hand, and Franklin handed him the orders. After reading them, he said, "The orders say at least a division. You have the flexibility of using a stronger force and attacking with both the First and Sixth Corps."

Franklin looked beaten down and was in a churlish mood. "It's obvious to me that we are only to make a diversionary attack. The main assault will be at Marye's Heights. Reynolds, you'll select one of your divisions to make the attack."

"I don't think one division is enough to take Prospect Hill," Meade said. "If we throw more divisions in later, it will be like Antietam. The attacks will occur in a piecemeal fashion."

FREDERICKSBURG: OVERVIEW

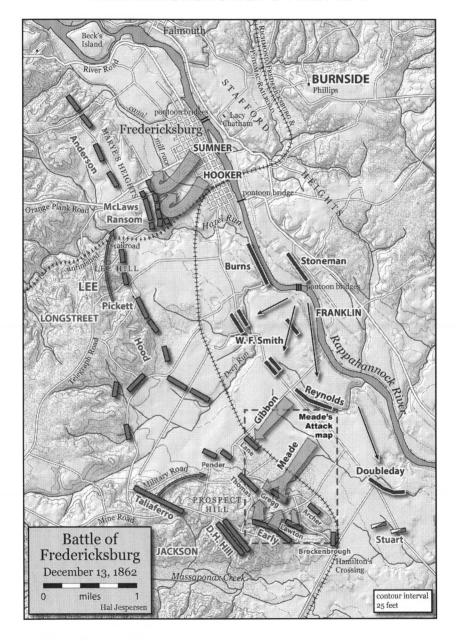

Beck's Island

Falmouth

River Road

STAFFORD

BURNSIDE
Phillips

canal pontoon bridges

Fredericksburg

Lacy
Chatham

SUMNER

HOOKER

pontoon bridge

Orange Plank Road

McLaws
Ransom

Hazel Run

HEIGHTS

railroad

unfinished

LEE HILL

Burns

Stoneman

LEE

pontoon bridges

Pickett

FRANKLIN

LONGSTREET

Hood

W. F. Smith

Deep Run

Rappahannock River

Reynolds

Gibbon

Meade's
Attack
map

Lane

Military Road

Pender

Meade

Doubleday

Taliaferro

PROSPECT
HILL

Thomas

Gregg

Mine Road

D.H. Hill

Early

Lawton

Archer

Stuart

Battle of
Fredericksburg
December 13, 1862

JACKSON

Brockenbrough

Hamilton's
Crossing

0 miles 1

Massaponax Creek

Hal Jespersen

contour interval
25 feet

Franklin waved his hand dismissively. "Burnside has changed his mind from yesterday, and the main attack will not be on Prospect Hill! We are only a diversion. I'm not going to send in more men than necessary."

As they left, Reynolds said, "Meade, your Reserves division will make the attack. Our intelligence advises that Lee has built a military road connecting Prospect Hill to Marye's Heights. Seize that military road and cut Lee's communications. Stonewall Jackson is defending Prospect Hill. You have a tough task in front of you."

Meade tried to keep his emotions in check as he responded to Reynolds. The Reserves had experienced horrific losses and were a shrunken unit. "We went into the Seven Days Battles with 11,500 men. Now, after Second Bull Run and Antietam, we're down to 4,500. I don't think the Reserves is a large enough force to take Prospect Hill."

Reynolds agreed. "I don't understand Franklin. Burn's orders were muddled, but they still gave Franklin discretion in determining how large of a force would make the attack. He's chosen to construe Burn's orders in the narrowest possible fashion." The two men looked at each other in silence. Then Reynolds announced, "Gibbon's and Doubleday's divisions will also assault Prospect Hill. I'm taking an expansive view of my orders."

CHAPTER 25

Meade summoned his brigade commanders, General Jackson and Colonels Magilton and Sinclair, and pointed across the farmland to the low hill covered with trees. "The Reserves are going to make a frontal assault on Prospect Hill. Gibbon's and Doubleday's divisions will support us."

Colonel Magilton asked, "Why are we attacking with such a small force? We have an enormous army here. Why not attack with the whole force available?"

Meade snapped, "I don't make those decisions. I only follow orders! Get your men ready to make the attack!"

Meade turned to Sinclair. "The Stage Road has thick hedges on either side and deep ditches beyond the hedges. Have your men cut down those hedges and use the cuttings to fill in the ditches so our artillery can cross and support the infantry attack."

Once Sinclair's men had made the road passable for artillery, Meade ordered the Reserves forward into the open field beyond the road. The sun was warming the frozen ground. The men had advanced four hundred yards when Rebel artillery opened up on their left flank. The Confederate artillerists had a good line of fire, and Meade watched a man die taking a direct hit from a Rebel shell. Human body parts were flung across the field.

Meade rode among his soldiers, yelling and frantically gesturing. "Get down! Get down!"

He had to silence those guns or their attack would be a failure before they had engaged the enemy.

Meade's three batteries roared into action. Doubleday's division advanced on the left, and their batteries joined in an artillery duel with the Confederates.

Federal artillery on Stratford Heights across the Rappahannock added their weight to the cannonading. After an hour of sustained bombardment, the Rebel cannons were finally silenced.

Reynolds rode to Meade. "The Federal artillery on Stratford Heights shelled Prospect Hill, but Stonewall Jackson did not return fire. He is probably hiding his battery positions from us. We are going to resume bombarding Prospect Hill. I will let you know when to advance."

Soon the intense cannonading resumed. For an hour, the Federal batteries pounded Prospect Hill, with no response from the Confederates.

Reynolds rode out and asked his commanders if they were ready to attack.

Meade and Gibbon responded yes. Doubleday was quiet.

Reynolds asked, "Doubleday, why are you hesitating?"

"I'm concerned that if I advance, the Confederates will make a flank attack. My division is protecting the army's left flank."

Reynolds responded, "Move forward if you can. Give Meade as much support as possible."

Meade went to his brigade commanders and told them, "Get the men out of the mud and ready to attack!"

The sun had come out, and the air temperature had warmed rapidly, turning the frozen ground to mud. The troops rose out of the muck for the first time in two hours. Meade watched his soldiers stretch their aching limbs. Their faces, hands, and bodies were covered in mud. They looked as dirty as farm animals that had been rolling in the mud. Meade thought, *They may look like mud hens, but they will fight like warriors.*

Meade and Gibbon got ready to advance. They formed a thousand-yard line of battle. Meade put Sinclair's and Jackson's men on the front line, with Magilton in reserve. The artillery batteries were placed between the two lines. He gave the order to advance, and they marched through the muddy fields toward the railroad.

FREDERICKSBURG: MEADE'S ATTACK

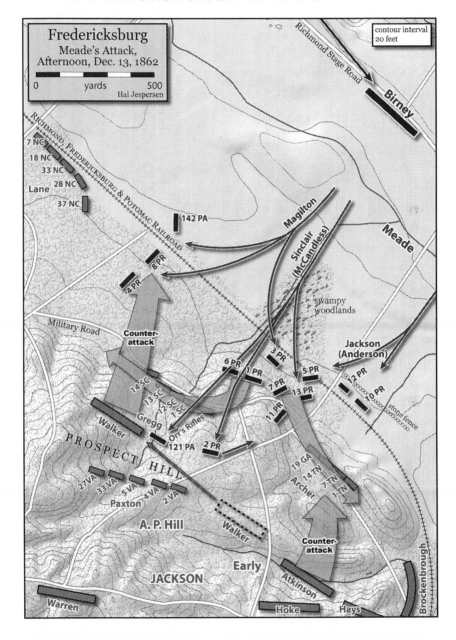

Fredericksburg
Meade's Attack,
Afternoon, Dec. 13, 1862

0   yards   500
Hal Jespersen

contour interval
20 feet

Richmond Stage Road

Birney

7 NC
18 NC
33 NC
28 NC
Lane
37 NC

RICHMOND, FREDERICKSBURG & POTOMAC RAILROAD

142 PA

Magilton

Sinclair
(McCandless)

Meade

8 PR

4 PR

swampy
woodlands

Military Road

Counter-
attack

3 PR

Jackson
(Anderson)

6 PR   1 PR

5 PR

2 PR

14 SC

13 SC

12 SC
1 SC

7 PR

13 PR

10 PR

stone fence

Gregg

Walker

Orr's Rifles

11 PR

PROSPECT HILL

121 PA   2 PR

27 VA   33 VA   5 VA   4 VA   2 VA

Paxton

A. P. Hill

Walker

19 GA   14 TN   7 TN
Archer   1 TN

Counter-
attack

Early

JACKSON

Atkinson

Brockenbrough

Warren

Hoke   Hays

There was no fire coming from Prospect Hill. Meade was not comforted by this. He thought it was unlikely that the Federal bombardment had silenced the Rebel batteries. Stonewall Jackson was probably waiting for the muddy soldiers to get within ideal range of his guns. Eight hundred yards from Prospect Hill, Meade got his answer. Rebel batteries thundered, and artillery rounds impacted the tightly formed lines. Men were cut in two, dismembered bodies littering the field. The attack faltered.

Meade rode forward, yelling and waving his arm for the infantry to fall back. "General Jackson and Colonel Sinclair, have your men retreat and lie down behind our batteries!"

The artillery duel resumed. Meade rode among his batteries, directing fire at the Confederate positions. The noise was deafening. Angry missiles howled and shrieked. Screams of wounded and dying men filled the air. Soldiers who manned the cannons and their artillery horses went down with ghastly wounds. Dirt and shell fragments filled the air all around him.

Meade left the batteries and rode along the line of his infantry troops, who were face-down in the mud, trying to protect themselves from the hellish cannon fire.

"Don't worry, boys. We are going to silence their guns soon, and then we will storm the hill and break the Rebel line!"

But it was more than an hour before Confederate fire slackened, ending the fearsome artillery duel. It was time to attack.

Meade ordered his men to resume their advance on Prospect Hill. The Reserves went forward, shoulder-to-shoulder. The Rebel cannon still functioning opened up. A steady volume of musket fire poured out of the woods. Minié balls and artillery shells filled the air, indiscriminately taking human life. The Reserves closed ranks as men fell. Meade rode his horse, cheering on his troops.

When the Reserves reached the railroad tracks, they quickly overwhelmed the Confederate pickets, who fled toward Prospect Hill. When the Union troops tried to move past the railroad, they were hit with a wall of lead that felled more brave soldiers and stopped their advance. Meade had his soldiers use the rail embankment for protection. They poured musket fire into the Confederates on Prospect Hill.

A fingerlike slice of swampy woods extended across the railroad tracks. Some of Sinclair's men had entered the woods and crossed the tracks. The ground was marshy, and the footing slippery. Oddly, the patch of forest seemed undefended. Sinclair found Meade.

"My men are in those woods to our left and have not encountered any Rebs."

"Take your brigade and attack through the woods." Meade then sent orders for Magilton and Jackson to send regiments in support of Sinclair.

Meade became worried when Lieutenant Dehon, who was sent to deliver the order to Jackson, didn't return. Meade rode to investigate. He learned that Dehon was killed as he was delivering the order. Seconds later, General Conrad Jackson was also killed.

A messenger arrived from Sinclair. They had breached the Rebel line and captured a portion of the military road that had been the objective of the assault. Meade felt a thrill of exhilaration. They had breached the great Stonewall Jackson's defensive line!

Prisoners from South Carolina soon began streaming past him.

Meade sent a message to Reynolds with an urgent request for reinforcements to support the breakthrough. If Franklin would throw the weight of Smith's Sixth Corps into the fight, they could rout the acclaimed Stonewall Jackson.

Sinclair sent word that the Reserves were vigorously attacking the exposed Confederate flanks and had punched a six-hundred-foot gap in the Rebel line. Meade was jubilant! A great victory was at hand if Franklin would act decisively.

But no reinforcements showed up, and Meade fretted. The roar of musket fire intensified; his men were being pushed out of the woods. The Rebels were making a counterattack! Without reinforcements, the battle would be lost. Time was critical. He dispatched a staff officer to hasten the reinforcements.

The staff officer returned. "Sir, I found General Birney on the Stagecoach Road. He refuses to advance!"

Meade was astounded. "What the hell is he thinking? If we don't receive immediate reinforcements, the day is lost!"

Meade raced to find Birney. When he found him, his anger came to a boil. He screamed at the Puritanical-looking, dour-faced man. "Why have you not honored my request for reinforcements? Don't you realize the opportunity for a glorious victory is hanging by a thread?"

Birney calmly responded, "I have no orders to advance from either Franklin or Reynolds. Reynolds ordered my division to this location, behind where you are attacking, but he did not issue an order for me to advance."

"My God, are you blind? My men are in a desperate struggle with Stonewall Jackson, and they need your support! Goddamn you! Common sense and military honor demand that you advance into the battle!"

"General Meade, you do not rank me, and I will not take orders from you!"

Meade remembered his promotion. "I've been promoted to major general, and I do rank you! I assume the authority of ordering you to reinforce my men. Now, show some grit and lead your men into the battle!"

Meade galloped back to the railroad. He saw the Reserves had been driven out of the woods and were making a stand at the railroad embankment.

Meade grabbed a battle flag and rode along the railroad tracks, urging his men to hold the line. He was oblivious to danger. There were too many Confederates to stop. Hand-to-hand fighting broke out, with muskets being used as clubs. Screams and oaths filled the air. The Rebel tide overwhelmed the Reserves, who broke and began retreating.

Meade did his best to make a fighting retreat, but his division was spent. Many men were out of ammunition, and some simply abandoned the fight and fled to the rear.

He passed Birney, who had finally taken the field and was marching to meet the counterattacking Confederates. The last of Birney's brigades to enter the fight was a gaudy Zouave outfit with white turbans and baggy red pants. Birney's men looked fresh and ready to put a jolt into the advancing Rebels.

Meade rallied the remnants of his troops. "Look at those red-legged devils entering the battle! Reserves, let us rally and join the fight!"

He succeeded in getting some of his weary men to fight alongside the Zouaves. The Confederate troops on the open farmland were taking terrific casualties from the Union cannons on Strafford Heights across the river and soon retreated to the safety of Prospect Hill.

When the battle ended, Meade found Reynolds. "Why didn't you honor my request for reinforcements? Did you think the Reserves could beat Stonewall Jackson all by themselves?"

Reynolds calmly replied, "I never received the request."

Meade had an overwhelming yearning to lash out at Reynolds. *Where in the hell had he been in the heat of battle that a messenger couldn't find him? Why hadn't he ordered Birney forward on his own account? Why hadn't he gone to Franklin and demanded the Sixth Corps enter the battle?*

Meade struggled to control his temper. "Where in the hell . . ." He bit his lip. No good could come from a verbal assault on Reynolds. He shook his head. "I'm too angry to have a rational discussion!" He took several deep breaths and tried to compose himself. "Was Doubleday engaged?"

"No. The Confederates never attacked him."

"Unbelievable! He was idle yet failed to send any men to support my attack!"

Meade suddenly felt bone-tired. He looked down at his boots and pants. They were splattered with mud and blood. Then he took off his slouch hat and shook it to dislodge the debris of battle. He noticed two prominent bullet holes near the top of the hat. He thanked God for bringing him unscathed through another day of violence.

CHAPTER 26

A day after the Battle of Fredericksburg, Meade's anger was still smoldering. He had placed Stonewall Jackson in a desperate spot. Reynolds, an old artillerist, had gotten himself immersed with the artillery and didn't receive Meade's message for help. He entered Reynolds's tent telling himself to control his temper. He was surprised to find their fellow Pennsylvanian, General Winfield Scott Hancock, paying a visit.

Hancock was a tall, well-built man with a firm jaw, deep-blue eyes, and a booming voice. During the Richmond campaign, McClellan had called him a superb commander, hence his nickname, "Hancock the Superb."

Reynolds said, "Win was just about to tell me about yesterday's battle on the north side of town."

Hancock's face darkened. "Burnside horribly mismanaged the attack on Marye's Heights. He's not fit to be the commanding general."

Reynolds asked, "What happened?"

"There is a sunken road at the base of the heights protected by a stone wall that had to be captured before we could scale the heights. The Confederate musket fire from behind that stone wall was so thick that whole rows of men fell like wheat cut by a scythe. That sunken road was unreachable. Nobody got closer than fifty yards. Confederate artillery had a horrific effect on our exposed men."

"Did Burnside call off the attack after it was clear that it was futile?"

"No. Burnside sent wave after wave, in one suicidal frontal assault after another. The ground was covered with the corpses of our soldiers."

Meade asked, "Wasn't it clear to Burnside that the attack was bound to fail?"

"His headquarters at Phillips House was away from the battle-field, and he couldn't see what was happening. Despite reports of the unfolding battlefield disaster, he stubbornly continued to order men to march to their death. When Hooker was ordered to join the assault, he went to Burnside and vigorously argued that continuing the attack was foolish and would only result in more squandered lives. Burnside dismissed Hooker's protest and ordered him to continue with the frontal assaults. The battle was a total debacle with astronomical casualties. None of the corps commanders want to serve under Burnside. Hooker is the most strident in his criticism."

Reynolds shook his head. "I don't think Burn can survive such a calamity. Pretty soon, we are going to be in Joe Hooker's army."

Camp opposite Fredericksburg, Va, December 16, 1862

My Dearest Margaret,

On the twelfth, we crossed the river: Sumner at the town, Franklin below, and Hooker remaining in reserve. On the thirteenth, it was determined to make an attack from both positions, and the honor of leading this attack was assigned to my division. I cannot give you all the details of the fight, but I will simply say my men went in beautifully, carried everything before them, and drove the enemy for nearly half a mile. But finding themselves unsupported on either right or left, and encountering an overwhelming force of the enemy, they were checked and finally driven back. As an evidence of the work they had to do, it is only necessary to state that out of 4,500 men taken into action, we know the names of 1,800 killed and wounded. I was myself unhurt, though a ball passed through my hat so close that if it had come from the front instead of the side, I would have been a goner.

Last night we had the humiliation to be compelled to return to this side of the river; in other words, we had to acknowledge the superior strength of the enemy and proclaim what we all knew before: that we never should have crossed with the force we have without some diversion being made on the James River in our favor. What will be done next I cannot tell. Burnside, I presume is a dead cock in the pit, and your friend Joe Hooker (fighting Joe) is the next on the list.

Your Loving Husband George

CHAPTER 27

The Army of the Potomac was in a bad way following the disastrous Battle of Fredericksburg. Morale was poor. Desertions were occurring with depressing frequency. Criticism of Burnside's leadership was rampant, led by the outspoken Hooker. Both Meade and Reynolds didn't think their friend Burnside could survive.

An aide handed Meade a telegram. It brought good news: he had been promoted to command the Fifth Corps. Meade felt a sense of deep pride in having achieved his professional ambition, a corps command.

He had his horse saddled. He needed to thank Burnside in person for following through on his promise. When he arrived at Phillips House, the commanding general was mounting his horse. Burnside called out, "George, it is good to see you. Will you join me for a ride to get a little exercise?"

"Of course. I came to thank you for my promotion to Fifth Corps commander."

"You deserved the promotion."

"How did Hooker and Butterfield handle the situation?"

"They were both upset. Hooker expects to replace me soon. I think he thought it was personal, demoting his friend when I had the power to do so." Burnside frowned. "I know that Hooker is working hard to undermine my authority so he can become commanding general."

Meade remained silent. He didn't want to discuss army politics.

After a while, Burnside said, "George, I trust your discretion, and I need to unburden myself to someone. Yesterday, the President called me to Washington. I was shocked when Lincoln told me a delegation of generals from the Army of the Potomac had visited him to have me restrained from further winter campaigning. I know the real reason they went to the President. They want me dismissed as commanding general. I demanded to know who these backstabbers were, but the President refused to divulge their names. I offered to resign, but Lincoln would not accept the resignation. So, in the presence of Halleck and Stanton, I wrote a letter demanding that the President dismiss all three of us, as none of us has the confidence of the people or the army. Stanton and Halleck stood mute, and Lincoln wouldn't accept my letter."

Meade said, "There are too many generals interested in intrigue in this army."

"Do you know who went behind my back to the President?"

"I don't know. I stay out of army politics."

"I bet that devious bastard Hooker is behind all these machinations."

Camp opposite Fredericksburg, Va, December 31, 1862

My Dearest Margaret,

It was very civil of Reynolds to call on you. He's a very good fellow, and I have had much pleasant intercourse with him during the past eighteen months. Considering how closely we have been together and the natural rivalry that might be expected, I think it is saying a good deal for both that we have continued good friends.

Today is our wedding anniversary and my birthday. Twenty-two years ago, we pledged our faith to each other, and I doubt if any other couple live who, with all the ups and downs of life, have had more happiness with each other than you and I. I trust a merciful Providence will spare us both to celebrate yet many returns of the day and that we shall see our children advancing in life prosperously and happily.

I had hoped to spend this day with you and the darling children, but my promotion to command the Fifth Corps and the number of generals that have been sent to testify before the Porter and McDowell courts have prevented my getting away. Should it be decided the army is to go into winter quarters, I may yet have a chance, though I hardly have much hope.

I have sent George's name to the President for appointment as one of my aides, with the rank of captain.

Your Loving Husband George

CHAPTER 28

Camp opposite Fredericksburg, January 2, 1863

My Dearest Margaret,

No one in Washington has the courage to say or do anything other than hamper and obstruct us. I am tired at this playing war without risks. I had a talk with Franklin yesterday, who is of the opinion we cannot go to Richmond on this line and there's no object in attempting to move on it. I agreed with him on the impracticality of this line, but I did not think for that reason we should stand still. I agreed with Franklin that the James River was our proper and only base, but as they were determined in Washington that we should not go there, we ought to attempt a practical, though less desirable line. We must encounter risks if we fight, and we cannot carry on war without fighting. That was McClellan's vice. He was always waiting to have everything just as he wanted before he would attack, and before he could get things arranged as he wanted them, the enemy pounced on him and thwarted all his plans. There is now no doubt he allowed the occasion to take Richmond slip through his hands, for want of nerve to run what he considered risks.

Such a General will never command success, though he may avoid disaster.

Your Loving Husband George

———————

In early January, Meade received a note from Burnside asking him to visit. Meade rode through the chilly winter air, thinking about how much he missed Margaret and the children. It was frustrating not to have had time to take leave to visit Philadelphia.

When he arrived at Burnside's headquarters, he gave an orderly his horse and entered the Phillips mansion.

Burnside had a satisfied look on his face. "George, please read this draft order."

Meade took the paper from Burnside and read the document.

GENERAL JOSEPH HOOKER, HAVING BEEN GUILTY OF UNJUST AND UNNECESSARY CRITICISMS OF THE ACTIONS OF HIS SUPERIOR OFFICERS AND OF THE AUTHORITIES, AND HAVING, BY THE GENERAL TONE OF THIS CONVERSATION, ENDEAVORED TO CREATE DISTRUST IN THE MINDS OF OFFICERS WHO HAVE ASSOCIATED WITH HIM, AND HAVING, BY OMISSIONS AND OTHERWISE, MADE REPORTS AND STATEMENTS WHICH WERE CALCULATED TO CREATE INCORRECT IMPRESSIONS, AND FOR HABITUALLY SPEAKING IN DISPARAGING TERMS OF OTHER OFFICERS, IS HEREBY DISMISSED FROM THE SERVICE OF THE UNITED STATES AS A MAN UNFIT TO HOLD AN IMPORTANT COMMISSION DURING A CRISIS LIKE THE PRESENT, WHEN SO MUCH PATIENCE, CHARITY, CONFIDENCE, CONSIDERATION, AND PATRIOTISM ARE DUE FROM EVERY SOLDIER IN THE FIELD. THIS ORDER IS ISSUED SUBJECT TO THE APPROVAL OF THE PRESIDENT OF THE UNITED STATES.

Meade was astounded that Burnside would try to dismiss Hooker from the army. He continued reading the draft order and saw that Hooker wasn't the only target of Burnside's wrath. Meade absorbed the implications of the draft order. "While Hooker's actions are reprehensible, I can't believe the President would dismiss him. He's an able general."

"You may be right, but I can no longer work with Hooker. I'm going to Washington to meet with the President and tell him in the most frank terms that it's either me or Hooker."

"You're also removing Franklin, Baldy Smith, and a whole slew of other generals from the Army of the Potomac."

"I'm getting rid of all disloyal generals. Franklin disobeyed my orders at Fredericksburg. After your attack faltered, I ordered him to attack with his entire force, and he ignored the order. Baldy Smith is just like Hooker. He's always criticizing his superiors. I don't want men like that in my army. Lincoln has no problem getting rid of officers who don't follow orders. You saw he upheld the court-martial conviction of Fitz John Porter."

"Porter had discretion not to attack! He's been targeted because of his association with McClellan. He has been treated disgracefully!"

Burnside looked surprised at the vehemence that Meade had displayed in defending Porter. "I wasn't there but will take your word that Porter is innocent."

Camp Near Falmouth, Va, January 26, 1863, 9:00 p.m.

My Dearest Margaret,

I went out to ride for exercise, and on my return at 6 p.m., I found an order awaiting me announcing that Major General Hooker is in command of the Army of the Potomac, and that Generals Sumner and Franklin had both been relieved and ordered to Washington. You will, doubtless, be anxious to know what I think of these changes.

With all my respect, and I may almost say affection, for Burnside—for he has been most kind and considerate toward me—I cannot shut my eyes to the fact that he was not equal to the command of so large an army. He had some very positive qualifications, such as determination and nerve, but was deficient in that enlarged mental capacity that is essential in a commander. Another drawback was a very general opinion among officers and men, brought about by his own assertions, that the command was too much for him. This greatly weakened his position.

As to Hooker, you know my opinion of him. I believe my opinion is more favorable than any other of the old regular officers, most of whom are decided in their hostility to him. I believe Hooker is a good soldier; the danger he runs is subjecting himself to bad influences, such as Dan Butterfield and Dan Sickles, who, being intellectually more clever than Hooker and leading him to believe they are very influential, will obtain an injurious ascendancy over him and insensibly affect his conduct.

Your Loving Husband George

CHANCELLORSVILLE

CHAPTER 29

Meade had decided to visit Hooker. The falling snow was swirling in the wind, visibility was poor, and Meade was riding slowly so his horse wouldn't go into a ditch. His gray beard had been turned white, and he pulled his slouch hat down just a little further to try to keep the snow out of his eyes. He was beginning to regret the decision to go out in such weather, and he let out a deep sigh of relief when he reached Hooker's headquarters.

When he got inside, he found a beaming Hooker. "Why, if it isn't George Meade."

"Joe, I came to congratulate you on being named commanding general."

Hooker warmly shook Meade's hand. "Thank you, George. It is an awesome responsibility. I feel confident I can lead the Army of the Potomac."

"How were you treated in Washington?"

"Handsomely. You know that Halleck and I can't stand each other. I was able to work out an arrangement with Lincoln to communicate directly with him and not go through Halleck." Hooker pulled a paper out of his pocket. "When I met with the President, he gave me this letter."

Executive Mansion
Washington, January 26, 1863

Major General Hooker:
General.

I have placed you at the head of the Army of the
Potomac. Of course I have done this upon what
appeared to me to be sufficient reasons. And yet I
think it best for you to know that there are some things
in regard to which, I am not quite satisfied with
you. I believe you to be a brave and skillful soldier,
which of course, I like. I also believe you do not
mix politics with your profession, in which you are
right. You have confidence in yourself, which is a
valuable, if not an indispensable quality. You are
ambitious, which, within reasonable bounds, does
good rather than harm. But I think that during Gen.
Burnside's command of the Army, you have taken
counsel of your ambition, and thwarted him as much
as you could, in which you did great a wrong to the
country, and to a most meritorious and honorable
brother officer. I have heard, in such way as to
believe it, of your recently saying that both the Army
and the Government needed a Dictator. Of course it
was not for this, but in spite of that, that I have
given you the command. Only those generals who gain
successes, can set up dictators. What now I ask of
you is military success, and I will risk the dicta-
torship. The government will support you to the utmost
of its ability, which is neither more nor less than it
has done and will do for all commanders. I much
fear that the spirit which you have aided to infuse
into the Army, of criticizing their Commander, and
withholding confidence from him, will now turn upon
you. I shall assist you as far as I can, to put it

down. Neither you, nor Napoleon, if he were alive again, could get any good out of an army, while such a spirit prevails in it.

And now, beware of rashness. Beware of rashness, but with energy, and sleepless vigilance go forward, and give us victories.

Yours very truly
A. Lincoln

"What an extraordinary letter."

Hooker took the letter back from Meade and returned it to his pocket. "I feel Lincoln wrote that letter to me like a father would to a son. Of course I didn't try to undermine Burnside. All I did was voice, perhaps too vigorously for the President, legitimate criticism of Burnside's failure as a commanding general. Fredericksburg was a military disaster. If what I said about Burnside helped persuade Lincoln to sack him, then I performed a valuable service for the country."

Camp Near Falmouth, Va, January 28, 1863

My Dearest Margaret,

There is report prevailing that the Provost Marshal of Washington is in the habit of systematically opening letters received and written by officers. I can hardly credit the statement. In writing to you, the wife of my bosom and the only confidential friend I have in the world, I have expressed opinions about men and things that would not be considered orthodox, but I maintain no government in the world would take advantage of such confidential intercourse to find a man *guilty, and I don't believe that any of my letters have been opened.*

Your Loving Husband George

CHAPTER 30

Meade had ridden out into the countryside for some exercise. A winter snowstorm caught him by surprise and conditions were quickly deteriorating. He was near Hancock's camp and decided to pay his friend a visit. For his winter quarters, Hancock had erected a stout log cabin, complete with chimney and fireplace.

When Meade entered the cabin, Hancock said, "George, you look like you could use a hot mug of coffee!" He added, "I need more coffee myself. I'm still recovering from Hooker's party last night. I didn't see you there."

Meade warmed himself before the crackling fire. "I attended one of Hooker's parties, but the atmosphere was not to my taste."

Hancock laughed. "You're a little too God-fearing for the likes of Hooker. He and his friends Butterfield and Sickles enjoy throwing a party. The liquor flows freely, and there are always plenty of women. Hooker has quite a reputation with women of loose virtue. Do you know what they call the Second Ward in Washington, the one that's filled with brothels?"

"No idea."

"Hooker's Division, because he spends so much time in that part of town! The ladies of the night are called Hooker's women!"

Meade didn't laugh. He was disgusted by Hooker's loose morals. "Hooker's lifestyle is not one I want to emulate."

"Sickles was holding court last night, telling the story of how he murdered his wife's lover in cold blood and got away with it."

Meade knew the basic story from the sensationalistic press coverage. "I would be interested in hearing Sickles's version," he said.

"Sickles lives in a house on Lafayette Square, across from the White House. He discovered that his young and beautiful wife, Teresa, was having an affair. He confronted her, and she admitted to the affair. Sickles made her write a full confession."

"I remember reading the confession in the paper."

"Funny thing about the confession. Sickles said the Judge excluded it from the evidence to be presented to the jury. The next day, the confession appeared in the newspapers."

Meade was offended. "What a scoundrel! Sickles must have leaked it to the press to poison the jury's mind."

"That's what I think too. Anyway, Teresa's suitor, Philip Barton Key, would stand outside Sickles's Lafayette Square house and signal her when he was available for a tryst by taking a handkerchief out of his pocket."

"Wasn't he related to Francis Scott Key, who wrote the 'Star Spangled Banner'?"

"Yes. He was his son."

"Sickles sought revenge for his wife's unfaithfulness?"

"Yes, but he had a double standard when it comes to affairs. Sickles was bragging about having many affairs during the marriage."

"The papers didn't report that he had been unfaithful to his wife."

"Sickles said that the prosecution wanted to introduce evidence of his affairs. His lawyers persuaded the Judge to exclude his affairs as being prejudicial to Sickles!"

"I don't understand our legal system. I would think that would have been relevant evidence."

"Sickles assembled an elite legal team of eight lawyers that included Edwin Stanton."

Meade was surprised. "Stanton was his lawyer?"

"Stanton was one of his lawyers. Sickles was quite effusive in praising Stanton's legal abilities."

"Did Sickles plan the murder?"

"Yes, he planned it. He stayed home with a friend, waiting for a day when Key would give the handkerchief signal. He didn't have to wait long; the day after his wife admitted her adultery, Key was outside the house, fluttering his hanky. Sickles had his friend detain Key in Lafayette Square while he armed himself. He approached Key and divulged his knowledge of the affair. When Sickles pulled out his gun, Key begged for mercy. But Sickles shot him multiple times. He then went to the Attorney General's house and confessed to the murder."

"Then it was premeditated murder. I thought he got acquitted by the jury on some novel legal argument involving temporary insanity."

"Stanton came up with a new legal theory that Sickles was so crazed with anger when he learned of the affair, he was not in his right mind when he committed the murder. The jury only took an hour to acquit him."

Meade shook his head. "This is the man that Hooker has promoted to command the Third Corps?"

"He is one of Lincoln's political generals, a Democratic politician who supports the war. Sickles is a favorite of Mrs. Lincoln. But to be fair, Sickles did recruit the Excelsior Brigade, and he has fought bravely on the battlefield."

"How is the Union going to win this war when a politician like Sickles, with no military training, gets promoted to a corps command over you, a West Point graduate and battle-tested general?"

Headquarters Fifth Army Corps, February 15, 1863

My Dearest Margaret,

I have not seen General Hooker for several days. Indeed his course toward me is so inexplicable in refusing me a leave of absence, and not vouchsafing any reason for it, that I feel indisposed to see him. Besides, I do not like his entourage. Such gentlemen as Dan Sickles and Dan Butterfield are not the persons I should select as my intimates, however worthy and superior they may be.

Your Loving Husband George

CHAPTER 31

In a city that had a distinct Southern flavor, Meade's favorite Washington hotel, Willard's, stood out. It was owned by two Vermont brothers who were staunch unionists. Federal officers always received a warm welcome. As Meade was checking in, he asked the front desk clerk, "Is General Burnside in residence?"

"He is. Would you like to see him?"

"Yes, if he would be so inclined."

"I will send your name up and get his response."

A few minutes later, Meade was ushered into Burnside's room. They warmly shook hands. Meade was introduced to Mrs. Burnside, who had come down from Rhode Island to spend a few days with her husband.

"Burn, since I was in Washington, I wanted to see how you're holding up."

"I'm glad to still have one friend among the senior generals of the Army of the Potomac," Burnside said ruefully. "I'm engaged in the most frustrating correspondence with Franklin concerning his conduct at Fredericksburg. Many in Congress and in the press are blaming him for failing to support your attack against Stonewall Jackson. Franklin wants me to whitewash him with the press for his lack of action. But I will not alter the facts."

"That's why I'm in Washington. I have been subpoenaed to testify before the Committee on the Conduct of the War. The Radical

Republicans dominate that committee, and they are out to get Franklin because of his close association with McClellan."

Camp Near Falmouth, Va, March 17, 1863

My Dearest Margaret,

I went up the day before yesterday to Washington. As usual, I stayed at Willard's. Finding Burnside was in the house, I sent up my name and was ushered into his room, where I found himself and Mrs. Burnside. The latter was a very quiet, lady-like, and exceedingly nice personage. She was quite pretty and rather younger than I expected to see.

Burnside was glad to see me, and we had a long talk.

The next morning, I went up to the capitol and presented myself to the committee. I found old Ben Wade, senator from Ohio, awaiting me. He said the committee wished to examine me in regard to the attack at Fredericksburg.

My conversations with Burnside and Wade satisfied me that Franklin was to be made respon-sible for the failure at Fredericksburg, and the committee is seeking all the testimony they can procure to substantiate this theory of theirs. I feel sorry for Franklin because I like him, and he has always been consistently friendly to me.

I sometimes feel very nervous about my posi-tion; they're knocking over generals at such a rate.

Your Loving Husband George

CHAPTER 32

Springtime brought a presidential visit to the Army of the Potomac. Hooker had invited the corps commanders to attend a reception and dinner to honor Lincoln. A spring storm caused Meade to arrive late—and dripping wet. Meade was cleaning the water and mud off his glasses when Lincoln, with the First Lady on his arm, approached.

"General Meade, this is my wife, Mary. You two have some things in common: fluency in French and a bunch of relatives fighting for the Confederacy!"

Mrs. Lincoln was short and portly with a round, attractive face. She smiled and looked up at Meade. *"C'est bon de te recontrer."*

"C'est un plaisir de vous recontrer."

The President clapped his hands and laughed. "Mrs. Lincoln is a big hit with the French diplomats. General Meade, when I send those diplomats to visit the Army of the Potomac, I will have you host them!" He continued, saying, "The troop review yesterday was most impressive. The men seem to be in good spirits."

"They were demoralized after Fredericksburg. General Hooker deserves a great deal of credit. He made beneficial changes in army policy. He instituted a furlough system, allowing men leave to go home and see their families. The furloughs have dramatically reduced desertions. Chief of Staff Butterfield created distinctive badges that have helped create an esprit de corps. Hooker established brigade bakeries, and the men get fresh bread four times a week. My men cheered lustily when they received their first batch of soft bread."

Lincoln smiled. "I love our troops. It lifts my spirits tremendously to hear such positive things about our army."

After the President and Mrs. Lincoln took their leave to continue socializing with the officers gathered for the reception, Meade sought Reynolds. "Have you heard anything concerning Hooker's plans for a spring offensive?"

"Not a word. That man is expansive when criticizing others and totally silent when it comes to his military plans."

After dinner, Lincoln joined Reynolds and Meade. "Did you know Robert E. Lee before the war?"

"We served with Lee in Mexico," Reynolds said. "He's brave, smart, daring, a fine engineer, and a natural leader. Many regarded him as the best soldier in the old army."

"That is what General Winfred Scott told me when I asked who should I place in command of the Union army after the attack on Fort Sumter," Lincoln replied.

Meade asked, "Did you offer Lee command?"

"Can you two keep a secret?"

Reynolds and Meade simultaneously said yes.

"I had Francis Blair invite Lee to his home on Lafayette Square. I instructed Blair to tell Lee that if he remained loyal, the command of the Union army was his. Blair told me they spoke for several hours. Lee said he opposed secession and would be glad to see the South give up slavery to save the Union but could not raise his sword against his native state of Virginia. Two days later, Virginia seceded, and Lee resigned his commission in the Federal army."

Meade wondered how the war would have evolved if Lee had accepted Lincoln's offer. He shook his head. With Lee's talent and the Union's greater resources, the war may have already been won.

Lincoln smiled. "My experiences here have added to my repertoire of stories. While inspecting various army camps, I have been transported in an ambulance over rough, corduroyed roads. Today on the roughest part of the road, the driver let fly a string of oaths at the mules pulling the ambulance. I asked the driver if he was an Episcopalian. The man looked startled. He said no, he was a Methodist. I responded that I thought he must be an Episcopalian because he swore just like Secretary of State Seward, who is a church warder!"

———————⟶

Falmouth, Va, April 9, 1863

My Dearest Margaret,

I have been very much occupied in the ceremonies incidental to the President's visit. He arrived here on Sunday in the midst of a violent snowstorm. I was invited to dine with General Hooker and to meet the President and Mrs. Lincoln. We had a very handsome and pleasant dinner.

You have seen the report of the Committee on the Conduct of the War. It is terribly severe upon Franklin.

The President looks careworn and exhausted. It is said he has been brought here for relaxation and amusement and that his health is seriously threatened. He expresses himself greatly pleased with all he has seen, and his friends say he has improved already.

Your Loving Husband George

CHAPTER 33

Camp Near Falmouth, Va, April 18, 1863

My Dearest Margaret,

General Hooker seems to be very sanguine of success but is remarkably reticent of his information and plans; I really know nothing of what he intends to do or when or where he proposes doing anything. This secrecy I presume is advantageous, as it prevents the enemy's becoming aware of our plans. At the same time, it may be carried too far; important plans may be frustrated by subordinates, from their ignorance of how much depends on their share of the work. This was the case at Fredericksburg. Franklin was not properly advised—that is to say, not fully advised—as to Burnside's plan. I am sure if he had been so advised, his movements would have been different.

Your Loving Husband George

Meade enjoyed the brisk April weather as he rode toward Hooker's headquarters. The roads were drying out. It was time to resume offensive operations.

After all the corps commanders arrived, Hooker addressed his top generals.

"We're ready for the spring campaign. There will be no more Fredericksburgs. We're going to avoid making frontal assaults on fortified positions. My maneuvers will force Lee to react to us.

"Slocum, Howard, and Meade will march twenty-five miles north, to Kelly's Ford on the Rappahannock. Our intelligence advises that Kelly's Ford is lightly defended. Once across the Rappahannock, they will march south and cross the Rapidan at Ely's Ford and continue south toward Fredericksburg. To conceal from Lee that the army is on the move, the four corps that camp on the Rappahannock, in full view of the Confederates, will initially not move.

"We will be on Lee's left flank, and he will either have to come out of Fredericksburg and fight or retreat. Sedgwick will stay at Fredericksburg and be prepared to fall on Lee's rear.

"General Stoneman will lead the cavalry on a raid south of Fredericksburg to disrupt Lee's communications and cut the railroad coming from Richmond that supplies his army."

When the meeting concluded, Hooker approached Meade. "What do you think of my plans?"

"They are bold. Lee will be surprised."

Hooker smiled. "My plans are perfect, and when I start to carry them out, may God have mercy on General Lee, for I will have none!"

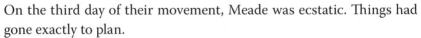

On the third day of their movement, Meade was ecstatic. Things had gone exactly to plan.

The troops had crossed Kelly's Ford on a pontoon bridge but had to walk through more than three feet of water in a strong current at Ely's Ford on the Rapidan. He had the men take off their pants and place their clothing and ammunition on their shoulders before entering the water. Some men were knocked over by the strong current and carried downstream. He had foreseen this and established a lifeguard line across the river. He was proud that, unlike in the other corps, no Fifth Corps soldiers had drowned crossing Ely's Ford.

After crossing the Rapidan, Meade sent Sykes's division to uncover US Ford on the Rappahannock. Sykes's men had little trouble driving off the Rebel pickets and opening US Ford as a link to the four army corps still on the north bank of the Rappahannock.

The army was in the Wilderness of Spotsylvania. Early settlers found iron ore and had cut down first-growth timber to make charcoal for fuel to run their furnaces and foundries. The area was covered with a second-growth mix of scrub oak, dwarf pines, hickory, and cedar trees. The woods were dark and gloomy, with thick undergrowth. Hardy souls had carved out a few clearings for farms. Meade wanted to march out of the Wilderness and into the more open land around Fredericksburg as quickly as he could. It was no place to fight a battle.

Meade reached Chancellorsville, a crossroads ten miles west of Fredericksburg that consisted of a single building: a large redbrick house that served as a country inn for travelers.

His orders were to wait at Chancellorsville for Slocum, who ranked him and would have command until Hooker arrived. When Slocum appeared that afternoon, Meade was exuberant.

"This is splendid, Henry! Hurrah for old Joe! We're on Lee's left flank, and he doesn't know it. Let's march out of these woods. Why don't I take the Orange Turnpike, and you take Plank Road? Or vice versa, as you may prefer."

"My orders are to stay here until I receive additional direction from Hooker."

"This is our opportunity to get out of this confining space to open country, where we can maneuver our troops and our artillery can have an effect on the battle."

"I understand why you want to move forward, but I have my orders. We are staying here until Hooker says we should move."

At 6:00 p.m., Hooker arrived and established his headquarters in the Chancellorsville house.

Hooker was in a jubilant mood. "George Meade, I told you my plans are perfect. I have outfoxed old Bobby Lee. God Almighty could not prevent me from winning a victory tomorrow!" Hooker took a paper out of his pocket and handed it to Meade. "Here. Review the order I am about to issue to the army."

Meade took the paper and read it quietly:

> IT IS WITH HEARTFELT SATISFACTION THE COMMANDING GENERAL ANNOUNCES TO THE ARMY THAT THE OPERATIONS OF THE LAST THREE DAYS HAVE DETERMINED THAT OUR ENEMY MUST EITHER INGLORIOUSLY FLY, OR COME OUT FROM BEHIND HIS DEFENSES AND GIVE US BATTLE ON OUR OWN GROUND, WHERE CERTAIN DESTRUCTION AWAITS HIM. THE OPERATIONS OF THE FIFTH, ELEVENTH, AND TWELFTH CORPS HAVE BEEN A SUCCESSION OF SPLENDID ACHIEVEMENTS.

Meade gave the order back to Hooker. "Joe, it has been a flawless campaign. Are we going to march out of the Wilderness tomorrow?"

"We're going to move in the morning. I want to secure the high ground behind Banks's Ford. Couch has already crossed US Ford. Sickles will be here tomorrow. Sedgwick will demonstrate in front of Fredericksburg to keep Lee confused as to our objectives. I'm leaving Reynolds at Fredericksburg, and he can either support Sedgwick or join us."

CHAPTER 34

It was a bright, beautiful morning, and Meade was eager to be on the move. He was pacing, his impatience growing by the minute. *Hooker is dithering,* he thought. *We should have been on the march at daybreak. The sooner we get out of the suffocating, tight spaces of the Wilderness, the better.*

Finally, at 10:30 a.m., Meade received the order to move out. He mounted Old Baldy, who had missed the Battle of Fredericksburg while recovering from his Antietam wound. A soft breeze rippled the Stars and Stripes. The drummer boys beat their instruments, and the men began to march.

Meade advanced Humphreys's and Griffin's divisions on River Road, with Sykes's division taking the Orange Turnpike. Slocum's Twelfth Corps took the Plank Road. The three roads ran parallel to each other. The three columns of troops were to converge at Banks's Ford with the objective of uncovering it and capturing the high ground above the crossing.

The narrow River Road forced his men into a mile-long line of march. Meade felt anxious as his column was engulfed by the forbidding forest. His thin, strung-out line was susceptible to an ambush.

After an hour, he heard cannon and musket fire coming from either the turnpike or the Plank Road or perhaps both. It seemed that Lee had decided to fight and not retreat.

After several miles, they reached the base of a hill defended by Rebel pickets. Meade ordered Griffin's division to take the hill. As Griffin's men advanced, the Confederates disappeared into the woods.

Meade rode to the top of the hill overlooking Banks's Ford. This was the high ground Hooker wanted to capture. He rode down toward the river and saw that Rebel pickets lightly defended Banks's Ford. They could easily be driven off.

When Meade arrived back on the top of the hill, an aide from Hooker was waiting for him. "General Meade, you are ordered to return to Chancellorsville."

Meade was stunned. "Retreat! There must be some mistake! Go back and tell General Hooker we have captured the high ground above Banks's Ford and that it makes no sense to retreat!"

When the aide didn't immediately move, Meade snarled, "Are you deaf? Return to General Hooker and advise him that we have the high ground and that we should not retreat!"

The chastened aide didn't reply. He turned his horse and galloped down the hill toward Chancellorsville.

Meade was still fuming when the same aide returned. "The commanding general orders you to return to Chancellorsville. General Sykes's and General Slocum's columns met heavy resistance, and they have been ordered to retreat to Chancellorsville as well."

"My God! If we can't hold the top of a hill, we certainly can't hold the bottom of it!"

But Meade did as he was ordered. When he reached Chancellorsville, he found Hooker in the big red house. Meade asked, "Why did we give away the high ground and retreat into the Wilderness?"

"Sykes and Slocum were having their flanks turned. I want to fight a defensive battle where Lee will have to attack us. I've got Lee just where I want him; he must fight me on my ground."

CHANCELLORSVILLE: MAY 1, 1862

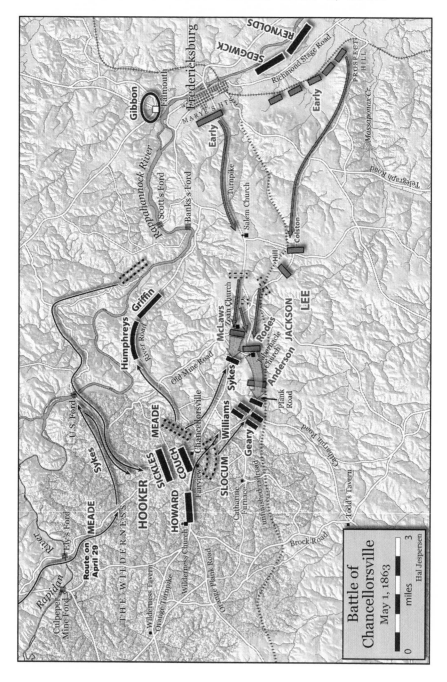

Battle of
Chancellorsville
May 1, 1863

0   miles   3

Hal Jespersen

CHAPTER 35

Meade's Fifth Corps was the left flank of Hooker's defensive line, facing east. Couch's, Slocum's and Sickles's corps formed an arc across Orange Turnpike to cover two clearings of high ground—Hazel Grove and Fairview—where Hooker had placed artillery batteries. Howard's Eleventh Corps extended the defensive line west along the turnpike and was the army's right flank.

Hooker paid Meade a visit. "George, will Lee attack or retreat?"

"Based on his history of aggressiveness, I believe he will attack."

Hooker looked surprised. "I think Lee will retreat. I created the Bureau of Military Intelligence—BMI, for short—and placed Colonel George Sharpe in charge. He has provided very useful information. Longstreet is not here and Lee has substantially less men than he had at the Battle of Fredericksburg. Sharpe estimates that Lee has sixty-five thousand troops. I have a hundred and twenty thousand men. It would be crazy for him to attack such a large force. Common sense dictates that Lee should retreat."

"Lee doesn't seem bothered by odds. Look how he divided his army at Second Bull Run and again at Antietam. By the way, what happened to Pinkerton? I thought he ran the intelligence operation."

"He quit when McClellan got relieved, claimed he was a civilian employee."

"Joe, what is going on with the Eleventh Corps? I heard the men are very unhappy that they're no longer commanded by a German."

"There are a lot of German immigrants in that corps. When the position became available, Otis Howard was the most senior general without a corps command. Howard is a strict disciplinarian and very religious. Those Dutchmen don't like him and call him 'Old Prayer Book.'" Hooker laughed. "And the men call you an Old Goddamn Snapping Turtle!"

Meade sighed. "I know that's what they call me. I'll give the men their due. There are times I pitch into people."

—————

The day wore on. Meade looked at the watch Margaret had given him as a birthday gift. Every time he checked it, he remembered how much he missed his wife and children.

It was 2:30 p.m., and things were quiet. He summoned an aide. "Go to Hooker's headquarters and see if there's any information about what the Confederates are up to."

When the aide returned, he told Meade what he had learned. "A Rebel column passed in front of Sickles's position, and he was given authority to attack it. That is happening now. Hooker believes that Lee is retreating, although he thinks it's also possible the Confederate column was marching to get on our right flank to make an attack. Hooker sent Howard a message to be prepared for a possible flank attack."

Hours passed and Meade's front remained quiet. Suddenly, at 6:00 p.m., musket and cannon fire erupted on the Union's right flank three miles away. Half an hour later, Meade was startled to see troops from Howard's Eleventh Corps running toward his line. Lee had again divided his army, and Stonewall Jackson had launched an audacious flank attack. Howard's men had broken. They were a disorganized, frightened mob fleeing the Confederates as fast as they could move.

Meade immediately had his troops and cannons turned west to face the Rebel threat. He corralled as many of the Eleventh Corps soldiers as possible and turned them around to face the enemy.

Meade knew that US Ford on the Rappahannock had to be protected. It was the lifeline that connected the divided Army of the Potomac. There was no time to wait for an order from Hooker. He rode

CHANCELLORSVILLE: MAY 2, 1862

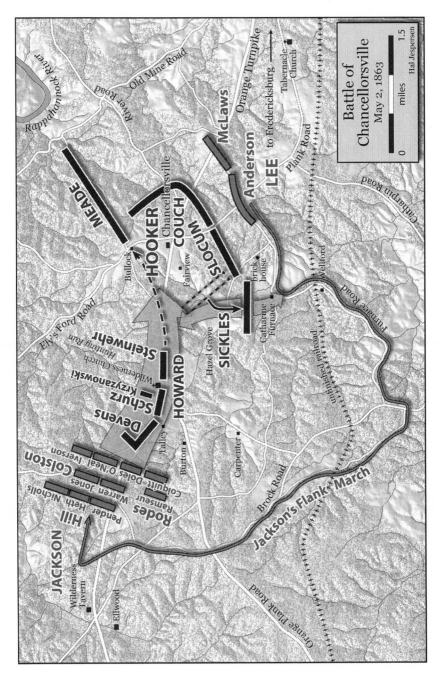

to General Sykes. "Take your men and position them west of US Ford and block any Rebel attempt to capture it."

Meade heard cannon fire coming from Hazel Grove and Fairview. Those guns should slow down the Rebel attack. Darkness fell without the Fifth Corps being engaged.

That night, Reynolds crossed US Ford. When he saw Meade, he asked, "What the hell happened today?"

"Stonewall Jackson marched in the woods in front of our position on the Orange Turnpike and around our right flank. Jackson came out of the Wilderness woods and crushed Howard's Eleventh Corps. Many of his men ran like scared animals. As night fell, Hooker was able to stabilize his lines."

"Didn't Howard have his men ready for a possible flank attack?"

"No. His men were totally unprepared. From what I've heard, he wasn't even with his corps when Jackson attacked. He was with Sickles, fighting what must have been Jackson's rear guard down near Catherine's Furnace. Howard came back and quite bravely tried to rally his men, even holding the Stars and Stripes with the stump of the arm he lost in front of Richmond."

Reynolds had a gleam in his eye. "Lee has divided his army again. I give him credit for being brazen. This gives Fighting Joe an opening to go on the offensive and destroy Lee's divided army! This battle can still be won."

"I doubt Hooker will attack. All he talks about is being on the defensive and having Lee attack him."

CHAPTER 36

Meade was up before dawn inspecting his new Fifth Corps line, which formed a lopsided ∪ with Reynolds's and Howard's corps. Couch's, Sickles's and Slocum's corps bulged out from the center of the line to protect the Hazel Grove and Fairview high ground.

Startling news had come from a Rebel prisoner. Stonewall Jackson had been shot by his own pickets in the dark, and Jeb Stuart was now in charge of Jackson's men.

Meade had known Jackson in Mexico. He was fervently religious, a stern disciplinarian, and had odd habits such as holding up what he believed was his longer arm to equalize his blood circulation. In battle he fought with the intensity of a zealot. Jackson had been an exceptionally successful general. Lee would miss him.

Meade heard musket and cannon fire coming from Fairview and Hazel Grove. The sound of the battle intensified. He rode in front of his line and through field glasses watched Confederate troops, led by Jeb Stuart, attack the Fairview salient from the west.

He and Reynolds had thirty-two thousand men that had seen no fighting. They were in a perfect position to launch a devastating flank attack. Meade thought this could be the decisive point of the battle. He anticipated receiving an order from Hooker to attack. Meade became exasperated when no order was received and set out to find Hooker.

While Meade rode toward Hooker, the Fairview position collapsed, and Union forces were withdrawn from Hazel Grove. The Confederate

CHANCELLORSVILLE: MAY 3, 1862

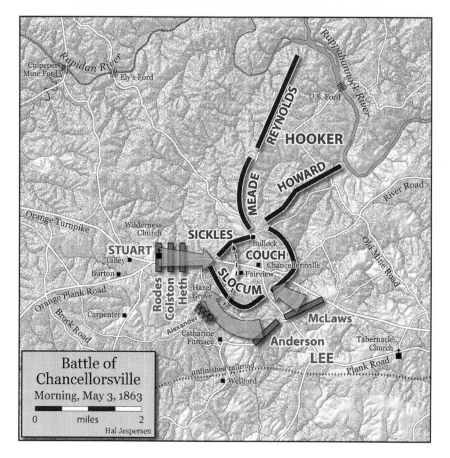

artillery, now on the Hazel Grove high ground, was having a terrible effect on Couch's, Sickles's, and Slocum's men. Union artillery was strangely ineffective, with many guns running out of ammunition and no cannons being brought forward from the Artillery Reserve.

Meade found Hooker lying on his back in a tent. An aide advised that Hooker had been watching the battle from the porch of the Chancellorsville house when a Confederate shell shattered a column that then struck the right side of his body, knocking him unconscious.

Hooker's eyes were open, but he looked dazed and exhausted.

"Joe, how are you feeling?"

"I'm in pain, and I feel a little groggy, but I still can command the army."

"Reynolds and I are perfectly positioned to make a crushing flank attack. Our troops are fresh and itching to get into the fight. We can change the tide of the battle in our favor."

"No attack," Hooker said wearily.

Meade was shocked. "Why won't you allow us to attack?"

"I've ordered Sedgwick to march from Fredericksburg and attack Lee's rear. We need to stay on the defensive until Sedgwick arrives."

"Joe, I have never seen a better opportunity to strike a decisive blow! We can destroy Stuart! Time is critical. We need to attack now!"

"No offensive until Sedgwick arrives."

Meade's anger was building. Hooker's fighting spirit had vanished. He needed to change Hooker's mind. "You will be making a huge mistake if you don't let us attack! Lee's divided army is vulnerable if we go on the offensive. Please give us permission!"

Hooker flared, his face turning red. "Stop arguing! I made my decision! Go."

Meade persisted. "I know you're suffering from the blow to your head. You're not thinking clearly. Let us attack. If it turns out to be a disaster, you can rightfully blame me."

Hooker snapped. "Get the hell out of here! You're not attacking!"

Meade left Hooker's tent angry and disgusted. *How could Hooker not see that this was the golden opportunity to severely punish Lee for dividing his army? Stonewall Jackson's flank attack must have really spooked him.* As he mounted his horse, he saw smoke in the distance. The Chancellorsville house was on fire.

Shortly after returning to his headquarters, Meade received orders to retreat to a new defensive position. The fight had gone out of Fighting Joe.

CHAPTER 37

The next morning, Hooker's army was north of the Chancellorsville crossroads and formed in a ∪ defensive formation, with one flank on the Rapidan and the other on the Rappahannock.

Reynolds looked exasperated and complained to Meade. "Can you believe how Hooker has become such a meek commander? He's making McClellan look aggressive. We have a significant advantage in troop strength, yet Lee is the aggressor."

Meade was also bewildered by Hooker's lack of action. Yesterday afternoon, Sedgwick and Lee fought a battle. Lee had to take troops away from Chancellorsville to fight Sedgwick. At the minimum, Hooker should have attacked Lee's weakened forces to take the pressure off Sedgwick, yet he had done nothing! The same thing was happening today. Lee was fighting Sedgwick, and Hooker had taken no action.

"I can't believe we weren't allowed to attack Stuart yesterday. I'm sure that blow to his head muddled his thinking, but he was already acting on the defensive before that happened." Meade began pacing. "Hooker is throwing away the opportunity to go down in history as the man who destroyed Lee! He devised a brilliant plan and succeeded in forcing Lee out of his Fredericksburg fortifications. The Army of the Potomac has never been stronger, and Lee has never been weaker. In the next six weeks, we are going to lose twenty-five thousand troops because their enlistments are up. Lee likely will have Longstreet back with his twenty-five thousand men. The time to be aggressive and attack is now!"

Reynolds didn't disagree.

Meade spent the day hoping that the pugnacious, aggressive, and combative Joe Hooker he knew would return. But the sun went down, and Hooker had done nothing.

Later that night, he was in a deep sleep when he was awakened by an aide. "General Meade. You and the other corps commanders have been summoned to General Hooker's headquarters tent."

Meade sat up and wiped the sleep from his eyes. "What time is it?"

"Quarter to midnight, sir."

Meade quickly dressed and rode to Hooker's tent. Inside, he found all the corps commanders except Slocum. Chief of Staff Butterfield and Chief Engineer Warren were also present.

Hooker's eyes were red. He looked haggard and dispirited. "Gentlemen, I have called you together to discuss whether we should attack or retreat across the Rappahannock. I have been waiting for Sedgwick to break through Lee's lines. Less than an hour ago, I received a dispatch that he was being pressed by the enemy and was retreating across the Rappahannock."

Reynolds asked, "Why wouldn't we go on the offensive?"

"Launching an attack in this forbidding terrain would be difficult and dangerous," Hooker replied. "Our men would have to advance in thin columns on narrow roads hemmed in by dense vegetation. These dark woods make it exceptionally hard to maneuver. The men have little visibility as to where they are marching and can't see what danger lurks in front of them." Hooker stood. "My orders from the President are to stay between the Army of Northern Virginia and Washington. We need to consider whether a failed offensive, which could destroy the Army of the Potomac, would endanger Washington. Butterfield and I are going to leave the meeting so you can talk candidly."

Hooker and Butterfield left.

Meade was appalled by Hooker's evident intention to retreat. His ire was up, and he took the initiative by speaking first. "We should attack Lee in the morning! The First and Fifth Corps have fresh troops eager to join the battle. Attacking in this Wilderness would be difficult, but Lee has aggressively attacked us, demonstrating that it can be done despite the challenges the terrain poses. Protecting Washington has become an excuse for this army not to take bold actions! We greatly outnumber Lee. We can make a decisive attack against the Rebels. We can't meekly retreat. Now is the time to go on the offensive!"

Reynolds, whose eyes were glazed over from lack of sleep, spoke. "We should stay and attack in the morning." He yawned, his head rolled to the side, and he fell asleep.

Howard said passionately, "The men of the Eleventh Corps were mortified when they were routed by Jackson's flank attack. We should stay and fight. The Eleventh Corps will redeem its honor on this battlefield!"

Sickles was next. "I believe we should retreat. It's more of a political than a military matter. A military disaster now for the Army of the Potomac following the debacle at Fredericksburg would have grave political consequences for the Lincoln administration. The President is committed to prosecuting this war vigorously and restoring the Union. Anything that weakens Lincoln poses a threat to ultimate victory. Common sense dictates that we avoid giving Lee an opportunity for a decisive victory in this godforsaken Wilderness by retreating to fight another day."

Couch was the last corps commander to speak. "Since crossing the Rappahannock, Hooker has not handled the army well. He has made many questionable strategic and tactical decisions. I'm not confident in his decision-making if we go on the offensive. We should retreat."

The men were arguing over the right strategy when Hooker and Butterfield returned. They polled each corps commander for his opinion.

Hooker looked surprised that the majority wanted to go on the offensive. With little hesitation and in a tired voice, he said, "We are going to retreat back across the Rappahannock."

Meade protested. "There is risk in withdrawing from an aggressive enemy like Lee. The only avenue of retreat is across the pontoon bridges at US Ford. If Lee pressed us, we could be caught straddling the river. It might be more dangerous retreating than attacking."

"I'm sure we can cross the river without losing a man or a cannon." Hooker smiled weakly. "General Lee would throw his hat in the air to have us withdraw. We will retreat tonight under the cover of darkness."

Camp Near Falmouth, Va, May 7, 1863

My Dearest Margaret,

I reached here last evening, fatigued and exhausted with a ten-days' campaign, pained and humiliated at its unsatisfactory result but grateful to our heavenly Father that, in His infinite goodness, He permitted me to escape all the dangers I had to pass through. The papers will give you all the details of the movement.

Today I was summoned to headquarters, where I found the President and General Halleck. He and Halleck spent a couple of hours, took lunch, and talked of all sorts of things, but nothing was said of our recent operations. No reference was made to the future, nor was any corps commander called on for an opinion. The President remarked that the result was in his judgment most unfortunate; he did not blame anyone. He believed everyone had done all in his power and that the disaster was one that could not be helped. Nevertheless, he thought its effect, both at home and abroad, would be more serious and injurious than any previous act of the war.

General Hooker has disappointed all his friends by failing to show his fighting qualities in the pinch. He was more cautious and took to digging quicker even than McClellan, thus proving that a man may talk very big when he has no responsibility, but it is quite a different thing, acting when you are responsible. Who would have believed a few days ago that Hooker would withdraw his army in opposition to the opinion of a majority of his corps commanders?

I have been a good deal flattered by the expressed opinion of many officers that they thought and wished I should be placed in command.

Your Loving Husband George

CHAPTER 38

The soldiers had returned to the Falmouth camps they thought would never see again. The men were dismayed at their generals' inability to defeat Lee.

Meade heard a commotion outside his tent and went to investigate. He saw a distinguished-looking civilian on horseback. The handsome visitor looked familiar. He realized it was Andrew Curtin, the Republican governor of Pennsylvania.

Meade knew Curtin from his days training the Reserves near Harrisburg and approached as the governor was dismounting. "Governor Curtin, it is good to see you again."

"I'm here to meet as many brave Pennsylvanians as I can. I'm up for election this fall, and I owe the troops some of my campaign time."

"I'm sure the men appreciate the effort you're making to see them."

"After Fredericksburg and Chancellorsville, many are asking whether their husbands, fathers, and brothers died for a war that cannot be won. It seems that Robert E. Lee wins every battle. Antiwar feelings are growing, and support for President Lincoln is eroding. I fear the Confederacy will win its independence. What is the spirit of the army?"

"Please join me in my tent, where we can have a private conversation."

Once they were alone, Meade said, "The men know that they are just as brave, courageous, and skillful soldiers as the Rebels. In the

Chancellorsville campaign, many of the men were disappointed when we retreated."

"Are you disappointed with General Hooker?"

"Confidentially, many senior officers have lost confidence in Hooker. He placed the army in an advantageous position to strike Lee a severe blow and then, inexplicably, became overly cautious. I was disappointed with many of the decisions he made on the Chancellorsville battlefield, including withdrawing the army when we should have gone on the offensive."

The flap of the tent moved aside as Reynolds entered. "I heard the governor was here."

Curtin warmly welcomed Reynolds. "It's good to see you again. I hope you're not still mad at me for causing you to miss the Battle of Antietam."

Reynolds smiled. "No grudges here."

"What's your opinion of Hooker?"

"He came up with a brilliant plan. But once we met the Confederate forces at Chancellorsville, he lost his nerve."

After Curtin took his leave, Reynolds said, "Meade, there is a groundswell of support for you to replace Hooker as commanding general. Couch, Slocum, and Sedgwick told me they would support you replacing Hooker. I would support you as well. Couch was impressed with how you handled yourself at Hooker's council of war."

"They visited me as well. Couch wanted me to join him in approaching Lincoln and demanding Hooker's removal. I refused. I have never worked to subvert a fellow officer, and I never will."

Camp Near Falmouth, Va, May 10, 1863

My Dearest Margaret,

I see the press is beginning to attack Hooker. I think these last operations have shaken the confidence of the army in Hooker's judgment. I have been much gratified at the frequent expression of opinion that I ought to be placed in command. I mention all this confidentially. I do not attach any importance to it, and I do not believe there is the slightest possibility of my being placed in command. I think I know myself and am sincere when I say I do not desire the command, hence I can quietly attend to my duties, uninfluenced by what is going on around me, while expressing, as I feel, great gratification that the army and my senior generals should think so well of my services and capacity as to be willing to serve under me. Having no political influence, being no intriguer, and indeed unambitious of the distinction, it is hardly probable I shall be called on to accept or decline.

Your Loving Husband George

CHAPTER 39

Meade entered the commanding general's headquarters. "Joe, you sent for me?"

Hooker's normally ruddy face was flushed even redder. "When I was in Washington, I was surprised to learn that I no longer have the confidence of the army. Governor Curtin has been telling everyone he sees that you believe I am incompetent to command this army. You have been intriguing behind my back to destroy my reputation!"

Meade was shocked that Governor Curtin had divulged the confidences he had shared during their private conversation. "I did confide in Governor Curtin that I was disappointed with some decisions you made during the Chancellorsville campaign. I believed our conversation was private and that he would not repeat to others what I had told him. I'm sorry that he has caused you anguish. But you know that I didn't hide my disagreements with your strategy decisions during the campaign. I protested leaving the high ground above Banks's Ford, I protested not being allowed to make a flank attack against Stuart, and I protested ending the campaign and retreating across the Rappahannock. I have the right to my private views."

Hooker stiffly replied, "You have done great harm to my reputation. But at least you're enough of a man to own up to your actions. You may return to your command."

Meade read the Richmond paper. Stonewall Jackson had died. This was surprising news. The Southern press had reported that Jackson had an arm amputated but was expected to recover and return to command. Though they were enemies, he respected Jackson as a skilled adversary. War was cruel. Jackson had just fathered a daughter. Meade felt sadness for his widow and the child who would never know her famous father.

He looked up as Hooker, with a scowl on his face, entered his tent and held up the paper. "Meade, are you responsible for this article claiming that the majority of my corps commanders protested retreating across the Rappahannock?"

"I'm not the source. I haven't spoken to any newspaper reporters."

"It's a lie that four of my six corps commanders opposed retreating! Hell, Slocum wasn't even present."

"You must recall that Slocum showed up as we were leaving the meeting. He was in favor of staying and going on the offensive."

Hooker waved his hand dismissively. "I don't remember that. I count you and Reynolds as helping me determine to retreat because you said it was unsafe and impractical to withdraw the army. Because I knew that it was perfectly safe to withdraw the army, that fact nullified your opinion for advancing."

Meade could not believe what he was hearing. "That is ridiculous! Your argument is total sophistry! I vigorously advocated staying and going on the offensive!"

"I'm going to the press and refute the lie that my corps commanders opposed ending the campaign."

"If you do that, I will most assuredly set the record straight with the truth! I believe Reynolds, Slocum, and Howard will as well."

Hooker abruptly turned and stormed out of the tent. Meade's temples were throbbing. He would have to be watchful. The commanding general was now an enemy.

Camp Near Falmouth, Va, May 19, 1863

My Dearest Margaret,

I am sorry to tell you I am at open war with Hooker. Yesterday he came to see me and referred to an article in the Herald stating that four Corps commanders were opposed to the withdrawal of the army. He said this was not so and that Reynolds and myself had determined him to withdraw. I expressed the upmost surprise at the statement. I said that my opinion was clear and emphatic for an advance, that I had gone so far as to say I would not be governed by any consideration regarding the safety of Washington, for I thought that argument had paralyzed this army too long.

The fact is, he now finds he has committed a grave error, which at that time he was prepared to assume the responsibility of but now desires to cast it off on the shoulders of others. The entente cordiale is destroyed between us, and I don't regret it, as it makes me more independent and free.

Such things are very painful and embarrassing, but I have always feared the time would come when they would be inevitable with Hooker, for I knew no one would be permitted to stand in his way. I suppose he has heard some of the stories flying around camp in regard to my having the command, and these have induced him to believe I am maneuvering to get him relieved so that I may step in his shoes.

Your Loving Husband George

GETTYSBURG

CHAPTER 40

Camp Above Falmouth, June 11, 1863

My Dearest Margaret,

This army is weakened, its morale not so good as at the last battle, and the enemy is undoubtedly stronger and in better morale. Still, I do not despair. If they assume the offensive and force us into a defensive attitude, our morale will be raised, and with a moderate degree of good luck and good management, we will give them better than they can send. War is very uncertain in its results, and often when affairs look the most desperate they can suddenly assume a more hopeful state.

I am removed from Hooker's headquarters. I know nothing of what is going on, neither of plans or surmises. In some respects that is convenient, as I am spared much speculation. In other respects, it is not so agreeable, because I like to form my own judgment on what is going on and make my preparations accordingly.

Your Loving Husband George

Couch had left the Army of the Potomac, refusing to serve any longer under Hooker. Hancock had been promoted to command the Second Corps. Meade and his newest aide were riding through scorching heat to Hancock's camp to congratulate him.

"Win, Hooker has finally done right by you!"

"Thank you, George. I feel confident that I will be up to the challenge." An aide handed Hancock a clean white shirt.

"How many of those white shirts do you wear a day?"

"In this Virginia heat and humidity, usually three."

"General Hancock, let me introduce you to my son and newest aide, Captain George Meade."

Hancock shook Captain Meade's hand and in a booming voice said, "Welcome to the Army of the Potomac. It is too bad you are on the staff of this irascible general who the men not-so-affectionately refer to as that Old Goddamn Snapping Turtle!"

His son looked surprised. "Does Mother know that's your nickname?"

"No, and you're not going to tell her!"

Hancock roared with laughter. "I bet Margaret would give you a real tongue-lashing if she knew your reputation for being crotchety."

Meade smiled tightly. "She would be decidedly unhappy."

After catching his breath, Hancock asked, "George, are you surprised that Hooker has allowed Lee to slip away, up the Shenandoah Valley?"

"I don't understand Hooker anymore."

"Hooker is in trouble. Halleck hates him. Word is that if Lincoln makes a change, it will be either you or Reynolds."

"I don't want the job. Reynolds would be an excellent choice."

"I hear Hooker's friends in Congress are unhappy with you. They think you used Governor Curtin as a proxy to hurt Hooker's reputation. You should be careful. Those Radical Republicans who control the Committee on the Conduct of the War enjoy destroying generals, especially ones they associate with McClellan. Look what they've done to Porter and Franklin."

"It wasn't my intention to harm Hooker. Governor Curtin betrayed my confidence."

Hooker had finally put the Army of the Potomac in motion heading north. Meade was surprised when his friend Reynolds rode up beside him. He had a serious look on his face and told him he needed to speak privately. They rode off the road and dismounted.

"Reynolds, do you have another secret?"

"Well, it's not a secret like my engagement to Kate. It's information I want kept confidential. You are the only person in the army that I'm going to tell about my visit to Washington."

"What were you doing in Washington?"

"I heard Lincoln was considering getting rid of Hooker and placing me in command. I went to Washington and told the President that I would only accept command if he could promise that Washington would not interfere with the operations of the Army of the Potomac. The administration would need to give me freedom to maneuver the army without silly restrictions, like having to stay between Lee and Washington."

"Did you convince the President to let go of his overblown concerns for the safety of Washington?"

"No. He refused to make any promises. I told Lincoln politely but firmly that if he offered me command, I would not accept."

"The President asked me what I thought of Hooker. I told him that Hooker had lost his nerve at Chancellorsville and missed a perfect opportunity to defeat Lee."

"Is Lincoln going to keep Hooker?"

"I think so. The President said he was not disposed to throw away a gun because it misfired once."

As they were mounting their horses again, Reynolds said, "Oh, I told Lincoln if he decided to replace Hooker, he should make you the commanding general."

CHAPTER 41

Meade breathed in the fresh air and enjoyed the soothing sounds of a fast-moving stream. He was surrounded by lush, green foliage and the rugged terrain of the Bull Run Mountains. For the fifth day, the Fifth Corps was camped in the mountains.

Meade was surprised by how sluggish Hooker was being in pursuing Lee. The Army of Northern Virginia was in Maryland near the Mason-Dixon Line and seemed certain to invade Pennsylvania. There was panic in the North. No troops from the Army of the Potomac had yet crossed its namesake river into Maryland. Hooker was allowing Lee to invade Pennsylvania without opposition. *Was Hooker afraid to face Lee in battle again?*

Camp at Aldie, Va, June 25, 1863

My Dearest Margaret,

I see you are still troubled with visions of my being placed in command. I thought that had all blown over, and I think it has, except in your imagination and that of others of my kind friends. I have no doubt great efforts have been

made to get McClellan back and advantage has
been taken of the excitement produced by the
invasion of Maryland to push his claims. But his
friends ought to know that his restoration is out
of the question so long as the present administration remains in office. I have no doubt, as you
surmise, that his friends would look with no favor
on my being placed in command. They could not
say I was an unprincipled intriguer who had risen
by criticizing and defaming my predecessors and
superiors. They could not say I was incompetent
because I have not been tried, and in so far as I
have been tried, I have been singularly successful. They could not say I had never been under
fire because it is notorious no general officer, not
even Fighting Joe himself, has been in more battles, or more exposed, than my record evidences.
The only thing they can say, and I am willing
to admit the justice of the argument, is that it
remains to be seen whether I have the capacity to
handle successfully a large army. I do not stand,
however, any chance because I have no friends,
political or others, who press or advance my claims
or pretensions, and there are so many others who
are pressed by influential politicians that it is
folly to think I stand any chance on merit alone.
Besides, I have not the vanity to think my capacity so preeminent, and I know there are plenty
of others equally competent with myself, though
their names may not have been so mentioned.
For these reasons, I have never indulged in any
dreams of ambition, content to await events and
do my duty in the sphere it pleases God to place
me in. I think your ambition is being roused and
that you are beginning to be bitten with the daz-
zling prospect of having for a husband a commanding general of an army. How is this?

I hear nothing whatever from headquarters and am as much in the dark as to proposed plans here on the ground as you are in Philadelphia. This is what Joe Hooker thinks is profound sagacity: keeping his corps commanders, who are to execute his plans, in total ignorance of them until they are developed in the execution of orders.

Your Loving Husband George

When Hooker finally issued orders to march into Maryland, Meade mounted Old Baldy and led his men through Leesburg, Virginia, and across a pontoon bridge at Edwards Ferry into Maryland.

Early the next morning, the Fifth Corps was on the march. There was no pontoon bridge over the Monocacy River, and the troops forded the waist-high water. They camped near Frederick. They had marched forty-five miles in two days. There had been little complaining; the men were happy to be again on Northern soil. They knew there would soon be a big fight with their nemesis, the Army of Northern Virginia.

CHAPTER 42

Meade was in a deep sleep on his cot when a visitor from Washington woke him at 3:00 a.m. Slowly coming awake, he saw a man wearing civilian clothes peering at him. He sat up and put on his spectacles. The man wore a monocle and looked familiar. It was Colonel Hardie, who was now on General Halleck's staff.

"General Meade, I have come to bring you trouble."

Trouble! Hooker and his friends on the Committee of the Conduct of the War must have trumped up some charges to have him arrested. He was going to be scapegoated like Porter.

Meade sat up. "Colonel Hardie, I have done my duty, and my conscience is clear. I have not engaged in any wrongdoing. What is the bad news you bring?"

Hardie handed Meade an envelope. "You'll know when you read this letter."

Meade tore open the envelope.

Headquarters of the Army,
Washington, D.C., June 27, 1863

Maj. Gen. George G. Meade,
Army of the Potomac:

General: You will receive with this the order of the President placing you in command of the Army of the Potomac. Considering the circumstances, no one ever received a more important command; and I cannot doubt that you will fully justify the confidence which the Government has reposed in you.

You will not be hampered by any minute instructions from these headquarters. Your army is free to act as you may deem proper under the circumstances as they arise. You will, however, keep in view the important fact that the Army of the Potomac is the covering army of Washington, as well as the army of operation against the invading forces of the rebels. You will, therefore, maneuver and fight in such a manner as to cover the Capital and also Baltimore, as far as circumstances will admit. Should General Lee move upon either of these places, it is expected that you will either anticipate him or arrive with him so as to give him battle.

All forces within the sphere of your operations will be held subject to your orders.

Harper's Ferry and its garrison are under your direct orders.

You are authorized to remove from command, and send from your army, any officer or other person you may deem proper, and to appoint to command as you may deem expedient.

In fine, General, you are entrusted with all the power and authority which the President, the Secretary of War, and the General-in-Chief can confer on you, and you may rely on our full support.

You will keep me fully informed of all your movements, and the positions of your own troops and those of the enemy, so far as known.

Very respectfully, your obedient servant,

H. W. Halleck
General-in-Chief

Meade was stunned. If there was going to be a change in command, he was sure it would have been Reynolds. There likely would be a major battle in a matter of days. He had not sought command, and in the circumstances, he didn't want it.

"I protest this order. Hooker has kept me in the dark. I have no inkling of his plans, and I'm totally ignorant about where the other army corps are. I'm not the best man to take control of the Army of the Potomac. Reynolds would be a better choice."

"General Meade, all the objections you have raised were antici-pated by the President and General Halleck. President Lincoln's deci-sion is final. You are now in charge of this nation's greatest army."

Meade said sardonically, "Well, I've been tried and condemned without a hearing. I suppose I shall have to go to the execution."

Meade had wondered what it be would like to command a grand army. He was going to find out more quickly than he would have liked. Did he have what it took to lead the Army of the Potomac to victory over Lee?

He stood and started dressing. Meade had always been honest with himself. He frankly didn't know if he could effectively manage the frac-tious Army of the Potomac. Would the weight of grave responsibilities be too much for him? Would he become timid when facing Lee, like Hooker had?

God had placed him in this position. He had to gather himself and rise to the great challenge of confronting Lee's invading army.

He thought of his precious Margaret. She was so wary of the vicious politics that swirled around commanding generals. She would be both proud and worried.

Meade, with his son George and Hardie, rode in the darkness to Hooker's headquarters. His mind was racing. He thought of his corps commanders. Were they competent? Could he trust them?

He would promote George Sykes to take over his Fifth Corps. Sykes was a career army man, a West Point graduate, and a man Meade could trust. Reynolds was his best friend in the army, a fine leader and a great general. Hancock was also a friend, and Hancock the Superb was a fitting nickname. Sedgwick and Slocum were competent but not special men like Reynolds and Hancock. Howard had been derelict in his duties at Chancellorsville, and while he had demonstrated personal bravery, Howard could not be trusted as a battlefield leader. Last, there was Dan Sickles. Meade had no respect for this political general and cold-blooded murderer. Sickles and Hooker were close friends. Meade could not trust Sickles either on the battlefield or in the cesspool of army and Washington politics.

At 5:00 a.m., they arrived at Hooker's headquarters at Prospect Hall. Hooker was dressed and prepared to see them. Hardie handed Hooker a letter, which Meade assumed advised him of his removal. Hooker frowned but didn't look totally surprised. Hooker sent for his chief of staff, Butterfield, and a meeting was held to review the status of the army.

After Butterfield identified the location of each corps, Meade exclaimed, "I'm surprised at how scattered the army corps are. The army is very dispersed."

Hooker looked offended. "They are not scattered. It's simply a function of a large army marching vigorously toward the enemy."

"Where is Lee and the Army of Northern Virginia?"

"We believe they're entirely in Pennsylvania," Butterfield said. "Lee has spread his army across the countryside, foraging for supplies. There are reports of Confederate troops in Carlisle, York, and the Cumberland Valley around Chambersburg."

Meade asked, "Do you think Lee will cross the Susquehanna River and attack Harrisburg?"

"I don't think so. Lee doesn't have bridging equipment," Hooker responded in a tired voice.

"There must be fords across the Susquehanna, and capturing Pennsylvania's capital would be quite a prize."

Hooker replied, "I don't see Lee crossing that river."

Meade asked, "What size are our forces?"

"We suffered seventeen thousand casualties during the Battle of Chancellorsville," Hooker replied. "Then we lost twenty-five thousand troops when their enlistments expired. When we left the Rappahannock to march north, we had about eighty thousand men.

I have been vigorously requesting that Lincoln, Stanton, and Halleck provide reinforcements. They have given the Army of the Potomac an additional fifteen thousand troops. Right now, total strength, including the cavalry, is around ninety-five thousand men."

"And the strength of Lee's army?"

"Ask Colonel Sharpe for the latest analysis," Hooker responded.

Hooker's shoulders had slumped, and he looked dejected. "Do you have control of the troops at Harper's Ferry?"

"Yes. They're under my command."

Hooker angrily exclaimed, "That Goddamn bastard Halleck! I demanded control over Harpers Ferry, and he refused to give it to me! He has hated me since our days in California! In a fit of anger, I offered my resignation to Lincoln." Hooker exhaled a deep breath. "The President accepted it. He wanted to make a change in command."

The meeting ended, and Hooker took his leave.

Meade came out of the headquarters tent and saw his son. "Well, George, I'm now in command of the Army of the Potomac."

His son beamed with pride. "Congratulations, Father! I'm so proud of you!"

Meade was happy that George felt joyous over the promotion. With his youthful exuberance, his son couldn't comprehend the crushing weight of the grave responsibilities that Lincoln had imposed upon him. He remembered McClellan talking about the pressure of having the fate of the nation on his shoulders. He now knew how McClellan felt.

"Thank you, son. I have a hard job in front of me, and I need to get started."

Meade went back into the headquarters tent and, sitting at Hooker's vacated desk, composed a telegram to Halleck.

FREDERICK, MD, JUNE 28, 1863—7 AM
GENERAL H. W. HALLECK

GENERAL-IN-CHIEF:

THE ORDER PLACING ME IN COMMAND OF THIS ARMY
IS RECEIVED. AS A SOLDIER, I OBEY IT, AND

TO THE UTMOST OF MY ABILITY WILL EXECUTE
IT. TOTALLY UNEXPECTED AS IT HAS BEEN, AND
IN IGNORANCE OF THE EXACT CONDITION OF THE
TROOPS AND POSITION OF THE ENEMY, I CAN
ONLY NOW SAY IT APPEARS TO ME I MUST MOVE
TOWARD THE SUSQUEHANNA, KEEPING WASHINGTON
AND BALTIMORE WELL COVERED, AND IF THE ENEMY
IS CHECKED IN HIS ATTEMPT TO CROSS THE
SUSQUEHANNA, OR IF HE TURNS TOWARD BALTIMORE,
TO GIVE HIM BATTLE. I WOULD SAY THAT I TRUST
EVERY AVAILABLE MAN THAT CAN BE SPARED WILL
BE SENT TO ME, AS FROM ALL ACCOUNTS THE ENEMY
IS IN STRONG FORCE. SO SOON AS I CAN POST
MYSELF UP, I WILL COMMUNICATE IN MORE DETAIL.

GEO. G. MEADE
MAJOR-GENERAL

CHAPTER 43

Meade needed to find a new chief of staff to replace Butterfield. Before the war, Butterfield had worked for American Express, a company that his father helped found. He was disliked by many officers, who viewed him as pompous. He was an intimate friend of Hooker and Sickles, and Meade could not trust or rely on him.

Meade sought out Seth Williams, the assistant adjunct general. "Seth, will you be my chief of staff?"

"I'm flattered that you asked me, but that's not a job I want. I have to say no."

Meade next went to Gouverneur Warren, his chief engineer. Warren was a small, slender man with dark, piercing eyes. "Congratulations! I understand you're a newlywed. How did you pull that off when Lee is invading Pennsylvania?"

"Hooker was most gracious. He let me go to Baltimore for the wedding on June 17. Emily and I had a one-night honeymoon at Willard's Hotel in Washington. Then I was back with the army."

"I need a new chief of staff. Will you do it?"

"I would not advise changing chiefs of staff in the middle of a campaign. In any event, I want a field command, not a desk job. I must respectfully decline."

It was unsettling having good men turn him down for such an important position. He next sought out General Andrew Humphreys, a fellow Philadelphian who commanded a division in Sickles's Third Corps.

"Humphreys, I need you to be my new chief of staff."

"I want to stay in the field. I must say no."

Completely frustrated and having an enormous amount of work to do, Meade resigned himself to the reality that for the coming battle, Butterfield would be his chief of staff.

Meade went to Butterfield and curtly said, "We have three army corps guarding Maryland mountain passes when Lee's entire army is in Pennsylvania. That makes no sense. Get orders issued to have those three corps march toward Frederick."

Meade summoned Alfred Pleasanton, who had replaced Stoneman as a commander of the Cavalry Corps. When he arrived, Meade said, "The Union cavalry has not performed as well as the Confederate cavalry during this war. As we speak, Jeb Stuart is doing another of his infamous rides around our army, with no one from the cavalry impeding him. We need more vigorous commanders. Do you have any suggestions?"

"Let me have a while to think."

"I want your suggestions in an hour!"

———————

Meade sat at the desk and drafted a communication to the army.

> *Headquarters of the Army of the Potomac*
> *June 28, 1863*
>
> *General Order, No. 66*
> *By direction of the President of the United States, I hereby assume command of the Army of the Potomac.*
> *As a soldier, in obeying this order, an order totally unexpected and unsolicited, I have no promises or pledges to make.*
> *The country looks to this army to relieve it from the devastation and disgrace of a foreign*

invasion. Whatever fatigues and sacrifices we may be called upon to undergo, let us have in view constantly the magnitude of interests involved, and let each man determine to do his duty, leaving to an all-controlling Providence the decision of the contest.

It is with just diffidence that I relieve in the command of this army, an eminent and accomplished soldier, whose name must ever appear conspicuous in the history of its achievements; but I rely on the hearty support of my companions in arms to assist me in the discharge of the duties of the important trust which has been confided in me.

George G. Meade,
Major-General, Commanding

Meade went to Butterfield and told him to have the communication distributed.

———————————⚔

Pleasanton returned. "General Meade, I suggest we promote three of the most competent and aggressive cavalry captains to brigadier generals and give them their own brigades to command in the coming conflict."

"What are their names?"

"Wesley Merritt, George Custer, and Elon Farnsworth."

"I will see that the men receive their promotions immediately. You are dismissed."

As Pleasanton left, Reynolds entered the tent. The old friends embraced.

"Congratulations, Meade! You have my full support."

"I was sure that if Lincoln was going to make a change, it would have been you. Look at Burnside. He twice turned down command, yet Lincoln ordered him to replace McClellan. When I was informed that I had been chosen for command, I immediately said you would be a better choice."

Reynolds laughed. "It's time for you to be my boss. I have confidence that you will rise to the challenge."

The normally taciturn Meade felt a surge of emotion. "Thank you, Reynolds. You're like a brother to me."

"Did Lincoln burden you with the need to protect Washington so that you can't maneuver the army freely?"

"Protecting Washington is an essential part of my orders."

"I'll take my leave. You must have a vast amount of work to do."

Meade found Colonel George Sharpe, who ran the BMI. He had a droopy mustache and clear, intelligent eyes.

"Colonel, I am keen on getting all the intelligence we can on the Rebels." Meade paused. He needed to know he had the right man for the job. "What are your qualifications to run an intelligence operation?"

"Before the war, I practiced law in New York and spent two years as a diplomat in Vienna. I was in Sickles's Third Corps when Hooker took command in January. Hooker came to me and said he had heard that I was intelligent, a Yale-educated lawyer, and asked me if I would be interested in creating an intelligence operation for him. I said yes, and he made me deputy provost marshal."

Sharpe rubbed his fingers through his mustache. "I learned that McClellan had used Allan Pinkerton, a civilian detective to gather intelligence. When McClellan was relieved, Pinkerton left with him. John Babcock, who was Pinkerton's second-in-command, served as an intelligence officer for Burnside. I made Babcock part of my organization and had him explain how Pinkerton operated. I was surprised when Babcock told me that Pinkerton would pass along tales he heard from prisoners and allegedly loyal citizens as to Confederate troop strength without doing any analysis to see if the claims were accurate. My experience is that prisoners and deserters wildly inflate Rebel strength. I suspect that Pinkerton gave McClellan grossly inflated estimates of the number of Confederates he faced."

Meade had thought that McClellan's estimate of Lee's troop strength seemed exaggerated during the Seven Days Battles, and here was evidence that it was likely so. "Have you done anything to get more accurate estimates of the number of Rebel soldiers?"

"Yes. I brought in people to not only gather raw data but also analyze the information in a systematic fashion. At the end of that process, I provide my assessments of the analyzed data."

"How do you gather and analyze intelligence?"

"BMI gathers information from numerous sources, including a network of spies, the interrogation of captured Confederates and deserters, Southern newspapers, cavalry patrols, telegraph intercepts, runaway slaves, Signal Corps observation stations, interceptions of Confederate flag signals, and captured letters and diaries. We have created charts of every Rebel regiment, division, and corps. If we get a report that the Thirteenth Mississippi Regiment battle flag passed through a town, we know that it is part of Barksdale's brigade, which is part of McLaws's division, which is part of Longstreet's corps. Thus, a single regiment sighting can provide a lot of information."

"How big is Lee's army?"

"We estimate that Lee has ninety-two thousand soldiers carrying muskets and two hundred seventy-five cannons. Those numbers don't include Jeb Stuart's six thousand cavalry troopers."

"Where is the largest concentration of Lee's army?"

"Around Chambersburg, Pennsylvania. Rodes is as far north as Carlisle and Early as far east as York."

"How far is Chambersburg from Frederick?"

"About fifty-five miles."

Meade left his meeting feeling confident in Sharpe.

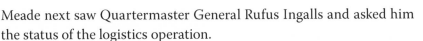

Meade next saw Quartermaster General Rufus Ingalls and asked him the status of the logistics operation.

"With Lee invading Pennsylvania, we moved our supply base from Aquia Creek to Baltimore," Ingalls said. "We are creating a field supply base at Westminster, Maryland, the terminus of a train line from Baltimore. I do my best to anticipate the army's needs. For example, with all the marching, the men are wearing out their shoes, so I ordered ten thousand pairs of shoes and socks sent here to Frederick."

"How large are our supply trains?"

"We have 3,652 supply wagons and 43,300 horses and mules. I'm confident we can meet the army's supply needs."

"Rufus, I know I can rely on you."

Meade went to Butterfield. "Do you have maps of the roads in Maryland and Pennsylvania?"

"I will provide you with all the maps we have."

Meade studied the road network and the current location of his army corps and thought about his instructions to protect Washington and Baltimore. He came up with a plan to move his army the next morning, June 29, starting at 4:00 a.m.

He sat down with Butterfield and went over the orders he wanted prepared for each corps commander. He would have the army press forward from their campsites around Frederick toward the Pennsylvania border, twenty-five miles north. It would be a hard day of marching for his men, but he needed to aggressively close the gap with Lee. Meade wanted to get Lee's attention and have him turn away from the Susquehanna River and Harrisburg. By the end of the day, his left flank would be at Emmitsburg, Maryland, and his right flank at Union Mills, Maryland. The distance between the two flanks would be twenty miles. While his line would not be continuous, it would cover the major roads Lee could take to attack either Washington or Baltimore.

The day seemed to never end. He had been bothered by the poor showing of the Union artillery at Chancellorsville, so he sent for Henry Hunt, Chief of Artillery.

"Hunt, what the hell happened to the artillery at Chancellorsville? I have never been in a battle where Union artillery was more poorly handled!"

"Hooker didn't allow me to do my job! I've never liked him. I cannot stand how he uses his political connections in Washington to sabotage the careers of his superiors and promote himself. Hooker stripped me of my duties and made me a mere artillery adviser. That conceited ass Dan Butterfield relayed Hooker's order emasculating my responsibilities in the most smug and condescending way imaginable. Hooker did not even allow me to be present on the Chancellorsville battlefield. After Chancellorsville, Hooker told me he had made a mistake and was going to restore my authority."

Meade wasn't shocked. He had heard stories about the conflict between Hunt and Hooker. He assured Hunt that he knew he was a damn good artillerist and said, "In the coming battle, I want you to do your job and exercise your full authority."

Meade summoned Provost Marshal Marsena Patrick. "Patrick, I understand our troops have been enjoying themselves a bit too much in Frederick. The whole army will be marching at four a.m. tomorrow morning. Have your men clear all our troops out of Frederick's bars and brothels and have them in their camps tonight, so they will be sober in the morning and ready to march."

CHAPTER 44

Right before the army began to move, Meade sat down to write his precious Margaret a letter. He hadn't slept since being woken by Hardie. There was simply no time.

Headquarters Army of the Potomac, June 29, 1863

My Dearest Margaret,

It has pleased Almighty God to place me in the trying position that for some time past we have been talking about. Yesterday morning, at 3:00 a.m., I was aroused from my sleep by an officer from Washington entering my tent. After waking me up, he said he had come to give me trouble. At first I thought that it was either to relieve or arrest me, and I promptly replied to him that my conscience was clear, void of offense toward any man; I was prepared for his bad news. He then handed me a communication to read, which I found was an order relieving Hooker from the command and assigning me to it. As dearest, you know how reluctant we both have been to see me placed in this position, and as it appears to be

God's will for some good purpose—any rate, as a soldier, I had nothing to do but accept and exert my utmost abilities to command success. This, so help me God, I will do, and trusting to Him, who in His good pleasure has thought proper to place me where I am, I shall pray for strength and power to get through with the task assigned me. I cannot write you all I would like. I am moving at once against Lee, a battle will decide the fate of our country and our cause. Pray earnestly—pray for the success of my country (for it is my success besides). Love to all. I will try to write often.

Your Loving Husband George

At 4:00 a.m., Meade led his army out of Frederick. His life had changed in a blink of an eye. Twenty-five hours ago, he was in a deep sleep, content with being commander of the Fifth Corps. Lincoln had chosen him to lead the Army of the Potomac at a time of crisis in the nation's history.

One Union military debacle after another was fueling a rising peace movement. Lincoln's political support for the war was eroding. Meade realized that if the Union army could not defend its homeland, public support for the war could plunge to an unsustainable level. While he differed with Lincoln on some military issues, he wholeheartedly supported the President's steely resolve to suppress the rebellion and reunite the country. He felt enormous pressure to deliver a desperately needed victory over Robert E. Lee to restore the peoples' confidence in the army and instill a belief that the war would be won.

Meade was the fourth commander of the Army of the Potomac in eight months. Lee had vanquished every Union commander he had faced: Pope, McClellan, Burnside, and Hooker. Lee and his soldiers were probably feeling that no Union commander could defeat them.

He wondered if he could win a battle against Lee and give the nation the victory it needed to renew support for the war. Doubts were seeping into his mind. He took a deep breath and sharply exhaled. There was no time for thinking about failure. He had to put all his energy and focus into the present and the tasks at hand.

Meade was smart, courageous, and a tireless worker. Those traits and his belief in the Almighty would have to carry him through the coming battle. The fate of his country was hanging in the balance.

At midmorning, he rode Old Baldy off the side of the road to take in the spectacle of his army on the march. A continuous line of soldiers marched on the dusty road, intermingled with horses, artillery, and wagons. Numerous flags flapped in the breeze. The road turned and twisted as it made its way across the rolling terrain. The Army of the Potomac resembled a giant blue snake as it moved toward Pennsylvania.

When the day's marching ended, Meade was generally pleased with the army's progress. Only Sickles's Third Corps had failed his expectations by covering a mere twelve miles, half the distance of other corps. He sent a sharp note of rebuke to Sickles. Better performance was expected going forward.

Meade had moved north at a fast and grueling pace to get Lee's attention and have him turn south. Lee would not want his divided forces attacked before he could concentrate his army. Meade had his cavalry out in front, looking for the Rebel army. He hoped soon to get Sharpe's BMI analysis to see whether his stratagem was working. If Lee turned south, a major battle could erupt within days. He issued orders for the next day for shorter marches so his troops would not be totally exhausted going into the coming battle.

Overall, he thought it had been a good day's work. The army had moved with alacrity under his direction. He was beginning to think that he had what it took to be a commanding general. Even though there was much work to do, he took time to write another letter to his wonderful and supportive wife.

Headquarters, Middleburg, Md, June 29, 1863

My Dearest Margaret,

We are marching as fast as we can to relieve Harrisburg, but we have to keep a sharp eye that

the Rebels don't turn around us and get at
Washington and Baltimore in our rear. They have
a cavalry force in our rear destroying railroads,
etc., to try to get me to turn back. But I shall not
do it. I am going straight at them and will settle
this thing one way or the other. The men are in
good spirits; we have been reinforced so as to have
equal numbers with the enemy, and with God's
blessing, I hope to be successful. Goodbye.

Your Loving Husband George

CHAPTER 45

The next morning, while on the march, Colonel Sharpe reported to Meade, "Lee is turning away from the Susquehanna River."

Meade smiled. "That's good news. Do we know where he is headed?"

"Our analysis suggests Lee may concentrate his forces east of South Mountain, probably around Gettysburg, a crossroads town. If Lee ends up in Gettysburg, its extensive network of roads would give him options; go around your right flank toward Baltimore or your left flank toward Washington."

Meade stopped and studied a map. He decided to set up his headquarters in Taneytown, Maryland. He was determined to keep his corps commanders informed of developments, unlike Hooker.

Circular, Headquarters Army of the Potomac, June 30, 1863

The Commanding General desires you be informed that from present information Longstreet and Hill are at Chambersburg, partly towards Gettysburg; Ewell at Carlisle and York. Movements indicate the disposition to advance from Chambersburg to Gettysburg.

The Commanding General believes he has relieved Harrisburg and Philadelphia, and

now desires to look to his own army and assume
position for offensive or defensive, as occasion
requires, or rest the troops. It is not his desire
to wear the troops out by excessive fatigue and
marches, and thus unfit them for the work they
will be called upon to perform.

By Command of Major General Meade.
S. Williams,
Assistant Adjutant General

———————————

Meade wanted the coming battle to be on ground of his choosing. Before getting to Taneytown, he had crossed Pipe Creek. It reminded him of Beaver Dam Creek, which had proven to be a formidable defensive position.

He summoned Warren and Hunt. "You both have a good eye for terrain. I want you to explore a possible defensive line along Pipe Creek from west of Middleburg to east of Manchester. A defensive line between those towns would cover the three major routes out of Pennsylvania toward Baltimore and Washington. The line would encompass Westminster and provide a train line for supplies." Warren and Hunt left, promising to conduct their surveys as quickly as possible.

Meade felt a growing anxiety. This battle had to be won. The Army of the Potomac could not suffer defeat on its own soil. Every man needed to know the gravity of the circumstances.

Circular, Headquarters Army of the Potomac,
June 30, 1863

The commanding general requests that, previ-
ous to the engagement soon expected with the
enemy, corps and all other commanding officers
address their troops, explaining to them briefly
the immense issues involved in the struggle. The
enemy are on our soil; the whole country now

looks anxiously to this army to deliver it from the presence of the foe; our failure to do so will leave us no such welcome as the swelling of millions of hearts with pride and joy at our success would give to every soldier of this army. Homes, firesides, and domestic altars are involved. The army has fought well heretofore; it is believed that it will fight more desperately and bravely than ever if it is addressed in fitting terms. Corps and other commanders are authorized to order the instant death of any soldier who fails in his duty at this hour.

By command of Major General Meade:
S. Williams,
Assistant Adjutant General

⎯⎯⎯⎯⎯⎯⎯▷

That evening, Meade issued orders for his corps commanders to continue their northward movement the next morning, July 1. He had made Reynolds Left Wing commander in control of the First, Third, and Eleventh Corps. Reynolds was directed to Gettysburg. Hancock's and Slocum's corps were to move toward Gettysburg. He sent Sedgwick to Manchester, Maryland, to prevent Lee from turning his right flank. Sykes filled the gap between Slocum and Sedgwick.

Darkness had fallen, and neither Warren nor Hunt had returned with an analysis of the potential Pipe Creek line. He took a few minutes to write another letter to his cherished Margaret.

Headquarters, Taneytown, June 30, 1863

My Dearest Margaret,

All is going well. I think I have relieved Harrisburg and Philadelphia, and Lee has now come to the conclusion that he must attend other matters.

I continue well, but I am much oppressed with a sense of responsibility in the magnitude of the great interests entrusted to me. Of course, in time I will become accustomed to this. Love, blessings, and kisses to all. Pray for me and beseech our Heavenly Father to permit me to be an instrument to save my country and advance its just cause.

Your Loving Husband George

At midnight, Warren reported to Meade. "Pipe Creek is excellent ground for a defensive line. A ridge runs behind the south side of the creek from Manchester to Middleburg that would provide high ground for our troops and artillery. For the most part, the land the Confederates would have to cross to attack is open, and Hunts's artillery would make the Rebels pay a heavy price. The slopes of the creek are steep and would be extremely difficult for infantry to cross in the face of artillery and musket fire. A good network of roads would allow you to go on the offensive if a Rebel attack was repulsed."

Meade believed the possibility existed that he could lure Lee into attacking an exceptionally strong defensive position. He found Seth Williams, his Assistant Adjunct General, and together they prepared a circular to be distributed to his corps commanders describing a Pipe Creek contingency plan. They worked till 5:00 a.m. preparing the details of the plan.

Meade took the text of the circular to Butterfield. "Have this circular prepared and distributed to the corps commanders."

Circular, Headquarters Army of the Potomac, Taneytown, July 1, 1863

From information received, the Commanding General is satisfied that the object of the movement of the army in this direction has been accomplished, viz: the relief of Harrisburg and the prevention of the enemy's intended invasion of Philadelphia beyond the Susquehanna. It is no longer his intention to assume the offensive until the enemy's movements or position should render such an operation certain of success.

If the enemy assume the offensive and attack, it is his intention, after holding them in check sufficiently long to withdraw the army from its present position, and form a line of battle with the left resting in the neighborhood of Middleburg, and the right at Manchester, the general direction being that of Pipe Creek.

For this purpose General Reynolds, in command of the left, will withdraw the force at present at Gettysburg, by the road to Taneytown and Westminster, and, after crossing Pipe Creek, deploy towards Middleburg.

General Slocum will assume command of the two corps at Hanover and Two Taverns and withdraw them via Union Mills, deploying one to the right and one to the left, after crossing Pipe Creek, connecting the left with General Reynolds, and communicating his right to General Sedgwick at Manchester, who will connect with him and form the right.

The time for falling back can only be developed by circumstances. Whenever such circumstances arise as would seem to indicate the necessity for falling back and assuming this general line indicated, notice of such movement will be at once communicated to these headquarters and to all adjoining corps commanders.

Corps commanders should make themselves thoroughly familiar with the country indicated, so that no possible confusion can ensue, and that the movement, if made, be done with good order.

This order is communicated, that a general plan, perfectly understood by all, may be had for receiving attack, if made in strong force upon any portion of our present position.

Developments may cause the Commanding General to assume the offensive from his present positions.

All true Union people should be advised to harass and annoy the enemy in every way, to send in information, and taught how to do it; giving regiments by number of colors, number of guns, generals' names, &c. All their supplies brought to us will be paid for and not fall into the enemy hands.

Roads and ways to move to the right or left should be studied and thoroughly understood. All movements of troops should be concealed, and our dispositions kept from the enemy.

By command of Major-General Meade.
S. Williams,
Assistant Adjutant General

Hunt had come by at 6:00 a.m. and confirmed Warren's report that Pipe Creek would be a splendid defensive position.

An hour later, Meade looked in on Butterfield. "Has the Pipe Creek circular gone out?"

"Not yet."

Meade was infuriated. Having rapid communication of his orders and circulars to his corps commanders was critical in maneuvering his large army. "You're working too slowly! Getting orders out quickly is an essential part of your job!"

CHAPTER 46

Reynolds was at Moritz Tavern on the Pennsylvania side of the Mason-Dixon Line, six miles south of Gettysburg. He had been asleep on the floor with a saddle for a pillow when an aide woke him before daylight and read him Meade's order to advance to Gettysburg. Reynolds felt a surge of adrenaline. He knew Lee might be concentrating at Gettysburg. He was only sixty miles from his boyhood home in Lancaster and was anxious to drive the Rebels out of Pennsylvania to protect his family and fellow citizens from the dangers of an invading army.

As Reynolds got dressed, he thought of his darling Kate. He longed to be with her and start their new life together. Before that could happen, there was a war to win. Because the day might bring a battle, he took the Catholic medal and gold ring she had given him and placed them around his neck.

Reynolds didn't envy Meade. None of his predecessors as commander of the Army of the Potomac had been able to defeat Lee. He hoped his friend could rise to the challenge of commanding such a large army with its political generals, internal power struggles, and interfering Washington politicians. Meade was brave, intelligent, energetic and had an engineer's mind for organization, but he had a temper and could be sharp with people who annoyed him. Reynolds smiled and thought that the conceited and pompous Butterfield was learning why the men called Meade a Snapping Turtle.

Reynolds knew that John Buford's cavalry regiment of 2,500 troopers had spent the night in Gettysburg. He looked forward to seeing Buford, a friend from the old army.

Reynolds issued orders for Howard's Eleventh Corps to follow to within supporting distance of Gettysburg and for Sickles's Third Corps to march to Emmitsburg, Maryland, ten miles south of Gettysburg, to protect the army's left flank.

He got his First Corps in motion heading north on Emmitsburg Road. Two miles from Gettysburg, he received a note from Buford. He was in a fight with the Confederates west of Gettysburg and urgently needed infantry support.

Reynolds went to the commander of his First Division, James Wadsworth. "Buford is in a fight at Gettysburg. I'm going to ride ahead to reconnoiter the field. Come up as fast as you can."

Reynolds galloped, with his staff, into Gettysburg. He rode through town and headed out Chambersburg Pike toward the sounds of battle. He learned Buford was observing the battle from atop the Lutheran seminary. Reynolds found the attractive redbrick seminary building with its white cupola. Buford was descending a ladder from the cupola.

Reynolds looked up at Buford and yelled, "What's the matter, John?"

"The devil's to pay! I have a good portion of A. P. Hill's corps coming down Chambersburg Pike. I don't have enough men to hold them off."

When Buford exited the seminary building, he huddled with Reynolds. "I got to Gettysburg yesterday and saw some very defensible high ground south of town. I figured it was worthwhile trying to impede the Rebels until the infantry got up here and determined whether this was the place to fight Lee." Buford spit out some tobacco juice. "This morning, Hill's men approached Gettysburg like they didn't expect a battle. Their initial nonchalance let our small force hold them off. Now they are taking us seriously and have deployed into battle lines. My men have been fighting off their horses as infantry since first light. They are on McPherson's Ridge, about half a mile in front of us. When it gets too hot there, they will fall back here to Seminary Ridge."

Reynolds had noticed the hills south of Gettysburg on his ride into town and thought it would be good ground for defensive fighting.

Having grown up in Pennsylvania, he was familiar with the ridge-and-valley contour of the terrain. The ripples in the land were like swells in the ocean. The cultivated farmland would be good for maneuvering troops and deploying artillery. He quickly determined the ground at Gettysburg was worth fighting for.

"Can you hang on until I get the infantry up?"

"I reckon so."

Reynolds sent a courier to Howard directing him to move the Eleventh Corps quickly to Gettysburg.

He turned to an aide. "Captain Weld, take a message to General Meade. Tell him that the enemy is attacking Gettysburg in strong force, and I'm afraid that the Confederates will seize the high ground south of town. I will fight here as hard and as long as possible. I will fight house-to-house and throw up barricades in town if necessary. Now, ride like the wind."

Reynolds galloped back to find Wadsworth's division. He bypassed Gettysburg's narrow streets by cutting across farm fields.

He found Wadsworth. "General, have your men march at the double-quick to the battle west of town. Bypass Gettysburg and go across the farmland. Have men cut down any fences that slow your progress."

Reynolds rode back to the raging battle. When James Hall's Maine battery came up, Reynolds led Hall to a location in front of Buford's battle line between Chambersburg Pike and an unfinished railroad cut.

"Hall, this position is exposed, but I want to draw the Rebel artillery fire toward you and not the deploying infantry. Do your best to drive off the enemy artillery. Once the infantry is deployed, I will pull you back to a safer position."

Reynolds directed the first infantry to arrive, Lysander Cutler's brigade, to relieve Buford's cavalry troopers on either side of Chambersburg Pike. Immediately after their deployment, the Confederates launched a ferocious attack that Reynolds did not have enough troops to repulse.

He desperately needed more soldiers on the field. He looked back and saw the black hats of the Iron Brigade advancing across the farm fields. Thank God! These were some of the best troops in the Union army. They were Western men from Wisconsin, Indiana, and Michigan. During the Battle of South Mountain, they had fought with such determination and valor that McClellan had exclaimed, "They must be made of iron." They stood out because they wore black hats rather than the blue kepis that adorned the heads of most Union troops.

Reynolds rode toward the Second Wisconsin, the lead regiment of the Iron Brigade. "Forward men, forward, for God's sake. Forward and drive the Rebels out of those woods!"

Reynolds turned and pointed the way. The men of the Second Wisconsin loaded their muskets and charged toward the forest. Reynolds followed the men on his horse. He heard musket fire and saw some of the black-hatted soldiers fall. The Second Wisconsin did not falter but continued their charge into the woods. He felt great pride in his men, who fought with such selfless bravery. Reynolds turned in his saddle to see if more of the Iron Brigade had come on the field. A minié ball struck him in the back of his neck, and he fell from his horse.

GETTYSBURG: JULY 1, 1863

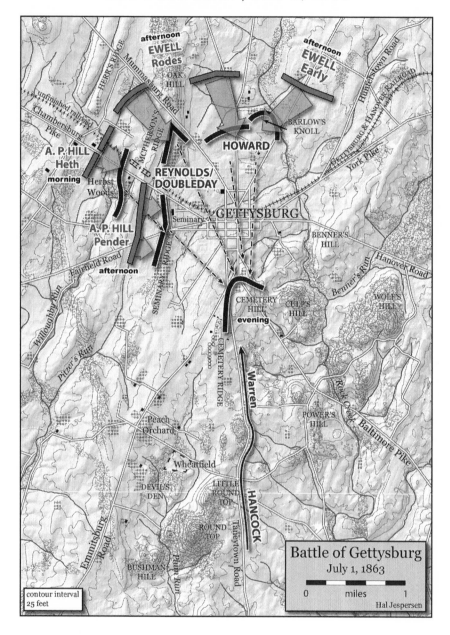

CHAPTER 47

Meade knew that Hancock's Second Corps would be marching through Taneytown and sent a message requesting Hancock pay him a visit. At 10:00 a.m., Hancock entered Meade's tent.

"Win, it is good to see you."

"Congratulations on your new command!"

"Thank you. I have hardly had time to sleep or eat. Do you remember at West Point being taught a tactic of inducing the enemy to attack you on ground you have chosen? The idea is to contact the enemy and then withdraw your forces to a predetermined defensive line. If the enemy is aggressive, like Lee, he will follow and give battle."

"That's what your Pipe Creek circular is all about."

"Precisely. My orders are to stay between the Rebel army and Washington and Baltimore. The Pipe Creek line does that perfectly, covering every major road south out of Pennsylvania toward those cities. It is a contingency plan. I want all corps commanders to understand its details if I determine to implement it." Meade valued Hancock's insights and judgment. "Stay in Taneytown. John Gibbon can lead the Second Corps in your absence."

———————

It was 11:30 a.m. when Captain Weld found Meade with Reynolds's message. "The First Corps is engaged in heavy fighting at Gettysburg. The enemy is advancing in strong force. General Reynolds fears the Rebels will seize the high ground south of town. He will fight as tenaciously as possible, even door-to-door in the town to keep the Confederates from getting the high ground."

"Reynolds is fighting like a tiger!" Meade exclaimed. "That is just like Reynolds. Is the whole Rebel army in Gettysburg or only a part of it?"

"All I can confirm is that A. P. Hill's corps was engaged."

"Did Reynolds order Howard and Sickles to advance to Gettysburg?"

"He ordered Howard to Gettysburg. I didn't hear any order for Sickles to move."

Meade thought that Reynolds must have left Sickles at Emmitsburg as protection for Washington should Lee disengage and head in that direction. Meade had to protect Baltimore and Washington. He couldn't leave his flanks vulnerable to a turning movement until he had confirmation that Lee was concentrating his army at Gettysburg.

Meade sent for his chief engineer, Warren. "Reynolds is in a battle at Gettysburg, trying to prevent the Confederates from securing high ground south of town. Go to Gettysburg and examine the ground Reynolds is fighting for. Report back your observations."

An hour later, another messenger arrived from the First Corps. He looked like he had been crying. "General Reynolds has been killed on the battlefield at Gettysburg."

Meade was stunned. Reynolds was dead! A wave of anguish and grief swept over him. He fought back tears. Reynolds was his best friend, a great general, and a true warrior who never considered personal risk when directing his men.

While still in shock, his mind turned to the practical. With Reynolds dead who would assume command at Gettysburg? The senior officer in the First Corps was Abner Doubleday, whose nickname was "Forty-Eight Hours" because it took him two days to complete an action that other generals did in a day.

When Howard got to Gettysburg, he would be the most senior officer and would take control. That was unacceptable. Howard had been completely unprepared for Stonewall Jackson's flank attack at Chancellorsville.

Meade thought, *Should I go to Gettysburg or stay at Taneytown? Butterfield had to be prodded to get orders out. He must know that efforts had been made to replace him. Was that why he was slow in performing his duties?*

Meade had taken the Fifth Corps from Butterfield. Now Lincoln had taken the Army of the Potomac from his close friend, Hooker. *Butterfield likely hated his guts and given the opportunity, would probably put a knife in his back.* So, for the time being, he would stay in Taneytown.

Meade sent for Hancock. When he arrived, Meade said, "Reynolds got into a fight in Gettysburg and has been killed."

"My God! I can't believe John Reynolds is gone."

"The Eleventh Corps should be at Gettysburg by now, which means that Howard will be senior and in command. After Chancellorsville, I don't trust Howard. I am sending you to Gettysburg to take command."

"But Howard ranks me."

"That's not an issue. Halleck gave me authority to assign commands without regard to seniority. You are a better general than Howard. I will give you a note authorizing your status, and you can show it to anybody who challenges you. I need to know if Lee is concentrating there, whether we secured the high ground that Reynolds died fighting for, your evaluation of the ground we hold, and your thoughts on fighting the battle there."

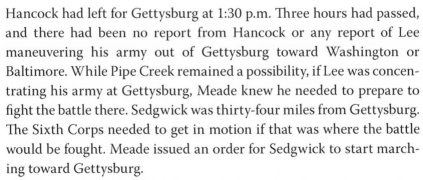

Hancock had left for Gettysburg at 1:30 p.m. Three hours had passed, and there had been no report from Hancock or any report of Lee maneuvering his army out of Gettysburg toward Washington or Baltimore. While Pipe Creek remained a possibility, if Lee was concentrating his army at Gettysburg, Meade knew he needed to prepare to fight the battle there. Sedgwick was thirty-four miles from Gettysburg. The Sixth Corps needed to get in motion if that was where the battle would be fought. Meade issued an order for Sedgwick to start marching toward Gettysburg.

Meade was taking full advantage of his authority to ignore seniority. Doubleday would expect to replace Reynolds, but he was slow and indecisive. Meade remembered Doubleday's failure to support him at Fredericksburg. He issued an order for John Newton, a Sixth Corps general, to come to Taneytown. Newton would replace Reynolds as the First Corps commander.

Major Mitchell, Hancock's Chief of Staff, arrived at 5:30 p.m. to update Meade. "When we arrived on the field, the First and Eleventh Corps were retreating through Gettysburg and were establishing a position on high ground south of town called Cemetery Hill."

Meade thought this must be the high ground Reynolds was fighting to protect.

"After Reynolds's death, the First Corps fought valiantly on ridges east of Gettysburg. When Howard's Eleventh Corps arrived, it took up a position facing west and north and fought with courage and tenacity. Howard got outflanked when a Rebel force under General Jubal Early came in from the north. The fighting was fierce, with many casualties on both sides. When the Union forces retreated through Gettysburg, many men were taken prisoner."

Early was part of Ewell's corps, and Meade now had confirmation that Lee was concentrating at Gettysburg. "What about the terrain? Does Hancock believe we should fight the battle at Gettysburg?"

"General Hancock has positioned the available troops to cover as much of the high ground as possible. He believes the ground is good for defense but could be turned by Lee. He said he could hold the position till dark to allow you to make a decision whether to concentrate at Gettysburg."

Meade now had the information he needed to determine where to fight. "Lee is concentrating his army at Gettysburg. We're partially concentrated there and hold good ground." Meade stood. "I have made my decision. We are going to give battle to Lee at Gettysburg."

Meade went to Butterfield. "Issue orders for all corps and the Artillery Reserve to immediately march to Gettysburg. Have General Newton proceed directly to Gettysburg. Have the supply wagons, except for ammunition, go to the Westminster supply base. I don't want to slow down the army's concentration at Gettysburg."

MOVEMENT OF THE ARMIES
TO GETTYSBURG

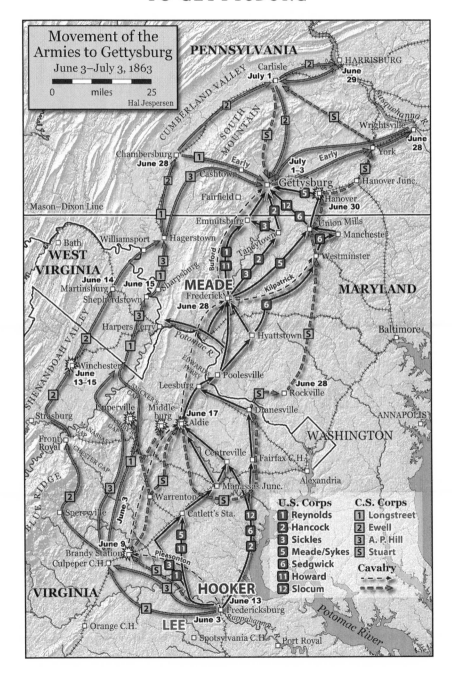

CHAPTER 48

As Meade was getting ready to leave for Gettysburg, Hancock returned to Taneytown.

"How did you find things in Gettysburg?" Meade asked.

"The First and Eleventh Corps both got pretty chewed up today. Reynolds's men fought bravely after his death. The Iron Brigade added to its growing legend but suffered severe casualties. The Eleventh Corps acquitted itself better today than they did at Chancellorsville. Howard had the foresight to place some of his men on Cemetery Hill, so there was a place to rally our men when they retreated."

"How did Howard handle your being given command of the field?"

"He was clearly unhappy, but he cooperated. I had a problem with Doubleday. Howard and Doubleday did not see the necessity of occupying the neighboring Culp's Hill, which, in my opinion, is critical ground for the Union forces to hold. I instructed Doubleday to place a division on Culp's Hill. He resisted, claiming his men were worn out. I told him that you had placed me in charge of the battlefield and that I had given him an order that he must obey. Doubleday was quite angry, but he did send Wadsworth's division to occupy Culp's Hill."

"How are the men's spirits?"

"Demoralized. Today was a Rebel victory. I did my best to reinvigorate the men. I stayed at Gettysburg until Slocum arrived and turned over command to him."

At 10:00 p.m., Meade set out on Old Baldy for Gettysburg. He was accompanied by Hunt and Warren, who had returned from his reconnaissance trip to Gettysburg.

"Warren, what is the terrain like in Gettysburg for establishing a defensive line?"

"We occupy two hills south of town. One is called Cemetery Hill because there's a small cemetery there. The open and relatively flat top will be a good location for artillery. We also hold Culp's Hill, which is east of Cemetery Hill and curves south. It's rocky and heavily wooded. Cemetery Ridge runs south from Cemetery Hill to a hill called Little Round Top. Cemetery Ridge is mostly open farmland and would be good ground for artillery. If you choose to form a defensive battle line running from Culp's Hill to Little Round Top, it would look like a fishhook, with the barb being Culp's Hill; the bend, Cemetery Hill; the shank, Cemetery Ridge; and the eye, Little Round Top."

"What are the Rebel positions?"

"They occupy the town of Gettysburg and have forces facing Culps and Cemetery Hills. They also are on Seminary Ridge, which is about a mile west of Cemetery Ridge."

Meade turned to Hunt, who had been listening to Warren's description of the ground. "When we get to Gettysburg, take control of your guns. Unlike Chancellorsville, I want you to actively manage the batteries in the coming battle. How many cannons are in the Artillery Reserve?"

"There are 18 batteries and 108 guns in the Artillery Reserve. Including the batteries attached to the corps, we will have 324 cannons at Gettysburg."

At midnight, Meade rode up Baltimore Pike under the moonlight to a small gatehouse entrance to Evergreen Cemetery. He was greeted by Howard, Slocum, and Sickles.

Meade asked, "Is this good ground to fight on?"

Howard responded, "It is excellent ground to defend."

Slocum and Sickles concurred.

Meade replied dryly, "I'm glad to hear it because it's too late to leave."

Meade had never been to Gettysburg and needed to get the feel of the land. He walked out on Cemetery Hill and looked west. He saw the campfires of the Confederate soldiers around Seminary Ridge. He then walked out beyond Baltimore Pike and, looking north, saw more Rebel campfires.

He asked Warren to show him the suggested defensive line. Together they rode under the moonlight, examining the terrain.

Meade returned to Howard's headquarters in the cemetery and addressed the logistics of having his whole army concentrated at Gettysburg.

Meade was on Old Baldy before dawn, accompanied by Hunt; his son, George; and Warren's aide, Captain Paine, for a detailed inspection of the land.

Meade addressed Paine. "Sketch the terrain we are surveying. I will identify on the drawing where I want each corps to deploy. Have copies of the sketch with my designations distributed to each corps headquarters. I don't want any confusion where they should position their men."

They rode south along Cemetery Ridge. There was a shallow valley between Cemetery Ridge and the Rebel-held Seminary Ridge to the west. Emmitsburg Road ran in a northeastern direction between the ridges.

"Hunt, what do you think of this land for your artillery?"

"It is lovely ground for my guns, nice and open with a little elevation. We can easily reach the Rebel positions on Seminary Ridge. Of course, their cannons can reach our positions as well."

Cemetery Ridge slowly descended, and by the time it reached Wheatfield Road, the land to its west along Emmitsburg Road was at a higher elevation. Past Wheatfield Road, Cemetery Ridge rose and became Little Round Top.

Meade rode to the crest of Little Round Top, which had commanding views of the land to the west, including Seminary Ridge. This would be his left flank. He rode over to rugged Culp's Hill. This would be his right flank. He liked the concave nature of his lines. During an attack, he could shuttle troops to places of stress.

His staff had found him a headquarters, a small white house on Taneytown Road owned by Lydia Leister, a widow. It was behind the center of Cemetery Ridge.

When Paine delivered his sketch, Meade placed Slocum on Culp's Hill, and the First Corps extended the line to Cemetery Hill, which

Howard held. The line then bent onto Cemetery Ridge to connect with Hancock. Sickles would connect to Hancock's left and extend the line to Little Round Top. Sykes's Fifth Corps would be held in reserve. Sedgwick was not expected to arrive until late in the afternoon. He gave the sketch with his designations to Paine for distribution to the corps commanders.

Meade had a strong position to defend. He thought of his friend Reynolds, who had sacrificed his life so the Union army would have this high ground. He was determined to honor Reynolds by defeating Lee.

CHAPTER 49

At seven in the morning, Meade met with Slocum and Warren in the Leister house. "I'm contemplating attacking Lee's left flank from the area around Culp's Hill. Examine the ground and report back your recommendations."

Slocum and Warren had few questions, and after examining a map of Gettysburg on Meade's desk, they left.

Meade studied the map. Baltimore Pike, which ran over Cemetery Hill, was a direct route to Westminster and the Union supply base. Meade knew Lee liked flank attacks. If he could turn the Union's right flank and capture Baltimore Pike, the Army of the Potomac would be cut off from its supply base and be in serious peril. Meade couldn't allow that to happen. He summoned his artillery chief, Hunt, and told him to examine the terrain on the right and see if there were areas that could be strengthened with batteries from the Artillery Reserve.

Hunt said he would, but before he left, he told Meade, "I need to alert you that, through some mistake, General Sickles's ammunition trains are miles away from Gettysburg."

"Can't Sickles do anything right? Now I am worried we will not have enough ammunition!"

"Don't worry." Hunt smiled. "I always bring extra ammunition."

After an all-night ride, General Newton arrived at 8:00 a.m. Meade told him he was putting him in command of the First Corps.

"Doubleday ranks me," Newton said. "He was the most senior officer in the First Corps after Reynolds, and by army precedent, he should command the First Corps."

Meade snapped, "I know that! I have authority to assign commands without regard to seniority. I think you are a better general than Doubleday, and I am putting you in charge of the First Corps. Now attend to your duties!"

"Yes, sir," Newton replied.

Geary's Division of Slocum's Twelfth Corps had spent the night on the Union left flank around Little Round Top. Meade ordered Geary to rejoin Slocum on Culp's Hill. Sickles's men would replace Geary's withdrawing troops.

An hour later, Meade thought he should review his left flank. As he came out of the Leister house, he saw his son. "George, visit Sickles and see if he has his men in line."

A little while later, his son returned. "General Sickles is unsure where to place his men."

Meade was annoyed. "Go back and tell Sickles that he is to connect with Hancock and occupy the ground that General Geary held last night!"

A half hour later, Sickles showed up at Meade's headquarters. Sickles was a rakish-looking man. He had a large mustache with ends that curled up. "General Meade, I need to clarify where to place my men. To my knowledge, Geary did not have a position last night."

Meade was exasperated. He pointed south, in the direction of Little Round Top. "General Sickles, you need to connect to Hancock's left flank and extend your line south to cover Little Round Top! Didn't you get Paine's drawing of where to place your corps?"

"I don't recall seeing it. Can you send someone from your staff to help place my artillery?"

Meade agreed. "I will send General Hunt."

"Do I have authority to place my corps in such a matter as in my judgment I deem most suitable?"

"Certainly. Within the limits of the general instructions I have given you. I leave to you the choice to occupy any ground within those limits."

After Sickles left, Meade went to Butterfield. "We know the main roads in and out of Gettysburg, but we also need to know all the connecting roads. Please have staff officers learn all the roads in the area and ascertain the positions of the ammunition supply trains and the Artillery Reserve batteries. Familiarize yourself with all the details so we are prepared to meet any contingency."

Slocum and Warren returned from their feasibility analysis of an attack on Lee's left flank. "Gentlemen, do we have good ground for going on the offensive?"

Slocum spoke up, shaking his head. "We don't recommend it. The ground in front of Culp's Hill is rugged, and any attacking force would be exposed to Ewell's cannons. The chance of a successful attack is not good."

Meade gave up the idea of attacking Lee. He issued an order for Sykes to move into a reserve position behind the left flank held by Sickles.

As the afternoon wore on, Meade received reports from lookouts on Cemetery Hill and Little Round Top about Confederate movements toward his flanks. A courier reported that Sedgwick was approaching Gettysburg.

Meade prepared a status report for Halleck.

Headquarters Army of the Potomac,
July 2, (3 p.m., near Gettysburg) 1863

Major General Halleck, General-in-Chief

I have concentrated my army at this place to-day. The 6th corps is just coming in very much worn out, having been marching since 9 p.m. last night. The army is fatigued.

I have to-day, up to this hour, awaited the attack of the enemy, I having a strong position for defense. I am not determined as yet in attacking him till his position is more developed. He has been moving on both my flanks apparently, but it is difficult to tell exactly his movements. I have delayed attacking to allow the 6th corps and parts of other corps to reach this place, and to rest the men. Expecting a battle, I ordered all my trains to the rear. If not attacked, and I can get any positive information of the position of the enemy which will justify me in so doing, I shall attack. If I find it hazardous to do so, or am satisfied the enemy is endeavoring to move to my rear, and interpose between me and Washington, I shall fall back to my supplies at Westminster. I will endeavor to advise you as often as possible.

In the engagement yesterday the enemy concentrated more rapidly than we could, and towards evening, owing to the superiority of numbers, compelled the 11th and 1st corps to fall back from the town to the heights this side, on which I am now posted.

I feel fully the responsibility resting on me, and will endeavor to act with caution.

George G. Meade
Major General

GETTYSBURG: JULY 2, 1863

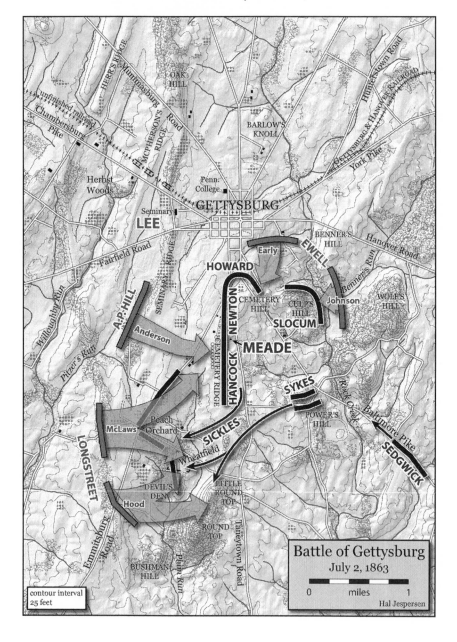

CHAPTER 50

Meade had called a 3:00 p.m. meeting of his corps commanders. Everybody had come except Sickles.

About fifteen minutes into the meeting, Warren burst in, slamming the door so hard he shook the windows. He rushed up to Meade. "Sickles has broken contact with Hancock's left flank! He's moved the Third Corps west of Cemetery Ridge, all the way to Emmitsburg Road!"

Meade was outraged that Sickles had blatantly ignored orders. He turned to Sykes. "Get the Fifth Corps moving forward toward Sickles. That insolent man has exposed the army to danger."

He ended the meeting, lamenting Lincoln's weakness for appointing political generals without military experience who felt free to disobey orders. How in God's name could Sickles be so foolish as to have broken contact with the rest of the army? Meade was worried. His army was no longer concentrated. If Lee should attack it could be destroyed in detail, unit by unit.

As Meade rode south on Cemetery Ridge, he beckoned for Warren to ride beside him. "Go to Little Round Top and see whether that fool Sickles has any troops on it!"

Shortly after dispatching Warren, Meade saw Sickles riding toward him from a peach orchard on Emmitsburg Road.

When they met, Meade's temper exploded. "You moved three-quarters of a mile in front of Cemetery Ridge and left Hancock's flank in the air! You posted your men where they are isolated. They have no connection to the rest of the army! Why did you move the Third Corps off Cemetery Ridge?"

"This is higher ground for my artillery. I was acting within the discretion you gave me."

"You were to connect with Hancock on Cemetery Ridge! There is no way in hell my orders gave you discretion to move out here!"

They rode to the peach orchard. Humphreys's division was facing Emmitsburg Road. Birney's division connected to Humphreys's and angled south through a wheat field, ending in a jumble of boulders called Devil's Den.

Sickles waved his arm toward Cemetery Ridge. "The area I moved from was low ground, at least fifty feet below this peach orchard. Being here prevents the Rebels from grabbing this high ground."

Meade looked around. Emmitsburg Road ran over a narrow ridgeline between Seminary and Cemetery Ridges.

In a sharp, curt voice he addressed his insubordinate commander. "General Sickles, it's true this is higher ground than where you were posted." Meade pointed west, toward South Mountain. "If you keep moving toward the mountain, you will find progressively higher ground. Higher ground doesn't always mean better ground. This is neutral ground between the two armies. Both our guns and those of the enemy control it." Meade pointed to the joinder of Sickles's two divisions. "General Humphreys's and Birney's lines connect like the apex of a triangle, forming a salient that can be attacked from both sides! Both of their flanks are in the air! This is an inherently weak position!"

Sickles was visibly angry at being so harshly spoken to. He asked through clenched teeth, "Should I pull back to Cemetery Ridge?"

Cannon fire erupted, and Rebel shells began to fall around them.

The disconnected Army of the Potomac was in grave danger. Meade knew his command skills were about to be put to the supreme test.

Meade yelled to be heard above the noise of the exploding shells. "I wish you could withdraw to Cemetery Ridge, but the Rebels are not going to allow it! You have no choice but to stay here. I will do my best to support you."

Sickles didn't respond, but he looked happy to be able to stay in his advanced position.

On his way back to Cemetery Ridge, Meade sent an order to Sykes to dispatch a division to support Sickles. Meade received a note from Warren saying that Little Round Top was unprotected. Unbelievable! Meade sent an order for Humphreys to leave the peach orchard and move to Little Round Top.

Ten minutes later, Meade received another note from Warren. He had gotten Strong Vincent's Fifth Corps brigade to occupy Little Round Top. Meade had been Vincent's corps commander until a few days ago and knew that he was a good officer.

Meade ordered Humphreys to turn away from Little Round Top and go back to the peach orchard.

Musket fire erupted from the wheat field where Birney was positioned. The Confederates had attacked. A battle raged in a field of breast-high, ripening wheat.

Sykes sent a note that Sweitzer and Tilton's brigades were moving to support Birney in the wheat field and that Vincent's brigade had been diverted to Little Round Top.

Meade returned to Cemetery Ridge and found Hancock. "George, did you order Sickles to march forward and leave a huge gap in our line?"

"Of course not. That damn scoundrel disobeyed my order to connect to your left flank! I need to support him to avoid a catastrophe! Please send one of your Second Corps divisions to that wheat field. We can't let the Rebels break our line."

"That son of a bitch Sickles should be court-martialed! He has gambled the fate of the Army of the Potomac as casually as he would place a bet in a game of cards!"

"That can wait till after the battle. We need to repulse Lee's attack, and Sickles needs to be supported."

"I'll send Caldwell's division."

Meade stayed on Cemetery Ridge, monitoring the battle. He received another note from Warren. He had secured more Fifth Corps reinforcements for Little Round Top: Hazlett's battery and the 140th New York.

Hunt rode up. "When I saw how exposed Sickles was, I gave him additional batteries before the fighting started. Do you want me to place some batteries on the area of Cemetery Ridge Sickles vacated?"

"Yes. Good idea."

Both sides were feeding more troops into the cauldron of violence that was the wheat field, control of which changed hands multiple times, leaving the ground covered in blue and gray corpses. Meade wasn't giving up the wheat field. He ordered Sykes to send in another division. Meade thought of the cornfield at Antietam. *This damn wheat field at Gettysburg is going to be as bloody as that awful cornfield.*

An hour and a half after the Confederate attack had begun, the Union lines were holding.

There had been an intense artillery duel between the Union batteries in the peach orchard and Rebel cannons, but there had been no infantry attack. That changed when Southern soldiers charged out of the woods and assaulted Humphreys's Emmitsburg Road line.

Through his field glasses, Meade saw the battle flag of Barksdale's Mississippi brigade. They charged right at Humphreys's cannons. Confederate soldiers fell, but their comrades kept charging. The Rebels overran some of the cannons, and the left flank of Humphreys's line began to break. Batteries began limbering up and retreating to avoid capture. Humphreys was a good commander, and the retreat of his left flank was orderly, with men stopping to turn and fire at the pursuing Confederates.

With Humphreys's line crumbling and Hancock's corps shrunken because Caldwell was off fighting in the wheat field, there were too few men to defend Cemetery Ridge.

Meade needed reinforcements. He had hesitated to weaken his right flank, which was protecting Baltimore Pike, out of concern that Lee would attack there when he saw troops leaving to repulse assaults on other parts of the Union line. But he had to save the center of his line and issued orders for Slocum and Newton to each send a division to Cemetery Ridge.

GETTYSBURG: WHEATFIELD

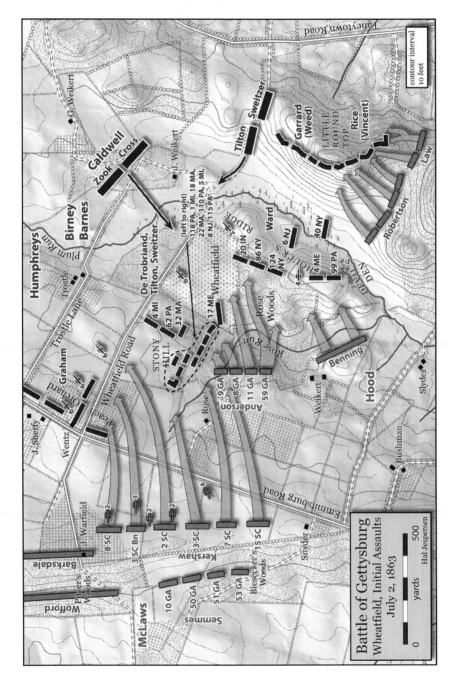

Battle of Gettysburg
Wheatfield, Initial Assaults
July 2, 1863

0 yards 500

Hal Jespersen

contour interval
10 feet

Meade found Hancock. "I have ordered reinforcements for Cemetery Ridge."

"They better get here Goddamn quick!"

The Rebels were desperately pressing the Union's left flank. Meade ordered Sykes to send his last division, the Pennsylvania Reserves, to Little Round Top and the wheat field.

A Third Corps aide appeared. "General Sickles's leg has been struck by a Rebel cannonball. He is being transported to a field hospital to have it amputated."

When Meade heard this, he sought Hancock. "I want you to take control of the Third Corps in addition to your Second Corps."

"Sickles is a Goddamn idiot! We are in danger of having our defensive line destroyed because he disobeyed orders and put his men in an untenable situation! Because of him, two of my best generals, Zook and Cross, have been killed in that fucking wheat field!"

Another Rebel brigade charged out of the Seminary Ridge woods. Wilcox's Alabamians hit the center of Humphreys's line. Ten minutes later, Lang's Florida brigade came out of the woods and charged Humphreys's right flank.

Meade realized that Lee had launched an *en échelon*, progressive attack. The successive waves of attacks were coming like hammer blows. Lee had forced him to commit his reserves and weaken his center to protect his left flank. The center of the Union Cemetery Ridge line was now in dire jeopardy.

Meade knew he could not lose this battle. He thought about the Sixth Corps, who were exhausted from an all-night march. He issued an order for Sedgwick to move his entire corps forward to support the left flank and Cemetery Ridge. He was not going to make the mistake of his predecessors and fail to get all his men into the battle.

The weight of the combined assault from the Mississippi, Alabama, and Florida brigades was too much, and Humphreys's line collapsed. Sickles's Emmitsburg Road defensive front had been destroyed.

The Confederates who had decimated Humphreys's division were advancing on Cemetery Ridge.

Hancock rode up. "George, I am taking Willard's cowards to stop Barksdale."

"Cowards?"

GETTYSBURG: CEMETERY RIDGE

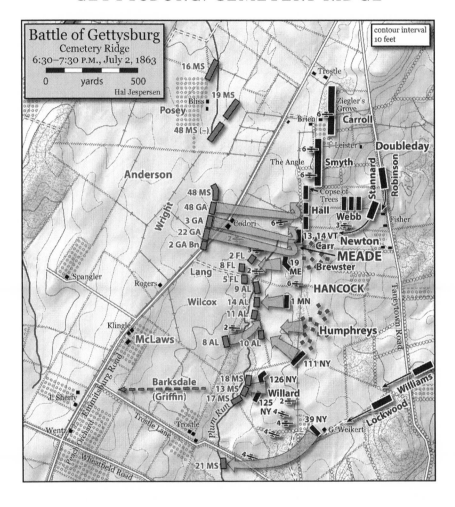

Battle of Gettysburg
Cemetery Ridge
6:30–7:30 P.M., July 2, 1863

0   yards   500

Hal Jespersen

contour interval
10 feet

"Those New Yorkers broke and ran when Stonewall Jackson attacked them at Harpers Ferry during the Antietam campaign. Today they are going to have a chance to be heroes."

Hancock led Willard's brigade off Cemetery Ridge, toward Barksdale's advancing Rebels.

They charged into the advancing Confederates. There was a great collision on the battlefield. Hundreds of soldiers wearing blue and gray were on the ground. Barksdale's men faltered, then retreated.

Wilcox's Alabama troops were moving toward Cemetery Ridge. Meade looked behind him to see if the reinforcements he had ordered from Newton and Slocum were in sight. They weren't.

When he turned back, he saw Hancock with the First Minnesota. They were the only Union troops available to take on Wilcox's advancing soldiers. Hancock sent the small Minnesota regiment, less than three hundred men, charging down Cemetery Ridge toward the Alabamans, who outnumbered the Minnesotans four to one. The First Minnesota slammed into the Confederates and, while taking horrific casualties, they stopped the Rebels from getting to Cemetery Ridge.

Meade felt great pride in Hancock's leadership and initiative in plugging gaps in the Union line. *He is truly Hancock the Superb!* he thought. *And what heroism by the New York and Minnesota soldiers! They had sacrificed themselves to save the day.*

While Hancock was orchestrating heroic charges, another Rebel brigade had come out of the Seminary Ridge woods. Wright's Georgians were fast approaching Hall's brigade, which constituted Hancock's left flank.

Ominously, two of Wright's regiments were moving past Hall, onto ground where the only men in blue were Meade and his small group of staff officers.

Meade straightened himself in his stirrups and pulled out his sword. His staff officers, including his son George, also pulled out their swords. Meade would not turn his back to the enemy. The gap in the line needed to be defended until reinforcements arrived.

Suddenly an aide shouted, "Here they come, General Meade!"

Meade turned and saw Newton galloping up Cemetery Ridge as he led Stannard's Vermont brigade. The Green Mountain Boys deployed into a battle line. Meade cheered the reinforcements. He sheathed his sword, took off his hat, and, waving it over his head, led the Vermonters forward. "Come on, gentlemen. Let's take it to these Rebels."

As he advanced, Old Baldy suddenly stopped. Meade looked down. Blood was spurting from his old warhorse's stomach. He dismounted and examined Old Baldy. It was a serious wound.

Then he saw his son George sprawled on the ground. His horse had been shot out from under him. George wasn't getting up. *My God! Has he been shot?* Meade rushed over to George. "Son, are you OK?"

After an agonizing minute, George sat up. "I think I will be OK, Father. I was stunned from being thrown from the horse."

Meade extended his hand and helped George stand.

An aide gave Meade a new horse. He mounted and started forward. The Georgians were retreating.

Newton rode up. "General Meade, we have saved Cemetery Ridge!"

Meade took in the scene. Everywhere, the Confederates were retreating toward Seminary Ridge. "Yes, but it was a damn close call."

Newton pulled out a flask of whiskey and handed it to Meade, who took a sip.

Meade heard the thunder of cannons and the rattling of musketry fire coming from the wheat field. "The day is not over. There still seems to be some fight left in the Rebels."

CHAPTER 51

Meade rode toward the sounds of the continuing battle on his left flank. He observed with dismay that the wheat field, strewn with bodies of Union and Confederate soldiers, had been captured by the Rebels. Georgia and South Carolina battle flags were advancing toward Little Round Top.

The Pennsylvania Reserves were positioned on the slope of Little Round Top, facing the approaching Confederates.

General Samuel Crawford, commander of the Reserves, grabbed a regimental battle flag and led his cheering men in a charge down the slope, toward the Rebels. The Confederates appeared shocked by the bold charge and retreated toward the wheat field.

Meade thought of his departed friend Reynolds, who had led a similar charge at Second Bull Run. How he wished Reynolds had been with him on the battlefield today.

The Reserves drove the Rebels back through the wheat field. The Confederates regrouped on the western side of that hellish ground, while the Reserves stopped behind a stone wall on the eastern border. It was ironic that after so much fierce and savage fighting, neither side controlled the wheat field.

An aide from General Howard appeared with a note that the Rebels were preparing to attack the Eleventh Corps position on Cemetery Hill, and he needed support. Meade sent an order to Newton to have Robinson's division rush to Cemetery Hill.

As Meade galloped toward Cemetery Hill, he looked toward Little Round Top and was happy to see Sedgwick present in force on his left flank.

On Cemetery Ridge, he encountered Hancock. "What's happening on the right flank?"

"Lee began an attack on Culp's Hill, and Howard sent reinforcements from Cemetery Hill. Now Lee is attacking both Cemetery and Culp's Hills. I ordered Carroll's brigade and a regiment from the Philadelphia Brigade to reinforce Howard on Cemetery Hill."

Meade was pleased. "Win, you have done brilliant work today."

"George, you proved your mettle by moving troops around like a chess master."

Meade valued Hancock's opinion, and the compliment made him feel proud. He had been too busy to reflect upon his performance. But Hancock was right. He had admirably handled the army.

The sun disappeared, and it grew quiet on Cemetery Ridge. Meade continued toward his right flank. Cannon and musket fire were coming from Culp and Cemetery Hills.

A note arrived from Howard. The Confederates had captured a portion of Cemetery Hill. Unbelievable! The Eleventh Corps was losing control of that key ground.

Under a rising moon, he heard shots, screams, and musket fire coming from Cemetery Hill. He surmised it must be a Union counterattack by the reinforcements he and Hancock had sent. Meade could see sheets of flame from the discharge of muskets. He was excited. *Could Cemetery Hill, the loss of which would be catastrophic, be secured?*

The fighting didn't seem to last long. A note arrived from Howard announcing that Cemetery Hill was totally in Union hands. Meade let out a sigh of relief.

He rode over to Culp's Hill. The fight was continuing under the moonlight. He found Slocum. "Henry, what is the status here?"

"During the day, our defenses got very thin because we sent reinforcements to other parts of the field. The Confederates have tried to take advantage. Many of our men have returned, and I am confident that we can hold the position."

Meade returned to his headquarters at 9:00 p.m. This was his fifth day in command of the Army of the Potomac. He'd had only five hours of sleep since Lincoln thrust him into command. Rather than being exhausted, he felt elated. Sickles's actions had placed the army in great danger. Time after time, his army had faced a crisis that could have resulted in its destruction. The men had fought with unparalleled enthusiasm and devotion to duty. Every Rebel assault had been thrown back. The great Robert E. Lee had not prevailed.

However, Union losses had been substantial. He thought that the number of dead and wounded had to approach those of Antietam, which had been the deadliest day of the war.

Meade craved information and summoned Colonel Sharpe. When Sharpe arrived at the Leister house, Meade asked, "How much of his army has Lee used?"

"From prisoner interviews, we believe Lee has put into combat every division but Pickett's."

Given the ferocity of the fighting, Meade wasn't surprised. The only fresh divisions he had were Sedgwick's.

"Any insight on what Lee might do tomorrow?"

"The Confederate prisoners believe they are winning the battle, and with one more push, the Union army will be driven off the field in defeat. If that's how Lee sees it, he will attack."

"Thank you, Colonel."

As Sharpe left, Warren entered Meade's small headquarters. Blood was leaking through a bandage on his neck.

Meade was concerned. "What happened to your neck?"

"A bullet grazed my throat on Little Round Top. It's a minor wound."

"Tell me about the Little Round Top fight."

"When I arrived, only the Signal Corps was on the hill. I saw a battery below, posted on top of Devil's Den. I rode down and had them fire a shot into the woods, causing enemy troops to look up. I saw glistening gun barrels and bayonets. It was an intensely appalling discovery. Our left flank was unprotected, and disaster loomed."

"That cold-blooded murderer Sickles! His insubordinate actions nearly destroyed this army!"

With disgust, Warren said, "I hate those fucking political generals!" He took a pitcher of water and filled a glass. "I rode behind Little Round Top and found Strong Vincent marching toward the wheat field.

At my direction, Vincent led his brigade to the defense of the hill. He finished deploying his men just minutes before the Rebels launched a ferocious attack. During the fighting, Vincent was mortally wounded."

Meade was sad. Vincent had been a brilliant young lawyer who had developed into a fine officer.

"I then found Charles Hazlett's battery. Little Round Top was too steep and rocky for his horses to haul up his guns. His men pushed and pulled their cannons up the steep slope of the hill. During the intense fight, Hazlett was killed."

Meade shook his head. "Hazlett was a good man."

"I went back, looking for more troops. I intercepted the 140th New York on the way to the wheat field. I told Colonel Paddy O'Rorke that Little Round Top was in imminent danger. Paddy led his men on the double-quick up the hill, and none too soon because our right flank was beginning to give. Paddy was killed as soon as he crested the hill. His men swung the battle in that portion of the field in our favor."

As the Fifth Corps commander, Meade knew these fallen soldiers well. He felt for their families. War was an ugly business. "We lost so many brave men today."

"On our left flank, Joshua Chamberlin's Twentieth Maine fought off repeated attacks. Finally, out of ammunition, Chamberlin led a bayonet charge down the hill and repulsed the Rebels. The Fifth Corps covered itself in glory holding on to Little Round Top."

Meade was determined to act more transparently than Hooker did. He called a meeting of his corps commanders for 11:00 p.m. at his Leister house headquarters.

Meanwhile, he prepared a status report for Halleck.

Headquarters Army of the Potomac, July 2, 1863—
11 p.m.

General Halleck:

GETTYSBURG: LITTLE ROUND TOP

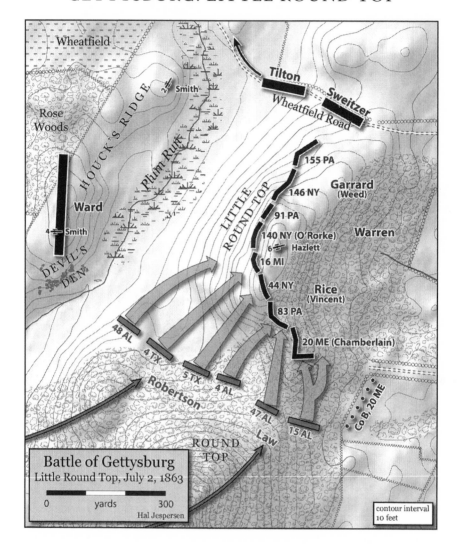

Wheatfield

Rose Woods

HOUCK'S RIDGE

2≣ Smith

Tilton

Sweitzer

Wheatfield Road

155 PA

Garrard (Weed)

146 NY

91 PA

LITTLE ROUND TOP

140 NY (O'Rorke)

Warren

6≣ Hazlett

16 MI

Ward

4≣ Smith

DEVIL'S DEN

44 NY

Rice (Vincent)

83 PA

Plum Run

20 ME (Chamberlain)

48 AL

4 TX

5 TX

4 AL

Robertson

47 AL

Law

15 AL

Co B-20 ME

ROUND TOP

Battle of Gettysburg
Little Round Top, July 2, 1863

0   yards   300
Hal Jespersen

contour interval
10 feet

The enemy attacked me about 4 p.m. this day, and after one of the severest contests of the war, was repulsed at all points. We have suffered considerably in killed and wounded. We have taken a large number of prisoners. I shall remain in my present position tomorrow, but am not prepared to say, until better advised of the condition of the army, whether my operations will be of an offensive or defensive character.

George G. Meade,
Major General

Meade's top generals gathered in a small, cramped room. Musket fire could be heard coming from Culp's Hill. Soon the room filled with cigar smoke.

Meade stood. "Gentlemen, I have called you together to ascertain the fitness of the troops and to get your thoughts on whether we should attack Lee or wait for him to attack us."

Birney said, "The Third Corps is badly used up and not ready for further action."

Meade responded, "Would each corps commander provide an estimate of the number of infantry troops fit for action?"

Butterfield tallied the responses. "There are fifty-eight thousand infantry soldiers available for battle tomorrow."

Newton, a well-respected engineer, spoke. "Gettysburg is no place to fight a battle."

Meade was startled. He considered the ground they held to be excellent terrain for defense and asked General Newton to explain.

"While we hold high ground that can be defended from direct assault, I'm concerned that Lee can turn our flank and get between us and Washington. Then we would have to fight a battle on ground of his choosing. I would rather defend a Pipe Creek line than to have to attack Pipe Creek with Lee defending it."

Hancock said in a commanding voice, "There is no way in hell we should leave Gettysburg! The Army of the Potomac has never fought better than today. The men fought with incredible valor and courage

on their home soil. It would demoralize the troops to retreat to Pipe
Creek. This is good ground to defend, and we proved it today."

Meade listened to an animated discussion of the pros and cons of
staying in Gettysburg and whether to attack or defend.

Butterfield interjected, "I propose we vote on three questions.
First, should the army remain in Gettysburg or retire to another location closer to our base of supply? Second, if the army stays, should it
defend or attack? And third, if it's decided to remain on the defensive,
how long should the army wait for an attack?"

Meade had not called his senior generals together for a council of war. He had already informed Halleck that he was staying at
Gettysburg. He firmly believed the army should stay and see if tomorrow Lee would attack their strong defensive position. But he was curious to see how the generals voted on Butterfield's questions, so he let
the vote proceed.

Meade was gratified when every general voted to stay and fight. All
voted to stay on the defensive, which he agreed with. A majority voted
to wait only one day to see whether Lee attacked before considering
other measures, which was a position he shared. He was happy with
the consensus achieved.

Meade ended the meeting. "Gentlemen, thank you. We will maintain our position and wait for Lee to attack."

As Gibbon was leaving, Meade pulled him aside "If Lee attacks
tomorrow, it will be in your front, the center of our line. He has made
attacks on both of our flanks and failed. He will assume that I have
weakened the center to reinforce the flanks."

Gibbon smiled. "If Lee attacks the Second Corps, we will be ready."

At 1:00 a.m., an aide from Slocum brought a note requesting permission for a morning attack on Rebels who had occupied breastworks
abandoned by troops sent to reinforce Cemetery Ridge.

Meade replied, "Attack at first light."

CHAPTER 52

At 4:30 a.m., Union cannons on Culp's Hill exploded with fury, pounding breastworks held by the Confederates. After fifteen minutes, the firing ceased. Before the planned Union assault started, the Rebels took the initiative and charged up the hill.

Culp's Hill was steep and rugged. Union defenders had created strong breastworks. Fierce Federal musket fire felled many Rebels as they struggled up the slope. By 5:30 a.m., the Confederate assault had been repulsed.

Meade worried about Howard's ability to hold Cemetery Hill. He ordered Robinson's First Corps Division and two Sixth Corps regiments to move behind Cemetery Hill. Given his interior lines, these men would be within supporting distance of Hancock on Cemetery Ridge.

He thought of Margaret and what a special relationship they had. Her love and support sustained him through arduous times. Writing her frequently helped him cope both with how much he missed her and the stress of his work.

Headquarters Army of the Potomac, Gettysburg,
8:45 a.m., July 3, 1863

My Dearest Margaret,

All is well and going well with the army. We had
a great fight yesterday, the enemy attacking and
we completely repulsing them; both armies are
shattered. Today at it again, with what results
remains to be seen. Army in fine spirits, and every-
one determined to do or die. George and myself
well. Reynolds killed the first day. No other of
your friends or acquaintances hurt.

Your Loving Husband George

When Meade heard the sounds of battle again from Culp's Hill, he surmised that the Confederates must have renewed their attack. He had
confidence in Slocum and decided to let him fight his battle without
looking over his shoulder.

Meade left the Leister house to inspect his lines. The day was hot
and muggy, and the air was still. He rode up Cemetery Ridge and found
Hancock, who immediately questioned him.

"Gibbon tells me you think Lee's going to attack the center of my
line?"

"That was my supposition last night. Right now, he is attacking
Culp's Hill. Lee is unpredictable. I need to and will have all parts of the
line well supported."

Hancock pointed at Seminary Ridge. "His men would have to travel
close to a mile of open ground under punishing artillery fire."

"Lee is a gambler, and his bets have paid off in the past. I think he
believes his men are invincible. I hope he attacks today. Our troops
have never been in better spirits. We are ready to lick the Army of
Northern Virginia."

Meade continued his inspection tour, riding along Cemetery Ridge and up the slope of Little Round Top. He dismounted and walked out on a rocky ledge. He took out his field glasses and studied the Confederate position on Seminary Ridge. The Rebels were massing their cannons in front of the woods. As he rode back toward his headquarters, he met his artillery chief.

"Hunt, have you observed that the Confederates are concentrating their artillery?"

"Yes. It's clear they are planning an artillery barrage."

"What preparations have you made to respond?"

"I'm in the process of inspecting every artillery piece. The ones not in good working order are pulled from the line for refurbishment and replaced with guns from the Artillery Reserve. I have placed additional batteries on Cemetery Ridge. My aides are making sure every battery has a full supply of ammunition."

"Do we have enough ammunition? Our batteries were in a hot fight yesterday."

"I always bring extra ammunition because your infantry commanders love to engage in artillery duels for the morale of their men. They expend shot and shell like there is an endless supply."

"Infantry troops like it when our batteries return enemy fire. It is good for their morale."

"While that's true, it's a waste of valuable ammunition. I took the liberty of instructing our battery commanders not to return Rebel cannon fire for fifteen minutes to conserve ammunition and to thereafter be conservative in their use of ammunition. The Confederates would be very happy if we depleted our ammunition and had nothing left to repulse an infantry assault."

Meade was impressed. "Hunt, your reasoning is sound. Continue with your preparations."

He received a note from Slocum. The Confederates had been pushed off Culp's Hill. The fighting had ceased.

As he passed back by the Second Corps line, General Gibbon hailed him. "General Meade, will you stop and have lunch with us?"

Meade couldn't remember the last time he had eaten. Hancock was there, along with one of Gibbon's aides. Meade agreed and took a seat on a cracker box.

Gibbon pointed to his aide. "You know Colonel Frank Haskell? He is my most trusted aide."

"Yes, I have met Haskell several times." Meade smiled at Haskell. "You're a lawyer turned warrior."

"You have a good memory. I was practicing law in Madison, Wisconsin, before I volunteered to fight for the Union."

"The commanding general and I go way back," Gibbon said. "What year did we meet in Florida?"

Meade had to think. It seemed like a long time ago. "It was 1849. I was a topographical engineer scouting locations for forts from Tampa to Fort Pierce to fight the Seminole Indians. The army was kind enough to name one of the bases Fort Meade."

Hancock interjected. "What in the hell is old Bobby Lee doing? I thought he would give us a real fight today."

"It's only midday. There's plenty of time for a battle," replied Meade.

After lunch, Meade returned to his headquarters. He was in the small front yard of the Leister house, speaking with an aide, when he heard a loud boom of a cannon from Seminary Ridge. Quickly 150 other cannons joined in. The noise was tremendous, and a great wave of sound passed over him. Soon cannonballs and shells began falling and exploding all around his headquarters.

A nearby caisson of ammunition exploded spectacularly, violently shooting fragments of shells in every direction. Horses tied to a fence were blown apart, their heads, legs, and innards spread over the ground. The house took a direct hit when a cannonball went through the roof and hit the map table. A cannonball landed up the ridge and grazed Meade's pants as it bounded down the slope. The shells kept coming, shrieking and whistling through the air.

Meade kept his composure. He had expected an artillery attack. The direction of the cannon shots suggested there would be an infantry attack on the center of his Cemetery Ridge line.

Some staff officers ran out of the house after it had taken another direct hit and sought shelter behind it. Meade calmly walked over to them.

"Are you trying to find a safe place? You remind me of the man who drove the ox team that took ammunition for the heavy guns onto the field at Palo Alto during the Mexican War. Finding himself within range, he tipped his cart and got behind it. Just then, General Taylor came along, and seeing this attempt at shelter, shouted, 'You damned fool! Don't you know you're no safer there than anywhere else?' The driver replied, 'I don't suppose I am, General, but it kind of feels so.'"

Meade laughed at his own humor.

Butterfield ran up to Meade. "We cannot keep our headquarters here. It's too dangerous."

Meade looked up at the sky and saw the continuing cascade of hostile spheres. "I suppose you're right. We need to move farther back."

CHAPTER 53

On Cemetery Ridge, Haskell found the sound created by more than a hundred cannonball shots and shells screeching and hissing in the air otherworldly. The air filled with sulfurous smoke, and Seminary Ridge became invisible. Incessant cannon flashes and exploding shells lit up the smoky air like summer fireworks. The ground shook with great vibrations. Tumultuous noise was all-pervasive, deafening, and ear-piercing.

The infantry clutched their guns and hugged the ground behind farmers' stone walls, seeking protection from the bombardment.

Many Rebel cannon shots landed down the ridge around Meade's headquarters, but some found targets on the crest. A fused shell appeared, suspended in air. Then it detonated over prone soldiers, dispersing flesh-piercing iron fragments that killed and maimed men. Another caisson, filled with ammunition, near Haskell, exploded and blew nearby artillerists and artillery horses to pieces.

Gibbon approached Haskell. "Let's show the men some leadership."

They strolled among the troops through the noise and violent explosions. "Haskell, I'm not a member of any church, but I've always had a strong religious feeling. In all these battles, I believe that I'm in the hands of God, and I should be unharmed or not, according to his will. For this reason, I am always ready to go where duty calls, no matter how great the danger." Gibbon asked a soldier lying behind a stone wall, "What do you think of this cannonading?"

"The boys are getting to like it!"

They walked to where Gibbon's line connected to Hays's division. There, the stone wall made a ninety-degree turn, creating an angle that could be attacked from both the front and side.

They saw Hancock at the battery of Alonzo Cushing, a baby-faced West Point graduate. They walked over and saw that Hancock was enraged.

"I don't fucking care that General Hunt ordered you to conserve ammunition! Your battery is part of the Second Corps, which I command, and I order you to return the Rebel cannon fire!" Hancock turned to Gibbon. "Hunt may be an expert on where to place his guns, but he doesn't know shit about the importance of returning enemy artillery fire for the morale of infantry soldiers!"

Haskell thought the Confederate cannon fire was aimed at their division, particularly an area around a copse of trees.

Union batteries were being more roughly handled than the infantry troops. Shattered cannons that had taken direct hits were covered in the blood and internal organs of dead artillerists and horses.

Amid the screams and cries of wounded gunners and with explosions all around him, Haskell watched General Hunt calmly directing the men of his Artillery Reserve. Destroyed batteries were being withdrawn and replaced with fresh ones.

After a hundred minutes, word came from Hunt for the Union batteries to stop firing.

The Rebel cannonading slowed, then ceased.

The smoke cleared. A quiet solitude enveloped the battlefield.

After a few minutes, Confederate soldiers marched out of the Seminary Ridge woods.

The men in gray and butternut quickly formed into three rows a mile wide, fifteen thousand strong. Defiant red Rebel battle flags hung in the still air as bayonets gleamed in the sun.

Haskell watched the Confederates move forward in perfect order as they marched in unison toward Cemetery Ridge. It was a magnificent, awe-inspiring sight. It was also maddening seeing those brave souls marching so resolutely because they wanted to destroy the Union. *They could not be allowed to succeed*, thought Haskell. *The rebellion must be crushed, and the nation reunited.*

PICKETT'S CHARGE

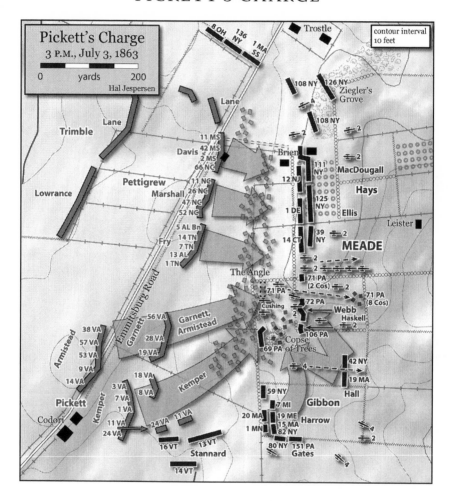

Pickett's Charge
3 P.M., July 3, 1863

0   yards   200
Hal Jespersen

contour interval
10 feet

Gibbon's troops calmly awaited the advancing Confederates. They were veterans. Haskell heard the click of locks as men raised the hammers of their guns, then the clank of muskets being placed on the stone wall facing the oncoming enemy.

As the Confederates advanced across open farm fields, a great roar of thunder arose from Union batteries along Cemetery Ridge, Cemetery Hill, and Little Round Top. The first cannonballs were solid shot. Haskell watched holes being torn in the Rebel lines, and human debris littered the ground. The holes in their ranks were filled in, and the Confederates continued moving forward.

Haskell noticed Cushing's guns were not firing. He looked around and realized none of the Second Corps batteries were firing. They must be out of long-range ammunition, having heeded Hancock's demand to keep firing during the long artillery duel.

As the enemy moved closer, the Union gunners changed to fused shells that exploded above the advancing infantry, inflicting gruesome casualties and creating more holes in the Confederate lines. Onward came the Rebel soldiers, not stopping to succor their fallen brothers. They kept advancing through a storm of iron, indifferent to the thinning of their ranks from monstrous Union artillery fire.

Gibbon rode his black horse along the line. In a calm but loud voice, he said, "Hold your fire until the Rebels reach Emmitsburg Road and start climbing the fences bracketing the road. Then commence firing."

Cushing and his surviving men pushed their cannons to the stone wall. Cushing had been hit with a shell fragment that tore into his abdomen and exposed his intestines. Cushing held in his intestines as he yelled for his men to load double canister rounds.

Hancock rode by, tall in the saddle and looking every bit a heroic general. "When the Rebels get within musket range, send them to hell!"

When the Rebels reached Emmitsburg Road, they climbed over rail fences too stout to be pulled down. Thousands of Union muskets fired, and the Confederates caught on the fences took terrific casualties. Some enemy soldiers stayed at Emmitsburg Road, which was sunken and gave them some protection from the devastating Union musket fire. Soon Rebel minié balls were finding victims on Cemetery Ridge.

Undeterred by the slaughter inflicted upon them by Union artillery and musket fire, Confederate officers rallied their men and charged up the clover-covered, gentle slope of Cemetery Ridge screaming the rebel yell. Many were cut down by musket fire, but the survivors kept coming. Cushing's battery was firing lethal canister rounds. Nothing was left of men who took a direct hit but bits of bone and blood. The Rebels targeted their fire at the Union cannons that were spewing forth so much death. Cushing went down, and his guns fell silent. Soon all of Hancock's batteries ceased firing.

Haskell had ridden the field, looking for Hancock and Gibbon. Both generals had been on their horses the last time he had seen them. Now, save for himself, there was not a mounted officer to be seen. *Both Hancock and Gibbon must have been shot!* He hoped they were alive. Then he felt a sharp pain in his right leg. A spent bullet had hit him.

A smoky haze covered Cemetery Ridge as the Confederates reached Hancock's Second Corps line, and vicious hand-to-hand combat raged along Cemetery Ridge. Muskets served as clubs and bayonets as swords. Oaths were screamed, and blood and gore covered the stone walls. Despite taking significant casualties, the Union line was holding.

Through the haze, Haskell saw with dismay that the Seventy-First Pennsylvania, positioned at the angle, had broken and fallen back. Confederates following Virginia battle flags rushed into the void. A Confederate general, with his hat on his sword, triumphantly put his hand on one of brave Cushing's silent cannons.

With the fate of the Battle of Gettysburg at stake, Haskell drew his sword and rode to the fleeing Seventy-First. "I order you to halt, face about, and fire into the enemy!"

Many men obeyed his command and turned back to face the Confederates. Haskell brought down the flat of his saber on those who failed to follow his orders.

General Alexander Webb arrived on foot and looked aghast that a regiment in his Philadelphia Brigade had broken. He aided Haskell in restoring their confidence. Webb brought forward his reserve brigades, the Seventy-Second and 106th Pennsylvania.

Webb's men, partially protected by the steep ridge line, fired into the spearhead of the Confederate attack that had penetrated the angle. Many Southerners, including the general who had desecrated Cushing's guns, were shot down.

Some Rebels, who were using the western side of the stone wall vacated by the Seventy-First Pennsylvania for protection, were firing deadly volleys into the Pennsylvanians on the edge of the crest.

Webb's ranks were thinning as casualties mounted. Haskell feared the Rebels would break through the center of the Union line. He rode to his left, looking for reinforcements. He found Norman Hall, commander of the Third Brigade.

"Webb is hotly pressed. He must have support, or he will be overpowered! Can you assist him?"

"Yes."

"You cannot be too quick!"

"I will bring my men at once!"

Hall led the Nineteenth Massachusetts and Forty-Second New York to aid the embattled Webb.

Haskell continued further left, looking for more reinforcements. He found fighting men in Harrow's brigade, who answered his call for help. Haskell led men from the Fifteenth and Twentieth Massachusetts, Nineteenth Maine, Eighty-Second New York, and the valiant First Minnesota on the double-quick into the fight at the angle.

When Haskell returned, only the Philadelphia Brigade's Sixty-Ninth Regiment was still holding the line at the stone wall, with their green Irish flag and blue Pennsylvania state flag firmly planted in the soil. They were battling the Confederate tide under duress, with both flanks exposed.

Webb's men were holding at the edge of the ridge, continuing their firefight with the Rebels behind the stone wall.

Confederates were pushing south, out of the angle and toward the copse of trees. Hall's troops had divided, with some supporting Webb and others battling the Rebels trying to break out of the angle.

The men from Harrow's brigade now added their weight, firing volleys into the Confederates advancing toward the copse of trees. Scores of soldiers from both sides were shot at point-blank range.

As Haskell rode toward Webb, his horse bucked, and blood poured from its chest. Haskell dismounted and continued on foot. He found Webb unsuccessfully trying to get his men to charge. Haskell found an officer of the Seventy-Second Pennsylvania on the slope of the ridge. "Sir, lead your men over the crest, and they will follow."

"I understand my place is in the rear of the men."

Frustrated with the lack of leadership, Haskell found a sergeant of the Seventy-Second Pennsylvania holding the severed lance of the American flag.

"Sergeant, forward to the wall with your color. Let the Rebels see the Stars and Stripes up close once more before they die!"

The color-bearer waved the flag over his head and rushed into a maelstrom of death.

Haskell screamed, "Will you see your color advance alone?"

Halfway to the wall, the gallant sergeant and his flag went down. His death put a jolt into Webb's men, and with a great roar, they surged forward into the angle and toward the stone wall, ignoring the groans and wails of their comrades who fell beside them.

Hall's and Harrow's men with frenzied screams joined Webb's charge and slammed into the Confederates advancing toward the copse of trees.

An intense fight boiled and seethed. Men fought like devils, stabbing, clubbing, swearing, and shooting in a furious, swirling fight. The Rebels were forced out of the angle, and the Union soldiers surged to the stone wall. It was too much for the outnumbered Confederates, who broke. Rebels who didn't retreat were killed or captured. The grand Rebel charge had failed.

CHAPTER 54

After leaving the Leister house, Meade moved farther down Cemetery Ridge. That was still a highly dangerous area, and Butterfield was hit in the neck by a shell fragment. Meade next moved to Slocum's headquarters, a mile south on Powers Hill. There, he couldn't communicate with the rest of the army because the soldiers relaying messages via flag signals had been driven off Cemetery Ridge by the bombardment. He then moved his headquarters to Cemetery Hill.

During these movements, Meade, anticipating an infantry attack on Cemetery Ridge, had Humphreys's and Ward's Third Corps divisions and Robinson's First Corps division begin moving to reinforce the center of Cemetery Ridge. Concerned that his batteries would run out of ammunition to repulse a Confederate charge, he ordered the batteries to cease firing. Meade's cease-fire order was issued mere minutes after Hunt's, to the same effect.

When the Confederate cannonade ended, Meade returned to his Leister house headquarters. He received word that a large cavalry fight was occurring in his rear. Lee had sent Jeb Stuart's cavalry around his right flank to attack his rear from the east as the Confederate infantry assault struck Cemetery Ridge from the west. A dispatch brought good news. Stuart had been repulsed.

After ensuring he had eighteen thousand reinforcements heading toward the center of his line to repulse any Confederate breakthrough,

Meade rode up and crested Cemetery Ridge behind Hays's division. The Rebels appeared to be retreating.

He asked a battery commander, "Has the enemy been turned?"

"General Hays has a Rebel battle flag."

"I don't care about their damn flag. Have the Rebels turned?"

"Yes, they're turning."

Meade could hear the battle raging south of him, where Gibbon's division was positioned.

As he rode south, he saw Union and Confederate troops engaged in vicious combat in the angle and along a stone wall. Suddenly the Confederates broke and retreated toward Seminary Ridge.

Meade looked for Hancock and Gibbon but didn't see them. He found Haskell. "Colonel, has the enemy been repulsed?"

"Yes, General Meade, the Rebels are retreating!"

"Thank God!"

Meade looked around. The immediate ground was covered with dead and wounded Confederate and Union soldiers. The Union batteries had suffered severely, many men and horses had been killed or wounded. Dead and dying Confederates were everywhere—in the angle, around the stone wall, on Emmitsburg Road, and in the farm fields. He saw Rebels running, walking, and limping back to Seminary Ridge.

Meade rode farther south and saw one of Hancock's aides. "Where is General Hancock?"

"He has been wounded."

Meade felt for his friend. "Is the wound life-threatening?"

"I don't think so. He was hit in the groin."

"Tell General Hancock that I regret exceedingly that he is wounded. I thank him on behalf of the country and myself for his services rendered today. Where is General Gibbon?"

"He has also been wounded."

My God, Reynolds dead and now Hancock and Gibbon wounded! He was losing his best commanders.

The men began to chant, "Fredericksburg, Fredericksburg!"

Meade surveyed the battlefield. The men were equating this failed Confederate charge to Burnside's disastrous frontal attacks against

Marye's Heights. The troops were right. The attack had been a disaster for Lee.

Catching sight of their commanding general, the men cheered, hurrahed, and threw their caps into the air. Meade was not a demonstrative man, and as he rode along Cemetery Ridge, he merely held his hand in the air. He was enormously gratified by the spontaneous and loud cheering of his men.

Meade was thinking about a counterattack. When he reached Little Round Top, he met with Warren, Sykes, Sedgwick, and Pleasanton. They walked out on a rocky ledge that provided a panoramic view of the battlefield.

Meade pointed toward the wheat field. "Sykes, launch a reconnaissance in force through that damn wheat field and probe the strength of Lee's right flank. I am issuing orders for the Sixth Corps troops I moved to support Cemetery Hill to return. We can launch an attack once we know the position and strength of Lee's forces." Meade turned to Pleasanton. "Have the cavalry support Sykes's troops."

Meade learned the Confederates had fallen back from the wheat field and formed a new battle line on higher ground along Emmitsburg Road. The Confederates were ready to defend an assault.

Time passed and Meade wondered where the Sixth Corps regiments were that he needed for a strong counterattack. It started raining. Daylight was waning, and the Sixth Corps regiments had not appeared. Meade determined there had been enough fighting for the day. There would be no counterattack.

As darkness fell and rain pelted him, Meade felt elated. On this day, he had bested Robert E. Lee!

That night Meade received a visitor: a flamboyantly dressed cavalry officer. His head was topped with a broad-brimmed sombrero, his neck was covered by a red scarf, and he wore a black velvet uniform with coils of gold lace. His golden hair fell in curls on his shoulders.

"General Meade, I came to thank you for making me a general, the youngest in the whole Union army!"

"General Custer, you were promoted for your good service. I understand you were in the middle of the cavalry battle with Jeb Stuart."

"We had a mighty cavalry fight with the Rebs this afternoon. There were charges and countercharges, and my Wolverines distinguished themselves. I led two countercharges. Though we were outnumbered, Jeb Stuart couldn't get past us."

Meade sniffed the air. "Are you wearing perfume?"

"I put cinnamon oil on my hair. Doesn't it smell nice?"

Meade laughed. "You young people have some curious practices."

CHAPTER 55

Headquarters Army of the Potomac, Gettysburg,
Pa, July 5, 1863

My Dearest Margaret,

I hardly know when I last wrote to you, so many
and such stirring events have occurred. It was
a grand battle and is in my judgment a most
decided victory, though I did not annihilate or
bag the Confederate army. This morning, they
retired in great haste into the mountains, leaving their dead unburied and their wounded on
the field. The men behaved splendidly; I really
think they are becoming soldiers. They endured
long marches and short rations and stood one of
the most terrific cannonading I ever witnessed.
Old Baldy was shot again, and I fear he will
not get over it. Two horses that George rode were
killed. I had no time to think of George or myself,
for at one time things looked a little blue, but I
managed to get up reinforcements in time to save
the day. The army is in the highest spirits, and of
course I am a great man. The most difficult part
of my work is acting without correct information
on which to predicate action.

Your Loving Husband George

———————⚔

Meade sent Sedgwick on a reconnaissance in force to discover whether Lee had retreated over South Mountain or had set up a battle line at the base of the mountain. Sedgwick reported that Lee's army was camped on the Gettysburg side of the mountain, apparently wanting the Union army to attack him.

The army was out of food for the men and forage for the animals. Meade stayed in Gettysburg and ordered supplies from the Westminster depot. On July 6, Lee disappeared over South Mountain, retreating toward Virginia.

Because a small force could hold the South Mountain passes near Gettysburg while the main body of Lee's army escaped, Meade decided to march south and use the same passes over South Mountain the army had used on the way to the Battle of Antietam.

The march was slowed by torrential rains that rendered the roads barely passable. Meade ordered forced marches, up to thirty miles a day. The tremendous pace was too much for many of the animals pulling supply wagons. Thousands of horses and mules died along the route. Many men had worn out their boots and were shoeless.

Meade had the cavalry harass and annoy Lee as much as possible. A cavalry raid destroyed the Confederate pontoon bridge across the Potomac River at Williamsport, Maryland, and heavy rains had raised the water level so the Potomac couldn't be forded. Lee's retreat had been stopped by the swollen Potomac.

———————⚔.

Headquarters Army of the Potomac, Frederick, Md, July 8, 1863

My Dearest Margaret,

The army is assembling at Middletown. I think we shall have another battle before Lee can cross the river. For my part, as I have to follow and fight him, I would rather do it at once and in Maryland than to follow into Virginia. I am truly rejoiced that you are treated with such distinction on account of my humble services. I see also the papers are making a great deal too much fuss about me. I claim no extraordinary merit for this last battle and would prefer waiting a little while to see what my career is to be before making any pretensions.

From the time I took command till today, now over ten days, I have not changed my clothes, have not had a regular night's rest and many nights not a wink of sleep, for several days did not even wash my face and hands, had no regular food, and was all the time in a great state of mental anxiety. I think I have lived as much in this time as in the last thirty years.

Old Baldy is still living and apparently doing well; the ball passed within half an inch of my thigh, passed through the saddle, and entered Baldy's stomach. I did not think he could live, but the old fellow has such a wonderful tenacity of life that I am in hopes he will.

Your Loving Husband George

GETTYSBURG: RETREAT

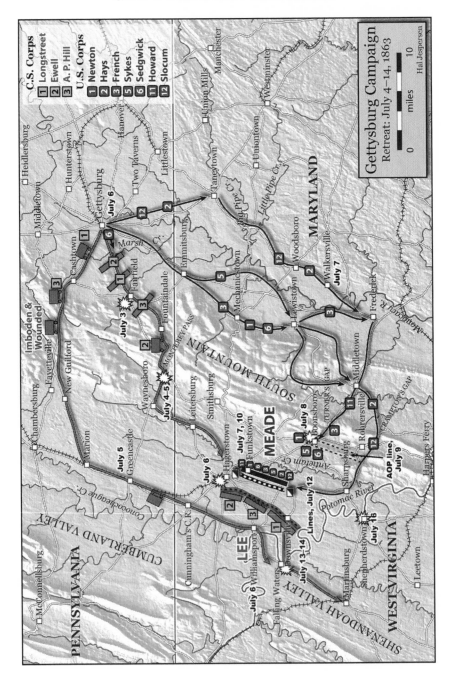

CHAPTER 56

Headquarters Army of the Potomac, South Mountain Pass, July 10, 1863

My Dearest Margaret,

Lee has not crossed and does not intend to cross the river, and I suspect in a few days again to hazard the fortune of war. I know so well that this is a fortune and that accidents, etc., turn the tide of victory, and, until the question is settled, I cannot but be very anxious. If it should please God again to give success to our efforts, then I could be more tranquil. I also see that my success at Gettysburg has deluded the people and the government with the idea that I must always be victorious, that Lee is demoralized and disorganized, etc., and other delusions that will not only be dissipated by any reverse that I should meet with but would react in proportion against me. I have already had a very decided correspondence with General Halleck upon this point, he pushing me on and I informing him that I was advancing as fast as I could. I am of opinion that Lee is in a strong position and is determined to fight before he crosses the river.

Your Loving Husband George

———————◡

On July 12, Meade found the Confederate army entrenched on a ridge running from Hagerstown to Williamsport, Maryland. He spent the afternoon surveying Lee's line. Because of dark, rainy skies and foggy conditions, it was difficult to get an accurate picture, but it was clear the Rebel army was in a strong position. A frontal assault would require troops to cross open land that had been flooded by heavy rains and attack uphill against an entrenched enemy. It was Gettysburg in reverse. What the papers were calling Pickett's Charge had been a catastrophe for Lee. He didn't want to repeat Lee's mistake.

That evening, Meade convened a meeting at his headquarters near Antietam Creek. In attendance were his new Chief of Staff, General Andrew Humphreys; Chief Engineer Warren; and his corps commanders.

"Gentlemen, I plan tomorrow to advance the army in a reconnaissance in force against the Rebel line. We can convert it into a major attack if we find a position that can be exploited. I know that the Confederates are strongly entrenched and that we have not had sufficient time to fully explore the ground, but we must bring Lee to battle. The waters on the Potomac are beginning to recede. We cannot allow him the option of escaping across the river."

Sedgwick said, "I strongly oppose attacking tomorrow. Lee's defensive position looks as strong as the one he had at Fredericksburg. It would be a mistake to attack blindly. We need to carefully explore his line and find the most vulnerable spot to attack."

Slocum followed. "I agree completely with John, it would be folly to advance tomorrow. We just won a glorious victory. We should not sully it with a senseless attack that would give Lee another victory."

Meade was dismayed. His two most senior corps commanders adamantly opposed his plan to bring Lee to battle. A short while ago, he had been in their position, and Hooker had ignored his advice. They had raised valid points, and Meade understood their caution. But there are times in war when risks must be taken.

"I'm for an all-out attack tomorrow," Howard said. "Our men are in high spirits. Lee's back is to the Potomac. A successful attack could destroy his army. Now is the time to be aggressive."

A contentious debate ensued. Finally, Meade called for a vote. The tally was five to two against making any advance.

Meade was unhappy that the majority of his corps commanders opposed his plan. Was it a mistake to attack without adequate reconnaissance? He didn't want to be blindly aggressive and suffer a debacle like Burnside's suicidal Fredericksburg attacks. He felt the heavy weight of his responsibilities. He decided to postpone the assault for a day to allow for a more thorough survey of Lee's defensive line.

"Tomorrow I will reconnoiter the enemy's position, and I'll decide when and where we will attack."

The next morning, Meade and Humphreys rode out in the mist toward the Confederate line. Meade noticed that Humphreys had a scrawny horse with an odd gait. "You're riding a pretty sorry-looking horse."

"I've had three horses killed. The one I lost at Gettysburg cost me two hundred dollars. I am through spending good money on fine-looking horses. I now buy the cheapest horse I can find."

Many of the fields the troops would have to cross were submerged in water, over two feet in some places. The water would slow men down and make them extremely vulnerable to artillery fire. Meade could see the ridge line bristling with cannons. Lee would have positioned his cannons to have the most lethal effect upon troops attacking across open ground.

Their inspection confirmed that the Rebels had erected a strong defensive line, and an attack would be costly in blood. They had not found a weak spot.

Halleck had told him to hold no more councils of war. He liked getting his senior generals' perspectives, and he valued their input, but Meade knew Halleck was right. He was in charge and was the one who had to make decisions.

"Humphreys, prepare an order for the army to advance in the morning."

The next morning, the Army of the Potomac was on the move toward the Rebel position. There was no cannon fire. Lee was escaping!

Meade immediately started in pursuit. Union soldiers captured two thousand prisoners. Federal cavalry had a sharp fight with Lee's rearguard at Falling Waters, where the Confederates had constructed a pontoon bridge. Confederate general James Pettigrew was killed, but Lee and most of his army made it safely across the Potomac.

The Union generals were inspecting the abandoned Confederate works. "Meade, these works are as strong as what Lee had at Marye's Heights. It would have been a bloodbath had we attacked," Humphreys said.

An aide approached Meade, handing him an envelope. "Sir, telegram from General Halleck."

> I NEED HARDLY SAY THAT THE ESCAPE OF LEE'S ARMY WITHOUT ANOTHER BATTLE HAS CREATED GREAT DISSATISFACTION IN THE MIND OF THE PRESIDENT. IT WILL REQUIRE AN ACTIVE AND ENERGETIC PURSUIT ON YOUR PART TO REMOVE THE IMPRESSION THAT IT HAS NOT BEEN SUFFICIENTLY ACTIVE HERETOFORE.

Meade was infuriated. He telegraphed back his response.

> HAVING PERFORMED MY DUTY CONSCIENTIOUSLY AND TO THE BEST OF MY ABILITY, THE CENSURE OF THE PRESIDENT CONVEYED IN YOUR DISPATCH, IS IN MY JUDGMENT, SO UNDESERVED I FEEL COMPELLED MOST RESPECTFULLY TO ASK TO BE IMMEDIATELY RELIEVED FROM THE COMMAND OF THIS ARMY.

WILLIAMSPORT AND FALLING WATERS

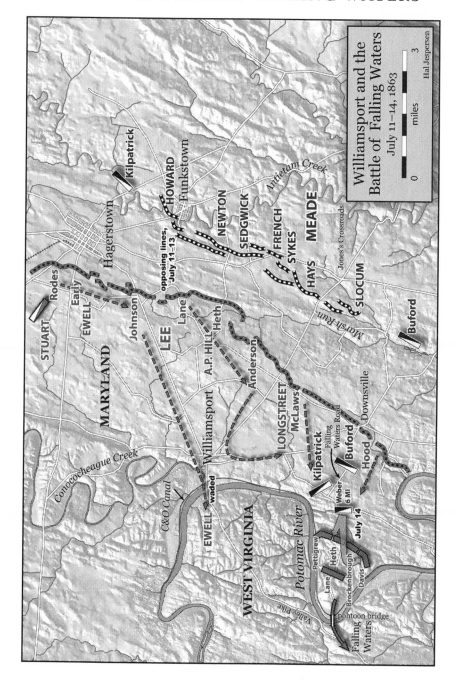

Williamsport and the
Battle of Falling Waters
July 11–14, 1863

Hal Jespersen

miles
0   3

Headquarters Army of the Potomac, July 14, 1863

My Dearest Margaret,

I found Lee in a very strong position, entrenched. I hesitated to attack him without some examination of the mode of approaching him. I called my corps commanders together, and they voted against attacking him. This morning, when I advanced to feel his position and seek for a weak point, I found he had retired in the night and was nearly across the river.

On reporting these facts to General Halleck, he informed me the President was very much dissatisfied at the escape of Lee. I immediately telegraphed I had done my duty to the best of my ability and that the expressed dissatisfaction of the President I considered undeserved censure. I asked to be immediately relieved. In reply, he said it was not intended to censure me but only to spur me on to an active pursuit and that it was not deemed sufficient cause for relieving me.

This is exactly what I expected: unless I did impractical things, fault would be found with me. I have ignored the senseless adulation of the public and press, and I am now just as indifferent to the censure bestowed without just cause.

I start tomorrow to run another race with Lee.

Your Loving Husband George

MINE RUN

CHAPTER 57

During breakfast, Meade was in a contemplative mood. "Humphreys, after Gettysburg I was being lionized by the press as a great hero, the general who defeated Lee. Ten days later, Lee escapes across the Potomac, and now the papers accuse me of being a timid, ineffectual general."

"Your reputation with the newspapers and Washington politicians is being savaged by that bastard Dan Sickles. I hear that he is presenting himself to anyone who will listen as the real hero of Gettysburg. He claims you were blind to the threat to your left flank and were saved by the brilliant performances of your corps commanders. The President visited Sickles the day he returned to Washington. I'm sure that he is doing everything he can to poison Lincoln's mind when it comes to your performance."

"Sickles probably should stand court-martial for insubordination, but having his leg amputated at Gettysburg makes him a sympathetic character. The President and Mrs. Lincoln like him. I'm just going to ignore him."

Headquarters Army of the Potomac, Berlin, Md,
July 18, 1863

My Dearest Margaret,

My army (men and animals) is exhausted; it
wants rest and reorganization; it has been greatly
reduced and weakened by recent operations. Yet,
in face of all these facts, well known to them, I
am urged, pushed, and spurred to attempting to
pursue and destroy an army nearly equal to my
own. This has been the history of all my predeces-
sors, that in time their fate would be mine. This
was the reason I was disinclined to take the com-
mand, and it is for this reason I would gladly
give it up.

Your Loving Husband George

A week had passed since Lee crossed the Potomac. Meade had been summoned to Washington and was in Halleck's office in the War Department. Halleck had a receding hairline, a prominent forehead, and bulging eyes. He had a reputation for being an intellectual, having written a number of books, including one on military theory. His nickname was Old Brains.

After small talk, Halleck said, "I wanted to clear the air with respect to your performance at Gettysburg and the subsequent pursuit of Lee's army. You handled your troops at Gettysburg as well, if not better, than any general has handled his army during the war. You brought all your forces into action at the right time and place, something no commander of the Army of the Potomac has done before."

Meade was surprised by the praise, given the caustic language in Halleck's telegrams. "Thank you for the kind words."

"You should not have been surprised or vexed at the President's disappointment at the escape of Lee's army. He thought that Lee's defeat was so certain that he felt no little impatience at his unexpected escape."

"I thought the President believed that I failed to do what I should have done to prevent the withdrawal of Lee's army. I believed it was my duty to give him an opportunity to replace me."

"Lincoln is not replacing you. Your short campaign has shown your superior generalship, and you merit the confidence of the government and gratitude of the country. I have lost none of the confidence that I felt in you when I recommended you for command. You need to go out and vigorously pursue Lee."

"Your confidence in me is very gratifying." As Meade stood to leave, he remembered Hooker's story that Halleck had become a lawyer while remaining an army officer. "General Halleck, did you attend law school after West Point?"

Halleck laughed. "I became a lawyer by accident. The army sent me to California in 1846 during the Mexican War. There was no civilian government. The army formed a military district. I was made military secretary of state with responsibility for addressing legal issues. When the war ended, there was a lot of controversy about land title, and I became an expert on Mexican law involving land ownership. When gold was discovered, soldiers began deserting to prospect. To keep officers during the gold rush, the army allowed them to have a second job. Americans were flooding into the new California territory. They wanted to buy land from Mexicans, and there were many disputes over who owned the land. Without formal legal training, I got admitted to the federal court in San Francisco." Halleck smiled. "I formed a law firm and did quite well."

Union, Va., July 21, 1863

My Dearest Margaret,

Your indignation at the manner in which I was treated on Lee's escape is only natural and is fully shared by me. I took command from a sense of duty. I shall continue to exercise it to the best of my humble capacity. I have no ambition or ulterior views, and whatever be my fate, I shall try and preserve a clear conscience.

Your Loving Husband George

CHAPTER 58

Meade read the letter from Margaret, and his mood darkened.

His son noticed. "Father, is something wrong?"

Meade looked up. "Sargie is not doing well."

"Poor Sargie. I wish we could do something to help him."

"We've done everything possible. I pray to God every night for Sargie's health to improve."

An orderly entered Meade's tent and delivered the latest newspapers. The lead story in every paper was the ugly draft riots that had paralyzed New York City.

George picked up a New York paper and began reading. "Father, the New York City draft riots are terrible. Working-class whites attacking blacks, and eleven black men have been hanged. The rioters even attacked the Colored Orphan Asylum."

Meade stood and began pacing. The army could no longer meet its needs with volunteers, and Congress had authorized a draft. Despicable Copperhead politicians had stirred up racial hatred, claiming that freed slaves would go north and take jobs from white workers. Days of out-of-control rioting had overwhelmed New York City's police. It had taken troops from the Army of the Potomac to restore a semblance of order. The draft was resuming in the middle of August, and Halleck was having him send even more soldiers to New York to deter further rioting.

"I'm nauseated by the Copperheads. They sow dissension, claiming the war can't be won, and give speeches that encourage desertions. They would be happy if the Confederacy became an independent nation." Meade stopped and lit a cigar. "It's hard to prosecute the war when the home front is divided by such unsavory politicians."

Headquarters Army of the Potomac, August 3, 1863

My Dearest Margaret,

The Government has ordered me to cease pursuing Lee, though I strongly recommended an advance. This is confidential, though the newspapers for some days have been announcing that I would have to assume the defensive. Halleck in a dispatch said it was because a considerable part of the army would be required to enforce the draft.

Your Loving Husband George

Meade had again been called to Washington. The summer heat and humidity were oppressive as he and Halleck left the War Department and walked across President's Park toward the White House. They entered the Executive Mansion and took a staircase to the second floor on the east side to go the Chief Executive's anteroom. Sitting behind a desk was John Hay, Lincoln's young secretary.

Halleck said, "Hay, please advise the President that we are here for the two p.m. meeting."

A moment later, they were ushered into the President's office. Meade's eyes were drawn to the floor-to-ceiling windows overlooking the south lawn. He could see the unfinished monument to Washington and beyond it, the Potomac. The office had a threadbare look to it. The rugs were worn and the furniture rickety. Lincoln got up from an old leather armchair, extended his long arm, and warmly shook Meade's hand.

"General, it is a pleasure to see you again. Stanton is running late, so I have time for a story. Last night Mrs. Lincoln was reminding me about how she is invariably right. That made me think of a story I heard from a southern Illinois preacher. During a sermon, he asserted that the Savior was the only perfect man who had ever appeared in the world, and there was no record, in the Bible or elsewhere, of any perfect woman having lived upon the earth. Whereupon, there arose in the rear of the church a persecuted-looking woman who said, 'I know a perfect woman, and I have heard of her every day for the last six years.'

"'Who was she?' asked the startled minister.

"'My husband's first wife.'"

Lincoln slapped his knee and broke out in uproarious laughter that Meade and Halleck joined.

Lincoln turned serious. "I understand you and Halleck have cleared up any misunderstanding over my reaction to Lee's escape. Lee and his army are the heart and soul of the Confederacy, fighting for their independence with dash and boldness against a larger and better-equipped foe. This war will not end until Lee's army is captured or destroyed. That is why I had such angst at his escape. I am grateful for what you accomplished at Gettysburg. I have confidence in you as a brave and skillful officer and a true man."

"Mr. President, thank you for your confidence. If you ever become unhappy with my performance or believe I am moving too slowly, please replace me with someone more to your liking," Meade said.

Halleck smiled. "I have no doubt you would rejoice with being relieved, but there is no such good fortune for you."

Stanton joined the meeting, apologizing for being late.

Lincoln asked Meade, "After we get past the next phase of the draft, what are your plans for attacking Lee?"

"I prefer maneuvering on Lee's flanks to draw him out of his fixed fortifications. If he falls back to protect Richmond, we can besiege him there or cross the James and capture the railroad hub of Petersburg, which would force Lee to abandon Richmond because without the railroads, he wouldn't be able to feed his army."

"Let me say that an attempt to drive the enemy slowly back into his entrenchments around Richmond, and then lay siege, is an idea that I have been trying to repudiate for a year," Lincoln replied. "We need to attack and destroy Lee's army on the battlefield." The President continued, saying, "The large-circulation newspapers in New York, Philadelphia, and Boston focus most of their attention on the eastern battles. The majority of the nation believes we are winning or losing the war depending on how the Army of the Potomac is doing. While the great victories achieved by Grant in the west, like capturing Vicksburg, are not ignored, the psyche of our people is most deeply impacted by the performance of your army. The country needs more victories from the Army of the Potomac."

"I will do my best to deliver those victories," Meade replied. "Can we address the issue of the base of operations?"

Lincoln responded, "What are your views?"

"The single-track Orange and Alexandria Railroad is woefully inadequate to support the army's needs and requires large numbers of troops for protection against Confederate raids. We need a water supply-base, and the best base of operations is the James River."

Stanton exploded. "There is no way in hell we are going back to the James River! That insufferably arrogant McClellan tried that strategy and failed."

Meade replied, "McClellan didn't fail because of his base of operations."

"Having the army based on the Virginia Peninsula would expose Washington and make it vulnerable to a Rebel attack," Halleck interjected. "It is critical that the Army of the Potomac stay between Lee and Washington."

Meade felt his temper rising and fought to control it. He replied tersely, "When McClellan was on the Virginia Peninsula, the Confederate army didn't attack Washington. It protected Richmond. The fear that Washington will be captured has risen to the level of paranoia! The city is well protected by numerous forts, and troops from the Shenandoah Valley and the Army of the Potomac can be dispatched to Washington if it's threatened."

"It is a justifiable paranoia," Lincoln said. "The capture of our capital by the Rebels would be catastrophic. It would be like England losing London or France losing Paris. Cries for a peace treaty recognizing the Confederacy as an independent nation would intensify to unimaginable levels."

Halleck said, "For now your supply base will remain the Orange and Alexandria Railroad."

———————

Headquarters Army of the Potomac, August 16, 1863

My Dearest Margaret,

They have taken over twenty regiments to quell the draft riots and as yet only sent us one hundred twenty miserable creatures, substitutes for drafted men. Such worthless material as these men are no addition to this army. If the draft is not heartily responded to, the Government had better make up its mind to letting the South go. I am no Copperhead. I am for vigorous prosecution of the war. The war cannot be prosecuted with any hope of success without a great deal of men who have their hearts in the business and who are determined to fight and to conquer, or die.

The manner in which I was received and treated in Washington was most gratifying to me. I believe I have the confidence of all parties.

Your Loving Husband George

CHAPTER 59

Watching Sickles ride up strapped to his horse led Meade to think about the quality of his corps commanders. William French had taken over Sickles's Third Corps and Gouverneur Warren now commanded Hancock's Second Corps. None of his current corps commanders merited his confidence and trust the way Reynolds and Hancock had.

An aide helped Sickles dismount and handed him crutches. "General Meade, I would like to be restored to command of the Third Corps."

"Missing a limb would hinder your ability to command."

"General Ewell, who has lost a leg, commands one of General Lee's corps. I am a good general, my men love me, I am brave, and I showed initiative at Gettysburg."

"You were insubordinate at Gettysburg! I'm inclined to deny your request because of your disability. But I will let you know soon the final decision. I will have the Third Corps honor you by marching in review."

A week later, Meade informed Sickles that he would not be reinstated to command the Third Corps.

———⚔———

Meade and Humphreys were having dinner when a tall young man with a receding hairline entered their mess tent. Meade looked up, and a smile brightened his face.

"Hullo, Colonel Lyman. How are you?"

Lyman spoke with a distinctive Boston accent. "General Meade, thank you for accepting me as a volunteer aide."

Humphreys asked, "How do you two know each other?"

"In the 1850s, the army assigned me to design and build lighthouses along the Florida coast. Lyman had recently graduated from Harvard and came to the Florida Keys to study tropical fish."

"We met in the winter of 1856 in Key West. I was working with Professor Louis Agassiz of Harvard, who sent me to Florida to study and collect starfish specimens for the Harvard Museum of Comparative Zoology. The then Captain Meade graciously invited me to stay on his boat. He was rebuilding the Sand Key lighthouse."

"Sand Key is a spit of land in the Florida straits, six miles from Key West," Meade said. "The previous lighthouse was destroyed in an 1846 hurricane."

Lyman smiled. "There is a beautiful coral reef at Sand Key with an amazing variety of tropical fish. It was a great location for my scientific studies."

Humphreys asked, "Lyman, you have the rank of colonel. What is your military experience?"

"I have no military experience. General Meade advised that I needed two horses, a man to look after the horses, and an officer's commission to be able to serve on his staff. I went to Massachusetts Governor Andrew, who is a family friend, and he made me a colonel."

Humphreys asked with a wry smile, "Are you politically connected in the Bay State?"

"My father was mayor of Boston."

"Lyman, I want you to mess with me and Humphreys. It is good to have an old friend on the staff."

Headquarters Army of the Potomac, September 2, 1863

My Dearest Margaret,

The conscripts are coming in now pretty fast. Today for the first time, over a thousand arrived.

They are generally pretty good men. I trust the example made of five deserters, who were shot on Saturday, will check the evil of desertion. This execution was witnessed by a very large number of soldiers, and I am told the only remark was "Why did they not begin this practice long ago?" Not a murmur against the justice or the propriety of the act was heard. Indeed, the men are the most anxious to see this great evil cured, as they know their own security will be advanced thereby.

Your Loving Husband George

CHAPTER 60

Meade read in the paper that General William Rosecrans's Army of the Cumberland had suffered a crushing defeat at the Battle of Chickamauga in northwest Georgia and retreated into Chattanooga. Braxton Bragg's Confederate army was now besieging Chattanooga. An aide handed Meade a telegram. He opened it. He was being summoned to Washington.

———————

Meade was in the President's White House office with Stanton and Halleck.

"Rosecrans retreated into Chattanooga with only six days of rations," Lincoln said. "The Confederates control Missionary Ridge and Lookout Mountain and have cut off the Union supply line. We cannot have him surrender because his men are facing starvation. I am not counting on Rosecrans breaking out. He seems confused and stunned, like a duck hit on the head. Stanton's idea is to raise the siege by taking troops from the Army of the Potomac and sending them west by rail."

"I understand that Rosecrans is in a tight spot, but I must protest weakening the Army of the Potomac," Meade replied. "I want to launch an offensive. As we speak, I have General Buford's cavalry exploring whether we can turn Lee's right flank. We are getting new troops from the draft, the men's spirits are high, it is good campaigning weather, and the army is itching for a battle. I understand that Grant and Sherman are moving toward Chattanooga. Their forces ought to be enough to break the siege."

Stanton said, "General Meade, your army has been idle since Gettysburg! We need to take troops from you to avoid a catastrophe in Tennessee!"

"I have been forced into idleness by having my army stripped of men to suppress the New York draft riots!"

"I would love for you to attack Lee, but Rosecrans's army must be saved," Lincoln replied. "I need to carefully evaluate what is the best course of action. I will let you know my decision by tomorrow."

Meade asked, "Can I again raise the issue of the army's base of operations? I have greatly studied this issue, and the James River is clearly the best base line of operations in Virginia."

Halleck responded, "We have been over this before. That would expose Washington and make it vulnerable to a Rebel attack."

Lincoln added, "I agree with Halleck."

Humphreys was irate. "They are taking the Eleventh and Twelfth Corps from us and sending them to Chattanooga! That's twenty-five thousand men!"

"I am not happy about it, but it's the President's call," Meade replied. "He needs to save Rosecrans's army."

Headquarters Army of the Potomac, September 24, 1863

My Dearest Margaret,

I was summoned to Washington, and the President advised that he was going to take a portion of the army away. I objected and reasoned against this.

This morning, orders came, taking troops away. Of this I do not complain. The President is the best judge where the armies can be best employed, and if he chooses to place my army strictly on the defensive, I have no right to object.

I am so sorry to see you so anxious about me because it is impossible to keep you constantly advised of what is going on, and your imagination undoubtedly makes matters worse. My position is of course liable to misconstruction as long as the public is ignorant of the truth, for the time will come when it will be enlightened, and then I shall be all right. Of course, if people believe that Lee has no army, and I have an immense one, it is hard to expect them not to inquire why I do not do something. But when they come to know that just as I was about trying to do something, my army was suddenly reduced to a figure a little greater than Lee's and that he occupies a very strong position, where the natural advantages in his favor more than equalize the difference in our forces, they will understand why I cannot do anything.

Concerning a supply base, there is no probability of their permitting me to go to the James River, as it uncovers Washington.

Your Loving Husband George

CHAPTER 61

Lee was on the move, trying to turn the Union's right flank. Meade was worried that Lee would get between him and Washington and decided the best course of action was to fall back to high ground at Centerville, Virginia, where he could take up a strong defensive position and wait for Lee to attack.

Warren's Second Corps was following the Fifth Corps, marching along the Orange and Alexandria line toward Centerville.

Near Bristoe Station, A. P. Hill, unaware that Warren was on his flank across the railroad tracks, launched an attack against trailing elements of the Fifth Corps.

Warren quickly deployed his men along the railroad embankment. Warren surprised and staggered Hill's men with deadly musket and cannon fire.

Hill regrouped and impetuously attacked across six hundred yards of open land. To Warren, it looked like a mini Gettysburg, with four thousand Confederates attacking across farmland where the Second Corp veterans of Pickett's Charge were waiting and ready. Union artillery opened up with frightful effect on the Rebels. The Confederates continued forward into a curtain of musket and canister fire. Only a handful made it to the Federal line, where they were killed or captured. It was a stirring victory for Warren and a stinging defeat for Hill.

Lincoln and Halleck wanted Meade to aggressively seek out Lee and bring him to battle. Having lost contact with Lee, Meade wired Washington that he didn't know where Lee was, and he thought the prudent course was wait for Lee to attack him.

An aide handed Meade a telegram from Halleck.

> LEE IS UNQUESTIONABLY BULLYING YOU. IF YOU PURSUE AND FIGHT HIM, I THINK YOU WILL FIND OUT WHERE HE IS.

Meade was furious and quickly responded.

> MAJOR-GENERAL HALLECK: YOUR TELEGRAM OF 7 P.M. JUST RECEIVED. IF YOU HAVE ANY ORDERS TO GIVE ME, I AM PREPARED TO RECEIVE AND OBEY THEM, BUT I MUST INSIST ON BEING SPARED THE INFLICTION OF SUCH TRUISMS IN THE GUISE OF OPINIONS AS YOU HAVE RECENTLY HONORED ME WITH, PARTICULARLY AS THEY WERE NOT ASKED FOR. I TAKE THIS OCCASION TO REPEAT WHAT I HAD BEFORE STATED, THAT IF MY COURSE, BASED ON MY OWN JUDGMENT, DOES NOT MEET WITH APPROVAL, I OUGHT TO BE, AND I DESIRE TO BE, RELIEVED FROM COMMAND.

"Lyman, at one time I thought it would be an honor to command the Army of the Potomac. Now I would sooner lead a division under the heaviest musketry fire than command this army!"

A day later, with his army strongly entrenched at Centerville, Meade watched Rebel pickets and cavalry examine the Union defenses. Two days later, Lee was gone, having chosen not to attack.

Meade had again been called to Washington and was in Lincoln's office with Stanton and Halleck.

Lincoln asked, "Can you explain why Lee was not brought to battle?"

"When I learned Lee was maneuvering on my right flank, I thought he was trying to get between the army and Washington and force me to give battle on ground of his choosing. To prevent this, I made long, forced marches late into the night to beat Lee to the key ground, the heights at Centerville. Given his aggressive nature, I was surprised when he did not attack. I suppose he concluded my defenses were too formidable, and he did not want to repeat Gettysburg."

Stanton said, "We cannot win this war if we don't fight the enemy!"

Lincoln had a melancholy look on his face. "General Meade, I appreciate your professional judgment and desire to have advantages going into combat. But the army needs to realize that time is a precious commodity in this war. There was a growing peace movement before your glorious victory at Gettysburg. The glow of that victory is fading, and again the clamor for peace is rising. The Confederate goal is to keep the war going long enough that Northerners will despair of ever crushing the rebellion and grant the South its freedom."

Lincoln paused. "We live in a democracy. Next year, there will be a Presidential election. If the war is going poorly and we continue to pay a heavy price in the deaths of our valiant soldiers, I will lose the election to a Peace Democrat, and the Confederacy will become an independent nation. That is why I so consistently urge you to give battle to Lee's army. The North has a much larger population than the South and can more easily replace battlefield losses. Even if you do not destroy Lee's army, every battle reduces his strength. Eventually, his army will be so worn down that it will be captured or destroyed."

Meade replied, "Mr. President, I understand the points you are making. I'll bring Lee to battle in November before winter conditions make campaigning impossible."

Lincoln sat back and smiled. "This morning when I looked in the mirror, I was reminded of this story. I was once accosted on a train by a stranger, who said, 'Excuse me, sir, but I have an article in my possession which rightfully belongs to you.'

"'How is that?' I asked, considerably astonished.

"The stranger took a jackknife from his pocket. 'This knife,' said he, 'was placed in my hands some years ago with the injunction that I was to keep it until I found a man uglier than myself. I have carried it from that time to this. Allow me now to say, sir, that I think you are fairly entitled to the property.'"

Meade joined the President and Halleck in uproarious laughter.

———o———

Headquarters Army of the Potomac, October 30, 1863

My Dearest Margaret,

You seem to be very much puzzled about my retreat, as you misname it. It was not a retreat but a withdrawal of the army and maneuvering into proper position to offer battle. It was made to prevent Lee from compelling me to fight at a disadvantage. I don't suppose I shall ever get credit for my motives, except with the army. The soldiers realize the necessity of not letting the enemy have the game in their hands entirely; hence they cheerfully submitted to all the hardships, such as night and forced marches, that I was compelled to impose upon them.

Lee has retired across the Rappahannock after completely destroying the railroad on which I depend for my supplies. His object is prevent my advance and in the meantime send more troops to Bragg in Tennessee. This was a deep game, and I freely admit that in the playing of it he has got the advantage of me.

Your Loving Husband George

CHAPTER 62

Chilly November winds were blowing. Meade was angry as he paced fiercely back and forth in front of the campfire, bent forward, his hands clasped behind his back.

Meade had devised a strategy of changing his supply base to Aquia Creek on the Potomac, and moving the whole army rapidly and secretly far to Lee's right. He would cross the Rapidan River at Banks's Ford and gain the heights below Fredericksburg. The Army of the Potomac would be between Lee and Richmond. Lee would have had to abandon his lines on the Rappahannock.

Meade stopped pacing and turned toward his chief of staff, who was sitting by the fire, warming his hands. "Humphreys, my plan has been rejected. Halleck responded that I had the tactical freedom to try and turn Lee's right flank, but Washington will not approve a change of base from the Orange and Alexandria Railroad."

"What bullshit!" Humphreys fumed. "This was a good plan, a bold plan. We would have been on Lee's right flank with the inside track to Richmond. True, we would have uncovered Washington, but I'm sure Jefferson Davis would have ordered Lee to protect Richmond, either by attacking us or falling back in its defense. Lincoln's fixation with protecting Washington is crippling our flexibility of movement."

Meade thought of Reynolds. This kind of Washington hindrance with the operations of the army was why he hadn't wanted command.

Headquarters Army of the Potomac, November 3, 1863

My Dearest Margaret,

There is no doubt that my failure to engage Lee in battle during his recent advance created great disappointment in which feeling I fully share. Now that I have clearly indicated what I thought feasible and practicable, my plan is disapproved. I think under these circumstances, justice to me and the true interests of the country justify their selecting someone else to command.

Your loving husband George

———

After brooding over the rejection of his plan, Meade came up with a new approach for attacking Lee. "Humphreys, I promised Lincoln I would launch an offensive before going into winter quarters, and I will do it along this miserable Orange and Alexandria line as Washington demands. We are going to breech Lee's Rappahannock line. He will have no choice but to abandon his entrenchments."

Meade surprised Lee. In coordinated attacks on November 7, he captured Kelly's Ford and Rappahannock Station, breaking the center of Lee's river defense. Rather than battle outside of his fortifications, Lee retreated south across the Rapidan River.

Meade read the telegram from the President and felt a sense of gratification.

MAJOR-GENERAL MEADE,

I HAVE SEEN YOUR DISPATCHES ABOUT OPERATIONS ON THE RAPPAHANNOCK ON SATURDAY, AND I WISH TO SAY, "WELL DONE."

A. LINCOLN

BRISTOE CAMPAIGN

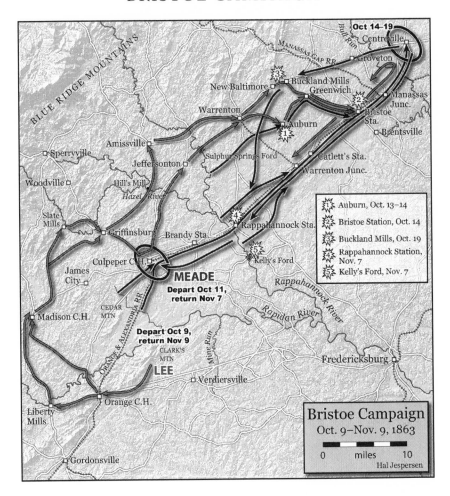

Bristoe Campaign
Oct. 9–Nov. 9, 1863

0   miles   10

Hal Jespersen

Headquarters Army of the Potomac, November 9, 1863

My Dearest Margaret,

The enemy occupied very strong positions on the Rappahannock. Thanks to their being deceived as to my capacity to move and to the gallantry of my men, we carried their strong works and forced passage of the river. I am more popular than ever, having been greeted with great cheering as I rode through the ranks. My having forced the passage of the Rappahannock and compelled Lee to retire to the Rapidan, will, I trust, convince the intelligent public that my retreat to Centerville was not to avoid battle and that Lee, who was not outflanked, or had his communications threatened, but was attacked in front, yet withdrew, is really the one who has avoided battle. I was greatly disappointed that Lee refused my offer of battle because I was desirous of effecting something decisive.

I received a telegram from the President expressing his satisfaction with my operations.

Your loving Husband George

The paper contained the text of the speech the President had delivered on November 19 as part of the dedication ceremony for the new Soldiers' National Cemetery in Gettysburg. Meade had been invited to the ceremony but had to decline because they were still in campaign season. He read the speech.

Lincoln's Gettysburg Address

Fourscore and seven years ago our fathers brought forth, on this continent, a new nation, conceived in liberty, and dedicated to the proposition that all men are created equal.

Now we are engaged in a great civil war, testing whether that nation, or any nation so conceived, and so dedicated, can long endure. We are met on a great battlefield of that war. We have come to dedicate a portion of that field, as a final resting place for those who here gave their lives, that that nation might live. It is altogether fitting and proper that we should do this.

But, in a larger sense, we cannot dedicate, we cannot consecrate—we cannot hallow—this ground. The brave men, living and dead, who struggled here, have consecrated it, far above our poor power to add or detract. The world will little note, nor long remember what we say here, but it can never forget what they did here. It is for us the living, rather, to be dedicated here to the unfinished work which they who fought here have thus far so nobly advanced. It is rather for us to be here dedicated to the great task remaining before us—that from these honored dead we take increased devotion to that cause for which they gave the last full measure of devotion—that we here highly resolve that these dead shall not have died in vain—that this nation, under God, shall have a new birth of freedom, and that government of the people, by the people, for the people, shall not perish from the earth.

Meade was impressed. Lincoln had given a powerful, brilliant address. He had elegantly paid homage to the brave soldiers who had made the ultimate sacrifice for their country and advocated that their deaths were cause to prosecute the war to a successful conclusion. "A new birth of freedom" perfectly captured the President's crusade to free the slaves.

CHAPTER 63

Meade devised a plan to avoid Lee's Rapidan entrenchments by cross-ing the river at lightly defended lower fords and then outflank the Confederates by quickly seizing Orange Plank Road and the Orange Turnpike, the best roads in the Wilderness. The objective was to force Lee out of his formidable river defenses and bring him to battle on ground not previously fortified. Speed was essential. If the army moved fast enough, Meade could take advantage of the Rebel army being strung out along the Rapidan and destroy it in detail before Lee could concentrate his troops.

———⚔———

Headquarters Army of the Potomac, November 25, 1863

My Dearest Margaret,

Yesterday it stormed, which required postpone-ment of the contemplated movement. It is of upmost importance to the success of any move-ment to have good weather this season of the year when the roads, after a day's rain, become impassable. I think if I advance we shall have *a great and decisive battle, with what result, He who reigns above alone can tell in advance. My army is in excellent condition, in high spirits, and confident of success if they can get anything of a fair chance. Let us trust it may please God to crown our efforts with victory, and to extend to me, as He has hitherto so signally done, His mercy and protection.*

Your Loving Husband George

———————◡

The men were issued eight days of rations, and the cumbersome wagon trains were left behind.

On November 26, the army began moving on a cold, moonlit night. Meade's plan to surprise Lee was spoiled by French's Third Corps's very sluggish movement, which caused traffic jams and slowed down the whole army.

Alerted that Meade was turning his right flank, Lee fought a delaying action, allowing him time to concentrate his army. It began raining, and the roads turned into quagmires.

Lee took full advantage of the delays and quickly built fortifications along Mine Run, a tributary of the Rapidan. The land in front of the steep banks of the stream had been cleared for eight hundred yards. The Rebel infantry was in a semicircle above the stream banks and behind stout breastworks sprinkled with cannons. The Confederates had the advantage of the high ground, prepared fortifications, and interior lines.

After surveying the Confederate line, Meade called a meeting with his corps commanders the night of November twenty-ninth. While disappointed that his stratagem hadn't worked as planned, he wasn't prepared to give up on his pledge to bring Lee to battle.

"Gentlemen, Lee's army is stretched thin. If we simultaneously attack both flanks, one of them may collapse. I'm issuing orders for a morning assault."

MINE RUN

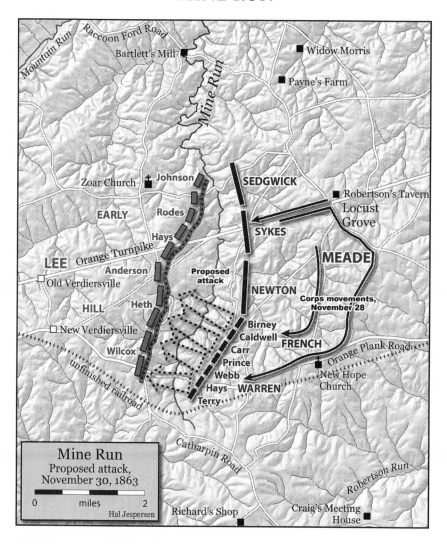

Mountain Run

Raccoon Ford Road

Bartlett's Mill

Widow Morris

Payne's Farm

Mine Run

Zoar Church

Johnson

SEDGWICK

Robertson's Tavern

Locust Grove

EARLY

Rodes

Hays

SYKES

Orange Turnpike

LEE

Anderson

Old Verdiersville

Proposed attack

MEADE

NEWTON

Corps movements, November 28

HILL

Heth

New Verdiersville

Wilcox

Birney

Caldwell

FRENCH

Carr

Prince

Webb

Hays

Terry

WARREN

Orange Plank Road

New Hope Church

unfinished railroad

Catharpin Road

Robertson Run

Mine Run
Proposed attack,
November 30, 1863

0   miles   2

Hal Jespersen

Richard's Shop

Craig's Meeting House

"Lee's defenses are frightfully strong," French said. "I don't think we should risk an attack."

Meade was irritated. "This is not a council of war. This meeting is to plan the details of the attack!"

"I have closely examined Lee's right flank. It appears vulnerable, its fortifications are not as strong as the rest of his line, and they appear thinly manned," Warren said. "I am confident, if given three additional divisions, of making a successful attack."

Warren was gaining Meade's confidence. He had performed brilliantly at Gettysburg. At Bristoe Station, he had rudely handled A. P. Hill, winning a victory for the Union army.

Meade decided to entrust Warren with leading the attack on Lee's entrenched defensive line. "In the morning, Warren's Second Corps, augmented with two divisions from the Third and one division from the Sixth, will attack Lee's right flank. If Warren has success on the right, the Fifth and Sixth Corps will assault the left flank. The attack will commence at eight a.m. with a one-hour bombardment of the Rebel line."

The next morning dawned frigidly cold. Several Union pickets had frozen to death overnight.

During breakfast, Humphreys received a dispatch. "Grant has finally broken the siege of Chattanooga. Bragg's army was routed and is in full retreat!

"That's great news!" Meade replied. "Grant has performed admirably in the west."

At 8:00 a.m., Federal cannons in the center and to the left of the Union line roared to life. Meade thought it strange that he didn't hear any cannon fire directed at Lee's right flank.

Shortly before 9:00 a.m., Captain Washington Roebling of Warren's staff rode up. "The enemy has so strengthened its position overnight that General Warren has determined it would be suicidal to attack. He has delayed it pending further orders."

Meade was shocked. "My God! Warren was given nearly half the army to make the attack!"

Meade rode the four miles to Warren's position. He found Warren looking very sad. "Why did you not attack?"

"With full apologies for taking matters in my own hands, the circumstances changed so dramatically overnight that I could not go forward with the assault."

"What changed?"

"Ride forward with me, and you will see."

As they rode forward through the ranks, Meade looked around. Something strange was stuck on the soldiers' uniforms. He turned to Warren. "What do the men have on their uniforms?"

"They have written their names on paper and pinned it to their uniforms so their corpses can be identified after the battle. They are not optimistic on surviving the attack."

Meade studied the Rebel line with his field glasses. The breastworks had been extended farther to the right, redoubts added, and abatis had been built in front. He saw newly placed cannons, and the works were fully manned.

"I calculate that it will take my men eight minutes to cross the open ground." Warren said. "Yesterday, because the defensive line looked assailable, I gauged the chances of success to be good. Now, with the enhancements to their fortifications and added cannons, that open ground is a death trap. The Rebels did an extraordinary amount of work overnight."

Meade was silent, studying the heights that Lee had so strengthened overnight. It was stronger than his position at Gettysburg and as strong as his position at Centerville, which Lee had refused to attack. Throwing brave soldiers against such strongly defended heights would result in a Fredericksburg-like debacle. The wounded would be exposed to overnight freezing temperatures. He was not going to send good men to their death in a senseless assault. He canceled the attack.

Meade was riding with Humphreys at the head of his army.

"This campaign will be seen as a fiasco, and there will be a great howl in the press and in Congress. I am sure to lose command. My conscience is clear. I know I made the right decision."

Headquarters Army of the Potomac, December 2, 1863

My Dearest Margaret,

I expect your wishes will now soon be gratified and that I shall be relieved from the Army of the Potomac. I crossed the Rapidan, intending to turn the right flank of General Lee and attack him or compel him to attack me out of his formidable river entrenchments. After reviewing all the circumstances, notwithstanding my most earnest desire to give battle, and in full consciousness of the fact that my failure to do so was certain personal ruin, I, having come to the conclusion that an attack could not be successful, withdrew the army. Failure of the Army of the Potomac to do anything, at this moment, will be considered of vital consequence, and if I can be held responsible for this failure, I will be removed to prove that I am. I therefore consider my fate as settled. But as I have told you before, I would rather be ignominiously dismissed than knowingly and willfully have thousands of brave men slaughtered for nothing. If I had thought there was any reasonable degree of probability of success, I would have attacked. I did not think so; on the contrary, I believed it would result in a useless and criminal slaughter of brave men and might result in serious disaster to the army. I have acted from a high sense of duty to myself as a soldier, my men as their general, and to my country and its cause, as the agent having its vital interests solemnly entrusted to me, which I have no right wantonly to play with and to jeopardize, either for my own personal benefit, or to satisfy the demands of popular clamor or interested politicians.

Yesterday I received a letter from Charlotte Ingram, my niece in Mississippi, telling me all her brothers lie on the battlefield, thus confirming the report that I had heard that Frank had been killed at Gettysburg. She says her parents are at Port Gibson, completely ruined, and they have all to begin anew in the world. Is this not terrible?

Your Loving Husband George

CHAPTER 64

Headquarters Army of the Potomac, December 11, 1863

My Dearest Margaret,

I have not heard a word from Washington, but from what I see in the papers and what I hear from officers returning from Washington, I take it my supersedure is decided upon. The only question is who is to succeed me. I understand the President and Secretary Chase are very anxious to bring Hooker back, but Halleck and Stanton will undoubtedly oppose this.

I will not go to Washington to be snubbed by these people; they may relieve me, but I will preserve my dignity.

Your Loving Husband George

⎯⎯⎯⎯⎯⎯⎯⎯

Meade looked up and smiled as Hancock entered his tent. "Win, it is wonderful to see you! Have you recovered from your Gettysburg wounds?"

"Enough to return to service. The bullet hit my saddle and pushed rusty nails into my groin. It is still very painful."

"Welcome back to the Army of the Potomac. I'm not sure how long I will be commanding general. The papers are filled with speculation on who will replace me."

"I think you're going to keep your command. I saw Halleck, and he told me that he saved you, that the officer who won the Battle of Gettysburg demands more consideration."

Meade was startled. He was sure his fate had been sealed at Mine Run.

"Are the rumors true that Lincoln is going to bring Grant east and make him general-in-chief of all the armies?"

"Yes, Lincoln is going to ask Congress to make Grant lieutenant general, the same rank George Washington had." Hancock handed Meade a newspaper. "You will want to scream when you read this."

Meade was incensed when he finished reading the article in Wilkes's *Spirit of the Times*.

"According to this article, Hooker planned the Gettysburg campaign, Butterfield wrote all the orders for the movements based upon Hooker's plans, and Sickles did all the fighting." Meade lit a cigar. "I presume, before long it will be clearly proved that I was not even present on the field!"

———

Headquarters Army of the Potomac, December 28, 1863

My Dearest Margaret,

You ask me about Grant. I knew him in the Mexican War, at which time he was considered a clever young officer but nothing extraordinary. I think his great characteristic is indomitable energy and great tenacity of purpose. He certainly has been very successful. The enemy, however, has never had in any of their western armies either the generals or the troops they have had in Virginia, nor has the country been so favorable for them as here. Grant has undoubtedly shown very superior abilities and is, I think, justly entitled to all the honors they propose to bestow upon him.

The President has written me that he desires to see me upon the subject of execution of deserters; so, as soon as I can get time, I shall have to go up to Washington.

Your Loving Husband George

CHAPTER 65

It was the last day of 1863, and Meade was alone with Lincoln in his White House office, discussing what to do with deserters.

"General Meade, you are a firm believer that deserters should be executed. I have a soft spot in my heart for our troops, and I have a hard time executing a man. Must I shoot a simpleminded soldier boy whom a wily agitator has induced to desert?"

"You're referring to Copperhead politicians like Clement Vallandigham?"

"A poisonous snake is a good label for men like Vallandigham. In his speeches, he encourages desertions. He and his ilk want to so weaken the army that it will not have the strength to suppress the rebellion. They want the Confederacy to gain its independence."

Lincoln looked pensive. "I have had to adopt strong measures, like the suspension of habeas corpus, arrests by the military, and trials in military tribunals. A jury too frequently has at least one member more ready to hang the panel than the traitor. I have taken those drastic steps because they are necessary to preserve the Union. I do not see how executing our own soldiers furthers the war effort."

"It's very bad for the morale of the troops shouldering the dangers on the frontlines to have their comrades desert in the face of the enemy and pay no consequence for their cowardly acts because you've pardoned them."

"My belief is that mercy bears richer fruits than any other attribute. Granting pardons and reprieves rests me after a hard day's work. When I find an excuse for saving some poor fellow's life, I go to bed happy that night as I think how joyous my action will make his family. I was even softhearted with Vallandigham. I commuted his prison sentence to expulsion to the Confederacy."

"Pardoning deserters encourages others to desert, because they think there will be no penalty to pay. I have not heard a murmur of dissent from our troops over executions of deserters."

"I have been thinking about the issue of the penalty. In many cases, execution is too harsh. We are dealing mostly with young men who deserve a second chance in life. I understand how strongly you feel that granting a full pardon is unfair to troops risking their lives fighting the Rebels. What do you think about sentencing a deserter to hard labor?"

"Sir, that's preferable to a full pardon."

"Would you have any suggestions for an appropriate location for a deserter's prison?"

Meade thought about where to send the cowards, someplace too far from home for families and friends to visit. He thought about the stifling heat and humidity of the Florida Keys.

"Fort Jefferson in the Dry Tortugas about seventy miles from Key West. The fort is still being built, and the prisoners could be put to work."

"Thank you, General, for your input. I am reminded of the story of the governor who went to the state penitentiary and heard the story of every inmate who thought he should be pardoned. One by one, the convicts appeared with stories of their innocence. When he got to the last prisoner, the governor asked, 'I suppose you're as innocent as these other fellows.'

"'No, I was guilty of the crime and got what I deserved.'

"The governor responded, 'I must pardon you, for I don't want such a wicked man as you to corrupt all these innocent men!'"

Lincoln and Meade shared a laugh.

Margaret had come down from Philadelphia, and that night, they had dinner at Willard's Hotel.

Meade looked adoringly at his wife. They were totally devoted to each other. He couldn't imagine living life without her. He ordered two glasses of champagne. When they arrived, he raised his glass. "To our twenty-third wedding anniversary. I am a blessed man to have found such a wonderful woman!"

Margaret raised her glass. "To the man who has filled my life with love and seven beautiful children. To your forty-eighth birthday!"

They spent the evening in their room rekindling the romance that made their marriage so strong.

The next day, they attended the traditional New Year's Presidential Reception in the oval-shaped Blue Room. George Washington began the tradition as a private affair. Thomas Jefferson opened the reception to the public. From 11:00 a.m. till noon, dignitaries from foreign embassies, Congress, and the Supreme Court were welcomed by the President and Mrs. Lincoln. At noon, the public was invited into the White House to greet the President and First Lady.

The Marine Corps band was playing as they entered the Blue Room.

"George, this is so exciting! All the foreign diplomats with their accents and medals. Everyone is dressed up in their finest clothes. Mrs. Lincoln looks pretty in her purple dress with white satin flutings. I like the flowers in her hair." Margaret paused, her face muscles tightening as they moved up the receiving line. "I won't embarrass you by saying anything impolite to the President. I am very angry with how shabbily he has treated you."

"My darling, you're too hard on the President. While we have our disagreements, he has always treated me with respect. I admire his steadfastness in fighting the rebellion."

When they reached Lincoln, he was quite welcoming. "Happy New Year, General and Mrs. Meade. It is an honor to receive the commander of the Army of the Potomac. Exactly one year ago, I signed the Emancipation Proclamation. Your army is fighting to make that promise a reality."

"Mr. President, the Union is going to prevail in this awful conflict and reunite the country. Then, as you so eloquently said at Gettysburg, there will a new birth of freedom for all Americans."

Meade was startled when the Marine Corps band began playing a lively rendition of "Dixie," the unofficial anthem of the Confederacy.

Lincoln laughed. "General Meade, you look astonished to hear 'Dixie' played in the White House. I have loved that song ever since I first heard it at a minstrel show in Chicago. That tune belongs to all Americans."

CHAPTER 66

It was a bitterly cold day in Philadelphia. Meade and Margaret were walking through and around Rittenhouse Square to get some exercise.

Margaret was agitated. "George, I don't trust those politicians in Washington. While Lincoln is gracious in person, he has not deferred to your military judgment, he rejected your plan of operations, and refused your request to change your base!"

"You're too harsh on Lincoln. He is a genuinely good man, unlike most of our politicians. He is doing his best in tough circumstances.

"Those wicked and deceitful congressmen treat you with scorn! Look at that resolution Congress passed thanking you for your service at Gettysburg. They have the names of Hooker, who wasn't even there, and Howard above yours! There's no mention of Reynolds and Hancock."

"Darling, I share your dislike for Congress. I have seen too many generals' careers destroyed by despicable and unethical politicians."

Meade felt weak. He touched his forehead. It was burning hot. "Margaret, we should go home. I think I have a fever."

Margaret looked horrified. "Do you have an illness like our precious Sargie?"

"I don't know what I have."

Meade was not worried about his own health. God would summon him when it was his time. He thought about his son, so young and promising. He fervently prayed for God to have mercy on Sergeant.

Dr. Hewson, the family physician, was summoned and examined Meade. "George, you have a serious case of pneumonia. Your Glendale wounds leave you susceptible to illnesses like this. You'll need to stay in bed for at least two weeks."

Meade was glad that his illness was temporary, and he would soon return to duty. "Dr. Hewson, is there any hope Sergeant will recover?"

"Unfortunately, nobody has identified a cure for tuberculosis. Because that terrible disease has killed so many people, scientists all over the world are searching for a cure. It's a slow-progressing disease, so you shouldn't lose hope. Perhaps a curative treatment will be discovered."

After three weeks of bed rest, Meade was well enough to travel. Stanton had requested his presence in Washington.

Meade entered the War Department and walked up the stairs to the second floor. Stanton had insisted on centralizing all telegraph operations for the war in an old library next to his office. His path to Stanton's office took him past the telegraph room, and today he spied the unmistakable form of the President reading a stack of telegrams. Lincoln looked up. "Ah, General Meade. Could I have a moment with you before you see the Secretary?"

"Of course, Mr. President."

"It is a good time for me to take a break. I was down to raisins."

Meade had a puzzled look on his face. "Down to raisins?"

Lincoln's eyes twinkled. "I need to tell a story for you to understand the meaning. Back in Springfield, there was a little girl who, on her birthday, was allowed to eat just about anything she wanted. The first food she ate was raisins. That night she became very ill. When the doctor arrived, she was casting up her accounts into a bowl held by her father. The doctor asked the parents what the child had eaten. The doctor then examined the contents of the vessel. On top were the raisins. He told the nervous parents that the danger was past as the child was down to raisins."

Lincoln chuckled. He held up a stack of telegrams. "It is my practice when I come to the telegraph office to take the telegrams from the box and start reading them from the top. When I reach the message in this pile which I saw on my last visit, I know that I need go no further. I am down to raisins."

Meade laughed.

"On a more serious note, I understand you have an ailing son."

"Yes. My oldest son, Sergeant, is very ill."

"Mrs. Lincoln and I lost two boys. Little Eddie died when he was four, and precious Willy got typhoid fever and died in the White house in 1862. We still have not recovered from those tragedies. I doubt we ever will. The most odious task a parent can ever face is burying a child. Our prayers are with you and your family."

"Thank you, Mr. President. Our faith in God is helping us cope with our fears."

Meade was into the second hour of an intense meeting with the strong-willed and action-oriented Stanton. "General Meade, we need to get rid of ineffective commanders."

Meade had been having similar thoughts. "Mr. Secretary, if we had fewer corps, we would need fewer corps commanders. I think larger corps would make for a more efficient fighting force. The First and Third Corps suffered disproportionate losses at Gettysburg. Their divisions could be merged into other corps."

"I have identified French, Newton, Sedgwick, and Sykes as men who should not be corps commanders."

"I won't object to losing French, or Newton, who have disappointed me since Gettysburg. I would strongly object to losing Sedgwick. He can be slow in moving his troops, but he is competent. His men love him—they call him Uncle John. I like Sykes, but there may not be a corps left for him."

"There will be a reorganization. You need to think about who you want in command."

Willard Hotel, 7:00 p.m., February 14, 1864

My Dearest Margaret,

I felt very badly at leaving you, but I tried to reconcile myself to what was inevitable and could not be helped. I spent all day at the War Department and the White House. The Secretary was, as he always is, very civil. He gratified me very much by saying there was no officer in command with so great a degree of implicit confidence of all parties as myself.

Your Loving Husband George

THE WILDERNESS

CHAPTER 67

Meade stepped off the train in Washington. He had a meeting in an hour with Stanton to continue the discussion about reorganizing the army.

As he walked through the train station, a colonel he knew approached him. "General Meade! I don't believe the stories that you intended to retreat at Gettysburg."

Meade was so startled that he couldn't respond. *Retreat from Gettysburg? What stories?*

When Meade saw Stanton, he was ready to explode. "What in the hell is going on? As soon as I got off the train, I heard a scurrilous rumor that I wanted to abandon the battlefield at Gettysburg!"

"The Committee on the Conduct of the War has been holding secret hearings on the Gettysburg campaign. Sickles alleged that you wanted to retreat to Pipe Creek and not fight at Gettysburg, that on July 2, you directed Butterfield to prepare an order for a retreat. Doubleday testified that he didn't get command of the First Corps because any anti-McClellan man didn't stand a chance with you. Yesterday some-one leaked the story to the press."

Meade was incredulous. "Sickles wants to rewrite history! Pipe Creek was a contingency plan that was never put into effect. Doubleday is notoriously slow. He would be a poor corps commander. His dislike of McClellan played no role in my decision. Am I going to be given the opportunity to testify to correct the record?"

"Senators Chandler and Wade planned an ambush. Yesterday they went to the President and demanded your dismissal. Lincoln refused. He suggested you be provided an opportunity to defend yourself. It's fortunate that you were coming to Washington. You are to appear before the committee tomorrow morning."

"Tomorrow? All my records from Gettysburg are at my Brandy Station headquarters. I would like to be organized and have my memory refreshed from the records before giving sworn testimony."

"If you delay your testimony, Sickles and his friends on the committee will say you're stalling for time because you have something to hide."

Meade's mind was racing. He valued his reputation as a brave officer who would never abandon a field to the enemy unless compelled by military necessity. He needed to rebut this scandalous allegation. He wouldn't yield an inch to Sickles. "I will appear and testify tomorrow."

When Meade arrived in the dank, windowless hearing room in the basement of the Capitol, only one committee member was present to question him: Senator Ben Wade of Ohio.

Meade raised his right arm and pledged to tell the truth. After preliminary questions, Wade asked, "Did you plan to retreat from Gettysburg before the battle on the second day?"

"I have understood that an idea has prevailed that I intended an order should be issued on the morning of July 2 requiring the retreat of the army from Gettysburg, which was not issued owing simply to the attack of the enemy having prevented it.

"I have no recollection of ever having directed such an order to be issued or of ever having contemplated the issuing of such an order. And it seems to me that to any intelligent mind who is made acquainted with the great exertions I made to mass my army at Gettysburg on the night of July 1, it must appear entirely incomprehensible I should order a retreat before the enemy had done anything to require me to make a movement of any kind."

"Did you want to fight the battle at Pipe Creek?"

"Being apprised that the enemy was concentrating his forces and that I might expect to come into contact with him in a very short time, I instructed my engineers to find some ground. I knew the existing position of the army and hoped that I might by rapid movement of concentration occupy and be prepared to give Lee battle on my own terms. The line of Pipe Creek was selected, and a preliminary order notified corps commanders that such a line might possibly be adopted and directing them, in the event of my finding it in my power to take such a position, how to move their corps and what their position would be along this line. From information received on July 1 that the enemy was concentrating at Gettysburg, I ordered the army to concentrate on the field of Gettysburg without any reference to and completely ignoring the preliminary Pipe Creek circular."

After testifying, Meade returned to the War Department and met with Stanton. "Mr. Secretary, do you believe the President will give in to Senate pressure to have me dismissed?"

"Lincoln won't dismiss someone because of Congressional pressure. The man is a political genius. After Burnside's debacle at Fredericksburg, Senate Republicans wanted the President to dismiss Secretary of State William Seward."

"Why?"

"Secretary of Treasury Salmon Chase, who hates Seward, led them to believe that Seward had too much influence over Lincoln, and if the war was going poorly, it had to be Seward's fault. Chase also told the senators that Lincoln didn't involve his Cabinet in major decisions, which was a false statement. A committee of nine Republicans met with Lincoln and demanded Seward's dismissal."

Meade found the underhanded, backstabbing ways of the capital's politicians repulsive. "Washington politics are so ugly and mean-spirited."

Stanton snorted. "That's an understatement. Where was I? Oh, Seward tendered his resignation, which the President did not want to accept. Lincoln set up a second meeting with the nine senators and his Cabinet, minus Seward. During the meeting, the President had members of the Cabinet discuss how they worked together in arriving at decisions. Chase was forced to admit that the Cabinet fully participated in decision-making. The senators stared coldly at Chase, knowing they had been lied to."

Stanton sat forward in his chair. "The next day, I was in the President's office when Chase announced that he had prepared a resignation letter. He obviously felt humiliated by the artful way Lincoln had outmaneuvered him. Lincoln's eyes lit up. He asked for the letter and snatched it out of Chase's hand. After reading it, Lincoln said, 'I can dispose of this matter now without difficulty.'

"The President refused to accept either Seward's or Chase's resignations, and both are still in the Cabinet, just the way Lincoln wanted it."

Meade said with admiration, "The President deftly finessed those senators and Chase."

"Lincoln is a clever leader," Stanton replied. "He knew there was not widespread public support for using the army to free the slaves when this horrible conflict began. He waited until our casualties had grown so severe that punishing the South for starting the war by freeing their slaves became an acceptable goal. The Emancipation Proclamation was a brilliant move. While controversial, it didn't significantly reduce public support for the war. It was a diplomatic triumph. Most people in Europe support abolition, making it near impossible for France or England to recognize the Confederacy."

Headquarters Army of the Potomac, March 6, 1864

My Dearest Margaret,

On arriving in Washington, I was greatly surprised to find the whole town talking about certain grave charges of Generals Sickles and Doubleday made against me in testimony before the Committee on the Conduct of the War. I was called before the committee. I spent about three hours giving a succinct narrative of events. Subsequently Mr. Stanton told me (this is strictly confidential) that there was and had been much pressure to get Hooker back in command and that thinking they might get me out (a preliminary step), they had gotten up this hullabaloo in the Committee on the Conduct of the War, but that I need not worry myself, there was no chance of their succeeding. The only evil that will result is the spreading over the country of certain mysterious whisperings of dreadful deficiencies on my part, the truth concerning which will never reach the thousandth part of those who hear the lies.

It is a melancholy state of affairs when persons like Sickles and Doubleday can, by distorting and twisting facts and giving a false coloring, induce the press and public to take away the character of a man who up to that time had stood high in their estimation.

Your Loving Husband George

CHAPTER 68

Humphreys angrily waved the newspaper he was holding. "Look at this article from the *New York Tribune*! It says you're on trial before Congress because Sickles testified you wanted to retreat and not fight at Gettysburg."

Meade shook his head. "There are similar articles in all the major newspapers. There is a concerted campaign by Sickles and his cronies to destroy my reputation. I doubt my good name will ever be fully restored, given the sheer volume of newspaper attacks."

"What Sickles is saying is untrue. The Committee on the Conduct of the War will discover the truth."

"That committee is not searching for the truth. Its members hate any general associated with McClellan! Zachariah Chandler, the senator from Michigan, hates me personally."

"Why?"

"In 1861 I was stationed in Detroit and commanded a small engineering staff doing a hydrographical survey of the Great Lakes. When the Southern states started seceding, Chandler organized a public meeting and invited all Union soldiers to attend and pledge their allegiance to the United States. I saw it as a political event, which as a soldier I should not be involved with. I refused to attend and counseled my staff not to go. As army officers, we had already taken an oath of allegiance, and civilian authorities had no power to compel a second oath. Chandler has hated me ever since."

That evening, Meade was walking with Lyman toward their mess tent. He was in a melancholy mood. He wanted to think about something other than vicious Congressional and press attacks. He thought of his time in Florida, designing and building lighthouses. It had been challenging but rewarding work. Lives depended on the quality of his structures. The hurricane that destroyed the Sand Key lighthouse that he had rebuilt had killed the keeper, his wife, and their four children. He felt a solemn responsibility to ensure that all his lighthouses were built with the strength to withstand the most ferocious hurricanes. So far, they had.

"Lyman, do you remember our days in the Florida Keys?"

"Of course. It so was quiet and peaceful there." Lyman paused, "You must find the war more exciting than your lighthouse work?"

"Yes, but I was happier building lighthouses than commanding this army with its political intrigues and limitations on maneuvers imposed by Washington."

When they entered the mess tent, Meade was delighted to learn one of his favorite dishes, *poulet au vin blanc*, was on the menu.

After dinner, Lyman sighed in contentment. "General Meade, your French cook is quite good. His meals remind me of the delicious home-cooked meals I had when staying with friends in the French countryside."

Humphreys smiled. "Our chief has good taste in cooks."

Lyman asked Humphreys, "Has General Meade told you how the US government used Spain's debts to his father to help finance the purchase of Florida?"

"No, but it sounds like a fascinating story."

"My father had a mercantile business in Cádiz, Spain, where I was born," Meade said. "He was successful in his business and became quite wealthy. Sometimes he accepted fine paintings in lieu of payment. He had works by Goya, Titian, and Rubens. When Napoleon invaded Spain, my father lent money to the Spanish monarchy. When he requested repayment, the King of Spain threw him into prison.

"At that time, Americans were moving into Spanish-controlled Florida, and the US wanted to purchase Florida." Meade took a cigar out of his pocket. "Spain insisted my father's substantial claims against

Spain be erased as part of the deal. The US government agreed, and in the Florida Purchase Treaty, all claims of American citizens then existing against Spain were assumed by the United States in exchange for Florida. My father was released from prison and returned to the United States."

Meade lit the cigar. "All his wealth was gone. The United States paid no money to buy Florida. It was entirely financed by forcing citizens like my father to forgo their claims against Spain. The US government never honored his claim for the debt that Spain owed him.

"After my father died, we were a prominent family without money. It was very hard on my mother. She went from living in a grand home surrounded by paintings by some of the world's greatest artists to being close to destitute."

Meade bent his head. When he looked up, his eyes were watery. "She always kept her dignity, but I was a sensitive child. She couldn't mask her depression from me."

Meade composed himself. "Life is full of twists and turns. I never dreamed of being a soldier. My mother had me go to West Point because it was a free college education."

Headquarters Army of the Potomac, March 8, 1864

My Dearest Margaret,

I am curious to see how you take the explosion of the conspiracy to have me relieved. Grant is to be in Washington tonight, and as he is to be Commander-in-Chief responsible for the doings of the Army of the Potomac, he may desire to have his own man in command, particularly as I understand he is indoctrinated with the notion of the superiority of the Western armies and that the failure of the Army of the Potomac to accomplish anything is due to their commanders.

Your Loving Husband George

CHAPTER 69

A short, plain-looking man with blue eyes, a neatly trimmed beard, and an air of determination approached Meade's headquarters at Brandy Station. Meade walked forward to greet him.

"General Grant, congratulations on your promotion to lieutenant general and on your glorious victories at Vicksburg and Chattanooga."

"And congratulations on your great victory over Lee at Gettysburg."

Meade produced two Cuban cigars, and both generals lit up and went into the headquarters tent.

"The last time we were together was during the Mexican War," Meade said. "I remember at Monterey how you rode through the streets, carrying dispatches while hanging off the side of your horse to avoid sniper fire."

Grant chuckled. "We had some close scrapes in that war. I recall that you were brevetted first lieutenant for your gallant conduct at the Battle of Monterey."

"Mexico was quite an introduction to war."

"You were in the Pennsylvania Reserves with George McCall?"

"Yes. McCall is a good man."

"McCall befriended me in Mexico. Just before we left Corpus Christi for the Rio Grande, a groom allowed my three horses to run off. I didn't have money to buy another horse. I was prepared to walk the two hundred miles with my men. On the day we left, the then Captain

McCall gave me a horse that he purchased so I could ride like the other officers."

"That's McCall—a great leader and a generous man." Meade gestured with his cigar. "You have had great success in the west. You may want to make a change in command, perhaps someone who you have worked with and have confidence in, such as General Sherman. Please do not hesitate to make the change if you think it's for the best. My only desire is to serve the nation to the best of my abilities wherever I may be placed. The work before us is of such vast importance that the feelings of one person should not stand in the way of selecting the right men for all positions. We must prevail in this terrible conflict and reunite the country."

"I have no thought of substituting any of my Western generals for you. You know your army, and you have proven that you can beat Lee. Sherman cannot be spared from the west."

Meade was surprised that he wasn't being replaced but was happy that Grant had confidence in him.

"Halleck advised that the Army of the Potomac was being reorganized, and you could provide me details," Grant said.

"We are eliminating the First and Third Corps, who suffered disproportionate losses at Gettysburg. Their units are being distributed to the Second, Fifth, and Sixth Corps. Hancock has recovered from his Gettysburg wound and has resumed command of the Second Corps. Warren has the Fifth and Sedgwick the Sixth Corps. Of the three commanders, Hancock is the best, Warren young and promising, and Sedgwick solid and dependable."

Grant nodded. "I understand you are not happy with the Orange and Alexandria Railroad as a supply base."

"That miserable, single-track railroad is wholly inadequate. A base on a navigable river controlled by the Union navy would be far superior."

"I don't disagree, but the administration seems fixated on the Orange and Alexandria Railroad."

"It's their paranoia for protecting Washington. If you have the authority, get a water supply base, preferably on the James."

Grant held his cigar in front of his mouth, lost in thought. "Can you explain why the Army of the Potomac has had so much trouble defeating Lee?"

Meade wasn't surprised by the question. Grant's Army of the Tennessee had won great victories at Vicksburg and Chattanooga and captured vast swaths of Confederate territory. It was natural for Grant to wonder why the Army of the Potomac had not matched his success.

Meade gathered his thoughts. "We both know Lee from Mexico. He's smart, bold, and a fine engineer. On the offensive, he is aggressive and is not afraid to take great risks. His only gamble that failed was Pickett's charge at Gettysburg.

"On the defensive, he uses the terrain to his advantage. The land between here and Richmond is excellent for defense. It is cut up with many streams and rivers, the banks of which are generally steep and difficult to cross without being bridged. The region is heavily timbered. The roads are bad, and they turn into deep mud pits after the least rain.

"Attacks against Lee when he is behind fixed fortifications have been failures with excessive casualties. We had an opportunity at Fredericksburg. My breakthrough of Stonewall Jackson's line was not supported."

Meade sighed. "Lastly we have been severely restricted in our ability to maneuver because Washington insists we serve as a blocking force, preventing Lee from having an opportunity to attack the capital."

Grant took in Meade's analysis with a stoic face. "No doubt Lee is a worthy opponent. In the spring campaign, once we contact Lee, there will be no turning back. We are going to hammer him until we destroy his army or he surrenders."

———

Grant and Meade shared the fifty-mile train ride on the Orange and Alexandria line to Washington. The President had invited them to dine with him Saturday evening at the White House.

As the train swayed and noisily clanked toward Washington, Grant said, "I don't care for the capital. I cannot walk through the lobby of Willard's Hotel without being accosted by newspaper reporters and politicians. I would be driven crazy if my headquarters was in

Washington." Grant puffed on his cigar. "When I am in the east, I will establish my headquarters in the field, near yours."

At dinner, Lincoln was regaling his guests with his homespun humor.

"General Meade, I understand you have been spending time testifying before the infamous Committee on the Conduct of the War. I have had my share of trouble with that committee."

"That committee has its conclusions made before it gathers any evidence," Meade replied.

Lincoln laughed. "So true. I may have made Senator Wade my enemy for life. He came to the White House a few weeks ago, demanding I cashier a certain general. I put him off for a while with a few stories. He was unhappy. 'Lincoln, everything with you is a story, story, story!' Senator Wade said I was the father of every military blunder the Union has made, that I am on the road to hell and am not half a mile off this minute. I responded, 'Senator, that is just about the distance from here to the Capitol, is it not?'" Lincoln burst into boisterous laughter. "Wade turned red and stormed out of my office."

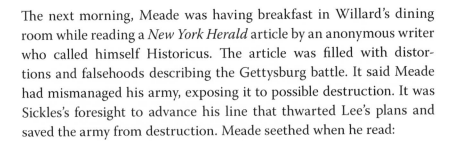

The next morning, Meade was having breakfast in Willard's dining room while reading a *New York Herald* article by an anonymous writer who called himself Historicus. The article was filled with distortions and falsehoods describing the Gettysburg battle. It said Meade had mismanaged his army, exposing it to possible destruction. It was Sickles's foresight to advance his line that thwarted Lee's plans and saved the army from destruction. Meade seethed when he read:

> It has been stated, upon unquestionable authority, that General Meade had decided upon a retreat and that an order to withdraw was penned by his chief of staff, General Butterfield, though happily its promulgation never took place.

What a vile lie! He folded the newspaper and stood. His reputation of being a brave soldier was being savaged.

Headquarters Army of the Potomac, March 14,
1864

My Dearest Margaret,

The President invited both General Grant and
myself to dinner. When I got to Washington, I
went before the committee and filed documentary evidence to prove the correctness of my assertion that I never for an instant had any idea
of fighting anywhere but at Gettysburg, as soon
as I learned of Reynolds's collision and obtained
information that the ground was suitable. Wade
was the only member present. He took great pains
to endeavor to convince me the committee was
not responsible for the newspaper attacks on me.
    I was very much pleased with General Grant.
In the views he expressed to me, he showed much
more capacity and character than I had expected.
I spoke to him very plainly about my position
and offered to vacate the command of the Army
of the Potomac in case he had a preference for
any other. This he declined in a complimentary
speech, but indicated to me his intention, when
in this part of the country, of being with my army.
So you may look now for the Army of the Potomac
putting laurels on the brows of another rather
than your husband.

Your Loving Husband George

Meade couldn't allow the lies and distortions in the Historicus article go unanswered. He sat down at his desk and wrote a letter to the War Department.

Headquarters Army of the Potomac, March 15, 1864

Col. E. D. Townsend
A. G. Washington, DC
Colonel.

I enclose herewith a slip from the New York Herald of the 12th inst., containing a communication signed "Historicus," purporting to give an account of the battle of Gettysburg to which I desire to call the attention of the War Department—and ask such action thereon as may be deemed proper and suitable.

For the past fortnight the public press of the whole country has been teeming with articles, all having for their object assaults upon my reputation as an officer, and tending to throw discredit upon my operations at Gettysburg. The character of the communication enclosed bears such manifest proofs that it was written either by some one present at the battle, or dictated by some one present and having access not only to official documents, but to confidential papers that were never issued to the Army, much less made public.

I cannot resist the belief that this letter was either written or dictated by General D. E. Sickles. An issue has been raised between that officer and myself, in regard to the judgment displayed by him in the position he took with his corps at Gettysburg. The prominence given to General Sickles' operations in the enclosed communication, the labored argument to prove his good judgment and my failings, all lead me to the conclusion he is either indirectly or directly the author.

As the communication contains so many statements prejudicial to my reputation, I ask that the Department ascertain whether General Sickles has authorized or endorses this communication, and in the event of his replying in the affirmative, I request of the President of the U. S. a court of inquiry that the whole subject may be thoroughly investigated and the truth made known.

I am, Very respectfully
Your obt. servant
Geo. G. Meade
Major General Comm'dg

CHAPTER 70

Headquarters Army of the Potomac, Easter Sunday, March 27, 1864

My Dearest Margaret,

I am very much distressed to hear of Sergeant's continued weakness. As to my going home, that is utterly out of the question. You must not expect to see me till next winter, unless as before, I am brought home on a litter. Whatever occurs, I shall not voluntarily leave the field.

You do not do Grant justice, and I am sorry to see it. I have no doubt Grant would have left me alone, but placed in the position he holds, with the expectations formed of him, if operations on a great scale are to be carried on here, he could not well have kept aloof. God knows I shall hail his advent with delight if it results in carrying on operations in the manner I have always desired they should be carried on. Cheerfully will I give him all credit if he can bring the war to a close.

Your Loving Husband George

Meade received regular reports of the ongoing "secret" hearings on the Gettysburg campaign. In addition to Sickles and Doubleday, other officers he had offended, Birney and Pleasanton, testified against him. Meade was gratified that Hancock, Warren, and Gibbon had testified in a supportive fashion.

A second article by Historicus appeared in the *New York Herald*, America's most popular newspaper, again castigating Meade as incompetent and singing the praises of the brave Sickles. What a nightmare. His reputation for being a courageous and skillful soldier was being destroyed.

As the avalanche of negative press continued, Meade was startled to read that Butterfield had testified that he had been directed to prepare an order of retreat. This was a blatant falsehood embedded in a sworn transcript and had to be rebutted. He sought and was granted permission to supplement his testimony.

Meade was again in Washington. He detested the city's politicians, except for Lincoln, who he had grown to admire for his personal warmth and political adroitness, and Stanton, who had his respect for efficiently managing the War Department. He trudged up the steps of the capital and then down into its bowels, to the dark and depressing Committee on the Conduct of the War's hearing room. When it was his turn to testify, Meade took a deep breath. He was going to set the record straight for all of prosperity.

"General Meade, you may make additional remarks."

"I utterly deny under the full solemnity and sanctity of oath, and in the firm conviction that the day will come when the secrets of all men shall be made known, I utterly deny ever having intended or thought, for one instant, to withdraw that army, unless military contingencies should develop during the course of the day which might render it a matter of necessity. I base this denial not only upon my own assertion, my own veracity, but

*also from the documentary evidence that if I intended
any such operation, I was at the same time doing things
totally inconsistent with any such intention.*

*"Soon after Butterfield arrived, I did direct him to
familiarize himself with the topography of the ground,
and I directed him to send out staff officers to learn all
the roads and know the location of the wagon trains
so we should be able to address any contingency that
might arise. That was the substance of the instructions
I gave to Butterfield: be ready, in case I should desire to
retreat or do anything else, to issue the necessary orders.*

*"I would call the attention of the Committee to the
absurdity that I prepared an order to retreat. If I had
directed such an order to be issued, why was it not issued?
With General Butterfield's capacity, it would not have
taken more than ten or fifteen minutes to prepare such
an order. We were furnished with what you call manifold
letter writers, so after the framework of an order is prepared, ten or a dozen copies may be made at once."*

Shortly after his testimony, Meade was excited to receive a letter from
the White House.

Executive Mansion Washington
March 29, 1864

Major General Meade
My dear Sir:

The Secretary of War has asked me to consider your
request for a Court of Inquiry concerning an article
that appeared in the Herald. It is quite natural that
you should feel some sensibility on the subject; yet
I am not impressed, nor do I think the country is
impressed, with the belief that your honor demands,
or the public interest demands, such an Inquiry.
The country knows that, at all events, you have done

good service; and I believe it agrees with me that it is much better for you to be engaged in trying to do more, than to be diverted, as you necessarily would be, by a Court of Inquiry.

Yours truly,
A. Lincoln

Meade wanted to fight back against Sickles' campaign of lies and distorted facts that was maligning his reputation, and he was disappointed in Lincoln's response. Stanton had delivered the President's letter and given him insight into Lincoln's thinking.

He sat down at his camp desk, and penned a letter to his cherished Margaret.

Headquarters Army of the Potomac, April 2, 1864

My Dearest Margaret,

I enclose for you a letter from the President. I feel quite sure the President meant to be very kind and complimentary in paying me the distinguished honor of writing a reply in his own hand, and under this conviction, I am bound to be satisfied. You will perceive that the main point of my request is avoided, namely, my desire that the Historicus article with my letter should be submitted to General Sickles, and if he acknowledged or endorsed it, then I wished court of inquiry, not otherwise.

Mr. Stanton told me the true reason, which was that it was concluded submitting my letter to Sickles was only playing into his hands; a court of inquiry might exonerate me yet would not necessarily incriminate him, and that on the whole, it was deemed best not to take any action.

Your Loving Husband George

CHAPTER 71

"Meade, do you know a Count Gurowski?"

"I know of him, General Grant. He's a Polish aristocrat who immigrated to America. He writes articles for Horace Greeley's *New York Tribune*. Gurowski has written, untruly, that I am under the influence of General McClellan."

"When I was in Washington, he cornered me in Willard's lobby and demanded I relieve you because of your relationship with McClellan, who he claims is a defeatist. The next day, Greeley himself accosted me, demanding your dismissal. I told both Greeley and Count Gurowski that I didn't care if you communicated with McClellan, that I was not relieving you, and I was not taking advice on who my generals should be from a newspaper."

"Thank you for your confidence and support. I have had little communication with McClellan other than some correspondence where he congratulated me on the Gettysburg victory."

Headquarters Army of the Potomac, April 6, 1864

My Dearest Margaret,

General Hunt has been up to Washington before the committee. After questioning him about the famous order of July 2, and him telling them he never heard of it, and from his position and relations with me, he would certainly have heard of it, they went to work in the most pettifogging way attempting to get him to admit such an order might have been issued without his knowing anything about it. This, after my testimony and that of Warren, Hancock, and Gibbon, evidently proves they are determined to convict me and that Butterfield's perjury is to outweigh the testimony of all others.

Your Loving Husband George

As commanding general of the country's largest army, Meade was inundated with visitors. Numerous politicians had seen fit to honor him with their presence at his headquarters.

He also had many European visitors who were fascinated by the American Civil War. Meade had hosted members of royal families and military officers from England, France, Russia, and the German states of Prussia and Bavaria. Even the Queen of England's personal physician had visited.

The people he most enjoyed welcoming were old friends from Philadelphia. He was happy when Judge John Cadwalader came to his Brandy Station headquarters.

"John, it's good to see you."

"I bring greetings from all your friends in Philadelphia. The people in our great city are outraged by how you have been treated by Congress and the press. How that scoundrel and murderer Sickles is given any credence is beyond me. Your dear Margaret has been greatly hurt by the unjustified attacks on you. My wife, Henrietta, and I; Mayor Henry; and many other leading citizens of Philadelphia have spent much time consoling Margaret."

"Thank you. These heinous attacks on my reputation have been harder on my family than on me. Your support and that of other Philadelphians means a tremendous amount to me, Margaret, and our family."

Headquarters Army of the Potomac, April 26, 1864

My Dearest Margaret,

Cadwalader arrived yesterday, and we paid a visit to General Grant. Cadwalader was not impressed. Grant is not a striking man, is very reticent, has never mixed with the world, has but little manner, and indeed is somewhat ill at ease in the presence of strangers, hence a first impression is never favorable. His early education was undoubtedly very slight. In fact, I fancy his West Point course was pretty much all the education he ever had, as since his graduation I don't believe he has read or studied any. At the same time, he has natural qualities of a high order and is a man who, the more you see and know him, the better you like him. He puts me in mind of Taylor, and sometimes I fancy he models himself on old Zac.

Yesterday I sent my orderly with Old Baldy to Philadelphia. He will never be fit again for hard service, and I thought he was entitled to better care than could be given to him on the march.

I have sent by Cadwalader a copy of my testimony before the committee. You must keep this private and sacred. If anything should happen to me, you will have the means of showing to the world what my defense was.

My relations with Grant continue friendly, and I see no disposition on his part to take advantage of his position.

Your Loving Husband George

CHAPTER 72

Meade entered Grant's headquarters at Culpeper Court House. Grant pulled two cigars out of his jacket. "Please join me in smoking one of these fine cigars. Ever since a newspaper reporter wrote that I was fond of Cuban cigars, citizens have sent me countless cigars. I smoke eighteen to twenty a day."

Meade happily joined Grant in enjoying the rich tobacco.

"I want to review my plans for the spring offensive. I agree with your assessment that Lee is strongly entrenched on the Rapidan and Mine Run and that the best approach is to flank him out of his fortifications. We are going to move around his right flank and force him to come out and fight or fall back to another defensive position."

Meade asked, "Did the administration give you a hard time before approving your plan?"

"During my first meeting with the President, he told me that all he had ever wanted from his top general was for him to take responsibility for prosecution of the war. McClellan and Halleck never filled their roles to Lincoln's satisfaction. When I told the President that I would accept accountability for defeating the Confederates, he clapped his hands in delight and told me I did not have to tell him what I proposed to do."

Meade couldn't believe his ears. "You have total freedom to maneuver?"

"I suppose I do, although I know that Halleck, Stanton, and Lincoln all want me to take an overland route and stay between Lee and Washington. I know you strongly favor, for good reasons, rivers for supply bases. By going to Lee's right, I allow for the possibility of using the Potomac and Chesapeake Bay tributaries for supplying the army. We can have our supply base move with the army."

"So Lincoln doesn't know your plans?"

Grant smiled. "Nobody in Washington knows what I am going to do, including Stanton and Halleck. I like keeping my plans close to the vest."

Grant puffed on his cigar. "Your object for the campaign is not Richmond. Rather, it is to destroy or capture Lee's army. Wherever we find Lee's army, we are going to attack it."

"My preference is to maneuver and look for openings for flank attacks. Frontal assaults against Lee, when he is in a fortified position, have led to the wanton slaughter of brave men."

"Maneuver has its uses, but we're not going to shy away from making frontal assaults just because Lee is in a strong defensive position. We're going to hammer his army every chance we get. I'm going to advance the Federal armies simultaneously on every front," Grant continued. "Butler and his Army of the James will push west toward Richmond."

"Don't expect much from Butler. He's a political general. He was a Massachusetts lawyer before the war and is a favorite of the Radical Republicans. He is good at politics but not soldiering."

"General Sigel will attack the Rebels in the Shenandoah Valley."

"Sigel is another political general bound to disappoint you. He's a favorite of the German immigrant community, and Lincoln wants his political support."

"You think I should replace Butler and Sigel?"

"Yes, if you have the authority."

"I'm not prepared to do that. The President has his reasons for giving them their commands, and 1864 is a Presidential election year."

Meade nodded. Politics trump military competence. He could see Lincoln's logic for keeping political generals that bolstered his reelection prospects. If he lost to a Peace Democrat, the Union war effort would have been in vain.

Grant continued, saying, "The Army of the Potomac has about a hundred thousand troops. We need a larger force to wage an offensive campaign. I have ordered General Burnside and his Ninth Corps of twenty-three thousand men to join us. He will report to me. I think it would be awkward for Burnside to report to you since he ranks you and used to command your army."

"I've always had a good relationship with Burnside. I would not find it awkward if he reported to me."

"Burnside will report to me. Have your staff prepare plans to move around Lee's right flank."

"We're going to have to cross through that godforsaken Wilderness, where we fought the Battle of Chancellorsville. Are we taking our supply wagons with us?"

"Yes. We're not sure where we're going to give Lee battle, so we will need provisions for at least two weeks."

"Our supply train will slow us down. We can get the infantry and artillery through the Wilderness in one very long day. With the supply wagons, it will take at least two days to get to open land where the infantry can maneuver and the artillery can be effective."

"We'll see what Lee does. Hopefully, we get through the Wilderness before he makes a move. If he chooses to fight there, we'll oblige him."

Two days later, Grant was at Brandy Station, meeting with Meade, Humphreys, and Sharpe. Heavy rain pounded Meade's headquarters tent.

Grant asked, "How big is Lee's army?"

"Lee has sixty-five thousand troops," Sharpe replied. "The Army of the Potomac has ninety-nine thousand soldiers, and Burnside's Ninth Corps close to twenty-three thousand men, so we will have close to a two-to-one force advantage."

"We'll cross the Rapidan by building pontoon bridges at Ely and Germanna Fords," Meade said. "On the chosen day, we will begin marching at midnight, and by four a.m., we should be prepared to cross the river. Lee is only protecting the fords with cavalry, which we can easily drive away. We should have the river bridged by six a.m."

Grant asked, "Do you think Lee might move on Washington?"

"Our intelligence strongly suggests that Jefferson Davis would order Lee to defend Richmond, so an advance on Washington is unlikely," replied Sharpe.

"Our goal will be to move south and get out of the Wilderness and into open terrain as quickly as possible," Meade said. "Then we'll turn west and confront Lee where we find him."

Meade looked at Grant. "Our assumption is you will order Burnside to follow close behind us."

"Burnside will be ordered initially to move here to Brandy Station to guard the supply depot and serve as a blocking force between Lee and Washington. Once we know that Lee is not moving on Washington, Burnside will be ordered to join you."

Grant lit a cigar. "How large is the logistical tail?"

Humphreys answered. "We have 4,300 supply wagons carrying food for the men and forage for sixty thousand horses and mules, 835 ambulances, and a herd of cows that can be slaughtered for beef. If we put all our logistical support on one road, the line would stretch fifty miles."

Grant smiled. "Gentlemen, you're well organized. We'll advance as soon as it stops raining and the roads dry out."

Headquarters Army of the Potomac, May 3, 1864

My Dearest Margaret,

Tomorrow we move. I hope and trust we will be successful and so decidedly successful as to bring about a termination of this war. If hard fighting will do it, I am sure I can rely on my men. They are in fine condition and most excellent spirits and will do all that men can do to accomplish the object. The telegraph will convey the first intelligence, though I shall endeavor to keep you posted. I beg of you to be calm and

resigned, to place full trust in the mercy of our
Heavenly Father, who has up to this time so signally favored us, and the continuance of whose
blessing we should earnestly pray for. Do not fret
but be cheerful, above all things don't anticipate
evil. It will come time enough. Give my love to all
the children. I shall think a great deal of you
and them, notwithstanding the excitement of my
duties.

Your Loving Husband George

CHAPTER 73

As the sun rose on May 4, 1864, Meade was on a bluff seventy feet above Germanna Ford. He took in a magnificent and stirring scene. Thousands of marching men in blue were crossing pontoon bridges, their flags flapping in the breeze. Hundreds of pieces of artillery were queuing up for their turn to cross.

A regimental band struck up "The Battle Hymn of the Republic." Thousands of voices broke into song.

> *Mine eyes have seen the glory of the coming of the Lord,*
> *He is trampling out the vintage where the grapes of wrath are stored,*
> *He has loosed the fateful lightning of His terrible swift sword*
> *His truth is marching on.*
> *Glory! Glory! Hallelujah!*
> *Glory! Glory! Hallelujah!*
> *Glory! Glory! Hallelujah!*
> *His truth is marching on.*

Meade felt pride in his men. They were ready to fight. He looked toward Clark Mountain and the Confederate signal station that was clearly visible. Lee knew the Union army was on the move. *What will that wily fox do?* Meade wondered.

When night came, every infantry unit and wagon train was precisely where they were planned to be.

Grant had pitched his tent within walking distance of Meade's. After dinner he walked over to pay his boss a visit. Grant was smoking a cigar before a blazing fire.

Grant handed Meade a cigar. "It was an excellent day's work. I was impressed with how efficiently you moved such a huge army and its supply train."

"Humphreys is a meticulous planner, and much of the credit should be given to him. Since the Rebels have not moved on Brandy Station, are you ordering Burnside up?"

"Yes, Burnside has been ordered to join us. I don't like that there's a gap between our forces."

"Burnside is not the fastest general when it comes to moving his troops."

"I have ordered him to do forced marches." Grant paused. "I have been impressed with Warren. He seems very bright."

"He was second in his class at West Point. He performed heroically at Gettysburg and did well at Bristoe Station. I have high expectations for him."

As Meade walked back to his tent, he thought about his relationship with Grant. While they got along just fine, he feared that the physical closeness of their headquarters would make it hard for Grant not to take over the Army of the Potomac. Meade sighed. Duty was paramount. He would be a good soldier, no matter what the future held.

CHAPTER 74

The next morning, Meade established his headquarters near the intersection of the Orange Turnpike and Germanna Plank Road. It was 7:15 a.m., and Humphreys was agitated.

"Warren is reporting Rebel infantry on the Orange Turnpike," he said. "Where is Sheridan and his cavalry? They should have warned us!"

"You're right. The cavalry failed to do its job. But I can't worry about that now. Grant wants us to pitch into the Rebels wherever we find them. I'm going to order Warren to attack."

"We don't know the size of the force Warren is facing. Don't you think we should wait for Sedgwick to come up? We should concentrate our strength. We don't want Lee destroying us in detail."

"Grant wants us to be aggressive. I'm prepared to take the risk of an immediate attack."

Warren was two miles away at the Wilderness Tavern. Meade decided to pay him a visit, and when he got there, he found Warren in a bad mood.

"Our Goddamn cavalry is missing in action!" Warren said. "We have men from Ewell's corps right in front of us and no warning from Sheridan! This was a bigger shock than finding no troops on Little Round Top!"

Meade tried to calm him. "Lee is outside of his fortifications, and we are going to engage him. If there is to be any fighting on this side of Mine Run, let's do it right off. Get your men ready to attack."

"I think it would be best to wait until Sedgwick is up. Without him my right flank will be exposed."

"Sedgwick is on the move, but we're not waiting for him. I want you to attack Lee as quickly as possible."

As he was leaving, Meade sent an orderly to inform Grant that he had ordered the attack. Another orderly went to Hancock and told him to stop at Todd's Tavern and wait for further developments.

When he returned to his headquarters, Meade received Grant's reply applauding his aggressive action. Meade smiled. Lincoln and Grant wanted a fighting general, and he was going to prove to them that he was one.

An hour later, Meade was having a cup of coffee when Humphreys exploded. "That son of a bitch Sheridan and his incompetent cavalry commanders! The Rebels are also on Orange Plank Road, and again no warning!"

Meade was incredulous. Without the cavalry doing its job, he was fighting blind. Confederate troops were between Warren and Hancock. He and Humphreys studied a map. Hancock was on Brock Road, which was the only road that connected him to the rest of the Army of the Potomac. The newly reported Rebel force was close to the intersection of the Brock and Orange Plank Roads. He needed to control that intersection, or his army would be cut in two. He issued an order for Sedgwick's lead division under General George Getty to march to the critical intersection and an order for Hancock to march north on Brock Road to join Getty.

Grant arrived at 10:00 a.m. and set up his headquarters on a knoll near Meade's headquarters. Grant sat on a tree stump, calmly smoking a cigar and whittling a stick with a penknife, while Meade, filled with nervous energy, paced back and forth as he described the morning's events.

At noon a note arrived from Getty. He had barely beaten the Rebels to the critical intersection. There had been a sharp engagement, and the Confederates had retreated. The Rebels were regrouping and likely would launch a new attack. He would do his best to hang on until

WILDERNESS: MAY 5, 1864

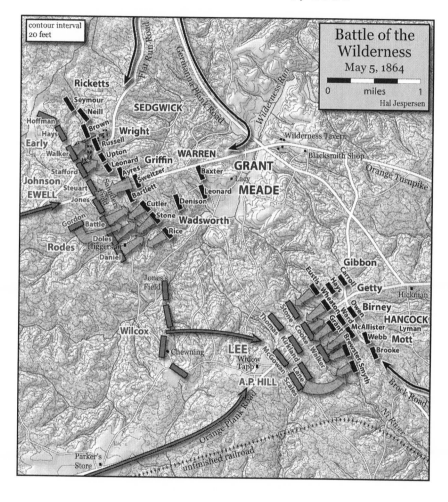

Hancock arrived. After bringing Grant up to speed, Meade walked back to his headquarters.

At 12:30 p.m., Grant visited Meade, and during lunch asked, "Has Warren launched his attack yet?"

"No. It's been five hours since he was ordered to. I have been urging him to move. He claims it's been difficult to get his battle line formed in the dense woods."

"Is he always so slow?"

"At Gettysburg he responded to a crisis with great swiftness. I think he's moving slowly with the hope that Sedgwick will come up to cover his right flank."

"If Warren can't move any faster, we need to consider replacing him."

Meade sent a message to Warren: No more delays. Attack immediately.

An hour later, he heard the crackle of musket fire and the roar of cannons. Meade and Grant rode to where Warren was engaged. There was fierce fighting in the woods and in Saunders Field, an abandoned farm clearing. Two New York Zouave brigades had taken heavy losses crossing the open field, which was covered with their brightly clothed bodies. Union forces had reached the Rebel breastworks on the edge of the woods on the far side of Saunders Field and were pushing the Rebels back. Meade and Grant returned to their headquarters.

At 2:30 p.m., a message arrived from Warren. The attack had been repulsed.

Twenty minutes later, division commander General Charles Griffin appeared at the knoll where Meade and Grant were conferring.

Griffin's face was red. He addressed Meade in a loud, angry voice. "This battle was a fucking disgrace! My division drove Ewell's Confederates three-quarters of a mile back into the woods. We would have been successful if we had any support. Horatio Wright was to attack on my right flank. That son of a bitch never showed up! On my left flank, Wadsworth's men performed miserably. I got no support from Warren! Both of my flanks were exposed, and we had to retreat, taking heavy casualties!"

Meade knew how Griffin felt. He had experienced the same anger when his Fredericksburg attack went unsupported.

"Charles, you and your troops did your best. Not every attack is going to be successful. Go back to your division and attend to your men."

After Griffin left, Grant asked Meade, "Who is this General Griffin? You should arrest him for such insubordinate talk."

"That's just his way of talking. He's a fine officer."

Meade looked for Lyman. "Take some orderlies and go down to the intersection that Getty is holding. Hancock should be arriving soon. Send me back periodic reports."

Lyman found Hancock on Brock Road at 4:30 p.m. There was a lot of musketry fire in the woods, and stray minié balls were annoyingly flying all around.

Hancock said, "Lyman, report to General Meade that it is difficult to bring troops up through these infernal woods. Only part of the Second Corps is up."

Lyman remained with Hancock, sending battle updates to Meade. A messenger arrived for Hancock. "General Getty is hard-pressed by A. P. Hill's men and is nearly out of ammunition!"

"Tell him to hold on. General Gibbon is coming on the double-quick!"

Minutes later, another messenger arrived. "General Hancock, Mott's Division has broken and is falling back."

Hancock roared, "Tell Mott to stop them from retreating!"

Union troops began pouring out of the woods. Hancock dashed among them. "Halt here! Halt here!" Hancock had such a presence that he was able to rally the demoralized men.

Colonel Samuel Carroll's brigade, who had saved Cemetery Hill the night of July 2, came up Brock Road and immediately disappeared into the woods. The roar of musket fire grew deafening. Twenty minutes later, Carroll came back on a litter, badly wounded.

General Alexander Hays's brigade arrived. Hays had red hair, a red beard, and a reputation for bravery. Waving a sword over his head, he led his men into the woods. Lyman was dismayed, when, minutes later, Hays's bloody and lifeless body was carried past him.

Lyman approached one of Hays's aides, who had hobbled out of the woods, blood pouring from his leg. "What's it like in there?"

"Pure hell. The fighting is close and savage. We are mere yards from the Confederates. Between the thickness of the underbrush and the smoke from the musket fire, the enemy is almost invisible. Both sides are firing blindly at what's in front of them. Troops from both sides are being slaughtered. When I got wounded, we had as many men dead as we had engaged."

When the vicious fighting ended at nightfall, Hancock held the critical intersection at Brock and Orange Plank Roads.

CHAPTER 75

At 4:30 a.m. the next morning, Lyman was again with Hancock, who was wearing his trademark clean white shirt.

"Yesterday you asked me to find out why we had no cavalry warning the Confederates were so close," Lyman said. "General Wilson, who Grant brought from the west with no cavalry experience, was responsible for patrolling in front of Warren. Wilson allowed the Rebel infantry to get between him and Warren. He had to fight his way through the Confederates and was not in position to provide a warning."

"Unbelievable!"

"Grant also brought Sheridan, the new Cavalry Corps commander, from the west. Like Wilson, Sheridan has no cavalry experience."

"So, the Army of the Potomac is the guinea pig while these Western men try to figure out how to do their jobs?"

"Unfortunately, yes. And I have intelligence for you from Colonel Sharpe. Longstreet's corps is not up but should arrive today."

Hancock smiled. "That's good news. Longstreet won't be here to support A. P. Hill when we attack this morning."

"Burnside will be on the field at five a.m. to support your attack."

"I hope that Burnside is on schedule for once in his life."

At 5:00 a.m., the dark woods exploded with musket fire, and the sounds of a furious battle filled the air.

At 5:30 a.m., Lyman received a note from Meade and frowned. "Burnside is behind schedule."

Hancock exploded. "I knew it! Burnside is always late! If he would attack now, we would smash A. P. Hill all to pieces! Goddamn Burnside for being so fucking unreliable!"

An hour later, the sound of musket fire had grown faint, and minié balls were no longer coming out of the woods. Lyman found Hancock with a huge smile on his face. "We are driving the Rebels down Orange Plank Road. Tell General Meade we are driving the Rebels most beautifully."

Half an hour later, the intensity of musketry fire grew louder. Lyman wondered if Longstreet's corps was up. He asked a Confederate prisoner being marched past him, "Do you belong to Longstreet's corps?"

"Ya-as, sir."

The fury of the battle grew, and the gunfire was louder and more intense. Wounded Union troops began flooding out of the woods. The flow of wounded soldiers kept increasing. Lyman stood in the intersection and did his best to turn back soldiers fleeing the battlefield. To those in great pain, he gave opium.

At 7:00 a.m., the Twentieth Massachusetts, the Harvard Regiment, advanced up Brock Road. Many of the officers and a number of the troops had attended Harvard. Some of these men had been Lyman's classmates at Harvard. Leading the regiment was his good friend Major Henry Abbott.

Lyman rode up beside Abbott. "The fighting has been vicious in those woods. Take care of yourself and good luck."

Abbott smiled. "Theodore, it is good to see you. After this battle, we can catch up on the latest Boston gossip."

Half an hour later, Lyman saw Abbott coming back on a litter, quietly breathing with the ashen color of death on his face. His friend was only twenty-two. He had entered Harvard as a fourteen-year-old prodigy. Abbott had risen to regiment commander after all his senior officers had been killed or wounded defending Cemetery Ridge against Pickett's Charge.

Their left flank was being pressed by Longstreet. The deafening sounds of battle reminded Lyman of an intense thunderstorm. Slowly the rattle of musket fire decreased.

WILDERNESS: MAY 6, 1864

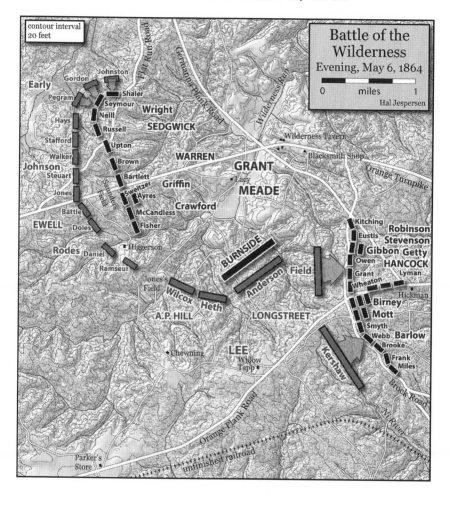

Hancock rode out of the woods. He was distraught. "Lyman, this morning the Confederates were on the verge of collapsing, and if Burnside had shown up, I'm certain we would have driven them out of these Goddamn woods. Then Longstreet and his corps pitched into our left flank, pushing us back, and it looked like the Rebels were going to win the day. Please advise General Meade that we learned from a prisoner that Longstreet has been shot by his own men. Their attack lost momentum without his leadership. Right now, there is an equilibrium on the battlefield. Both sides have suffered frightful losses in these gloomy woods."

A few minutes later Lyman received a note from Meade. "General Hancock, Burnside has finally arrived and will be attacking shortly."

Hancock took out his watch. "It's two p.m. Burnside is seven hours late!"

———⚬———

At 4:00 p.m., Meade sent an order for Hancock to vigorously attack at 6:00 p.m.

Before Hancock could attack, the Rebels launched an offensive up Orange Plank Road. Union troops had constructed breastworks of logs and dirt that were protected in front by abatis. Repeated Confederate charges were beaten off until a brush fire started. The fire quickly became a fast-moving blaze, and the wind blew the flames toward the Federal breastworks. Wounded men caught in the fire were burned alive, and their dying, soul-rendering wails filled the air.

Soon the center of the Union line was ablaze, and the men fell back. Confederates screaming the rebel yell leaped through the flames, charging after the retreating Federals. Hancock had the foresight to place a battery behind the center of the Union line. The guns roared to life, firing canister rounds into the Rebels, inflicting great casualties and stopping their advance. Union troops counterattacked back over their works, and the Confederates retreated.

"Lyman, advise General Meade that the enemy has been repulsed after a ferocious attack. Our ammunition is virtually exhausted, our losses have been severe, and our men are worn out from intense fighting," Hancock said. "In these circumstances, my opinion is adverse for attacking, but I await his order."

Meade responded by canceling the 6:00 p.m. attack.

Lyman returned to headquarters and was having dinner with Meade when, at 7:00 p.m., a messenger arrived. "Sir, Sedgwick's right flank has been turned," he said. "The Rebels are coming down Germanna Plank Road. You and your staff should retreat to avoid capture."

Meade set down his fork. "I will send our troops held in reserve to meet the threat. We are not retreating anywhere," replied Meade.

When the fighting ended that night, Sedgwick's right flank was secure.

SPOTSYLVANIA
COURT HOUSE

CHAPTER 76

The next morning, before dawn, Meade walked the short distance to Grant's headquarters tent to confer with his superior. It had been a frustrating two days for Meade. Despite the fierce fighting and a large number of casualties, the Union army had failed to break Lee's lines.

"We are stalemated here," Grant said. "We are going to disengage from Lee and move south out of the Wilderness to Spotsylvania Court House. We need to beat the Confederates to that crossroads town. If we do, we will be between Lee and Richmond. He'll have no choice but to attack us on ground of our choosing. Prepare for a march tonight."

"Did you hear that Longstreet was shot and wounded by his own men yesterday?"

"I heard. Before the war, we were close friends. Longstreet was best man at my wedding. He is a good commander. Lee will miss him."

As the day progressed, Lee did not attack. Meade thought that finally, Lee had lost his appetite for fighting blindly in the godforsaken woods.

———————

Meade ordered Sheridan's cavalry to clear the Rebel cavalry off Brock Road, which led to Spotsylvania Court House. The infantry was to begin marching at 8:30 p.m., and he didn't want the movement impeded by Confederates.

At 8:00 p.m., Meade received a note. Sheridan had handsomely repulsed the Confederate cavalry at Todd's Tavern.

Meade led the Army of the Potomac south on Brock Road. The fires kindled by the battles in the forest were still burning. Wounded soldiers from both sides had been consumed in the blazes. The sickening smell of burned human flesh filled the air. The night was dark and the going slow on the narrow road.

At 1:00 a.m., Meade reached Todd's Tavern. He was shocked to discover two of Sheridan's cavalry divisions camped there, with most of the men asleep.

One of the cavalry commanders, General David Gregg, came out to greet Meade.

But Meade was not in the mood for greetings. "Why in the hell are you not doing your job? Your troopers are supposed to clear Brock Road to Spotsylvania Court House so the infantry can march there without being obstructed by Confederates! Wake your men up, get them on their horses, and make sure the road is clear!"

"We are awaiting orders from General Sheridan."

"Sheridan has been derelict in his duties! I'm the Commanding General of the Army of the Potomac, and I have given you a direct order! Now get moving!"

Meade sent a curt note to Sheridan advising him of the orders he had issued to his cavalry commanders.

Confederate cavalry led by Fitzhugh Lee, General Lee's nephew, blocked Brock Road two miles south of Todd's Tavern. All efforts by Union cavalry to dislodge the Rebel cavalry failed. At 3:00 a.m., Warren's corps had to stop because the road was blocked. Finally, Warren had his infantry push the Rebels down Brock Road. Lee fought every inch of the way.

When the sun came up, the day grew hot and humid. At 8:30 a.m., Lee's cavalry was still fighting its rearguard action when Confederate infantry arrived and stopped Warren's advance short of Spotsylvania Court House.

SPOTSYLVANIA COURT HOUSE: MAY 7–8 , 1864

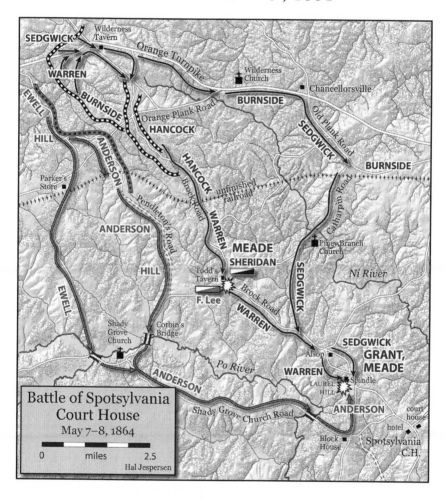

Battle of Spotsylvania
Court House
May 7–8, 1864

0   miles   2.5

Hal Jespersen

Phil Sheridan was five feet five, with fierce eyes, dark hair, high cheekbones, and a fiery temperament. At noon, Sheridan entered Meade's headquarters tent and in a loud, insubordinate tone said, "How dare you give orders to my cavalry commanders!"

"You didn't follow my orders to clear Brock Road! I found your commanders without orders. I'm the commanding general of this army! I had every right to give them orders! You have been derelict in your duties!"

"I never got an order to clear the road!"

"I don't know how that is possible." Meade said, "I apologize for calling you derelict in your duties. But your cavalry has done a poor job in this campaign. Wilson completely failed to detect the Rebel infantry in the Wilderness! Last night, your men were sleeping while the infantry was doing an all-night march!"

Sheridan moved close to Meade, who towered over him by seven inches, and pointed his finger toward Meade's face. "I'm not going to take any fucking shit from you! After Gettysburg, you meekly chased Lee and then let him escape across the Potomac! You then disgracefully failed to bring him to battle! Warren's performance was pathetic! He should have easily beaten the Rebels to the Spotsylvania Court House! I could whip Jeb Stuart if you would only give me the freedom to do so!"

Meade was not going to stand there and exchange insults with this short, arrogant man. He abruptly left, and while walking to Grant's nearby tent thought about who should replace Sheridan as Cavalry Corps commander.

He found Grant studying a map. "I must report that General Sheridan has spoken to me in the most insubordinate fashion."

After Meade related their conversation and noted how disappointed he was with Sheridan's performance, Grant was lost in thought. "Sheridan said he could whip Jeb Stuart if he were given the freedom to do so?"

"Yes."

"Well, he usually knows what he's talking about. Let him start right out and do it."

Meade was stunned. Grant had not supported him. Favoring his Western friend was more important than supporting the command structure. As Meade returned to his headquarters, he was still in shock. Grant had eviscerated his authority over Sheridan. He no longer had control over his cavalry.

—————⊸

Warren had been stopped at Laurel Hill, farmland north of Spotsylvania Court House. Grant decided that when Sedgwick was up, he and Warren would attack.

What Meade had feared—that Grant would assert himself and begin taking control of the Army of the Potomac—was happening. He had mentally prepared himself for this and would fight the way Grant wanted. Winning the war was more important than his wounded ego.

Sedgwick was slow to arrive, and both he and Warren looked worn out. This was their fourth straight day of intense operations, and the strain was showing. Their troops looked fatigued from all the hard fighting and the overnight march.

Meade rode out to inspect the Rebel lines. Earthworks were sprouting like mushrooms. It was incredible how fast the Confederates could erect formidable defenses.

Grant joined Meade in the inspection of the Confederate works. On their horses, they made inviting targets, and soon minié balls were buzzing around them. Meade had been under fire so often that he was unfazed. Grant was just as unflappable.

—————⊸

Warren was in a cranky mood. "That fucking Sheridan and his cavalry are useless. It's because of them that we didn't beat the Rebels to Spotsylvania Court House."

Meade replied, "Let's focus on what's in front of us."

Sedgwick and Warren were giving excuses for delaying the attack. Grant was visibly annoyed. Finally, at 6:30 p.m., the attack commenced.

The frontal assault uphill across plowed fields brought a hail of bullets, cannonballs, and shells from Laurel Hill. Losses were frightful because the soldiers were easy targets on the open ground. The few men who made it up the hill to the Confederate works were killed or captured. The battlefield was covered with Federal corpses.

———⌐

His son approached. "Father, you need to get some rest. You're about to fall over."

"This campaign has been so frustrating. Hancock is the only corps commander who has performed well. Sedgwick is constitutionally slow. Warren has been a disappointment. He has a brilliant mind but can be ponderously slow in preparing to attack. Burnside is always late." Meade paused and gave his son a stern look. "What I just told you is confidential. You cannot tell anybody. Understood?"

"Of course, Father."

CHAPTER 77

The next morning, Meade and Grant were discussing plans for a renewed attack when a distressed Sixth Corps aide approached.

"General Sedgwick has been killed by a Confederate sharpshooter!" Meade was shocked. "What happened?"

"He was inspecting a section of our line where Rebel sharpshooters have killed many officers. Bullets started whizzing around us, and a sergeant standing next to General Sedgwick hit the ground. The general said, 'Why are you dodging? Those sharpshooters couldn't hit an elephant from the distance they're shooting from.' The next moment, a bullet struck the general below his eye, killing him."

Grant decided to let the army have a day of rest so they could be resupplied with ammunition and mourn Sedgwick. On Meade's recommendation, Horatio Wright, Sedgwick's best division commander, was promoted to command the Sixth Corps.

———————⊃

Grant and Meade studied Lee's formidable defensive position. The line was four miles long, with a bulge in the middle shaped like a mule's shoe to cover high ground. The left flank was on the Po River, the right flank across Fredericksburg Road. The Rebels had erected stout breastworks out of rail fences and timber covered with dirt and with abatis in front. Menacing cannons were visible all along the line.

Meade pointed toward the Confederate line and said, with great intensity, "Lee has a stronger defensive position than I had at Gettysburg! I think we should maneuver around him and head to the James River. If we cross the James, we could capture the Petersburg rail hub. That would force the Confederate government to abandon Richmond."

Grant, who was usually calm and composed, replied in a flat but firm voice, "Lee is here, and we are going to attack him here."

Meade wanted Grant to see what he saw. It was not necessary to give Lee battle on ground of his choosing. "Lee would be ordered to follow us. There would be a chance of having a battle outside of his fortifications."

Grant remained placid. "General Meade, I understand and respect your strong feelings. Our goal in this campaign is to constantly engage the Rebel army. We are attacking Lee here."

Meade sighed. Since Grant was unwavering in his commitment to give battle, he would deploy his army in the most judicious fashion possible. "I think we should attack Lee's flanks and avoid frontal assaults across open ground."

"See if Hancock can cross the Po River and turn his left flank. I will have Burnside explore turning his right flank beyond Fredericksburg Road."

Meade took his leave to plan the movement.

With Sheridan's entire Cavalry Corps unavailable, away seeking glory and newspaper headlines, Hancock and Burnside had to do their own reconnaissance.

For Hancock to attack, he would have to cross the Po twice because of the bends in the river. By the morning of May 10, Hancock had made one crossing and was on the bank of the Po across from Lee's left flank.

Like he had at Mine Run, Lee reacted to the turning movement by strengthening his threatened flank with additional troops. Hancock advised Meade that he was not optimistic about making a successful attack.

As Meade told Grant about Hancock's predicament, Grant sat silently, smoking his cigar. Then he said, "Lee must have weakened his line on Laurel Hill to support his left flank. Have Hancock pull two divisions back and place them beside Warren, leaving one division opposite Lee's left flank to keep him from shifting forces back to Laurel Hill. I want a five p.m. attack on Laurel Hill."

"Leaving a single division on the Po without support is dangerous. It could be overwhelmed by a Confederate attack."

"We are leaving it there. I want Lee to feel his flank is threatened."

When Meade left Grant's tent, he found Horatio Wright waiting for him. "General Meade, one of my officers has an idea for breaching Lee's defensive line. You know Colonel Emery Upton."

"Yes, Upton did fine work in November at Rappahannock Station."

"He thinks that the best way to attack a fixed position is to reach it as quickly as possible. He believes it's foolish to stop and fire on the enemy during the charge. I would like to test that theory."

"I'm willing to try it. Pick twelve of your best Sixth Corps regiments and assign them to Upton. That should give him five thousand men that he can lead in a charge against the salient bulge in the center of Lee's line. If he breaks through, we'll have troops ready to support him. I will have our engineers pick the best spot to attack. Come with me. I want to review the plan with Grant."

Grant readily approved.

Meade was with Hancock planning the 5:00 p.m. assault when a message arrived that Barlow's division, the one left behind on the Po, was under attack.

"This is what I feared," Meade said. "Go down there and save Barlow and his men."

Hours later, Barlow had been extracted back across the Po, having suffered significant losses.

At 3:00 p.m., Meade entered Grant's tent. "Warren wants to attack early, at four p.m. I have been on him for being slow, so now he wants to impress us by accelerating an attack."

"I'm glad he is showing some aggressiveness. Let him attack early."

At 4:00 p.m., Warren's Fifth Corps and Gibbon's division of the Second Corps charged across the farm fields toward Laurel Hill. They were met with heavy artillery and musket fire. Casualties were high, few soldiers reached the Rebel abatis, and none breached the breast-works. The assault quickly fell apart, with survivors retreating to safety.

Meade watched the failed attack with Lyman.

"Making a frontal attack uphill, across open ground against such a strongly fortified position, is madness," Lyman said. "Such assaults only result in the death of thousands of brave men. You showed great courage in calling off such an attack at Mine Run."

"I explained to Grant that making frontal assaults against Lee once he's had a chance to fortify a position has proven futile and results in excessive casualties. Maneuvering Lee out of his fortifications has been my consistent suggestion. Grant hasn't found my advice appealing." Meade paused. "I'm not averse to making a frontal assault if the risk–reward factor makes sense. I led a frontal assault at Fredericksburg and breached Stonewall Jackson's line. I'm in favor of the assault Colonel Upton will lead later today. My engineers found where he can conceal his troops in woods only two hundred yards from the Confederate position. The plan is to rush across the open ground without stopping to fire. I think it has a chance of success."

Meade and Grant rode out of the woods to observe Upton's assault. At 6:00 p.m., Upton led his men out of the woods in a sprint toward the enemy line. The Confederates reacted immediately, and Union troops began falling. Their comrades kept running, not pausing to fire back. In an agonizing minute, the first troops reached the abatis. They crawled through the sharp, pointed wooden obstacle, taking more casualties. An officer climbed to the top of the Rebel breastwork, held his sword overhead, and screamed "Follow me!"

Moments later, his bullet-ridden body fell backward, landing on the abatis. More and more Federal troops reached the breastwork, and vicious hand-to-hand fighting broke out, bayonets were thrust, muskets swung, heads cracked, and blood flowed. Upton led his men into the Confederate trenches, killing hundreds of Rebels, capturing hundreds more, and seizing a battery. Upton's charge had been startlingly successful.

Meade was thrilled that Upton's daring assault had breached the Confederate line and ordered General Gershon Mott's division of Hancock's Second Corps to race across the field to support Upton.

Mott's men charged toward the Confederate line. They were met with heavy cannon and musket fire, and many men were cut down. Halfway across the field, they broke and retreated. Meade was furious. It was the most feeble charge he had witnessed in the war. No other readily available troops could be sent to support Upton.

Without support, Upton was in an untenable position. He didn't have enough men to hold his position and was forced to retreat to the Union line.

CHAPTER 78

Battlefield, Spotsylvania Court House, 9:00 a.m., May 11, 1864

My Dearest Margaret,

I have only time to tell you we are safe—that is, George and myself. We have been fighting continuously for six days and have gotten, I think, decidedly the better of the enemy, though their resistance is most stubborn.

Return thanks to the Almighty for the gracious protection extended to us. Let us try to deserve its continuance.

I am quite well and in good spirits and hope we shall continue to be successful and bring this unhappy war to an honorable close.

Your Loving Husband George

In the afternoon, Grant entered Meade's tent. "I want Hancock to attack the tip of the mule shoe salient at the center of Lee's line. He is our best corps commander, and his leadership will give us the best chance of success. We will use Upton's method of rushing the Rebel breastworks without stopping to shoot. He was able to make a breach using five thousand men. Hancock will attack with twenty thousand. Most of Hancock's corps is on our right flank, so prepare an order for them to move tonight under cover of darkness to a position opposite the mule shoe. While Hancock attacks the tip of the salient, Burnside will attack the bulge in the line from the east. Warren's and Wright's corps need to be prepared to attack on a moment's notice."

"I would not recommend any further attacks by Warren on Laurel Hill. The Confederate position is impregnable. Good men are dying for no advantage."

"It's a strong position. When Hancock and Burnside attack tomorrow morning, Lee is likely to shift forces from Laurel Hill to the points being attacked. In those changed circumstances, a new attack may be successful. We have to keep hitting Lee until we find a crack in his defenses."

That night, the skies opened, and torrents of rain poured down, subjecting the Second Corps to a miserably wet, cold, and muddy march to get into position for the assault.

At 4:35 a.m., Hancock attacked. His four divisions raced forward. As the darkness lifted, the Federals could see the red earth of the Confederate works on the crest of a ridge. The Rebels surprisingly allowed the Union troops to reach the abatis without strong opposition. Hancock's men worked their way up the ramparts. Vicious and violent fighting ensued. Men were run through with bayonets, and muskets fired at point-blank range. The morning's first light saw hand-to-hand combat, screams, oaths, and dead soldiers piling in heaps in the narrow confines of the Rebel entrenchments. The Virginians of the Stonewall Brigade, at the epicenter of the attack, were quickly overwhelmed, and prisoners were taken, including two generals.

The Rebels had built traverses, dirt and wooden mounds that separated troops, as a precaution to contain a breach in their line. The intense fighting went from traverse to traverse.

Meade began receiving positive reports from Hancock while Grant sat nearby, smoking a cigar. When news arrived that Hancock had

SPOTSYLVANIA COURT HOUSE: MAY 12, 1864

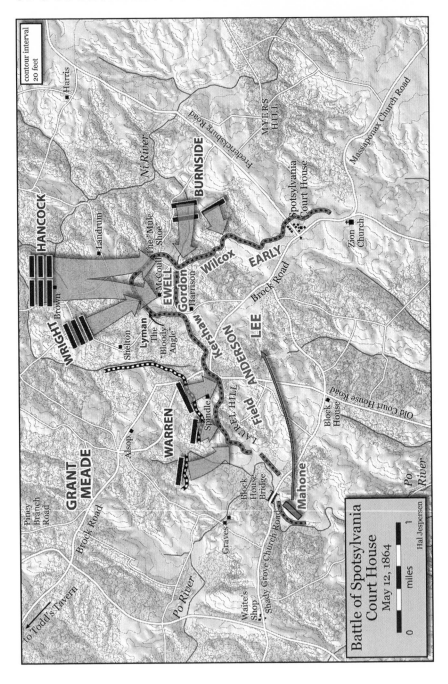

Battle of Spotsylvania
Court House

May 12, 1864

Hal Jespersen

captured more than two thousand prisoners, Grant exclaimed, "That's news I like to hear!"

At 5:30 a.m., a telegraphed message arrived from Hancock that the Rebels were strongly counterattacking. He asked for the Sixth Corps to be sent in on his right flank. Meade immediately ordered Wright to attack.

At 6:30 a.m., a captured Confederate general appeared at Meade's headquarters.

Meade stood and extended his hand to the stout, stern-faced Confederate. "General Allegheny Johnson, I remember you warmly from our adventures in Mexico."

Johnson shook Meade's hand. "I have fond memories for the brotherhood we shared in Mexico. I am most horribly mortified to have been captured. Our men stacked muskets facing the sky, and the heavy rain overnight dampened the powder, resulting in many of our muskets misfiring. Your men were able to get into our works without much opposition."

Grant walked over and shook the captured Confederate's hand. "General Johnson, you exhibited great bravery in Mexico." He pulled a cigar out of his pocket and handed it to Johnson. "This Cuban tobacco is excellent."

Grant, Meade, and Johnson spent some pleasant minutes reminiscing about their experiences in the Mexican War.

Meade called for Lyman. "Go to where Wright's Sixth Corps is fighting and keep me informed of what is happening."

As Lyman rode toward the fighting at the mule shoe, the whistling and groaning sounds of falling Confederate shells enveloped him. Noise from thousands of muskets became a continuous roar. He rode through a pine forest as bullets clicked off trees. He stopped at the edge of the woods, dismounted, and placed his orderlies behind trees.

Lyman walked out of the woods and saw Wright had attacked the western angle of the salient. Hancock had attacked the center of the salient. It was a chaotic scene. Federal troops pressed against the Rebel breastworks, trying to join their compatriots inside the Confederate entrenchments.

Lyman continued forward and found General Wright in a shallow depression close to the west angle of the salient. The small depression provided some protection from the bullets and shells flying overhead. Wright's leg had been hit by a shell fragment.

"From the reports I've received, it's pure hell in that bloody angle," Wright said. "The Confederates have made repeated and desperate counterattacks to hold the middle of their line. We keep sending in more of our men. Our advance has been stalemated. The fighting is so intense and in such close quarters, dead bodies are piling on top of each other."

It started raining, and the ground turned to mud. Lyman stayed near the bloody angle till 10:30 a.m., when he returned to see Meade.

Dripping wet from rain and covered with mud, Lyman found Meade in an irritable mood.

"Grant had me order Warren to attack Laurel Hill again. He delayed the attack, and Grant became very annoyed. He told me that if Warren didn't promptly attack, I should replace him with Humphreys. Warren finally attacked and was repulsed with terrible losses. I understand why he was reluctant to make another attack. But when I give him an order to attack, he must obey it! Grant gives me orders that I don't agree with, but I execute them to the best of my ability."

Lyman replied, "I feel bad for Warren. He knows each attack leads to the slaughter of brave men for no good purpose."

Meade sent an order for Warren to report to headquarters.

"General Meade, you wanted to see me?"

"Warren, since we crossed the Rapidan, you have been too slow to implement your orders to attack!"

"Repeated attacks on an impregnable position is crazy. They only lead to senseless deaths! I have a hard time ordering men to their death when there is no possibility of success!"

"It is not your position to pick and choose which orders you implement enthusiastically! You do not have authority to modify your orders by delaying the time to attack. That's insubordination. You provided good service at Gettysburg and Bristoe Station, but you'll lose your command if you don't follow the orders you are given!"

Hour after hour, both sides continued to pour men into the mule shoe's bloody angle. It had become a vortex of death. The fighting lasted till 2:30 a.m., when the Rebels retreated to a new defensive line six hundred yards south of the salient.

CHAPTER 79

The battle had lasted twenty-two hours and resulted in thousands of casualties. Lyman had an insatiable curiosity and had returned to survey the aftermath of the fighting. At the angle where Wright's Sixth Corps had fought, Lyman met Colonel Lewis Grant of the Vermont Brigade, who was also examining the battlefield. Lyman was stunned by the scope of the carnage. Both the Federals and Rebels had suffered appalling losses. In the small area of the bloody angle, bodies were everywhere. There were mounds of gray- and blue-clad corpses four and five deep. Wounded soldiers lay buried and writhing under dead men. The musket fire had been so intense and continuous that mature trees had been cut down.

Lewis Grant said, "Yesterday I fought in this Goddamn angle. From transverse to transverse, nothing but logs and dirt separated our men from the enemy. Our troops would reach over the logs and fire in the faces of Rebels and stab them with their bayonets through the crevices. Men were shot through holes in the logs. Men mounted the top of the works and with muskets rapidly handed to them, kept up a continuous fire until they were shot down, then others would take their places and continued the deadly work."

General Hancock's adjunct, Francis Walker, joined them. "Never before since the discovery of gunpowder has such a mass of lead been hurled into a space so narrow."

*Headquarters Army of the Potomac, 8:00 a.m.,
May 13, 1864*

My Dearest Margaret,

*By the blessing of God, I am able to announce
not only the safety of George and myself, but a
decided victory over the enemy, he having abandoned last night the position he held so tenaciously yesterday. Our losses have been frightful; I
do not like to estimate them. Those of the enemy
are fully as great. I have not time to write much.
God's blessing be with you and the dear children!
Pray earnestly for our success.*

Your Loving Husband George

At lunch Grant said, "General Meade, I'm impressed with the grit and tenacity of Lee's troops. Joe Johnston would have had his men retreat long before Lee did. As bad as the cause they are fighting for is, their gallantry cannot be denied."

"From my first battle, I have admired the indomitable fighting spirit and courage of Southern troops. I'm proud that our boys on battlefield after battlefield have matched the Rebels in bravery and steadfastness."

"The hardest part of being a general is responsibility for the deaths of so many brave men. But I see no other way. We must keep after them, and it's very hard. It means aching hearts back home." Grant lit a cigar. "Lee must have weakened his right flank to feed troops into the bloody angle. Burnside is in the best position to attack his right flank, but I'm losing confidence in him. Prepare orders for Warren and Wright to march tonight and be in position for a four a.m. attack down Fredericksburg Road."

"The men have been fighting almost continuously for over a week. They're fatigued. I would suggest giving them a day to rest."

"I appreciate your concern for the men. The way to win this war is to keep pressure on Lee. I'm not going to let up. We will attack his right flank tomorrow at four a.m."

That night, the weary soldiers of the Fifth and Sixth Corps were pelted with heavy rain as they trudged through darkness and knee-deep Virginia mud. Many of the men were too exhausted to keep up and fell out of the march.

At 4:00 a.m., only 1,200 of Warren's 15,000 men had reached the starting point for the attack. The attack was delayed. Slowly the men trickled in. By 7:30 a.m., 3,800 men had arrived. Not one of Wright's soldiers had made it to the staging area.

At 10:00 a.m., Grant and Meade conferred and called off the attack.

"This incessant rain has made the roads almost impassable," Grant said. "The deep mud makes moving the troops and artillery ponderously slow. We need to wait for the rain to stop and the roads to dry before we launch another attack."

That evening, Grant entered Meade's tent dripping wet. "It's a monsoon out there. Here is a copy of a dispatch I sent Stanton."

> General Meade has more than met my most sanguine expectations. He and Sherman are the fittest officers for large commands that I have come in contact with. If their services can be rewarded by promotion to the ranks of Major Generals in the regular Army the honor would be worthily bestowed, and I would feel personally gratified. I would not like to see one of these promotions at this time without seeing both.

Meade felt a surge of emotion after reading the dispatch. Finally, some positive recognition from Grant! While he was a major general in the volunteer army, without Lincoln accepting Grant's recommendation and subsequent Senate approval, he would not have that rank in the regular army when the war ended.

"General Grant, thank you for your support. It is very meaningful to me."

"You have earned it. You manage the maneuvering of troops and logistics of a huge army very well. You are a good officer, sharply focused and highly energetic in the performance of your duties. You beat Lee at Gettysburg, a singular accomplishment for the Army of the Potomac."

It kept raining until the morning of May 17, when the sun appeared and the roads dried up.

"General Meade, the Confederates must have learned that we massed men on their right for an attack on May 14." Grant tapped ash off the tip of his cigar. "Lee has likely shifted troops in anticipation that that is where we will next attack. We are going to surprise Lee by attacking his left. We cannot count on Warren to attack at the time he is told to, and Burnside has proven ineffective. We will use Hancock's and Wright's corps for the assault. Prepare orders for a four a.m. attack tomorrow morning."

That afternoon, Meade rode out, and using field glasses, inspected the portion of the Rebel line to be attacked. The Union soldiers would have to cross three-quarters of a mile of open ground that sloped upward to the Confederate works, which looked quite imposing. There would be an opening artillery barrage to soften up the Southerners. Meade wasn't optimistic. The usual result of frontal attacks against fortified positions was the senseless slaughter of the attacking force.

At 4:00 a.m., Union artillery fired hostile missiles through the morning fog toward the Rebel line. The Confederate artillery responded, and the ground shook with explosions.

Forty-five minutes later, Meade ordered Hancock and Wright's thirty thousand men to advance. As the infantry columns appeared out of the fog, Rebel cannoneers went to work. Whole swaths of Union men went down. The Federals dressed their ranks, moved to a double-quick pace, and continued toward the Rebel line.

As they moved closer, the Confederate works exploded with musket fire, and the Rebel gunners switched to canister shells. The veteran Union troops absorbed brutal losses, and the advance slowed, then stalled.

Grant joined Meade in observing the battle. Their men were pinned down, taking murderous fire from the Confederates.

At 8:45 a.m., Grant called off the attack.

———————⟡

During lunch Humphreys said, "It is outrageous that Grant has stolen your army. He has usurped your powers."

"I don't see it that way," Meade responded. "Once Grant made the decision to establish his headquarters within walking distance of my headquarters, it was only a matter of time before he took control. It's better that the army have one master than two men quarreling for control."

"I respect Grant. He has some good qualities, such as being tenacious as hell," Lyman said. "He also has weaknesses, like his fondness for frontal assaults and letting his Western friend Sheridan go hunting for Jeb Stuart, leaving the army blind without cavalry for reconnaissance."

"Phil Sheridan is headstrong and arrogant, and he hates me," Meade replied. "But I'll give him credit for being a fighter. He managed to kill Jeb Stuart at Yellow Tavern. Losing Stuart is a huge loss for Lee."

Humphreys asked, "What do you think about Franz Sigel's defeat at the Battle of New Market in the Shenandoah Valley? He managed to get beaten by VMI cadets."

"I told Grant that Sigel was a military liability. He only has a command because Lincoln wants the German vote."

———————⟡

Headquarters Army of the Potomac, May 19, 1864

My Dearest Margaret,

Yesterday on advancing, we found the enemy so strongly entrenched that even Grant thought it useless to knock our heads against a brick wall and directed a suspension of the attack. We shall now try to maneuver again to draw the enemy out of his stronghold and hope to have a fight with him before he can dig himself into an impregnable position.

We have recent Richmond papers containing Lee's congratulatory address to his army, so you see both sides claim having gained the advantage.

Yesterday I had a visit from Senators Sherman, of Ohio, and Sprague, of Rhode Island; both were very complimentary to me and wished me to know that in Washington it was well understood these were my battles. I told them such was not the case. At first I had maneuvered the army, but gradually, from the very nature of things, Grant had taken control and it would be injurious to the army to have two heads.

Your Loving Husband George

COLD HARBOR

CHAPTER 80

The Army of the Potomac moved around Lee's right flank and headed south, causing Lee to abandon Spotsylvania Court House. Lee moved south and established a new defensive position on the North Anna River.

Meade was tired of frontal attacks with their enormous casualties and scant results. He wanted to convince Grant to maneuver Lee out of his fortifications. That evening, he visited Grant's headquarters and told him what he was thinking.

"If we follow Lee to the North Anna River, you will find him in an impregnable position. Now is the time to surprise him by crossing the James and capturing Petersburg."

"There is a logic to your suggested strategy," Grant said. "Capturing Petersburg would be a significant blow to the Confederacy's rail network and diminish their industrial capacity. It could force the Confederate government to abandon Richmond and strengthen the President's reelection prospects." Grant rubbed the back of his neck. "Tempting as your approach sounds, we are going to continue with our strategy of finding and attacking Lee. The quickest way to end this war is to destroy or capture his army."

Meade was riding with Lyman under dark clouds. "Before we started the spring campaign a delegation of distinguished Philadelphians visited me at Brandy Station. They wanted to give me a spacious townhome near Rittenhouse Square. They thought that the victor of Gettysburg deserved a fine home. I refused the gracious offer, on the general principle that I have always held, which is that a public man makes a mistake when he allows his generous friends to reward him with gifts. I did tell them that if it should be God's will that I should fall in this war, then anything they could do for Margaret and the children would be most gratefully and thankfully received."

Rain began falling. "Yesterday I got a letter from Margaret, saying that after I refused the house, they returned to Philadelphia and offered the home to her, and she accepted. They recorded the deed in her name. She says it is too late to give the house back."

Lyman chuckled. "I guess your wife doesn't want to live with her mother anymore."

Meade laughed. "That's true for sure."

They came to a traffic jam: a wagon supply train was blocking the infantry's advance.

"Find me the quartermaster responsible for this supply train being out of position!" Meade ordered Lyman.

When Lyman returned with the offending officer, Meade lashed out. "Don't you understand your orders? Your wagons are not to impede the infantry's movement! Pull your wagons off the road until the infantry has passed!"

While Lyman liked and respected Meade for his intelligence, courage, and indefatigable energy, he didn't like his temper. His chief was a thin old Christian gentleman with gunpowder in his disposition. Meade would explode at subordinates and others who didn't perform their duties to his exacting standards. Lyman had experienced Meade's sharp tongue. His staff functioned efficiently. Nobody wanted to elicit their boss's anger.

Headquarters Army of the Potomac, 8:00 a.m.,
May 23, 1864

My Dearest Margaret,

The enemy refuses to fight unless attacked in
strong entrenchments; hence when we moved
on his flank, instead of coming out of his works
and attacking us, he has fallen back and taken
up a new position behind the North Anna River.
In other words, he performed the same opera-
tion that I did last fall when I fell back from
Culpeper—and for which I was ridiculed—that is
to say, refusing to fight on my adversary's terms.
 I am sorry you will not change your opinion
of Grant. I think you expect too much of him. I
don't think he is a very magnanimous man, but
I believe he is above any littleness, and whatever
injustice is done me, I believe is not intentional on
his part. It arises from the force of circumstances.

Your Loving Husband George

———————

Grant and Meade had stopped for a roadside conference. A teamster passed them, violently flogging his horses. Grant lost his normally calm demeanor. He mounted his horse and galloped toward the man who was abusing the animals.

Shaking his fist, Grant yelled, "You scoundrel! We don't mistreat our horses!" Turning toward an aide, he said, "Have the provost marshal take this man in custody and tie him to a tree for six hours as punishment for such brutality."

———————

Grant and Meade established their headquarters at Mount Carmel Church. Boards were laid across the aisle to make a work table. The two generals sat beside each other, writing out orders and dispatches.

Assistant Secretary of War Charles Dana, who before the war had been the managing editor of Greeley's *New York Tribune*, received a dispatch from General Sherman for Grant. Before delivering it to Grant, Dana, with evident glee, read aloud from the dispatch.

> *"The Army of the West has fought enough to be entitled now to maneuver, and if Grant could inspire the Potomac Army to do a proper degree of fighting, the final success cannot be doubted."*

Meade's eyes widened behind his glasses. "General Grant, I consider that dispatch an insult to the army I command and to me personally! The Army of the Potomac does not require your inspiration or anybody else's inspiration to make it fight!"

They found Lee in a strong, fortified position behind the North Anna River. After a series of small clashes, Lee established a defensive line shaped like an inverted V. To attack both flanks at the same time required that the army be divided by the river. Grant, thinking Lee was retreating, advanced on both sides of the river. The army was in a precarious position; if Lee attacked one half of the army, it would be impossible for the other half to provide rapid support. Realizing his mistake before Lee took advantage, Grant disengaged and ordered another flanking movement to Lee's right.

Headquarters Army of the Potomac, May 30, 1864

My Dearest Margaret,

We are within sixteen miles of Richmond. I trust to the blessing of God we will at last succeed, and if we do, I think from the tone of the Southern press, and the talk of the prisoners, that they will be sensible enough to give it up. They are fighting cautiously but desperately, disputing every inch of ground, but confining themselves exclusively to the defensive.

Your Loving Husband George

CHAPTER 81

Lee had established a new defensive position along Totopotomoy Creek. Grant and Meade established their headquarters in a large, Georgian-style house.

"Meade, having Burnside report to me has led to inefficiencies. Unless you object, I'm going to integrate the Ninth Corps into the Army of the Potomac," Grant said.

"I have no objection. Burn and I go back a long way."

"Sheridan's cavalry has captured the crossroads of Cold Harbor. I've ordered him to hold it at all hazards. It appears that Lee is shifting some of his infantry to Cold Harbor. Since Butler's Army of the James has been inactive, I borrowed Baldy Smith's Eighteenth Corps. Smith landed at White House Plantation and is marching to Cold Harbor to relieve Sheridan. Please send one of your corps for additional infantry support." Grant paused. "You were right about Butler. He has been a disappointment."

"Can't you get rid of him?"

"Maybe after the election. Lincoln values his political support."

Meade shook his head. He admired the President's ability to handle a quarrelsome Congress and a strong-willed Cabinet, but he despised Lincoln's political generals.

Meade said, "Our troops are very close to the Confederates along Totopotomoy Creek. We must be careful in how we disengage. This evening, I will send Wright on a night march. I know Cold Harbor

from the Seven Days Battles. It is close to where we fought the battle
of Gaines Mill."

"Why do they call it Cold Harbor?"

"The story I heard is that there was a tavern there, and the owner
only served cold meals."

The next morning, Wright's men arrived at Cold Harbor, exhausted
from a fifteen-mile march on a hot and humid night over rough, dusty
roads. They found the Confederate infantry dug in behind strong
breastworks. Baldy Smith had not arrived. Meade and Grant, back at
their headquarters near Totopotomoy Creek, decided to wait for Smith
before attacking.

Headquarters Army of the Potomac, 6:00 p.m., June 1, 1864

My Dearest Margaret,

We are gradually getting nearer to Richmond. Our advance is within two miles of Mechanicsville, which is the place where the fighting commenced in the Seven Days Battles. The Rebs keep taking up strong positions and entrenching themselves. This compels us to move around their flank after trying to find some weak point to attack. This operation has now occurred four times, crossing the Rapidan, the Wilderness, Spotsylvania Courthouse, and North Anna. We shall have to do it once more before we get them into their defenses at Richmond, and then we will begin the tedious process of a quasi-siege, like that at Sebastopol; which will last as long unless we get hold of their railroads and cut off their supplies. Then they must come out and fight.

Whilst I am writing, the cannon and musketry are rattling all along our lines, over five

miles in extent. We have become so accustomed to
these sounds that we hardly notice them.

The papers are giving Grant all the credit of
what they're calling successes. I hope they will
remember this if anything goes wrong.

Your Loving Husband George

———————◡

At 6:30 p.m., Smith and Wright launched their attacks at Cold Harbor. Two hours later, Meade received a note from Wright saying that Lee was bringing in reinforcements.

Meade and Grant conferred and determined that Hancock should make a night march to Cold Harbor and connect to Wright's flank, extending the Union line to the Chickahominy River.

As the night wore on, Meade became annoyed that he had received no communication from Baldy Smith. Around midnight, an aide from Smith arrived announcing that the Eighteenth Corps was in a precarious position. It was almost out of ammunition, medical supplies, and forage for its animals.

Meade asked, "Didn't General Smith bring with him sufficient supplies for a battle with the Confederates?"

"When General Grant ordered us to leave the Army of the James, we did so in a hurry and brought limited supplies."

Meade was incredulous. "If General Smith was not going to come prepared for battle, why in the hell did he come at all?"

He issued an order to Wright to send some supplies to Smith.

The night ended with stalemates at Totopotomoy Creek and Cold Harbor.

CHAPTER 82

Grant was being his usual aggressive self and wanted Hancock to attack the morning of June 2, immediately after his arrival from an all-night march. At 6:30 a.m., Meade received a note from Hancock. The lead elements of the Second Corps had reached Cold Harbor. The night march in the heat and humidity had led to much straggling, and it would be hours before he would be able to attack.

At 7:30 a.m., Meade left for Cold Harbor, where he visited Hancock.

"My troops are exhausted from all the intense fighting and hard marching," Hancock told Meade. "These all-night marches in this heat wear men out. They're too weary to attack."

"I will send a note to Grant and ask him to postpone it."

Grant agreed to postpone the attack until the next day. When Meade returned to headquarters, he found Grant eager to strike Lee a blow. "Move Warren's and Burnside's corps to Cold Harbor. Tomorrow at four-thirty a.m., have Hancock, Wright, and Smith charge straight ahead and drive Lee off the battlefield. Have Warren and Burnside attack Lee's left flank."

"I had our engineers study Lee's line. He is as strongly entrenched as he was at Spotsylvania."

"I'm sure Lee has erected stout defensive works. We are going to hammer him tomorrow with five army corps. Our constant attacks have weakened Lee. We are going to find a weak spot and break through."

It was a foggy, misty morning. Meade sent Lyman to Hancock with instructions to send back reports.

When Lyman arrived at Second Corps headquarters, Hancock was with General John Gibbon and Colonel Frank Haskell.

"I'm tired of these frontal assaults against Lee," Gibbon said. "He's a master of defensive fortifications. We have lost thousands of good men in these wasteful attacks. When is Grant going to figure out they don't work?"

"I don't disagree, but these attacks have adversely impacted Lee's army," Hancock replied. "The South does not have the population to replace Lee's losses, while the North can replenish our army with more soldiers. Grant knows the ugly math favors the Union. We have our orders, and we need to follow them."

Lyman noticed many soldiers were writing out their names on pieces of paper and pinning them to their uniforms. Lyman asked Haskell, "What are those men doing?"

"They think they're going to be killed in the attack, and they want their bodies to be identifiable so their next of kin can be informed."

Lyman shook his head. These brave souls would do their duty even though they expected to die.

He turned to Haskell. "I heard you became a regimental commander."

"I went back to Madison in February and recruited a new regiment, the Thirty-Sixth Wisconsin. I became their commander and trained them at Camp Randall. This morning, I was promoted to brigade commander."

"Are you participating in the charge?"

"Yes, and I will be leading my brigade from the front. I'm not the type of officer who leads from behind."

COLD HARBOR: JUNE 3, 1864

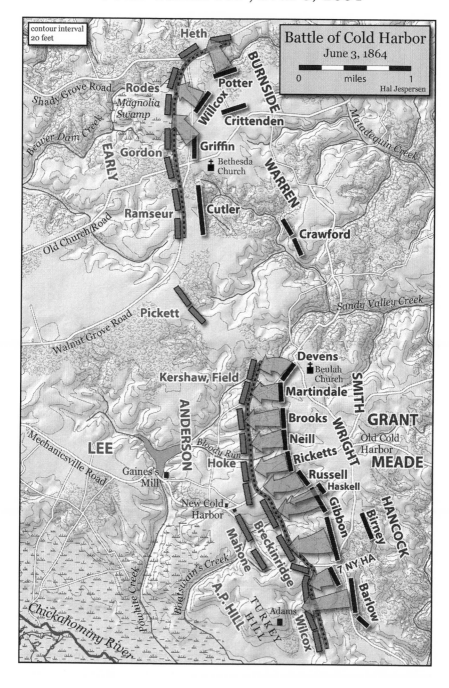

contour interval
20 feet

Heth

Shady Grove Road

Rodes

Magnolia
Swamp

Beaver Dam Creek

Willcox

Potter

BURNSIDE

Crittenden

Matadequin Creek

EARLY

Gordon

Griffin

Bethesda
Church

WARREN

Old Church Road

Ramseur

Cutler

Crawford

Walnut Grove Road

Pickett

Sandy Valley Creek

Devens

Beulah
Church

SMITH

Kershaw, Field

Martindale

GRANT

ANDERSON

Brooks

WRIGHT

MEADE

LEE

Mechanicsville Road

Bloody Run

Neill

Ricketts

Old Cold
Harbor

Hoke

Gaines's
Mill

Russell

Haskell

HANCOCK

New Cold
Harbor

Gibbon

Birney

Mahone

Breckinridge

7 NY HA

Black Swain's Creek

Pouncey Creek

A. P. HILL

TURKEY
HILL

Adams

Wilcox

Barlow

Chickahominy River

Battle of Cold Harbor
June 3, 1864

0   miles   1

Hal Jespersen

At 4:30 a.m., a cannon was fired, signaling the beginning of the attack.

A Union skirmish line disappeared into the fog and mist to drive off the Rebel pickets. Musket fire was heard; the pickets had been engaged. Confederate artillery began shooting, and Union batteries responded. A few minutes later, the Federal cannons stopped firing because the infantry was about to charge.

Haskell led his brigade forward. Once he saw the Rebel works through the mist, he raised his sword over his head. "Follow me, men. Charge!"

His brigade surged forward across an open farm field and was met with a sheet of lead from muskets and cannons. There were multitudes of grunts and cries of pain as men began falling. The charge soon faltered and then stopped under withering Confederate fire. His men were dropping to the ground for safety and to return fire. He shouted to be heard above the din of battle and gestured for the men still standing to lie down for protection. Haskell stood, studying the Confederate breastworks, looking for a weakness. A minié ball slammed into his temple, and his lifeless body fell to the blood-soaked ground.

———————

Meade grimly reviewed reports of dreadful losses. At noon, Grant called off the attack and directed that the most advanced positions should be held and strengthened.

Meade had grown weary of Grant's style of warfare, a meat-grinding war of attrition. It had been less than a month since the campaign began. The constant attacks had generated enormous casualties. The figures Meade received were depressing: eighteen thousand in the Wilderness, twenty thousand at Spotsylvania, and another eight thousand in smaller-scale battles around North Anna River and Totopotomoy Creek. Countless more today. Greater than fifty thousand casualties in less than a month!

Lyman returned to headquarters highly agitated. "General Meade, we have not learned any lessons from Spotsylvania! Why in the name of God would we launch frontal assaults against the Confederates after they have had time to entrench and build formidable defensive positions! One of the survivors told me it felt like they had charged into a volcanic blast of lead! Our men were slaughtered!"

"Grant always believes that the next attack is the one that will break Lee's army. I don't like frontal attacks on fortified positions any more than you do, but I have my orders and execute them to the best of my ability."

That night, the Union men who had charged the Rebel lines and survived slept within a stone's throw of their enemy, with the bodies of the dead and wounded between them.

CHAPTER 83

A day and a half passed without a truce. Wounded Union soldiers caught in no-man's-land between the lines were dying. At 3:00 p.m., Meade sent for Lyman.

Lyman found Meade lying on a cot, holding an envelope. "Take this note from Grant to Lee under a white flag. We want a ceasefire to retrieve our wounded and bury our dead. General Hancock will tell you where you can pass through the Rebel line."

Hancock was wearing his customary crisp, white shirt and reposing on his cot. "Colonel, you can't try and cross the enemy line on my front. It's too hot here, and you would likely get killed. Your best bet is to go to the left, where there are only pickets. An officer will tell you where you can pass through the enemy's line."

Hancock called for a staff officer. "Find something white that can be used for a flag and get a bottle of whiskey that Lyman can give the Rebs."

Lyman proceeded to his left with a white flag and an alcoholic gift. He found General Birney, who provided a guide, Colonel Charles Hapgood of the Fifth New Hampshire. Hapgood was tall and sinewy and had bullet holes in his hat and trousers.

They rode past the Union breastwork and found the Union picket line in a pine woods.

The colonel manning the picket line asked, "Do you know where you're going? Two officers have just been killed here."

"I know where I am going!" Hapgood responded. "There're some bullets that come through these woods, but none to hurt."

Lyman wondered about the definition "of none to hurt."

Hapgood pointed through the trees to the woods across a farm field.

"The trees in those woods are full of Rebel sharpshooters. If we try to cross this field, they will shoot us. We need to exit the woods further to our left, where we will be in shouting distance of their pickets."

Hapgood got them within a hundred yards of the Confederate pickets. He bravely stepped out of the woods waving the white flag and yelled, "We have a message for General Lee!"

After much delay, orders were issued for the pickets on both sides to cease firing. As the sun was setting, they crossed through the Rebel line.

Lyman was met by Major Thomas Wooten of the Fourteenth North Carolina. Wooten had a quiet dignity and spoke in a cultured voice that impressed Lyman. He was the sort of man you would meet in a good Boston club. Wooten sent Grant's letter to Lee. The only unpleasant aspect of Lyman's stay behind Confederate lines was the stench from unburied cavalry horses.

During the temporary truce, Union and Confederate pickets socialized like old friends.

At 10:00 p.m., a messenger arrived: Lee was preparing a response. Lyman didn't need to wait. The answer would cross at the same point on the picket line.

———————⌐

Headquarters Army of the Potomac, 9:00 p.m., June 5, 1864

My Dearest Margaret,

The enemy has tried his hand once or twice on the offensive and in each case has been repulsed and severely punished. The sound of artillery and musketry has just died away. I don't believe the military history of the world can afford a parallel to the protracted and severe fighting which this army has sustained for the last thirty days. I feel satisfaction in knowing my record is clear and that the results of this campaign are the clearest indications of my sound judgment, both at Williamsport and Mine Run. In every instance that we have attacked the enemy in an entrenched position, we have failed, except in the case of Hancock's attack at Spotsylvania, which was a surprise discreditable to the enemy. Likewise, whenever the enemy has attacked us in position, he has been repulsed. I think Grant has had his eyes opened and is willing to admit now that Virginia and Lee's army is not Tennessee and Bragg's army. Whether the people will ever realize this fact remains to be seen.

I am sorry, very sorry, to hear what you write of Sergeant, but God's will must be done, and we must be resigned.

Your Loving Husband George

Lee would only agree to a ceasefire if Grant did so under a formal flag of truce, an admission by Grant that he lost the battle. They passed nine notes over two days before Grant agreed to a truce.

"General Meade, I'm disgusted that we allowed our wounded to die because of generals' egos," Lyman said. "I was on the battlefield when we performed the grim task of picking up our fallen soldiers. Dead bodies had bloated under the hot Virginia sun and were in such an awful condition that it was impossible to recognize anyone except for papers found on them. When fighting ended on June 3, an estimated five hundred wounded Union soldiers were between the lines. Only two of our men were found alive."

"I don't think it was intentional on either Grant's or Lee's part, but their bickering let brave men needlessly die."

"During the ceasefire, I was struck with how friendly the Johnnie Rebs and Billy Yanks were. They were laughing and talking like the best of buddies, trading Yankee coffee for Southern tobacco. Now they will go back to trying to kill each other."

"We are all Americans, with a common language, religions, and institutions. The soldiers also have the shared combat experience of this sanguinary conflict. It is slavery that separates North and South."

CHAPTER 84

Meade was exhausted. He normally had boundless energy but not this morning. A month of constant, brutal combat with astronomical casualties had worn him down. When he heard Hancock's loud voice outside of his tent, he smiled. A visit from Win would help refresh him.

Hancock entered Meade's tent. "George, you look like shit. You need to get more sleep."

Meade laughed. "You always give me sage advice."

"A touch of frivolity would take your mind off this brutal war for a few minutes. Philadelphia's holding a fair to raise money for the US Sanitary Commission. One of the fund-raising events is a contest where people who pay a dollar can vote for their favorite general. The general getting the most votes is going to be awarded a ceremonial sword."

"Who do you think is going to win the sword?"

"My money is on you, the victor of Gettysburg."

"I've gotten very negative press since Gettysburg. You have always gotten positive press. I think Hancock the Superb has a greater chance of winning."

"You're from Philadelphia, and I'm from Norristown. I think the hometown advantage will put you over the top." Hancock sat down on a camp chair. "George, two years ago, we were here on this exact ground, close to Richmond. Why in the hell did Lincoln remove the Army of the Potomac from the Virginia Peninsula in 1862?"

Meade shook his head. "My guess would be his fear for Washington's safety coupled with his unhappiness with McClellan's performance."

———————⚬

Meade reread the article in the *Philadelphia Inquirer* by reporter Edward Cropsey with growing anger. It said that at the end of the Battle of the Wilderness, he was going to retreat across the Rapidan but had been overruled by Grant.

> History will record that one eventful night during the present campaign, Grant's presence saved the army and the nation too; not that General Meade was on the point of committing a blunder unwittingly, but his devotion to his country made him loath to risk the army on what he deemed a chance. Grant assumed responsibility and we are still "on the road to Richmond."

It was a total falsehood. He had never suggested retreating.

Meade snapped at his son. "George, find the reporter who wrote this malicious and libelous story and have him report to me!"

A short while later, Cropsey entered Meade's tent. "General, you asked to see me?"

"Did you write the article saying I wanted to retreat after the Wilderness Battle?"

"Yes. I wrote that article."

"It's a wicked lie! What was your source for printing such a falsehood?"

"It was the talk of the camp. Everybody said you wanted to retreat and regroup like Burnside after Fredericksburg and Hooker after Chancellorsville, but Grant insisted on moving south, looking for another battle with the Rebs."

Meade exploded. "That is a total fabrication! I'm going to make an example out of you as a deterrence to others from publishing false stories!"

Meade walked Cropsey out of his tent and handed him over to two soldiers.

"Take this man to Provost Marshal Patrick. Tell him to come up with a fitting punishment for a man who writes false news stories."

Patrick placed Cropsey on a mule facing backward, with a placard hung around his neck that said "Libeler of the Press." Cropsey, led by a bugler and a drummer playing "The Rogue's March," was paraded through the soldiers, who heckled and laughed at him. Cropsey was then expelled from the Army of the Potomac's camp.

———————

Grant looked contemplative. He held his cigar in front of his mouth, and the smoke curled in wisps in front of his face.

"Meade, we are stalemated again. We're going to make another flanking move. I know you favor crossing the James and capturing Petersburg."

Meade felt a sense of gratification. A strategy he had been advocating for two years was finally going to be implemented. "Do you want me to start planning for such a maneuver?"

"You can start making preliminary plans. I haven't made a final decision. I am concerned with the challenges of bridging a wide tidal river like the James."

"That's a big job, but this army has the best engineers in the world. If anybody can do it, they can."

———————

Headquarters Army of the Potomac, 9:00 p.m., June 9, 1864

My Dearest Margaret,

I fully enter into all your feelings of annoyance at the manner in which I have been treated, but I do not see that I can do anything but bear patiently till it pleases God to let the truth be known and matters set right. Now, to tell the truth, Grant has greatly disappointed me, and since this campaign, I really begin to think I am something of a general.

We find Lee's position again too strong for us and will have to make another movement, the particulars of which I cannot disclose.

Your Loving Husband George

———⚬———

At breakfast Lyman asked, "Have you seen the Democratic papers? They are calling Grant a butcher because of the enormous casualties. There is so much mourning for our dead soldiers that Lincoln said, 'The heavens are hung in black.' Copperheads are using the horrific casualty figures to demand that peace be made with the South."

"I saw the papers," Meade replied. "While I don't agree with all of Grant's tactics, as a nation, we need the strength to persevere until we are victorious and the country is reunited."

"So many soldiers have been killed in these last three battles that the government is running out of burial sites around Washington," Humphreys said. "They are going to turn Lee's Arlington plantation into a military cemetery."

———⚬———

Grant decided to move on Petersburg, and Meade and Humphreys were working feverishly planning the maneuver. It was going to be the most complicated move the Army of the Potomac had ever made. They would secretly disengage from the Confederates at night. Baldy Smith would march to White House Plantation and be transported by the navy back to the Army of the James. The four corps of the Army of the Potomac would march across the Chickahominy and then the James, if the engineers could successfully bridge it.

———⚬———

Headquarters Army of the Potomac, June 12, 1864

My Dearest Margaret,

Today we commence a flank march to unite with Butler on the James. If it is successful, as I think it will be, it will bring us to the last act of the Richmond drama, which I trust will have but few scenes in it and will end fortunately and victoriously for us.

Both George and myself are quite well, though the heat, hard service, bad water, and swampy regions are beginning to tell on the health of the army.

Your Loving Husband George

PETERSBURG

CHAPTER 85

Meade stood on a bluff overlooking the James River. *What a spectacle!* he thought. The engineers had used ninety-two pontoon boats anchored in the river and braced by three schooners to build a twenty-one-hundred-foot long, thirteen-foot wide bridge. The edges of the river were boggy, and huge cypress trees had been cut down to build causeways over the swampy ground. Navy gunships patrolling the river were ready to thwart any Confederate effort to oppose the crossing. Everywhere he looked under the cloudless blue sky, there were Federal troops. Bands played and sunlight sparkled off bayonets as soldiers marched down the steep bank and across the pontoon bridge. Grant had found some ferries to move men across the river. Men waiting their turn to cross were frolicking in the James.

They had slipped away from Cold Harbor under the cover of darkness. When Lee reacted in the morning, Union forces blocked Rebel cavalry from following. There was not a Confederate soldier in sight. Meade smiled. Old Bobby Lee didn't know where the Army of the Potomac was.

By June 15, the entire Army of the Potomac had crossed the James, and Hancock's corps was leading the march to Petersburg.

Grant approached Meade. "I have ordered Baldy Smith to capture Petersburg. I know Hancock is on the way, but I don't want to wait for him to get there. Smith has a large enough force to capture the city."

Reports came back from Smith that he had captured some of the Confederate defensive works but had failed to take Petersburg.

The next morning, Meade received an order from Grant to go to Petersburg and take command. Meade and his staff rode through land untouched by war, passing beautiful plantation homes.

"The Southern aristocracy lived fine lives on the backs of their slaves," Lyman said. "When the war is over and the Union has won, there will be no more slavery. Their way of life is going to dramatically change."

"My brother-in-law, Henry Wise, is a former governor of Virginia and is now a Confederate general. He was always smug and sanctimonious about the superiority of the Southern way of life. Secessionist politicians like him led their states out of the Union. I have little sympathy for the hardships they are going to face in the future."

"Have you noticed that the poor people we meet seem mostly indifferent to the impact the war is having on their lives? The bitterness toward Northerners increases with how high a person is in Southern society."

"I guess that is because those at the top are going to lose almost everything, while those at the bottom have little to lose."

At 2:00 p.m., Meade arrived at Hancock's headquarters in front of Petersburg and found his friend in pain. "Win, are you sick?"

"It is that Goddamn Gettysburg wound! If I spend much time in the saddle, it becomes very painful."

Early in the war, the Confederates had built substantial breastworks in front of Petersburg. Meade rode out in front of Hancock's position and with field glasses surveyed the Rebel position. It appeared formidable. They had cleared hundreds of yards of land for clear fields of fire.

Grant wanted an attack. A frontal assault across open ground was the only choice. Meade felt there was a chance of success. Sharpe's BMI had reported that the defenses were thinly manned. He ordered Smith and Hancock to jointly assault the Confederate position at 5:00 p.m.

Hancock breached the Rebel line and captured three Confederate batteries. The Confederates counterattacked, and darkness ended the fighting.

———⚔———

Field of Battle near Petersburg, Headquarters, Second Army Corps, Midnight, June 17, 1864

My Dearest Margaret,

I reached this field yesterday, having been placed by General Grant in command of all troops in front of Petersburg. We find the enemy as usual in a very strong position, defended by earthworks, and it looks very much as if we will have to go through a siege of Petersburg.

Hancock and I have great fun over the sword contest at the fair. We laugh and joke a good deal about it, and whenever a paper comes, we look for the state of the vote. The last date we have is the fourteenth, and that shows me about one hundred fifty ahead, which, as I have been behind him all the time, is the source of much merriment.

I wish Sargie would get well enough to travel; he might pay me a visit now that the weather is warm. I don't suppose Sargie cares much about seeing war, but I and George would like hugely to see him. Weather is getting quite warm. I continue in excellent health and spirits.

Your Loving Husband George

———⚔———

Overnight the Confederates had fallen back to a new defensive line.

Meade launched three more assaults during the day. All were repulsed with grim casualty counts.

"General Meade, our men are worn out from such an intense campaign of combat," Lyman said. "The carnage at Cold Harbor and Spotsylvania is fresh in their minds. Their hearts are not in making more frontal assaults."

"This is not the army that entered the Wilderness in May." Meade shook his head. "Too many of our best officers and soldiers are buried between the Rapidan and the Chickahominy."

OVERLAND CAMPAIGN

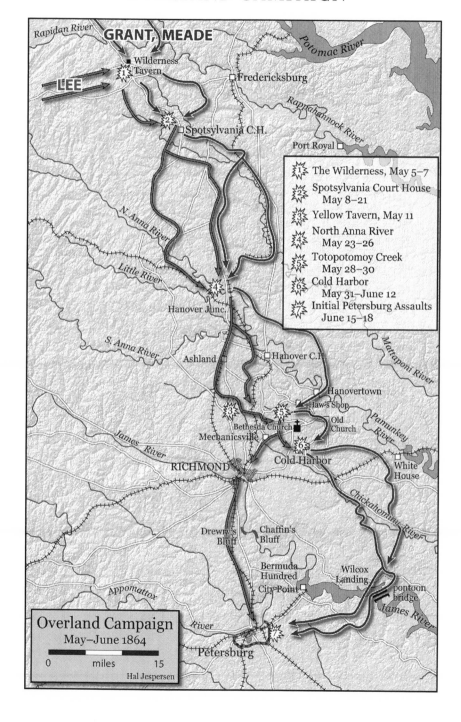

GRANT, MEADE

Rapidan River

Wilderness Tavern

1 The Wilderness, May 5–7

LEE

Fredericksburg

2 Spotsylvania C.H.

Port Royal

1 The Wilderness, May 5–7
2 Spotsylvania Court House
   May 8–21
3 Yellow Tavern, May 11
4 North Anna River
   May 23–26
5 Totopotomoy Creek
   May 28–30
6 Cold Harbor
   May 31–June 12
7 Initial Petersburg Assaults
   June 15–18

N. Anna River

Little River

4 Hanover Junc.

S. Anna River

Ashland   Hanover C.H.

Hanovertown

3   5   Haw's Shop

Bethesda Church   Old Church

Mechanicsville

6 Cold Harbor

James River

RICHMOND

White House

Chickahominy River

Drewry's Bluff   Chaffin's Bluff

Bermuda Hundred

City Point

Wilcox Landing

pontoon bridge

James River

Appomattox

River

7

Petersburg

Overland Campaign
May–June 1864

0   miles   15

Hal Jespersen

Rappahannock River

Potomac River

Mattaponi River

Pamunkey River

CHAPTER 86

Through sweltering heat, Meade and Lyman rode toward Grant's headquarters at City Point. Grant had chosen the junction of the Appomattox and James Rivers for his base of operations. It was vindication for McClellan, Meade, and many others who had long advocated for a supply base on the James River.

"General Meade, have you noticed that Grant has three facial expressions: deep thought, calmness, and great determination, like he is going to drive his head through a brick wall?"

Meade laughed. "Lyman, you are the most observant person I know. It must be your scientific training."

They found City Point bustling with activity. Wharves, warehouses, and hospitals were under construction.

"General Grant, consistent with your orders, we have prepared strong defensive works across from Rebel fortifications, which can be defended with a relatively small force," Meade said. "Large parts of our infantry are available for offensive operations."

"Excellent. We are giving up frontal assaults for a partial siege operation. To force Lee out of his fortifications, we need to cut the two remaining railroads into Petersburg. Use Hancock's and Wright's corps to extend our line southwest and then attack and occupy the Weldon Railroad coming up from North Carolina."

"Hancock has been incapacitated by his Gettysburg wound. Birney is temporarily in command of the Second Corps."

"Damn. Hancock is our best commander. I hope he recovers quickly."

Grant lit a cigar. "Every attack we have made has weakened Lee. The BMI reports that Lee's losses as a percentage of his army are greater than ours, and we have replenished our army with far more men than the South has provided Lee. We are going keep pressuring him till his army collapses."

———————————

As he rode toward Wright's headquarters, Meade reflected on how his strategy for flanking Lee out of his fortified positions and forcing him to fall back to Richmond had been rejected by the Washington brain trust. The casualty count since crossing the Rapidan was astounding—sixty-five thousand men! *If his strategies for maneuver and avoiding frontal assaults had been accepted, the army could have reached Petersburg last year, with tens of thousands fewer casualties.*

Meade was at Wright's headquarters when the First New Jersey Brigade band played "Hail to the Chief." He had no knowledge of a Presidential visit. He walked outside, and there was Lincoln in his customary all-black dress.

"General Meade, it is a pleasure to see you."

"It is always an honor to see you, Mr. President. Your visits to the army provide a morale boost to the men. They know you care about them."

"It is also good for my morale."

"Sir, this is Colonel Lyman, an officer on my staff."

Lincoln and Lyman shook hands.

"I was in Philadelphia for the Sanitary Fair and saw your lovely wife, Margaret. She reminds me a little of Mrs. Lincoln, two ladies with strong personalities."

Meade laughed.

"I met General Sheridan today. I know people think I look strange, but I have nothing on Sheridan. He is a little chap, a foot shorter than me, with a round head, red face, legs longer than his body, and not enough neck to hang him by."

Meade and Lyman joined the President's laughter.

Lincoln continued, "Some of Sheridan's cavalry horses are quite worn out, which reminds me of a story. When I was a lawyer riding circuit court back in Illinois, I became friendly with a certain Judge. We often talked about horse trading. One day I proposed we make a horse trade with certain stipulations: neither party would see the other's horse until it was produced in the courtyard of the hotel I was staying at, and both parties must trade horses. On the designated day, a crowd gathered, anticipating some fun. The Judge got there first. The crowd laughed uproariously as he led, or rather dragged, at the end of a halter the meanest, boniest horse that ever pressed turf. It was blind in both eyes. Then I came along carrying over my shoulder a carpenter's horse. The crowd roared with laughter. I silently surveyed the Judge's animal and then said, 'This the first time I ever got the worst of it in a horse trade.'"

Lincoln, Meade, and Lyman laughed so hard, they had tears in their eyes.

Lyman asked, "Mr. President, how did you get the nickname Honest Abe?"

"It dates from the time I had a general store in the little frontier settlement of New Salem, Illinois. The store failed, and my partner fled the area to avoid responsibility for repaying our debt. After that dismal experience, I became a lawyer and began making a little money. It took me fifteen years, but I repaid all the debt. That's how I got the moniker Honest Abe."

Headquarters Army of the Potomac, June 21, 1864

My Dearest Margaret,

On the eighteenth, I attacked the enemy with my whole force but could not break through their lines. Our losses in three days of fighting under my command amount to 9,500, killed, wounded, and missing. As I did not have over sixty thousand men, this loss is severe and shows how hard the fighting was.

Mr. Lincoln honored the army with his presence this afternoon and was so gracious as to say he had seen you in Philadelphia.

Your Loving Husband George

CHAPTER 87

Meade was surprised to see Burnside riding toward his headquarters.

They greeted each other warmly. "George, Colonel Pleasants of the Forty-Eighth Pennsylvania has a plan for building a mine under the Confederate fortifications at Pegram's Salient, filling it with explosives, and blowing a hole in the Rebel line that our infantry can attack through. He was a mining engineer before the war, and many of his men are Pennsylvania coal miners."

"Burn, how long would the mine be?"

"Over five hundred feet."

"I will review it with Grant. If he approves, I will do whatever I can to assist."

The next day, Meade saw Burnside. "You can proceed with the mining project. Some of our engineers have doubts whether it will work. There are concerns whether a military mine that long can be ventilated with fresh air. The longest military mine in history was built during the Sepoy Mutiny in India. And it was only four hundred feet." Meade lit a cigar. "But Grant and I feel it is worth making the effort. We are hopeful that Yankee ingenuity can solve the technical challenges."

The final vote was in. Meade was pleased. He was Philadelphia's favorite general. He had received 3,442 votes to Hancock's 1,506. McClellan garnered 297 and Grant 177 votes.

"Congratulations, George! You had a late surge and crushed me."

"Win, it was a pleasant surprise."

More good news came in the mail. Margaret reported that Old Baldy's health was improving since he began living a peaceful life on a Pennsylvania farm. Meade smiled. He loved that old warhorse.

Grant showed up with two French officers, Colonel de Chenal and Captain Guzman, who had a commission from the French emperor to observe the great American Civil War.

"Lincoln told me to bring these two distinguished French officers for you to host," he said.

"It will be my pleasure."

Grant stayed for dinner, during which Meade and Lyman conversed in French with their guests.

At the end of dinner, Grant said in English, "I apologize for not speaking French. If the grades in my French class at West Point had been turned upside down, I would have graduated high in French!"

Headquarters Army of the Potomac, June 24, 1864

My Dearest Margaret,

We suffer from the loss of superior and other officers. Hancock's corps has lost twenty brigade commanders. We cannot replace the officers lost with experienced men, and there is no time for reorganization or careful selection.

In flags of truce, and on all occasions that we meet Rebel officers, they always begin conversations by asking when is the war going to be over, expressing themselves as most heartily tired and anxious for peace. I believe these two armies would fraternize and make peace in an hour, if the matter rested with them.

I still believe, with the liberal supply of men and means which our superior resources ought to furnish, we will win in the long run. But it is a question of tenacity and nerve, and it won't do to look behind or to calculate the cost in blood and treasure; if we do so, we are lost and our enemies succeed.

I am well and seem to improve on hard work.

Your Loving Husband George

Wright and Birney were on the move, extending the Union line west across Jerusalem Plank Road. Once their movements were completed, Wright's Sixth Corps would advance to Globe Tavern and make a lodgment on the Weldon line.

The rugged terrain, dense woods, thick underbrush, and swamps made it difficult for Birney to extend his line to connect with Wright's. On June 22, the Rebels exploited the gap in the lines with a devastating attack on Birney's exposed left flank.

Meade reacted to the crisis by sending two brigades from Warren's Fifth Corps to bolster Birney. By evening, the Federal line was stabilized. Meade ordered Wright to advance on the railroad at 4:30 a.m. the next day.

He summoned Lyman. "Tomorrow you will spend the day with Wright."

Lyman found Wright in a state of anxiety. "I'm concerned that the Rebels will make a flank attack on me today like they did to Birney yesterday."

Wright was still fretting over a surprise enemy assault when a diminutive Vermont captain reported that his eighty sharpshooters had reached the Weldon Railroad and driven off a Rebel cavalry patrol. Wright ordered a picket line advanced to the railroad to aid the

Vermont men in ripping up the rail line. He slowly advanced the Sixth Corps forward, constantly on the lookout for a Confederate attack.

When Wright learned a mile-long Confederate column was moving down the Weldon Railroad from the direction of Petersburg, he sent a note asking Meade what he should do. Meade responded that Wright should advance and engage the Rebels. If he thought it impossible to advance, he should withdraw. He needed to act promptly.

Wright appeared nervous. "Lyman, I fear that I'm going to be caught in a Rebel trap."

"You need to move forward and protect the men who are ripping up the railroad."

"Yes, but I need to be sure I don't get blindsided."

Hours passed, and despite notes from Meade directing him to take a decisive action, Wright didn't move forward or issue an order withdrawing the men destroying the rail line. As a result, four hundred Union soldiers were taken prisoner.

At 8:00 p.m., Wright withdrew to the position he had started from in the morning. The vast majority of the Sixth Corps had not been engaged.

Lyman returned to Meade's headquarters frustrated and angry. "General Wright was inept and feeble today! He was constantly afraid a Confederate flank attack would appear out of thin air. We should have seized the Weldon line today!"

Meade sighed. "I share your frustration with Wright's performance. He is a good solider. Birney's misfortune yesterday spooked him."

<hr />

Headquarters Army of the Potomac, July 3, 1864

My Dearest Margaret,

Today is the anniversary of the last day's fight at Gettysburg. As I reflect on that eventful period, and all that has elapsed since, I have reason to be satisfied with my course and cause to be most thankful. The longer this war continues, the more will Gettysburg and its results be appreciated. Colonel de Chenal says in Europe it was looked on as a great battle.

I am glad to hear the good news about Baldy, as I am very much attached to the old brute.

Your Loving Husband George

CHAPTER 88

An oppressive heat wave had descended on the opposing armies, with temperatures hovering over a hundred degrees. Perspiration dripped off Meade's forehead as he mounted his horse. He liked visiting the headquarters of his corps commanders. He relished the personal contact and the insights he received from his top generals. Today he was seeing his favorite commander, Hancock.

As his entourage rode along the dusty road, Meade sought out his volunteer aide, who had a sharp and insightful mind. "Lyman, what is your opinion of the Army of Northern Virginia?"

"They're as brave a set of men as any who have ever gone into battle. Instead of being exasperated at Southerners by fighting them, I have a great deal more respect for them now than I ever had in peacetime."

"I've always respected their courage."

"People in Boston say Southerners must be immoral and corrupt to be fighting to save slavery. While their cause is odious, the Southerners I have met in the Rebel army strike me as honest and moral as any Northerner."

They found Hancock lying down in a covered wagon, attired in his customary white shirt. Meade mounted the front seat of the wagon.

"Win, how are you feeling?"

"Better. I heard that Stanton wants to replace you with me as commander of the Army of the Potomac, but Grant opposes a change."

"Thanks for the warning. This is a thankless job if you get it."

Lyman knew they would be there at least an hour. Meade and Hancock enjoyed each other's company. After forty minutes, Meade stood to go but Lyman didn't budge; he knew Meade would sit back down and continue his conversation. It was his routine when he visited Hancock.

⸻⚬

Meade had been summoned to City Point. He rode there with George.

His son asked, "Father, is there any truth to the stories that Grant has a drinking problem?"

"In the old army, and in this war, rumors have circulated of Grant being drunk. I think Grant knows he has a weakness and resists temptation. His chief of staff, Rawlins, is vigilant in seeing that no one tempts him with a drink. I have spent countless hours with Grant, and he has always been sober."

City Point was a hive of activity. Numerous ships were docked, off-loading supplies. A railroad was being constructed to shuttle supplies to the front lines.

"General Meade, we need to send a corps as quickly as possible to Washington to defend against Jubal Early's army moving up the Shenandoah Valley." Grant shook his head. "After losing the Battle of Lynchburg, General Hunter inexplicably retreated into West Virginia, leaving a clear path for Early to attack Washington."

"Is Halleck telling you that his worst fears have been realized and that Washington will be captured because the Army of the Potomac is not in position to block the Rebel advance?"

Grant laughed. "Halleck is worried sick. I'm not overly concerned. I don't think Early has a large enough force to capture Washington."

"I will send Wright by steamer to Washington."

⸻⚬

Headquarters Army of the Potomac, July 23, 1864

My Dearest Margaret,

I had a visit today from General Grant, who was the first to tell me of the attack in the Times based upon my order expelling two correspondents. Grant expressed himself very much annoyed at the injustice done to me, which he said was glaring, because my order distinctly states that it was by his direction these men were prohibited remaining with the army. He acknowledged there was an evident intention to hold me accountable for all that was condemned and to praise him for all that was commendable.

The stories you hear about me, some of which have reached camp, are mere canards. I have never had any quarrel with either General Hancock or Smith. Hancock is an honest man, and he always professes the warmest friendship for me. I never doubt his statements; and I am sure I have for him the most friendly feeling and the highest appreciation of his talents. I am perfectly willing at any time to turn over to him the Army of the Potomac and wish him joy of his promotion.

I am a good deal amused at your fear that I will be become entangled with politicians. I rather fancy I should be considered too independent and intractable for the purposes of any of these gentlemen.

Your Loving Husband George

Meade and Lyman were returning from a visit with General Benjamin Butler, whose Army of the James was besieging Confederate forces north of the James.

Lyman asked, "Have you seen a stranger-looking sight than Butler? A bald head set on a stout, shapeless body; squinting crossed eyes; and arms and legs that look like they are attached to the wrong body."

Meade laughed. "He is one of Lincoln's political generals. A War Democrat from Massachusetts is helpful to Lincoln in a Presidential election. He's not much of a general, but he's adept at the political game."

"I'll say. He outmaneuvered Baldy Smith, who lobbied Grant to give him Butler's command. Smith ended up in New York, far from the battlefield." Lyman laughed. "Smith the Bald tried the Machiavelli against Butler the Cross-eyed and got floored in the first round!"

CHAPTER 89

Colonel Pleasants solved the air-quality problem by placing a canvas partition near the mine entrance that separated the tunnel air from outside air, while allowing the miners to enter and exit the tunnel. A wooden duct was laid through the partition to draw in outside air and repeatedly extended to the front of the tunnel. A vertical exhaust shaft was dug 120 feet down the tunnel. A small fire was kept burning beneath the ventilation shaft that heated the stale air. Because hot air rises, the bad air was drawn out of the tunnel and up the exhaust shaft while fresh air was drawn into the tunnel via the duct.

A smiling Burnside welcomed Meade to Ninth Corps headquarters. "I told you Pleasants could do it."

"He showed real Yankee creativity in solving the ventilation challenge," Meade said. "We are giving you eight thousand pounds of explosive black powder to pack the mine. General Hunt will provide artillery support, and General Ord's Eighteenth and Warren's Fifth Corps are prepared to support you if your attack breaches the Rebel line."

Meade began pacing. "For the operation to be successful, it is imperative that your men capture the crest on Cemetery Hill behind the Confederate line. If we can secure and hold that crest, Lee's army will be cut in two."

"Why have you rejected my plan to use Ferrero's division of colored troops to lead the attack? They are the freshest troops in the Ninth Corps."

"We've never made this type of attack before. The first troops in will need to seize and hold the crest. Speed in securing the crest will be essential. Lee is sure to vigorously counterattack any breakthrough, like he did at the bloody angle at Spotsylvania. The soldiers leading this assault need to be combat-tested veterans. The colored troops have not seen any fighting. Experience in this war has repeatedly shown that troops seeing their first combat don't perform as well as veterans."

Meade paused. "I want the colored troops to get combat experience, and I want them to participate in the attack, but not as the spearhead. If we give the colored troops their first taste of warfare leading such a dangerous operation and the attack turns out to be a failure, the Radical Republicans in Congress would accuse me and Grant of using the colored soldiers as cannon fodder to be slaughtered by the Rebels."

Burnside wasn't satisfied. "I'm going to appeal to Grant."

"Fine. Grant will have the final word."

Grant supported Meade.

The mine was set to explode two days later at 3:30 a.m. At the appointed hour, nothing happened. Two of Pleasants's men bravely entered the mine and found a break in the fuse. They spliced and relit the fuse.

At 4:44 a.m., there was a deep rumbling sound. The ground trembled like an earthquake, a tongue of red-and-yellow flame shot into the air, and a mushroom cloud of red earth, Rebels, and cannons rose two hundred feet before falling back to earth. The blast created a crater 130 feet long, 75 feet wide, and 30 feet deep, with steep walls. Men not killed were buried alive, some with their legs kicking in the air and others with only their arms exposed.

Grant was with Meade, and they were connected to Burnside by telegraph. A note intended for Burnside was inadvertently delivered to Meade. Union soldiers were not advancing past the crater.

At 5:40 a.m., Meade had Humphreys telegraph Burnside.

> THE GENERAL COMMANDING LEARNS YOUR TROOPS ARE
> HALTING AT THE WORKS WHERE THE MINE EXPLODED,
> AND HE DIRECTS THAT ALL YOUR TROOPS BE PUSHED
> FORWARD TO THE CREST AT ONCE.

BATTLE OF THE CRATER

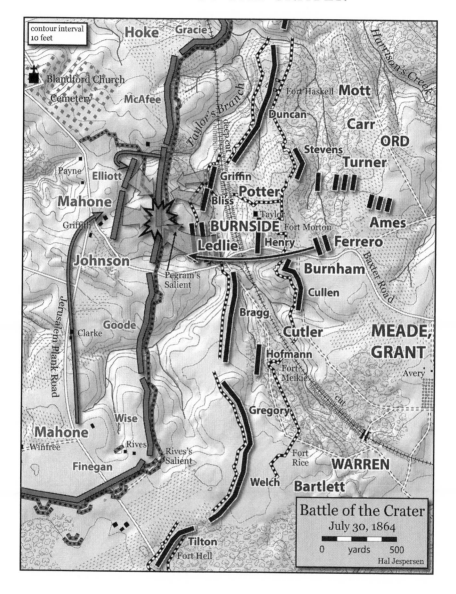

contour interval 10 feet

Hoke
Gracie
Harrison's Creek
Blandford Church
Cemetery
McAfee
Fort Haskell
Mott
Duncan
Carr
Taylor's Branch
deep cut
ORD
Stevens
Turner
Payne
Elliott
Griffin
Potter
Mahone
Bliss
BURNSIDE
Fort Morton
Ames
Griffith
Taylo
Henry
Ferrero
Ledlie
Johnson
Burnham
Baxter Road
Pegram's
Salient
Cullen
Goode
Bragg
Clarke
Cutler
MEADE,
GRANT
Hofmann
Fort
Meikie
Avery
Jerusalem Plank Road
cut
Wise
Gregory
Mahone
Winfree
Rives
Fort
Rice
WARREN
Rives's
Salient
Finegan
Welch
Bartlett
Tilton
Fort Hell

Battle of the Crater
July 30, 1864

0   yards   500

Hal Jespersen

At 6:00 a.m., Meade telegraphed Burnside.

> PRISONERS TAKEN SAY THERE IS NO LINE IN THEIR
> REAR, AND THAT THEIR MEN WERE FALLING BACK WHEN
> OURS ADVANCED. OUR CHANCE IS NOW. PUSH YOUR
> MEN FORWARD AT ALL HAZARDS—WHITE AND BLACK—
> AND DON'T LOSE TIME IN MAKING FORMATIONS, BUT
> RUSH FOR THE CREST.

At 6:50 a.m., Meade telegraphed Burnside.

> EVERY MINUTE IS MOST PRECIOUS AS THE ENEMY
> UNDOUBTEDLY ARE CONCENTRATING TO MEET YOU ON
> THE CREST. THE GREAT POINT IS TO SECURE THE
> CREST AT ONCE, AT ALL HAZARDS.

Burnside responded.

> I AM DOING ALL IN MY POWER TO PUSH THE TROOPS
> FORWARD, AND IF POSSIBLE, CARRY THE CREST. IT
> IS HARD WORK, BUT WE HOPE TO ACCOMPLISH IT.

Meade learned that Burnside's men had filled the crater, failed to advance, and were being savagely counterattacked by the Confederates, who were shooting down into the crater. An incredible opportunity to shorten the war was being wasted.

At 7:30 a.m., Meade replied.

> WHAT DO YOU MEAN BY HARD WORK TO TAKE THE
> CREST? I UNDERSTAND NOT A MAN HAS ADVANCED
> BEYOND THE ENEMY'S LINE WHICH YOU OCCUPIED
> IMMEDIATELY AFTER EXPLODING THE MINE. DO YOU
> MEAN TO SAY YOUR OFFICERS AND MEN WILL NOT
> OBEY YOUR ORDERS TO ADVANCE? I WISH TO KNOW
> THE TRUTH, AND DESIRE AN IMMEDIATE ANSWER.

Burnside replied.

I DO NOT MEAN TO SAY THAT MY OFFICERS AND MEN WILL NOT OBEY MY ORDERS TO ADVANCE. I MEAN TO SAY IT IS VERY HARD TO ADVANCE TO THE CREST. I HAVE NEVER IN ANY REPORT SAID ANYTHING DIFFERENT FROM WHAT I CONCEIVED TO BE THE TRUTH. WERE IT NOT INSUBORDINATE, I WOULD SAY THAT THE LATTER REMARK OF YOUR NOTE WAS UNOFFICERLIKE AND UNGENTLEMANLY.

At 9:30 a.m., Humphreys messaged Burnside.

THE MAJOR GENERAL COMMANDING HAS HEARD YOUR ATTACK HAS BEEN REPULSED, AND DIRECTS THAT IF IN YOUR JUDGMENT NOTHING FURTHER CAN BE EFFECTED, THAT YOU WITHDRAW.

At 10:30 a.m., an angry Burnside entered Meade's headquarters. "How dare you question whether my officers and men obey my orders! It was highly insulting! You questioned my veracity! I deserve respect!"

"This morning's attack was a debacle! You had responsibility for directing the assault. I learned of problems with the assault from sources other than you! There was no leadership at the crater. General Ledlie's division spearheaded the attack. I learned he wasn't with his troops. He was found behind our line in a drunken stupor! The attack is being suspended."

Headquarters Army of the Potomac, July 31, 1864

My Dearest Margaret,

Our attack yesterday was a failure. The mine had been dug by a Pennsylvania regiment of coal miners in Burnside's corps, and to this offi- cer was entrusted the assault. The mine was most successfully exploded, throwing into the air, and subsequently burying, four guns and a South Carolina regiment. Our column immediately took possession of the crater and part of the enemy's first line, but instead of immediately pushing on and crowning the hill, which was the key to the whole of the enemy's position, our men crouched in the crater and could not be got forward. Burnside and myself had a dispute, he not willing to admit his men would not advance. At the same time it was evident to all no progress was being made.

The affair was very badly managed by Burnside. It has produced a great deal of irritation and bad feeling. I have applied to have him relieved.

Your Loving Husband George

CHAPTER 90

Meade read the newspaper with disgust. "Lyman, look at this article. I'm being blamed for the failure of the Battle of the Crater!"

"I overheard two reporters talking," Lyman said. "All the war reporters have vowed not to print anything positive about you in their papers. They will only write negative stories. I think it is in reaction to the way Cropsey was treated."

Meade frowned. "I admit that was a mistake. The press has great power in this country. I have virtually disappeared unless they can associate my name with a fiasco like the mine attack."

Lyman asked, "Has the President responded to your request for a court of inquiry?"

"Yes. Lincoln approved it. Hancock will serve as president of the court. I learned Burnside let his division commanders draw straws as to who would lead the attack! That drunkard Ledlie drew the short straw. Grant has relieved Burnside. General John Parke will be the new Ninth Corps commander."

Lyman stood up and started to leave. "Oh, did you see that Sheridan has been appointed Commander of the Army of the Shenandoah?"

Meade replied in an irritated tone, "I knew that was happening. Grant led me to believe that I would have that command and be able to operate outside of his shadow. I asked Grant why Sheridan got the command. He said Lincoln expressed every willingness to give it to me, but he feared my removal from the command of the Army of the

Potomac might be misunderstood by the public as a demotion for the victor of Gettysburg."

Meade was tired of being under Grant's thumb. He liked and respected Grant, and they worked well together. But he had little strategic freedom. He wanted to be his own man again. He would have welcomed the Shenandoah Valley command.

Headquarters Army of the Potomac, August 9, 1864

My Dearest Margaret,

The attempt to implicate me in the recent fiasco was truly ridiculous. Still, the public must in time be influenced by these repeated and constant attacks, however untrue and unjustifiable they may be. Have you ever thought that since the first week after Gettysburg, now more than a year, I have never been alluded to in public journals except to abuse and vilify me?

I hope the dear children will enjoy themselves at Cape May. I should be so happy if I could only be there with you to indulge in those splendid sea baths and take our old walks on the beach. Let us keep up our spirits, have brave hearts, trust in God's mercy and goodness, and believe that so long as we try to do our duty, all will be well in time.

Your Loving Husband George

CHAPTER 91

Meade was in City Point to confer with Grant, who was lost in thought. "The Battle of the Crater was one of the saddest chapters in this terrible war. I'm revolted by the stories of Confederates murdering in cold blood the colored troops who surrendered."

Meade had been shocked when he learned of the Confederate brutality. "What savage and reprehensible conduct by the Rebels!"

The men were silent for a time.

Grant said, "But we must continue to look forward. We're going to keep the pressure on Lee. Have Hancock cross the James and threaten Richmond. That will draw troops away from Petersburg's defenses. Then send Warren to capture a piece of the Weldon Railroad."

"I'll visit Warren and impress upon him the necessity of being vigorous and aggressive in his movements."

"Good. Warren has a brilliant mind, but he is far too slow in marshaling his forces to attack." Grant picked a paper off his desk. "I have been in a tug-of-war with Halleck. There is going to be another draft next week. He wants me to send thousands of troops north to be in position to put down possible riots. I objected, not wanting to weaken our position at Petersburg." Grant handed Meade a telegram. "This was Lincoln's response."

I HAVE SEEN YOUR DISPATCH EXPRESSING YOUR
UNWILLINGNESS TO BREAK YOUR HOLD WHERE YOU

ARE. NEITHER AM I WILLING. HOLD ON WITH A
BULL-DOG GRIP, AND CHEW & CHOKE, AS MUCH AS
POSSIBLE.

Meade laughed. "Lincoln has quite a way with words."

Meade was at Fifth Corps headquarters. "Warren, we are going to make another attempt to get a lodgment on the Weldon Railroad. We know Lee's tactics now. As soon as he learns we are trying to cut the Weldon line, he'll send a mobile strike force out of his Petersburg fortifications and vigorously attack you. You need to be prepared to fend off his attack."

"I'll get the job done. Once my men get on that railroad, the Rebels aren't going to push us off."

"This is an opportunity to redeem your reputation, which has fallen since we crossed the Rapidan. Move your forces with speed and aggression."

"I hated those suicidal frontal assaults Grant kept ordering. I know I was slow to attack. It got to be too much! Our best men dying for no purpose!"

Warren successfully cut the Weldon line at Globe Tavern and made good on his promise, stubbornly fighting off three days of vigorous Confederate attacks to retake it.

Parke's Ninth Corps line was extended and connected with Warren, forcing Lee to extend his line to avoid being flanked.

Meade read the paper and saw Sheridan and Sherman had their promotions approved by Lincoln. He was shocked that his name was absent.

When he saw Grant he asked, "Why was my promotion to major general not approved with the others?"

"That was my decision. I decided to delay your appointment because if it was made on the same day as Sherman's, you would rank

GLOBE TAVERN

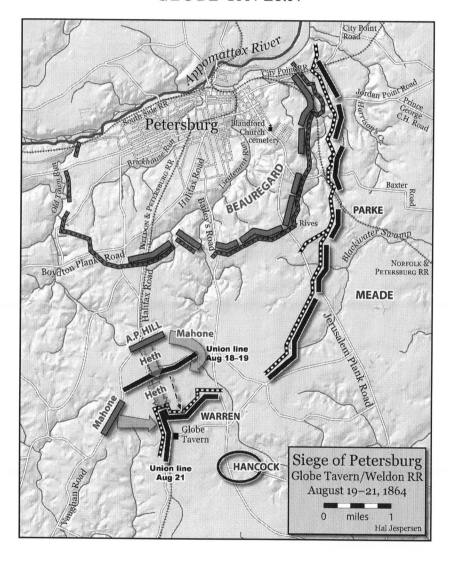

Siege of Petersburg
Globe Tavern/Weldon RR
August 19–21, 1864

0   miles   1

Hal Jespersen

him. I want Sherman to rank you. I should have told you what I was doing before you read about it in the newspaper."

Meade was dumbstruck by Grant's overt favoritism of his Western friends. What really rankled was that son of a bitch Sheridan would rank him!

Grant pulled out two cigars and both generals lit up. "Don't worry. Your promotion will come through. You have my support and that of the President and Secretary Stanton."

Meade fought to keep his tone professional. "I appreciate your candor and your high regard for Sherman, who you know so well from the Western Theater battles. I can accept with equanimity Sherman ranking me, but the fact that Sheridan will rank me is unfair! I have successfully commanded a large army and beaten Lee at Gettysburg. I have shouldered more responsibility and accomplished more than Sheridan has!"

Grant nodded. "I get your point and understand why you believe you should rank Sheridan. I will discuss your complaint with Stanton and the President."

Headquarters Army of the Potomac, August 24, 1864

My Dearest Margaret,

I see you have heard of the promotion of Sherman and Sheridan, and noted the absence of my name. The whole substance of the explanation was Grant desired to advance his favorites, Sherman and Sheridan. I did not care much about the appointment except to prove to the ignorant public that they had been imposed upon by a lying press. Grant really thinks he is one of my best friends and can't conceive why I should complain of a little delay in giving me what he tells me I am certainly to have. Every other officer in this army, except myself, who has been recommended for promotion for services in this campaign has been promoted. It is rather hard I am to be the only exception to this rule.

General Grant has been to Fortress Monroe and returned with his wife and children. He seems very much attached to his children, and his wife is said to possess a great deal of good sense and to have exercised a most salutary effect over him.

I have been for several days very much occupied, in the saddle all day, superintending the movements culminating in our securing a permanent lodgment on the Weldon Road.

I shall make an effort to get off for a few days to have a peep at you and the children.

Your Loving Husband George

CHAPTER 92

Meade stood on the street, looking at his wife's new home on Delancey Place. It was a large, four-story redbrick townhome. When he knocked on the door, Margaret opened it. They embraced, and he felt a wave of emotion. Margaret was not only his wife but also the rock of the family and his closest confidant.

"George, I'm so happy you're home! I love you so much! This terrible war has kept you from me."

"I so miss you and the children. I hope it ends soon. Those Rebs are a tenacious lot and refuse to give up. But I'm confident of ultimate victory."

They entered the house, and Margaret said, "Do you like our new home?"

"You mean your home."

She laughed. "I wasn't surprised that you turned down the house. You're scrupulously honest and ethical. When they offered it, I thought about what my father would have advised. I concluded that he would have told me to accept the house in my name. Women may not be able to vote or serve on juries, but they can own property."

Meade smiled. Margaret had an independent streak. "How is Sargie doing?"

She started crying. "He has gotten worse. I think he's going to die."

Meade hugged her tightly. He took out a handkerchief and dried her tears. "We have and will do everything we can for him. We must be strong and believe in the mercy of God."

He found Sargie in his bedroom. He looked pale and sickly and was constantly coughing. Sargie forced himself out of bed, and they hugged. "Father, it is good to see you."

"And it is wonderful to see you. Your mother and I are doing everything in our power to help improve your health."

"I know. I want to be a lawyer, like Grandfather. I'm fighting this illness with all my strength so I can fulfill my dream."

They conversed for an hour, and Meade left Sargie's room with tears in his eyes.

After dinner with the children, Margaret and Meade went for a walk around Rittenhouse Square.

Margaret held his arm. "Grant treats you with disdain by favoring his Western cronies! He has unfairly promoted Sherman and Sheridan over you! He allows that horrible, uncouth Sheridan to disrespect you!"

"My darling, you're being too hard on Grant. Yes, he has his favorite sons, but he is fundamentally a good man."

But Margaret was hot with anger. "My criticisms of Grant are fair! He takes credit for the successes you achieve with your army and saddles you with the blame for any disasters, like that horrible Crater Battle! Can't you ask to be relieved of command of the Army of the Potomac?"

"My duty is to the country. I will not voluntarily leave the frontline of our struggle to suppress the rebellion. I bear the injustices with dignity."

After four emotional days in Philadelphia, Stanton summoned Meade to Washington.

As Meade approached Stanton's office on the second floor of the War Department, he saw Lincoln in the telegraph room.

"General Meade, it is good to see you. When you finish your business with Stanton, come pay me a visit in the White House."

Meade said he would. After he greeted him, Stanton said, "You were understandably upset that the President didn't announce your promotion to major general on the same day as Sherman and Sheridan. I deferred to General Grant. I want to assure you that your promotion will come through. Congress will have to approve it, but with my support, as well as Grant's and Lincoln's, it will happen."

"Thank you, Mr. Secretary. Having your confidence is very meaningful to me."

"I understand you have a son who is very ill."

"My oldest son has tuberculosis."

Stanton's face paled. "My first wife, my beloved Mary, died from tuberculosis." Stanton's eyes filled with tears. "We were young and in love, and I cried like a baby when she died." Tears rolled down Stanton's cheeks.

Meade was moved by the show of emotion from the normally brusque and businesslike Stanton. "Mr. Secretary, losing loved ones is so painful. Take solace in your faith in God to help you through such dark times."

Stanton nodded. He took out a handkerchief and dried his cheeks. "What do you think of the Democrats nominating General McClellan as their Presidential candidate?"

"As an army officer, I don't believe I should be involved in politics. I have never supported or endorsed a political candidate."

"Last week Lincoln told me he didn't expect to win reelection. Then Sherman took Atlanta, and his prospects have improved dramatically. I think the Democrat peace platform pushed through by disloyal Copperheads will help the President get reelected. Most Americans don't want to see the deaths of so many brave and patriotic soldiers be for nothing. They will support Lincoln in his steadfastness to see the war through to a successful conclusion. How do you think the soldiers will vote?"

Meade considered the question. If McClellan won, and if he honored the Democratic pledge of peace, he would negotiate a treaty allowing the Confederacy to become an independent nation. Most soldiers fervently wanted the Union restored. Any peace agreement that let the South go free would be repugnant to them.

"McClellan was loved by the Army of the Potomac, but so is Lincoln. The younger soldiers reverently call him Father Abraham. They know from his frequent visits to the army that he sincerely cares about them. The soldiers desire peace, but not at any price as demanded by the Democratic platform. I think Lincoln will get a significant majority of the soldier vote."

"General Meade, thank you for coming over to the White House. I know you're upset with this promotion business, which we are going to address. Has it had a negative impact on your relations with Grant?"

"We have a good working relationship. We are both professionals dedicated to winning the war, and minor irritations don't affect the positive way in which we interact. I respect Grant, and I believe he respects me."

"I am happy to hear that you two are getting along. I have the same situation with my Cabinet members. Sometimes we butt heads, but there is an understanding that we have to work together to win the war. Take Stanton. At times he treats me rudely, but he is absolutely indispensable to the war effort. He works day and night, very efficiently managing the War Department. I have total confidence in his abilities, so I put up with his irritability and not laughing at my stories. Speaking of humor, have you heard of Petroleum V. Nasby?"

"I have not, Mr. President."

"There is a chap in Ohio who has been writing a series of letters in the newspapers using that name. I'm going to invite Petroleum to come visit, and I intend to tell him if he will communicate his talent to me, I will swap places with him!"

The President picked up a pamphlet. "Let me read you an example of his humor.

> *"I see in the papers that the goverment hez institooted a draft and that in a few weeks hundreds uv thousands uv peeceable citizens will be dragged to the tented field. I know not wat uthers may do, but ez for me, I can't go."*

Lincoln chuckled. "Here are some of his reasons why he can't be drafted.

> "I hev lost, sence Stanton's order to draft, the use uv wun eye. I'm holler chestid, am short-winded, and hev alluz hed panes in my back and side. I am afflicted with kronie diarrear. I hev verrykose vanes. I dont suppose that my political opinions wich are prossekooshn uv this unconstooshnel war, wood hev any wate with a draftin orfiser; but the above reesons why I can't go, will, I maik no doubt, be suuffshent."

The President laughed heartily.

―――――――――●

Headquarters Army of the Potomac, September 10, 1864

My Dearest Margaret,

I have been received with the greatest kindness both by the President and Stanton. Stanton said I might rest assured that my major generalcy would in due time be given me.

At my request, your brother Willie's appointment was immediately made out and given to him.

When I told Stanton of Sargie's ill health, he at once said if I wanted to send him to Cuba or New Orleans, he would place at my disposition a government steamer to take him out there.

I think the best place to go is the Island of Madeira. We must accommodate ourselves to things as they are, and not as we would have them, and yield everything in the hope that dear Sargie will be benefitted by the change of scene and air, and under the blessing of God, his health restored. I dream about you all the time and cannot dismiss you from my thoughts day or night.

I wish you would dismiss all politics from your mind, I think you allow yourself to be unnecessarily harassed about such matters. I fancy we should be happy, never mind who is President, if God will only spare my life, restore me to you and the children, and graciously permit dear Sergeant's health be reestablished.

Your Loving Husband George

CHAPTER 93

Meade read a dispatch from Stanton announcing that Sheridan had won a brilliant victory over Early's Rebel forces at Fisher's Hill in the Shenandoah Valley.

While he was happy for the Union cause, Meade couldn't help being envious that Sheridan had been set free with an independent command while his freedom of action had been superseded by Grant's close proximity.

He resented how the newspapers showered "Fighting Phil" with accolades and rarely mentioned that, in the battles against Early, Wright's Sixth Corps, which was part of Sheridan's Army of the Shenandoah, did most of the fighting.

It bothered Meade that the press ignored his contributions to the prosecution of the war. While he didn't seek publicity like Sheridan did, he felt his services should be fairly recognized.

His son entered his tent. "General Grant is here for your meeting."

"Please show him in."

George reentered the tent with Grant. "General Meade, I want to say in the presence of your son that he has earned a very admirable reputation in my headquarters as a young man who can be relied on."

Meade filled with fatherly pride. Coming from Grant, who was not known for his flattery, this was a wonderful compliment!

"Thank you, General Grant. I am very proud of the services George has provided the Union cause."

After Meade's son took his leave, Grant said, "Have Warren push farther west toward the Southside Railroad. I will have Butler's Army of the James threaten Richmond. We are going to choke and chew on Lee until he breaks."

"What do you make of the Rebel army adding old men and mere boys to its ranks?"

"It is a sign of desperation. They are robbing the cradle for men. Grandfathers and grandsons are fighting together."

"Lee is getting stretched thin. The rate of desertion has grown exponentially. Many deserters freely admit the South has no chance of winning."

"Jefferson Davis was stubborn and headstrong in Mexico. He will not give up. We will have to capture or destroy Lee's army to bring this war to a conclusion."

Headquarters Army of the Potomac, October 7, 1864

My Dearest Margaret,

I see the papers announce my narrow escape. It was a pretty close shave. Whilst I was on horseback on the field, talking to General Griffin and surrounded by my staff and escort, a shell fell in our midst, grazing Humphrey's horse, striking my left leg just below the knee, and embedding itself in the ground in the center of the group of officers, covering them all with earth but without exploding or injuring a soul. A more wonderful escape I never saw. At first I thought my leg was gone because I felt and heard the blow plainly, but it only rubbed the leather of my riding boot without even bruising the skin. How would you like to have me back minus a leg and on crutches?

Let us hope Providence will always be as merciful and protecting as in this instance; I take it was only God's will that saved my leg and perhaps my life.

I note all you say of politics, but in the army, we take but little interest except earnestly to wish the election was over. It is generally believed that McClellan has very little chance.

Your Loving Husband George

It was 4:15 a.m., the skies were dark, and a cold rain was falling. Meade was observing Hancock's battle to capture Boynton Plank Road. The Rebels were putting up an obstinate fight.

At 8:00 a.m., Grant joined Meade in observing the battle. Federal and Confederate batteries were exchanging cannon fire. Meade and Grant were both calm among the shriek and whistle of falling shells. A fused shell fell out of the sky and struck the back leg of Grant's horse but failed to explode.

"It's a good thing the Rebs manufacture such poor-quality shells," Meade said.

"It's getting pretty hot here. We should leave before we get all our horses killed," Grant replied.

After several days of hard fighting, Hancock failed to cut Boynton Plank Road.

CHAPTER 94

Would the despicable newspaper attacks never end? Meade wondered. The *New York Independent*, Henry Ward Beecher's paper, contained a vicious attack blaming Meade for Grant not being more successful.

> The advance was arrested, the whole movement interrupted, the safety of an army imperiled, the plans of the campaign frustrated—and all because one general, whose incompetence, indecision, half- heartedness in the war have again and again been demonstrated . . . Let us chasten our impatient hope of victory so long as Gen. Meade retains his hold on the gallant Army of the Potomac; but let us tell the truth of him . . . [he] holds his place by virtue of no personal qualification, but in deference to a presumed, fictitious, perverted, political necessity, and who hangs upon the neck of Gen. Grant like an Old Man of the Sea whom he longs to be rid of, and who, he retains solely in deference to the weak complaisance of his constitutional Commander-in-Chief.

Meade put down the newspaper. He caught the next military train to City Point. He found Grant at his desk. "Have you seen the assault on me in the *Independent*?"

"Yes. It was most unjust."

"Could you issue a statement that I'm retained as the commander of the Army of the Potomac because of my competence? That I am not foisted on you by the President?"

"I could do that. What would be more effective would be the President's announcement of your promotion to major general. I will speak to the President about having that happen sooner rather than later."

"There is a bitter hostility toward me on the part of certain supporters of the President and I do not want to embarrass Mr. Lincoln or to retain command by mere sufferance. Unless some measures are taken to satisfy the public and silence the persistent clamor against me, I should prefer being relieved."

"You take these newspaper attacks too seriously. At the beginning of the war, the newspapers said that I was a drunkard and Sherman was insane. After the Battle of Shiloh, my camp was inundated with reporters. I quickly learned that the papers are partisan—Democrat or Republican—and reporters play very loose with the facts and false stories are common. History is not based on newspaper stories."

Headquarters Army of the Potomac, October 31, 1864

My Dearest Margaret,

I have reason to believe you are in error in imputing any sympathy on the part of Grant with my detractors. It is true he has not exerted himself to silence or contradict them, but this arises from a very different cause. Grant is very phlegmatic, holding great contempt for newspaper criticism, and thinks, as long as a man is sustained by his own conscience, his superiors, and the Government, that it is not worth his while to trouble himself about the newspapers. Differently constituted, with more sensitiveness in his nature,

I don't doubt he would have taken some action and given publicity to such opinions of my services as would set to rest these idle stories.

I undoubtedly do not occupy the position I did just after Gettysburg, but when you compare my position with my numerous predecessors, McClellan, Pope, Burnside, and Hooker, my retaining command is even more creditable than the exaggerated laudation immediately succeeding Gettysburg. Most persistent efforts have been made by influential men, politicians, and generals to destroy me, without success. I think you will find reason to be grateful and satisfied, even though you should desire to see more justice done. I might have been treated much worse, and my present status does not justify my being discontented.

I am very much distressed to hear that Sergeant does not seem well enough to bear a sea voyage.

Your Loving Husband George

CHAPTER 95

"I'm happy the country had the good sense to reelect good-natured, iron-willed Old Abe," Lyman said during breakfast.

"Lincoln's reelection ended the last hope the Confederacy had of gaining its freedom," Meade replied. "He will ensure the war is prosecuted to a victorious conclusion."

"We have let Lincoln learn from his misfortunes and mistakes—not a bad school for a sensible man."

———

Headquarters Army of the Potomac, November 11, 1864

My Dearest Margaret,

I note all you write of dear Sergeant and of his condition. It is hard for me to know that he continues so sick and that I cannot be with you to assist in taking care of him and trying to keep up his courage and spirits. I never doubted Sergeant's firmness of purpose and moral courage.

Grant is not a mighty genius, but he is a good soldier, of great force of character, honest and upright, of pure purposes. I think he's without political aspirations or certainly not influenced by them. His prominent quality is unflinching tenacity of purpose, which blinds him to opposition and obstacles—certainly a great quality in a commander when controlled by judgment but a dangerous one otherwise. Grant is not without his faults and weaknesses. Among these is a want of sensibility, an almost too-confident and sanguine disposition, and particularly a simple and guileless disposition, which is apt to put him, unknown to himself, under the influence of those who should not influence him and desire to do so only for their own purposes. Take him all in all, he is, in my judgment, the best man the war has yet produced. I like Grant, and our relations have been very friendly. There is a difference between us. I am oversensitive, and he is deficient in sensibility.

Your Loving Husband George

Grant had unexpectedly appeared at Meade's headquarters. Meade assumed the visit meant they would be launching a new offensive.

"General Meade, I was in Washington and met with the President concerning General Sheridan ranking you. He was very receptive to correcting what we both believed was an injustice to you. The President is going to make your appointment to major general retroactive to August 19, the date Warren captured the Weldon Railroad."

Meade was happy to finally, if belatedly, have his efforts recognized. It also validated his judgment that Grant was an honest man who kept his promises. He was particularly pleased that he would rank Sheridan.

"Your support and that of President Lincoln and Secretary Stanton mean so much to me. You're all honorable men. The country is lucky to have such men leading us through this terrible conflict."

———————⚔

Meade was visiting Hancock, who was lying on his cot in a freshly pressed, crisp white shirt. Meade sat down on a camp chair.

"Win, Grant talked to me about the possibility of you recruiting and commanding a corps of veterans. What are your thoughts?"

"The idea is to recruit twenty thousand experienced soldiers who have been mustered out of the army. Stanton believes successful recruitment requires the new corps commander be a well-known and respected general. He flattered me by saying I am the best man for the job." Hancock paused. "I still haven't recovered from my Gettysburg wound and need some time away from the battlefront. I'm going to accept the offer."

Meade was emotional. "Win, you are a friend and a great commander. At Gettysburg, you were truly magnificent. You'll be missed."

"I'm sad to leave the Army of the Potomac before the war has been won. I will always cherish our times together, especially Gettysburg. Images of our heroic soldiers defending Cemetery Ridge are indelibly etched in my mind."

———————⚔

Headquarters Army of the Potomac, November 25, 1864

My Dearest Margaret,

Grant virtually acknowledged that my theory of Sheridan's appointment was the correct one, and had the matter been suggested at the time, I would have been appointed a few days in advance. As justice is thus finally done me, I am satisfied. At one thing I am particularly gratified and that is this evidence of Grant's truthfulness and sincerity. I am satisfied he is really and truly friendly to me. He says Stanton is as staunch a friend of mine as ever and that the President spoke most handsomely of me.

Your Loving Husband George

CHAPTER 96

The White House announced Meade's appointment as a major general in the regular army. He would be the fourth-highest officer in the army, ranked only by Grant, Halleck, and Sherman. He still needed Senate confirmation, which was a concern, given the bitter enmity against him by some prominent senators.

Meade was riding through a cold, rainy mist to visit Horatio Wright. Grant had brought the Sixth Corps back to the Army of the Potomac for its winter encampment.

When he arrived, Meade and Wright warmly shook hands. "What was it like being part Sheridan's Army of the Shenandoah?" Meade asked.

"Sheridan is a fearless warrior. He loves fighting and inspires confidence in the men. We really beat up Jubal Early."

"He doesn't much care for me."

Wright didn't immediately respond. "I will be honest. Sheridan made some disparaging comments about you."

"That's not surprising. I will give him his due, he is a good fighter. And I'll admit I am happy Sheridan is no longer with the Army of the Potomac. He is too much about himself."

Meade read the telegram and smiled. More well-deserved recognition for his son.

"George, here's a dispatch confirming your appointment to major by brevet, for gallantry and meritorious conduct! I'm proud of you."

His son had a huge smile on his face. "Thank you, Father. It has been an honor to be part of your staff. Your praise means everything to me."

Lyman entered Meade's tent. "Senator Zachariah Chandler is here and wants to see you."

"Invite him in."

When Chandler entered, Meade said, "Senator, to what do I owe the honor?"

"I am here with three other members of the Committee on the Conduct of the War to take testimony to determine who should be held accountable for the disaster that was the Battle of the Crater."

"There's no need for you to do that. A Military Court of Inquiry found that General Burnside poorly managed the attack."

"We believe there is evidence that Burnside was scapegoated."

"That is utterly ridiculous."

"Congress has the authority to investigate, and that is what we're going to do. Here is a list of witnesses we want to take testimony from."

Meade studied the list. "Except for me, all these men are close friends of Burnside. I will give you names of additional men you should take testimony from to get a full picture of what happened."

Headquarters Army of the Potomac, December 20, 1864

My Dearest Margaret,

Messers. Chandler and Harding, of the Senate, and Loan and Julian, of the House, all members of the Committee on the Conduct of the War, made their appearance to investigate the Mine affair. They gave me a list of witnesses to be called,

from which I saw at once that their object was
to censure me, as all the officers were Burnside's
friends. They called me before them. After numer-
ous questions by Mr. Loan, who evidently wished
to find flaws, I was permitted to leave. I asked the
committee to call before them General Hunt and
Colonel Duane; these officers came out laughing
and said as soon as they began to say anything
that was unfavorable to Burnside, they stopped
them and said that was enough, clearly showing
they only wanted to hear evidence of one kind. I
presume their object is to get some capital to oper-
ate with to oppose the confirmation of my nomi-
nation in the Senate.

Your Loving Husband George

———————————

Meade arrived in Philadelphia on a cold and dreary New Year's Eve. He found Margaret very depressed.

"Sargie is getting weaker. I'm so scared he's going to die."

Meade hugged her. "If it is God's will to take him, we must prepare ourselves for the grief that we will suffer."

He went up to his son's room. The young man had lost weight. His breathing was shallow, and he did not have the strength to raise his head.

Meade sat on the bed and held his son's hand. "Sargie, I'm so happy to see you. When I'm gone, I miss you terribly."

Sergeant smiled weakly. "I missed you too, Father. I wish I had the strength to stand up so we could embrace."

Meade spent hours by his son's side while he fell in and out of a fitful sleep. It was painful to think about how much he would miss Sargie if God took him, something that now seemed inevitable. Then he thought of the sorrow felt by the thousands of families who had lost loved ones defending their country. Meade stood up feeling emotionally drained. No matter the circumstances, losing a loved one was heart-wrenching.

That evening, Meade and Margaret made their annual New Year's Eve champagne toast.

Meade was feeling sad when he held up his glass. "To our twenty-fourth wedding anniversary. I am blessed to have married such a wonderful woman. And to our firstborn, who has shown such dignity and grace in battling his affliction."

Margaret held up her glass. "To your forty-ninth birthday. I am a fortunate woman to have found such a wonderful husband." Looking desolate and with despair in her voice, she said, "I pray for a miracle to save our son."

Meade stayed in Philadelphia until January 9, when Grant summoned him to Petersburg.

CHAPTER 97

Headquarters Army of the Potomac, January 10, 1865

My Dearest Margaret,

I found my recall to be as expected. Grant received information of Lee sending off two divisions and is under the impression it is the commencement of the evacuation of Richmond. I explained to Grant Sergeant's condition and my earnest desire to remain with him. He promised to let me return to Philadelphia as soon as this affair was settled.

The great subject of discussion in the army is the relieving of General Butler. He was relieved by the President at Grant's request.

It is hardly necessary I should tell you how much I have suffered since I left you. All I can do is earnestly pray to God to have mercy on dear Sergeant and yourself and to give you strength to bear up under the affliction you are visited with.

Your Loving Husband George

The report of Lee evacuating Petersburg and Richmond proved false. Meade was with Grant at City Point waiting for his ship to begin the journey to Philadelphia.

Meade asked, "Have you decided who is taking over the Army of the James?"

"General Edward Ord."

"I know Ord from the Pennsylvania Reserves. He is a good solider."

"Take care of your son and comfort your wife. I pray for your son's return to health. I can only imagine the pain you and Margaret are suffering."

"Thank you. Our faith in God is helping us cope."

———————

It was after midnight, and snow was falling in thick flurries. Meade now had a key to the Delancey Place house. He let himself in. Margaret had stayed up, waiting for him.

"George, darling, I'm so happy to see you!"

He hugged her. "I love you so much! How is Sargie doing?"

She started crying. "He is dying."

He held her tightly. "We must pray for God's mercy."

The next morning, he entered Sargie's room. His son's breathing was labored. Meade sat on the bed and held Sargie's hand.

"Father, I know I am dying." Sargie coughed so hard, his frail body shook. "I have lived my life as fully as God has allowed. I'm at peace with being taken."

Meade had tears running down his cheeks. "Sargie, I'm so proud of you. You have faced adversity with great courage. You're an inspiration to your family and all who know you. You need to keep fighting. We are praying to God for you."

Meade had spent three days with his ailing son when a telegram arrived from Stanton recalling him to Petersburg.

———————

Headquarters Army of the Potomac, February 1, 1865

My Dearest Margaret,

I found on my arrival last night that three distinguished gentleman, Mr. Alexander Stephens (vice president of the Confederacy) Mr. R. M. T. Hunter (formerly a United States senator from Virginia), and Mr. Campbell, of Alabama (formerly a justice United States Supreme Court) were in our lines, having been passed in by General Grant, on their expressing a wish to go to Washington. They do not profess to be accredited commissioners but state they are informal agents, desiring to visit the President and ascertain if any measures are practicable for termination of the war. I called this morning, with General Grant, on them and remained after General Grant left. Mr. Hunter asked what we propose to do with the slaves after freeing them. I replied that this was undoubtedly a grave question, but not insurmountable; that they must have labor and the negroes must have support; between the two necessities I thought some system could be devised accommodating both interests, which would not be so obnoxious as slavery.

Judge Campbell asked about your family. Mr. Hunter spoke of Mr. Wise and said he had brought two letters, one of which I enclose.

When they came within our lines, our men cheered loudly and the soldiers on both sides cried out lustily, "Peace! Peace!"

I judge from my conversation that there's not much chance of peace. The selection of three of the most conservative Southern men indicates *most clearly an anxiety on the part of Mr. Davis to settle matters if possible.*

I thought my last visit was, excepting dear Sergeant's sickness, most happy, but I cannot be happy seeing my noble boy suffering as he does. I think of him all the time, and feel at times like asking to be relieved that I may go home to help you nurse him. May God in His mercy restore him to health is my constant prayer!

Your Loving Husband George

The Confederate peace commissioners had been taken to Fortress Monroe and met with Lincoln. They had since returned to Richmond. Meade didn't know the results, but given that both sides had artillery going full blast, there evidently had been no peace agreement.

CHAPTER 98

Meade read Sharpe's latest intelligence report. It painted a grim picture for Lee. The Rebel army was poorly supported, food supplies were scant, men were famished, and morale was dropping. Lee's army was shrinking, with hundreds of men deserting nightly. Most deserters freely admitted the war could not be won. Lee's army was so depleted that he had asked that the slaves be freed so they could be armed and fight for the Confederacy.

Meade sat back. Here was clear evidence that the war had to end soon. The Union naval blockade had strangled the Southern economy. Sherman's burning of Atlanta and devastating march to the sea had added to Southern woes.

Meade said to his son, "Let's go for a walk. I need some exercise."

As he stepped out of his tent into the brisk February air, Meade thought about Sharpe's report. It seemed that it was only Lee's army that was keeping the Confederacy from collapsing.

A soldier from the telegraph office approached and handed Meade a telegram. He read it and smiled at George.

"The Senate has confirmed my appointment to major general by a vote of 32 to 5!"

"Congratulations, Father!"

A couple of days later, Meade was reading the paper. Predictably, the Committee on the Conduct of the War had exonerated Burnside and condemned him for the botched Battle of the Crater.

Within an hour, he received a dispatch from Grant.

Grant to Meade: Feb. 9, 10 a.m.

The Committee on the Conduct of the War have published the result of their investigation of the Mine explosion. Their opinions are not sustained by knowledge of the facts nor by my evidence nor yours either do I suppose. Genl. Burnside's evidence apparently has been their guide and to draw it mildly he has forgotten some of the facts. I think in justification to yourself who seem to be the only party censured, Genl. Burnside should be brought before a Court Martial and let the proceedings of the Court go before the public along with the report of the Congressional Committee.

Meade smiled. Grant was a man of rectitude.

Later in the day, Meade saw Grant at City Point. "Thank you for your dispatch. I believe that after the acknowledgment of my services by the President's nomination, and the large Senate vote in my favor, I can stand the biased report of the committee."

Grant said angrily, "It is disgusting that those congressmen on the committee have no interest in the truth."

Headquarters Army of the Potomac, February 9, 1865

My Dearest Margaret,

I note you have seen the report of the Committee on the Conduct of the War, about the Mine. You have done Grant injustice; he did not testify against me; the committee has distorted his testimony, my own, and that of everyone who told the truth in order to sustain their censure. Immediately on the appearance of this report, Grant sent me a dispatch; from it you will see what he thinks of the course of the committee and Burnside's testimony.

Four days ago, to prove war existed, whatever might be the discussions about peace, I moved a portion of my army out to the left. Warren attacked the enemy, and after being successful all day, he was toward evening checked and finally compelled to retrace his steps in great disorder. The next morning, notwithstanding it was storming violently, Warren went at them again and succeeded in recovering most of the ground occupied and lost the day before. On the whole, it has been favorable to our side; we have extended our line some three miles to the left. I was in the saddle each day from early in the morning till near midnight.

We must all endeavor to be resigned to God's will. We cannot avert the severe affliction with which it has pleased Him to visit us. All we can do is bear it with humility and resignation, preparing ourselves, as I believe my beloved son is prepared.

Dear Margaret, let me rely on your exhibiting in this, the greatest trial you have had in life, true Christian fortitude. Bear up, in the consciousness that you have devoted all the energy of a tender mother's love to check and avert the fatal disease that is carrying off our firstborn; all that human power could do has been done. Our boy has had warning, and not only his good life but the consciousness that he knew and was prepared for the change. That should sustain us in that parting *that had to be encountered one day, for we all must die in time.*

Your Loving Husband George

———————

Meade left Petersburg at noon February 21 and arrived in Philadelphia at 10:00 p.m. on February 23. Sergeant died at 11:00 p.m. on the twenty-first.

He entered the somber house. He and Margaret embraced. She sobbed, "Sergeant is gone!"

Meade felt a profound sorrow and a sense of overwhelming, enormous lost. For some inexplicable reason, God had taken their precious firstborn.

Meade felt his wife's heaving body against his chest. "Margaret, we have to accept it was God's will. Sergeant is in heaven."

Meade had been in Philadelphia for three days, doing his best to comfort his wife and children, when a telegram came from Stanton directing him to come to Washington.

———————

"General Meade, my condolences on the death of your son."

"Secretary Stanton, our faith in God helps Margaret and I grieve the passing of our beloved son."

"I apologize for ordering you away from Philadelphia. There have been reports of unusual Confederate activity, and with Grant away, you need to be in Petersburg."

———————

*War Department, Washington City, 12:00 p.m.,
February 27, 1865*

My Dearest Margaret,

*I hardly dare think of you and your lonely con-
dition, surrounded by so many associations of
our beloved boy. God have mercy on you and send
you submission and resignation! No human reasoning can afford you or myself any consolation.
Submission to God's will, and the satisfaction
arising from the consciousness that we did our
duty by him, is all that is left us.*

*I wish you would think favorably of my propo-
sition to take a trip to the army. I think it would
arouse you and distract your mind.*

Your Loving Husband George

CHAPTER 99

Margaret had agreed to visit with the children. Mimi Lyman was coming from Boston. Assorted relatives and prominent Philadelphia citizens were also coming. The traveling party numbered twenty-five.

Meade and Lyman took the military train to City Point. The ship carrying their families arrived the evening of March 22. Meade was excited to see his wife and five wonderful children waving at him from the deck of the ship. After the ship docked, Meade and Lyman boarded.

"Margaret, I'm so happy that you came and brought our wonderful children with you!"

"You were right. I needed a distraction, and visiting a war zone certainly qualifies. The children are quite excited to be so close to the war."

General and Mrs. Grant came on board and stayed for dinner.

The ship's dining room was small and had nautical-themed decorations. After they were seated, Margaret said, "Julia, you're fortunate that the press treats Ulysses so much better than they do George."

"Mr. Grant has gotten more than his share of bad press. After Cold Harbor, the Democratic papers called him a butcher. Such mean-spirited articles are quite hurtful."

"Well, Ulysses has also gotten a lot of positive press, particularly in the *New York Herald*," Margaret responded.

Meade interjected, "I admit that unfair and libelous press attacks bother me. General Grant ignores newspaper attacks."

"It wasn't always so," Grant said. "After the Battle of Shiloh, the Northern press said I had lost the battle, which wasn't true. The Confederates got the better of us the first day. The second day, we counterattacked and drove the Rebels off the field. It was a Union victory. The papers also claimed I was drunk during the fighting, which was a perverse lie."

Grant paused to light a cigar. "After all the horrible press, Halleck came to Tennessee and took over my army. I remained with the army but had little responsibility. It was humiliating. I asked to be relieved and was given a posting in California, where I would be far removed from the vicious Northern press. Sherman visited and convinced me I was making a huge mistake. If I went to California, I would sit out the war. He told me I had to develop a tougher skin. Sherman persuaded me to change my mind. Since then, I've ignored abusive and false press attacks."

Meade thought it was ironic that Grant had been upset when Halleck had taken over his army, since Grant had done something similar to him. The difference was that Grant gave him major responsibilities, and his plate was full of work.

After dinner, the Grants left the ship. As they were walking to their cabin, Margaret said, "Grant seems very infatuated with Julia."

"I hear they have a good marriage. In one respect, she reminds me of you. Grant's staff refers to Julia as the boss of the family."

Margaret laughed.

Meade and Lyman stayed with their wives overnight on the ship.

The next morning, Meade's guests took a military train to the Petersburg front. Ambulances at the train station transported the traveling party to his headquarters.

Meade gave his guests an overview of Union operations.

"Petersburg was chosen for attack because it is a key rail hub. The Southside Railroad is the last line the Rebels control. When it's captured, Lee will have to abandon Petersburg and Richmond because he won't be able to feed his troops.

"We have built a partial siege line that through a series of battles has been extended south and west of Petersburg for twenty miles. Forts have been built about every half mile along the line—forty-one in total. These are strong points containing cannons and housing troops.

"Our supplies arrive by boat at City Point and are brought to the front on the rebuilt City Point Railroad, which has been extended behind the entire length of the Union line. The train transports our wounded to hospitals at City Point.

"It's dangerous work for soldiers who man the fortifications. Artillery shells and sniper bullets are daily perils. The most hazardous duty is manning the picket line in no-man's-land between the lines.

"Conditions are often miserable. Summer heat crossed a hundred degrees, and winter brought freezing rain and snow. Wet weather makes the trenches muddy and filthy. Most nearby trees have been cut down to erect fortifications. The barren landscape has led to extremely dusty conditions. When the wind blows, the men are covered in dust and look like ghosts.

"Now we will go on a tour."

Some of the visitors, including a few ladies, rode horses. The rest traveled by ambulance. Their first stop was Fort Haskell.

Meade addressed the group. "All our forts are named for gallant soldiers who died in battle. This fort is named for Colonel Frank Haskell. At Gettysburg, he gave invaluable service in helping repulse Pickett's Charge. He died leading an attack at Cold Harbor."

Meade's guests spent the afternoon touring Union fortifications.

They ended the day with dinner back on the ship. Again, Meade and Lyman stayed the night.

The next day, they sailed up the James and boarded Admiral David Porter's flagship for lunch. Afterward Porter put the visitors in small boats behind a towing tug, and they were taken to see the ironclads.

On the way back to City Point, Meade said, "Margaret, the President and First Lady are due to arrive at City Point sometime today. Tomorrow there will be a grand review for Lincoln."

"The President was most gracious when I saw him at the Sanitary Fair in Philadelphia. I know you're pleased he appointed you a major general in the regular army."

"The North would not be on the verge of victory without Lincoln's deft political skills and unwavering will to see the nation be one again. The country owes him a great deal of gratitude."

It seemed like a dream to have Margaret and his children with him. The children were having a wonderful time interacting with the soldiers and sailors, seeing the fortifications, and running around the navy ships. It was a special time, being able to share a portion of his world with his precious Margaret and darling children.

When they reached City Point, the Lincolns had not yet arrived. Meade and Lyman again dined on the ship and stayed overnight.

At 7:30 a.m., Meade received a telegraph with startling news. At 4:30 a.m., the Rebels had launched an attack and captured Fort Stedman!

The telegraph line had been cut, explaining the delay in learning of the attack. The garrisons at Forts Haskell and McGilvery, on either side of Fort Stedman, had stood firm, and a counterattack had recaptured Fort Stedman and taken nineteen hundred Rebel prisoners.

Meade told Margaret, "I'm afraid that our idyllic respite is over. The Confederates made a surprise attack this morning. I must go to the front. I need to send you and the children back to Philadelphia. I pray that the next time we see each other, the war will be over."

Margaret was crying. "I understand. Duty calls." She wiped tears from her eyes. "It has been a wonderful trip, one I and the children will never forget. I love you dearly."

"I love you with all my soul."

They embraced and kissed. Then Meade and Lyman boarded a train for the front.

After disembarking at the train station named for him, Meade found General Parke, whose Ninth Corps had lost, then recaptured Fort Stedman.

Parke summarized the battle. "The Rebels approached our men on picket duty claiming they were deserting. Confederate desertion has become so common that our soldiers thought it was nothing unusual. They overwhelmed our pickets and caught us by complete surprise. They quickly captured Fort Stedman and turned its guns on Forts Haskell and McGilvery. The Rebel infantry attacked Fort Haskell. The fighting was intense, but those lads at Fort Haskell fought off the Confederates. General Hartranft's division was in reserve. He launched a punishing counterattack that recaptured Fort Stedman. The Rebels retreated to their line."

Meade received a telegram. The President and Mrs. Lincoln were coming to the front, along with General and Mrs. Grant. He wasn't finished entertaining dignitaries.

In the early afternoon, the Grants and Lincolns arrived at Meade's headquarters.

"General Meade, Mrs. Lincoln and I would like to have a private word with you."

They moved away from the larger group.

"You have our deepest condolences on the passing of your son," Lincoln said. "We have lost two beloved sons to illness. We know the deep pain and grief that you and Mrs. Meade are suffering."

Mary Lincoln was sobbing. "We lost the most darling boys. Losing a child is the worst feeling in the world!"

"You're right, Mrs. Lincoln." Meade replied. "I have never felt more pain than when my firstborn passed. I look to God for strength to get me through the valley of death. Thank you both for your kindness." Meade continued, "Mr. President, I have a dispatch for you from General Parke."

Lincoln pointed to a large group of Confederate prisoners awaiting transport to the rear. His eyes twinkled, and he seemed energized. "There is the best dispatch you can show me from General Parke!"

The next day, Meade took the train back to City Point. When he entered Grant's headquarters, he found the lieutenant general in a contemplative mood.

"When the war ends, Lincoln doesn't want us being vindictive toward the Confederates. The faster the Rebels return their allegiance to the Union, the better."

"The President is very sagacious, but he is going to have a battle with the Radical Republicans," Meade said. "They want to severely punish the South."

"Lincoln is a true leader. He wants what's best for the country."

"I haven't always agreed with Lincoln's military strategy, but I respect his political skills," Meade said. "The country is fortunate to have a man like Lincoln guiding it through such turbulent times."

Grant nodded his agreement. "We're going to start the spring campaign on March 29. Sheridan is returning from the Shenandoah Valley. He will have an independent command and report to me. He will need infantry support from the Army of the Potomac."

"Of course." While Meade would be a good soldier and willingly support Sheridan, he doubted Sheridan, that prima donna, would provide any support to the Army of the Potomac. "Lee's army has had tremendous desertion. His lines have to be stretched paper-thin."

Grant smiled. "We're going to force Lee out of his fortifications, and then we are going to bag his army."

Headquarters Army of the Potomac, March 26, 1865

My Dearest Margaret,

Your visit seems so like a dream I can hardly realize you have been here.
   The President and party came about 1:00 p.m. Mrs. Lincoln spoke very handsomely of you and referred in feeling terms to our sad bereavement. The President also spoke of you and expressed regret that your visit should have been so abruptly terminated.

Your Loving Husband George

CHAPTER 100

On March 29, heavy rain pelted Warren's men as they trudged through deep Virginia mud. Humphreys, who had been given the Second Corps when Hancock left, followed. Together they had thirty-five thousand men. Their objective was to meet up with Sheridan's cavalry and capture the Southside Railroad. Meade accompanied Warren. Parke's and Wright's corps stayed in the trenches in front of Petersburg.

Sheridan's cavalry had advanced to Dinwiddie Court House and got into a fight with Fitzhugh Lee's cavalry and Pickett's infantry, and was in a tight spot. On White Oak Road, Warren faced fierce Rebel resistance. Warren finally broke through the Confederate defense and was ordered to march to Sheridan and provide support for the beleaguered cavalry.

On April 1, Picket disengaged from Sheridan and fell back to the crossroads of Five Forks. Warren was ordered to Five Forks to coordinate an attack with Sheridan's cavalry.

Meade established temporary headquarters near Gravelly Run, a small stream, and established telegraph communications with Grant.

SIEGE OF PETERSBURG:
MARCH 28–APRIL 1, 1865

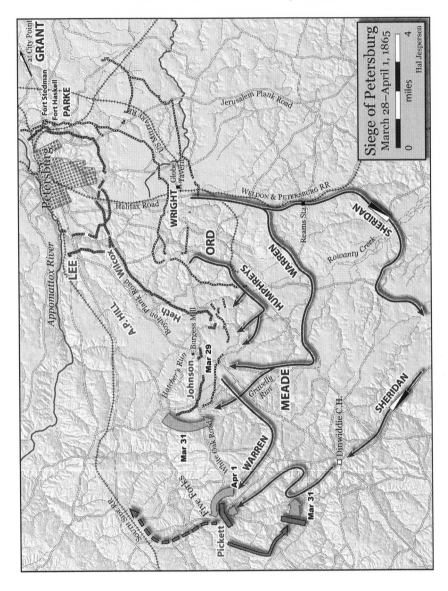

Headquarters Army of the Potomac, April 1, 1865

My Dearest Margaret,

We have been moving and fighting the last three days, I have not gone to bed till after one or two in the morning; then I am up at five. We have had considerable fighting with the enemy out of his works, and we have invariably driven him. I think this time we will reach the Southside Railroad, and if we do so, I should not be surprised if Lee evacuated his Petersburg lines and withdrew north of the Appomattox.

Your brother Willy was wounded yesterday. He left this morning, and I sent George to accompany him to City Point, and if necessary to Philadelphia.

Your Loving Husband George

———————

Meade read the telegram and felt a wave of elation. Warren and Sheridan had crushed Pickett at Five Forks! Lee's army was beginning to crumble.

A telegram came from Grant. He wanted a 1:30 a.m. artillery barrage of the Rebel line in Petersburg, and at 4:30 a.m., an all-out frontal assault on Rebel fortifications by Parke and Wright.

At midnight, a soaked, mud-covered, and disconsolate Warren entered Meade's headquarters.

"Why are you looking downcast?" Meade asked. "You just had a most glorious victory!"

"That son of a bitch Sheridan relieved me and placed Griffin in charge of the Fifth Corps!"

"What?"

"After the battle was over and we had thrashed Pickett, I got a note from Sheridan relieving me without explanation. I found Sheridan and asked him to reconsider his decision. He had a smug look on his face. He looked at me like I was an annoying fly that he could easily swat away. He waved his arm in a dismissive fashion and said, 'Hell! I never reconsider my decisions!' That short, stumpy bastard despises the Army of the Potomac. He wants all the glory for himself."

Meade was stunned. "Warren, in the past, you have come close to being relieved because you have been too slow to attack, but here in Petersburg, you have done good duty. You captured and held the Weldon Railroad."

"I got to Sheridan as fast as I could. With all this rain, Gravelly Run overflowed its banks, so it was impossible to ford, and we had to a build a temporary bridge."

"Relieving you in these circumstances, and at this point in the war, is most unfair. I am going to ask Grant to reinstate you."

Warren had a sad look on his face, like his life had been stolen from him. "Grant is not going to reverse one of his favorites. I am disgraced, and my career is ruined."

CHAPTER 101

At 1:30 a.m. on April 2, a bitterly cold, pitch-black night, Union cannons opened fire. When the bombardment ended, Horatio Wright made a bold decision. He moved his troops into no-man's-land well before the planned assault. He advanced them within a few hundred yards of the Confederate works. His men laid silently on the freezing ground, undetected, waiting for the signal to attack.

At 4:30 a.m., Parke's soldiers left the protection of their fortifications and rushed across no-man's-land toward the Confederate lines. Parke's men reached the Rebel line and engaged in fierce hand-to-hand fighting but could not break through.

At 4:40 a.m., Wright's men charged forward and with their head start smashed through the thinned Rebel line, creating a half-mile gap. Fourteen thousand Union soldiers poured through the opening. Lee's defensive line had been gashed open.

That night, Lee's army abandoned Petersburg and Richmond.

At 6:00 a.m. on April 3, Meade and Lyman triumphantly rode into Petersburg on Boynton Plank Road. All along their route, they were met with loud cheers and hurrahs from the Federal troops, who took off their caps and waved them excitedly at Meade as he rode past. The cries of "Hurrah for Meade!" filled his heart with joy. They rode through the center of town and reached Market Street.

SIEGE OF PETERSBURG:
BREAKTHROUGH, APRIL 2, 1865

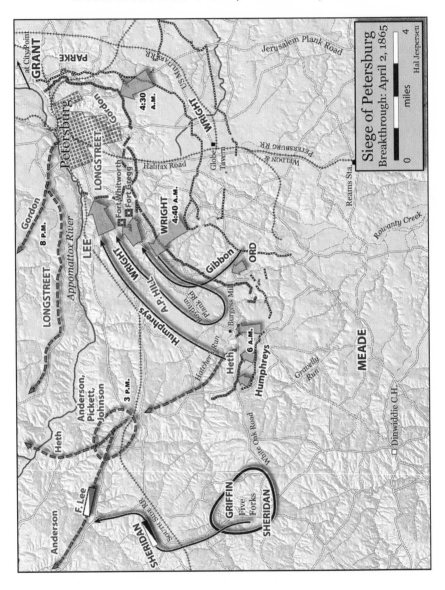

"For all the world, this street looks like Salem, Massachusetts—the same good, square, brick houses with gardens around them," Lyman said.

"Salem of the witch trials?"

"Yes. It's a quite charming town."

They continued to Cemetery Hill, Burnside's objective in the Battle of the Crater. They got off their horses and examined the crater that was close to the crest of the hill. Meade shook his head. They should have won that battle last July and shortened the war.

"Look at these deserted Rebel breastworks," Lyman said. "I give Grant credit. For more than nine months, in heat and cold, in rain and snow, by day and by night, he kept pressuring the Confederates until their line finally collapsed."

"The end of the rebellion is near. Grant won't let up until he has bagged Lee's army."

They returned to the center of town and found Grant sitting on the porch of a large house.

Meade asked Grant, "Could we have a word in private?"

They stepped away from their staffs.

"Would you consider reinstating Warren? He was relieved after winning a significant victory. The torrential rain caused the delay in getting to Five Forks. He performed heroically at Gettysburg, thrashed A. P. Hill at Bristoe Station, and captured the Weldon line. Sheridan's action humiliated Warren and is a death knell for his career in the army. I know he has often been late to begin a battle, but at this point in the war, given his good and sometimes brilliant service, he doesn't deserve to be treated this way."

"I understand that Warren has contributed to Union successes, but he has been habitually hours late going into combat. I gave Sheridan authority to relieve Warren. At Five Forks, Warren was hours behind schedule in arriving and then took hours organizing his men before going into battle. I am not overruling Sheridan."

Grant waved his cigar. "Let's discuss the pursuit of Lee. I'm going to have Ord's Army of the James stay south of Lee to block him from joining forces with Johnston's Confederate army in North Carolina. Sheridan's cavalry is going to try to get in front of Lee. I want the

Army of the Potomac to relentlessly follow Lee and attack him at every opportunity."

While Meade was unhappy that Sheridan's unfair treatment of Warren would be allowed to stand, he put aside his personal frustration to concentrate on the job at hand. "We will aggressively pursue Lee and bring him to battle or force him to surrender."

Headquarters Army of the Potomac, April 3, 1865

My Dearest Margaret,

The telegraph will have conveyed to you, long before this reaches you, the joyful intelligence that Petersburg and Richmond have fallen and that Lee, broken and dispirited, has retreated toward Lynchburg and Danville. We are now moving after Lee, and if we are successful in striking him another blow, I think the Confederacy will be at an end.

The last estimate of our prisoners amounted to fifteen thousand, and deserters and stragglers are being picked up by the thousands. Let us hope the war will soon be over.

Your Loving Husband George

APPOMATTOX

CHAPTER 102

On April 4, Meade led the Army of the Potomac in pursuit of Lee. Around midmorning, Meade got the chills and felt nauseous. Then he became dizzy. He couldn't stay on his horse.

"George, please help me get down. I don't think I can do it myself."

As soon as Meade's feet touched ground, he vomited. He kept vomiting till nothing was left of his breakfast. His head was spinning, and he sat down on the side of the road.

"George, please get an ambulance for me to travel in."

That evening at 9:30 p.m., a message was received from Sheridan. He was at Jetersville Station on the Southside Railroad. The Rebel army was just north of his position. He thought Lee's army could be captured if the infantry hurried up. Meade ordered Humphreys and Wright to do a night march to Jetersville, which was fifteen miles away.

Early the next morning, still feeling quite ill, Meade got in an ambulance and traveled to Jetersville to see Sheridan. He caught up with Humphreys, who was hot with anger.

"That Goddamn bastard Sheridan. He tells you it's an emergency to get the infantry to Jetersville. We get on the march in the middle of night and the road is blocked by Sheridan's supply wagons. We are six hours behind schedule, and my men are exhausted."

When Meade got to Jetersville, Lyman and George helped him out of the ambulance.

Meade was shaky on his feet, and his son held his elbow to steady him. "General Sheridan, where is General Lee?"

"I believe Lee is at Amelia Court House. I had Griffin's Fifth Corps dig in here at Jetersville, blocking Lee's movement south." Sheridan appraised Meade. "You look quite ill. You should go to a field hospital. I could take over the Army of the Potomac."

Meade wasn't about to allow Sheridan take over *his* army. He was determined to be leading the Army of the Potomac when the war ended. He had a coughing fit, spitting phlegm out of his mouth. "I'm a little sick, but I'm keeping up with the pursuit of Lee."

Humphreys's men arrived in Jetersville late in the afternoon, tired and worn out. Grant arrived in the evening, and it was determined that the next morning, Meade would advance on Amelia Court House while Sheridan would push ahead and try to get in front of Lee.

At daybreak, Union troops marched along the Southside line. On the way to Amelia Court House, they discovered that Lee had moved farther west toward Farmville.

Meade turned west in pursuit. Lee's army was shrinking by the hour as stragglers dropped out of the march, either too tired to keep up or quitting the war, sensing the end was near.

Humphreys caught the Confederate rearguard. For twelve miles, through woods, fields, and swamps, the Second Corps engaged in a running battle with the Rebels. Humphreys captured thirteen Confederate battle flags and seventeen hundred prisoners.

Wright advanced on Meade's left flank, and at Sailor's Creek, he caught General Ewell, who had stopped because Sheridan's cavalry was blocking his advance. After some fierce fighting, Ewell surrendered his eighty-five hundred men. Lee's army was disintegrating.

At 8:30 p.m., Meade saw a dispatch from Sheridan announcing that his cavalry with two divisions of the Sixth Corps had captured Ewell. There was no mention of Wright being on the field.

"Lyman, look at Sheridan's dispatch," Meade said. "Wright did most of the fighting and captured Ewell, yet he gets no credit. Sheridan also ignores the brilliant work done by Humphreys."

Lyman shook his head. "I'm sure his failure to mention Wright and Humphreys was intentional. Tomorrow's newspapers will be all about Fighting Phil."

The next morning, Meade's infantry followed Lee's retreating and dwindling army. What was left of Lee's army crossed the Appomattox on the Southside Railroad's High Bridge. Humphreys's Second Corps was in close pursuit.

The Confederates set fire to the High Bridge and the wagon bridge below it. The Second Corps put out the fires on the wagon bridge, preserving the span. Meade's men crossed the river and continued their pursuit of Lee.

Stragglers and deserters continued dropping out of Lee's army. Many had not eaten in days.

Meade followed his troops in an ambulance, covered in a blanket. He felt every sharp jolt delivered by the rough and uneven roads.

During a break in the pursuit, he saw his son approach the ambulance with a sad expression. "Father, Uncle Willie has died!"

Meade was shocked. Willie's wound hadn't appeared life-threatening.

"Do you know what happened?"

His son was crying. "He caught an infection in the hospital at City Point."

Poor Margaret. First Sergeant and now her brother, to whom she had been extremely close. Meade wished he could go Philadelphia to console her, but that was impossible with the chase on to catch Lee.

That evening, Grant arrived at the house Meade's staff had found for him, and they had dinner together.

"How are you feeling, old fella?"

"I'm improving," replied Meade.

"I sent a note to General Lee today exploring his interest in surrendering."

Grant handed Meade a copy of the note.

April 7, 1865
General R. E. Lee, Commanding, C. S. A.:

General: The result of the last week must convince you of the hopelessness of further resistance on the part of the Army of Northern Virginia in this struggle. I feel that it is so and regard it as my duty to shift from myself the responsibility of any further effusion of blood, by asking of you for the surrender of that portion of the Confederate States Army, known as the Army of Northern Virginia.

Very respectfully,
Your obedient servant,

U. S. Grant
Lieutenant-General
Commanding Armies of the United States

"Hopefully Lee surrenders, and this terrible war ends."

"Until he does, we will continue to pursue and attack him. Sheridan is doing his best to get in front of Lee. Ord and Griffin are marching south of the Appomattox to prevent Lee from turning south and getting into North Carolina. Keep on Lee's tail with Humphreys's and Wright's men. We're going to put Lee in a box."

Headquarters Army of the Potomac, April 7, 1865

My Dearest Margaret,

Though late at night, I seize the time to send you a few lines. I have been nearly all the time quite under the weather, with a severe bilious catarrh. Thanks to my powerful constitution and the good care of my attending physician, together with excitement of the scenes I have passed through, I have managed not to give up but to be on hand each day. Richmond is ours, and Lee's army is flying before us, shattered and demoralized.

Yesterday we took over ten thousand prisoners and five generals, among them General Ewell.

We are now at Farmville, on the Appomattox, Lee having started for Danville, but we cut him off and forced him back toward Lynchburg.

George is quite well, and has, with Lyman and Dr. McParlin, taken good care of me.

Your Loving Husband George

———⚬———

Late that night, Lee's response arrived.

April 7, 1865
To Lieut-Gen U. S. Grant, Commanding Armies of the United States

General: I have received your note of this date.
Though not entirely of the opinion you express of the hopelessness of further resistance on the part of the Army of Northern Virginia, I reciprocate your desire to avoid useless effusion of blood, and there-fore, before considering your proposition, ask the terms you will offer, on condition of its surrender.

R. E. Lee, General

CHAPTER 103

Grant responded to Lee the next morning.

April 8, 1865

To General R. E. Lee, Commanding CSA

General: Your note of the last evening in reply to mine of the same date, asking the condition on which I will accept the surrender of the Army of Northern Virginia, is just received.

In reply, I would say that peace being my great desire, there is but one condition I would insist upon, viz:

That the men surrendered shall be disqualified for taking up arms again against the Government of the United States until properly exchanged. I will meet you, or designated officers to meet any officers you may name, for the same purpose, at any point agreeable to you, for the purpose of arranging definitively the terms upon which the surrender of the Army of Northern Virginia will be received.

Very respectfully, your obedient servant,

U. S. Grant
Lieut.-General, Commanding Armies of the United
States

Grant left to visit Sheridan.

———————

Lee marched his beleaguered and starving army toward Appomattox Station, where he hoped to find a train with food supplies. Meade followed behind Lee, while Sheridan, Ord, and Griffin pushed to beat Lee to Appomattox Station.

That evening a messenger from Lee came to Meade's headquarters with a response for Grant.

April 8, 1865

General: I received, at a late hour, your note of to-day in answer to mine of yesterday.

I did not intend to propose the surrender of the Army of Northern Virginia, but to ask the terms of your proposition. To be frank, I do not think the emergency has arisen to call for the surrender.

But as the restoration of peace should be the sole object of all, I desired to know whether your proposals would lead to that end.

I cannot, therefore, meet with you with a view to surrender the Army of Northern Virginia, but as far as your proposal may affect the Confederate States forces under my command and tend to the restoration of peace, I should be pleased to meet you at 10 a.m. tomorrow on the old stage road to Richmond, between the picket lines of the two armies.

Very Respectfully, your obedient servant,

R. E. Lee
General, C. S. A.

Meade called out, "George, take this note immediately to General Grant!"

That night, General Custer's cavalry won the race to Appomattox Station and captured the supply train with the food rations meant for Lee's army.

The next day, April 9, was Palm Sunday. Grant responded to Lee's note.

April 9, 1865

General R. E. Lee, Commanding C. S. A.:

General: Your note of yesterday is received. As I have no authority to treat on the subject of peace, the meeting proposed for 10 a.m. to-day could lead to no good. I will say, however, General, that I am equally anxious for peace with yourself, and the whole North entertains the same feeling. The terms upon which peace can be had are well understood. By the South laying down their arms, they will hasten the most desirable event, save thousands of human lives, and hundreds of millions of property not yet destroyed.

Sincerely hoping that all our difficulties may be settled without the loss of another life.

Very respectfully,
Your obedient servant,

U. S. Grant
Lieutenant-General United States Army

That morning, Lee's effort to advance to Appomattox Station was repulsed by Sheridan and Ord.

When Lee received Grant's note, his small, unfed army had been caught in a vise, his way forward was blocked, and Meade was fast approaching his rear.

Lee's response came to Meade's headquarters.

April 9, 1865

Lieutenant General U. S. Grant

General—I received your note of this morning on the picket line, whither I had come to meet you and ascertain definitively what terms were embraced in your proposal from yesterday for the surrender of this army.

    I now ask for an interview in accordance with the offer contained in your letter of yesterday for that purpose.

Very respectfully, your obedient servant,
R. E. Lee, General

Meade sent George to find Grant and deliver Lee's note.

———————

At 2:00 p.m., Meade's ambulance arrived at the front line. Humphreys was forming a battle line in preparation for an attack.

A Confederate with a white flag came through the picket line with a note from Lee asking for a ceasefire. Meade ordered one. *This had to be the end. Lee's shrunken army couldn't go on. Could it?*

At 4:00 p.m., word came that Lee had surrendered!

Meade had a rush of adrenaline and with his son's help, managed to get on his horse.

He rode through the troops, waving his slouch hat over his head and yelling, "Boys, your work is done! Lee has surrendered!"

The men wildly cheered him! He felt an enormous emotional release. He thanked God that the terrible conflict was over and the country would be one again! Through God's grace, he had survived the carnage and would return to Margaret and the children.

Meade soaked in the happiness of his men. Muskets were discharged, cannons fired, and bands were playing. Meade felt joy—four years of bloodshed were over! The rebellion had been crushed, and the nation would be reunited!

APPOMATTOX CAMPAIGN

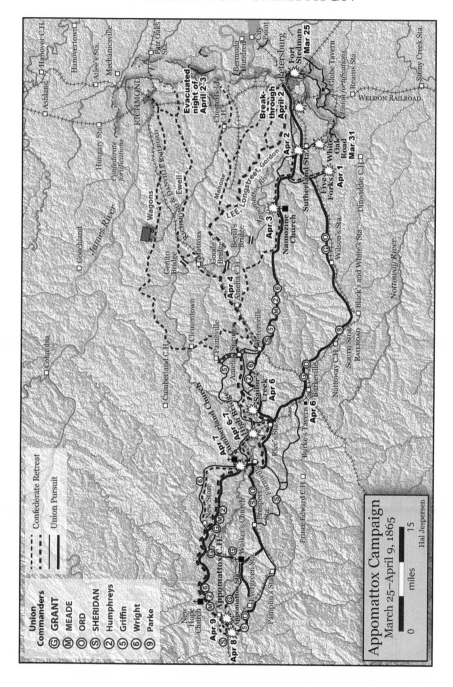

Appomattox Campaign
March 25–April 9, 1865

Hal Jespersen

CHAPTER 104

The next morning, Meade, George, and Lyman crossed the picket lines and were riding to the Confederate encampment.

Lyman asked, "Do you feel snubbed by General Grant not inviting you to the surrender meeting with General Lee? Sheridan and Ord were there. It's outrageous that nobody from the Army of the Potomac was present!"

"It was Grant's decision. I give thanks to God that the war is over."

"Father, technically the war is not over. Johnston's army is still in North Carolina."

"I can't imagine that Johnston won't soon surrender to Sherman. With Lee's surrender, for all intents and purposes the war is over."

They met General Lee riding out from his camp. He was a stately looking man, tall, erect, and strongly built, with clear brown eyes, a neatly trimmed beard, and thick white hair. He was wearing a blue military overcoat and a gray hat.

Meade took off his hat. "Good morning, General Lee."

Lee stared at him. "Sir, you look familiar, but I cannot place you."

"I am General Meade."

"George Meade? I didn't recognize you with all that gray in your beard."

"You're the cause of most of that gray! General, this is my son George and my aide, Colonel Lyman."

Lee courteously saluted. "It is good to make your acquaintance. General Meade, please come back to my camp. It has been many years since we have seen each other. You know so many of our officers from the old army and the Mexican War. I'm sure there are many men who would like to see you."

"General Lee, thank you for the invitation. I look forward to seeing old friends."

When they got to the Confederate camp, Lee and Meade sat on chairs in front of Lee's tent before a blazing fire.

"General Meade, I was surprised you were not at yesterday's surrender meeting."

"It was Grant's show, and I was not invited."

"Grant gave us liberal terms. Would you like to see the surrender agreement?"

"Yes, I would."

Lee summoned an aide, who brought the document and handed it to Meade.

Headquarters Armies of the United States
Appomattox Court House, Virginia, April 9, 1865

General R. E. Lee
Commanding CSA

General:

In accordance with the substance of my letter to you of the 8th instant, I propose to receive the surrender of the Army of Northern Virginia on the following terms, to wit: Rolls of all the officers and men to be made in duplicate, one copy to be given to an officer to be designated by me, the other to be retained by such officer or officers as you may designate. The officers to give their individual paroles not to take up arms against the Government of the United States until properly exchanged, and each company or regimental commander to sign a like parole for the men of their commands. The arms, artillery, and public *property to be parked and stacked, and turned over to the officers appointed by me to receive them. This will not embrace the side-arms of the officers, their private horses or baggage. This done, each officer and man will be allowed to return to his home, not to be disturbed by United States authority so long as they observe their paroles and the laws in force where they may reside.*

U. S. Grant
Lieutenant-General

Meade looked at Lee. "Grant's terms that Confederate soldiers will not be disturbed by US authorities would seem to preclude treason trials. That is a good thing. It's time for our country to be one again. Virtually all Union officers and soldiers, including me, have great respect for the Southern soldiers. As Lincoln so eloquently said in his second inaugural address, 'with malice toward none.' Now is the time for reunification, not recriminations."

"I'm personally prepared for reunification, but the war is not over. General Johnston has a sizable army in North Carolina, there are Confederate troops in other parts of the South, and Jefferson Davis has not given up."

"Don't you think Johnston will surrender now? It would be criminal to shed more blood at this point."

Lee paused. "I think he will surrender."

"Davis fled Richmond and is on the run. Your army was the heart and soul of the Confederacy. Now that it has been captured, the war has to end."

Lee looked solemn. "Your point is well taken."

"General Lee, do you remember in Mexico when General Winfred Scott took his staff and all his engineers on a cruise of Veracruz Bay on that small steamship *Petrita*?"

Lee's eyes gleamed. "I will never forget it!"

Meade thought back to that memorable day in 1847 when General Scott had scouted the Mexican defenses to find a place on the coast for an invasion landing. He boldly had the *Petrita* sail close to the fortress San Juan de Ulúa.

Lee continued. "It was a mistake to get so close to that old Spanish fort. The Mexicans started hurling cannonballs at us, and a few came close to hitting the mark. I came closer to dying than I ever did in this war."

"There were a lot of future commanding generals on that ship. George McClellan and Joe Johnston were with us."

A loud, gruff voice said, "It's true! George Meade is in our camp!"

Meade looked up and saw the burly figure and smiling face of General Longstreet.

He stood up and shook Longstreet's hand. "Pete, it is good to see you. I'm glad you recovered from being shot in the Wilderness."

"I was luckier than Stonewall Jackson."

"Grant thinks a lot of you."

"We were close before the war. I saw Grant yesterday after the surrender. It was like seeing a long-lost brother." Longstreet paused. "I remember our adventures in Mexico. We were such a brotherhood there. You were the brave topographical engineer who advanced in front of the infantry to find weak points in the Mexican defenses before our attack on Monterey."

Meade spent a delightful three hours catching up with friends from the old army who had fought for the Confederacy.

Headquarters Army of the Potomac, Appomattox Court House, April 10, 1865

My Dearest Margaret,

The telegram will have announced to you the surrender of Lee and the Army of Northern Virginia. This I consider virtually ends the war. I have been today in the Rebel camp; I saw Lee, Longstreet, and many others, among them Mr. Wise. They were all affable and cordial. Mr. Wise looked old and feeble and said he was very sick, had not a mouthful to eat. I secured him the privilege of an ambulance to go home, and, on my return to camp, immediately dispatched George with an ambulance load of provisions to him. He inquired very affectionately about yourself, your mother, and all the family.

The officers and men are to be paroled and allowed to go home, where they all say they mean to stay.

I have been quite sick, but I hope now, with a little rest and quiet, to get well again. I have seen but few newspapers since this movement commenced, and I don't want to see any more for they are full of falsehood and of undue and exaggerated praise of certain individuals who take pains to be on the right side of reporters. Don't worry yourself about this; treat it with contempt. It cannot be remedied, and we should be resigned. I don't believe the truth ever will be known, and I have a great contempt for history. Only let the war be finished, and I returned to you and the dear children, and I will be satisfied.

Your Loving Husband George

CHAPTER 105

Being an unpaid volunteer, Lyman could leave the army any time he wished. Now that Lee had been defeated, he felt it was time to go home to his family in Boston. He should be overflowing with joy and thankfulness at the victory over Lee but found himself boiling and fuming over the neglect of Meade and the undeserved prominence given to Sheridan.

When he entered his tent to pack up, he found an envelope on his desk.

Headquarters Army of the Potomac
April 11, 1865

Lt-Col. Theo. Lyman, A.D.C.

Colonel:
In parting with you after an association of over twenty months, during which time you have served on my Staff, I feel it due to you to express my high sense of assistance I have received from you, and to bear testimony to the zeal, energy, and gallantry you have displayed in the discharge of your duties. I shall ever preserve the liveliest reminiscences of our intercourse, and wherever our

separate fortunes may take us, I shall ever have a deep interest in your welfare and happiness, which, by the blessing of God, I trust may long be continued.

Most Truly Your Friend

Geo. G. Meade
Maj-Genl. U.S.A.

Lyman felt tears welling in his eyes. The recognition from Meade, who didn't hand out compliments freely, was meaningful. He carefully folded the letter and placed it inside a notebook that had cataloged his wartime experiences.

Headquarters Army of the Potomac, Burkesville, Va, April 12, 1865

My Dearest Margaret,

Your indignation at the exaggerated praise given to certain officers, and the ignoring of others, is quite natural. I have fully performed my duty and have done my full share of the brilliant work just completed, but if the press is determined to ignore this, and the people determined, after four years' experience of press lying, to believe what the newspapers say, I don't see there is anything for us but to submit and be resigned. Grant I do not consider so criminal. With Sheridan, it is not so. His determination to absorb the credit of everything done is so manifest as to have attracted the attention of the whole army, and the truth will in time be made known. His conduct toward me has been beneath contempt and will most assuredly react against him in the minds of all just and fair-minded persons.

My army is being assembled around this place, where I presume we will await events in North Carolina. The prevailing belief is that Johnston, on learning the destruction of Lee's army, will either surrender or disband his.

Your Loving Husband George

———————————⊸

Six days after Lee's surrender, Meade was still enjoying the afterglow of the great Union victory. Grant had gone to Washington, and Meade attended to the details of refitting the army if Joe Johnston didn't do the sensible thing and surrender to Sherman.

His son entered Meade's tent, all the color drained from his face. With a trembling hand, he held out a telegram. "Father, I bring terrible news."

Meade's body tensed, and he felt a jolt of fear. Had something horrible happened to Margaret or one of the children? He silently took the paper from his son's hand.

Meade read the telegram from Stanton in shock and disbelief.

PRESIDENT LINCOLN WAS MURDERED AROUND TEN O'CLOCK LAST NIGHT IN HIS PRIVATE BOX AT FORD'S THEATER BY AN ASSASSIN WHO SHOT HIM THROUGH THE HEAD WITH A PISTOL BALL. THE ASSASSIN OF THE PRESIDENT LEAPED FROM THE BOX BRANDISHING A DAGGER, EXCLAIMING SIC SEMPER TYRANNIS! AND NOW VIRGINIA WAS REVENGED. MR. LINCOLN FELL SENSELESS FROM HIS SEAT AND REMAINED IN THAT STATE UNTIL TWENTY-TWO MINUTES AFTER SEVEN O'CLOCK, AT WHICH TIME HE BREATHED HIS LAST BREATH.

Meade bent his head in despair. His sense of personal loss was profound. He had grown fond of Lincoln. He had admired the President's good nature, sharp wit, intelligence, and supreme political skills. Meade felt a sense of dread. *What kind of policies would come out of Washington without Lincoln's guiding hand?*

Meade slowly walked to his camp desk. He sat down in a daze. He had to inform the men that their beloved Father Abraham had been cruelly taken from them.

Hdqrs, Army of the Potomac, April 15, 1865

The major-general commanding announces to the army the death, by assassination, of the President of the United States. The President died at 7:22 this morning.

By this Army this announcement will be received with profound sorrow, and deep horror and indignation. The President, by the active interest he took in the welfare of this Army, and by his presence in frequent visits, endeared himself to both officers and soldiers, all of whom regarded him as a generous friend.

An honest man, a noble patriot, and sagacious statesman has fallen! No greater loss, at this particular moment, could have befallen our Country. Whilst we bow with submission to the unfathomable and inscrutable decrees of Divine Providence, let us earnestly pray that God, in his infinite mercy, will so order, that this terrible calamity shall not interfere with the prosperity and happiness of our beloved country!

George G Meade
Major-General, Commanding

CHAPTER 106

Johnston surrendered his army to Sherman. The new President, Andrew Johnson, determined the Union armies should celebrate victory by parading through Washington. Sheridan was supposed to lead the Grand Review, but Grant sent him to Texas because a Rebel army there had not surrendered.

At 9:00 a.m. on May 23, 1865, a beautiful sunny day, a signal gun fired, and Meade led the eighty thousand men of the Army of the Potomac from Capitol Hill down Pennsylvania Avenue, past huge, adoring crowds.

The infantry marched twelve men wide across the broad avenue. Sunshine sparkled off their bayonets. The marching men and the cavalry stretched seven miles.

The mood was festive and celebratory. The city's school students stood on the Capitol steps and terraces and sang patriotic songs as troops passed.

For this day, the Army of the Potomac was Meade's. He felt a deep sense of pride and accomplishment. He had seen the horrific conflict through to a victorious conclusion. The United States was one nation again. It was God's will that he survived the national bloodletting.

What a glorious day! He felt the cheers and adulation of the crowd pulse through his body.

He saw the Stars and Stripes flying from buildings decorated with Fourth of July bunting. Thousands of people lining the street were joyously waving American flags at Meade and his men. He thought of those brave souls who hadn't survived to march in the victory parade. Hundreds of thousands of Union soldiers, like his friend Reynolds, had not died in vain.

Meade was proud of his inner strength and toughness that helped him survive the dirty politics of Washington and malicious press attacks. The machinations of men like Dan Sickles and the blatant bias of the Committee on the Conduct of the War had not brought him down.

He thought of his family. George had proven a good soldier, courageous in the face of the enemy. Meade was proud of him. Margaret had been a tower of strength. Her love and support had helped sustain him through all the ups and downs. She had endured Sergeant's passing with Christian fortitude and grace.

Meade wondered about his legacy. His contributions to winning the war were the equal of any Union general, save Grant. Before Gettysburg, Lee had appeared invincible. If he hadn't beaten the great Southern warrior when Lee and his army were at their zenith, there may have been a different ending to the war. The harsh political and newspaper smears had tarnished his reputation. Because of the news boycott, he had virtually disappeared during the last year of the war. Would history forget him?

As the White House came into view, he felt a sense of great loss. Lincoln's indomitable will and political acumen had led to victory.

When Meade reached the White House, he saluted President Johnson and Lieutenant General Grant, who were in the reviewing stands. He dismounted and joined Grant and General William Tecumseh Sherman, whose Western army would march tomorrow.

Sherman warmly shook Meade's hand. "Your Potomac boys are mighty impressive-looking soldiers. I don't think my ragged Westerners will make as good an appearance when they march."

Meade laughed. "General Sherman, I am confident your men will do you proud."

Meade spent the next six hours saluting his men as they marched past. He had fought with them and bled with them and was leading at the forefront when victory was achieved over their archnemesis, Lee and the Army of Northern Virginia.

AFTERWORD

JOHN REYNOLDS'S FIANCÉE, KATE HEWITT

Reynolds's body was taken to his sister Catherine's home in Philadelphia, where his family found Kate's Catholic medal and gold ring around his neck. On the morning of July 3, before Pickett had charged at Gettysburg, Kate appeared to pay her respects. Catherine and her sisters welcomed their beloved brother's fiancée. After Reynolds's burial in Lancaster, Hewitt applied for admission to the Sisters of Charity Convent in Emmitsburg, Maryland. Hewitt stayed at the convent for three years but did not become a nun. She never married.

GEORGE MCCLELLAN

He had a successful business career and was elected governor of New Jersey.

AMBROSE BURNSIDE

He was elected governor of Rhode Island and later to the US Senate, where he was serving at the time of his death.

JOSEPH HOOKER

Hooker led President Lincoln's Springfield, Illinois, funeral procession. After the war, he suffered poor health.

WINFIELD SCOTT HANCOCK

In 1870, he ordered the Second Cavalry at Fort Ellis to provide a military escort for General Henry Washburn's exploration of the Yellowstone

Region. The expedition was a major impetus for creating Yellowstone National Park. Mount Hancock in the park is named for him. He was the Democratic nominee for president in 1880. He lost the election to James Garfield.

HENRY HALLECK
On his death, he left a large inheritance to his wife, the granddaughter of Alexander Hamilton.

EDWIN STANTON
He stayed on as Secretary of War under President Johnson. A conflict developed with Johnson. Congress passed a law making it illegal for the President to fire the Secretary of War without Senate consent. Johnson dismissed Stanton, leading to his impeachment by the House of Representatives. When the Senate fell one vote short of convicting Johnson, Stanton resigned and resumed his law practice. In December 1869, he was nominated to the Supreme Court by President Grant. Stanton died five days after receiving the nomination.

DANIEL SICKLES
Until his death at age ninety-four in 1914, he advocated that he was the true hero of Gettysburg and continued denigrating Meade. For his actions at Gettysburg, in 1897, he was awarded the Congressional Medal of Honor. He donated his amputated leg to the Army Medical Museum and Library. The museum, now known as the National Museum of Health and Medicine, still displays Sickles's leg. He played an important role in preserving the Gettysburg Battlefield. When he was reelected to Congress, he sponsored legislation creating the Gettysburg National Military Park.

FRANKLIN HASKELL
Two weeks after the Battle of Gettysburg, he wrote a long letter to his brother describing the battle. Fifteen years after the battle, his letter was published in a seventy-two-page pamphlet. In 1898, the letter was reprinted as part of a history of Dartmouth College's class of 1854, which included Haskell. The description of Pickett's Charge in this novel is taken in part from Haskell's letter.

GOUVERNEUR WARREN

Warren requested a court of inquiry to exonerate him from the stigma of Sheridan's action. Numerous requests were ignored or refused until after Grant's Presidency. President Hayes ordered a court of inquiry that convened in 1879. The Court found Sheridan's relief of Warren unjustified. The results were published after Warren's death.

PHILIP SHERIDAN

He led the army in the Indian Wars in the West. The quote, "The only good Indians I ever saw were dead" is attributed to Sheridan, although he denied saying it. He advocated for the extinction of buffalo herds to keep Indians on reservations. In 1886, when Congress cut off funding for Yellowstone National Park, Sheridan ordered the US cavalry into the park. The military operated the park until the National Park Service took it over in 1916. Mount Sheridan in the park is named for him.

ROBERT E. LEE

Lee was indicted but never tried for treason. Grant vigorously interceded with Stanton and President Johnson, arguing that his parole of Lee at Appomattox had to be honored. Johnson issued a proclamation of amnesty and pardon to the Confederates who had participated in the rebellion with certain exceptions, which included Lee. Lee signed an Amnesty Oath, but it was not accepted, and he was denied citizenship and the right to vote. In 1975, Congress posthumously restored Lee's citizenship.

Lee's Arlington plantation was seized by the Federal government for the failure to pay a special tax levied on the property of insurrectionists. Today it is Arlington National Cemetery.

Lee promoted reconciliation and became president of what is now Washington and Lee University.

ULYSSES S. GRANT

He was elected President in 1868, running as a Republican, and was reelected in 1872. He created the Justice Department and used it to prosecute the Ku Klux Klan, which was using violence to deny freed blacks their civil rights. Although Grant was honest and did not use public office for personal gain, corruption scandals marred his admin-istrations. After his Presidency, friends bought him a home on New York's Upper East Side. He was deceived in business and lost all his money. He was broke and dying of throat cancer when his friend Mark Twain urged him to write his memoirs, which were a critical and com-mercial success and provided money for his widow. He and his wife, Julia, are entombed in New York's Riverside Park in North America's largest mausoleum.

MEADE'S SON GEORGE
He remained in the army until his father's death. He resigned from the army and became a successful Philadelphia businessman.

THEODORE LYMAN
He continued his scientific pursuits. He was a member of the American Academy of Arts and Sciences and the National Academy of Sciences and an overseer of Harvard University. He acquired hundreds of acres of land to preserve the spawning grounds of the sea-run red brook trout. The Lyman Reserve, near Wareham, Massachusetts, is open to the public. He was an acute observer. His letters to his wife during the time he was Meade's aide were published under the title *Meade's Headquarters*. His private notebooks were published under the title *Meade's Army*.

OLD BALDY
The warhorse outlived his master by ten years. At Meade's funeral, Old Baldy followed the caisson carrying Meade's casket as the rider-less horse. After the warhorse's death, two soldiers dug up his body and took the head to a taxidermist. Old Baldy's head is on display at Philadelphia's Grand Army of the Republic Museum and Library.

GEORGE GORDON MEADE
The Committee on the Conduct of the War's *Gettysburg Report* was issued May 22, 1865, the day before the Grand Review. While critical of Meade, public interest in such reports had waned.

Grant assigned Meade command of the Military Division of the Atlantic, headquartered in Philadelphia. Living on Delancey Place, he took daily walks with Margaret. He was appointed a commissioner of Fairmount Park and took a deep interest in the development of the park. He enjoyed riding through the park on Old Baldy.

After the Reconstruction Acts of 1867, which set conditions the eleven seceding states needed to meet for readmission to the Union, Meade was assigned a command overseeing reconstruction in Georgia, Alabama, and Florida, with his headquarters in Atlanta. In 1869 he returned to command in Philadelphia. Meade was bitterly disappointed when his junior in rank, Sheridan, was promoted over him to the position of lieutenant general.

He remained on active duty until 1872. At fifty-six, he caught pneumonia and died in his wife's Delancey Place home. His pallbearers were Generals Sheridan, Humphreys, Wright, and Parke. President Grant and General Sherman were among the many dignitaries who attended Meade's funeral. He is buried in Philadelphia's Laurel Hill Cemetery beside his wife, Margareta, whom he called Margaret. She outlived him by fourteen years.

There are statues of Meade on Old Baldy at Gettysburg and Philadelphia. A statue honoring Meade stands in front of the Federal Courthouse in Washington. Fort Meade, Maryland is named in his memory. The General Meade Society in Philadelphia hosts events honoring Meade's service to his country.

Meade's letters to Margaret were edited by his son George and his grandson and namesake, George Gordon Meade. They were published in 1913 under the title *The Life and Letters of George Gordon Meade, Major-General United States Army*. Every letter in this book is from this publication. The letters have been edited for brevity, and some have been combined for narrative flow. Margaret's letters to George have never been made public.

LIST OF ORIGINAL SOURCE MATERIALS

Meade's letters to Margaret.

The pencil notes Meade received during the Battle of Antietam promoting him to command of the First Corps.

Burnside's proposed order dismissing Hooker.

Lincoln's letter to Hooker making him commanding general of the Army of the Potomac.

Halleck's letter to Meade with instructions for commanding the Army of the Potomac.

Meade's letter to Halleck accepting command.

Meade's June 28, 1863, letter to the Army of the Potomac.

Meade's Gettysburg circulars.

Meade's July 2, 1863, letters to Halleck.

Halleck and Meade telegrams on Lee's escape across the Potomac.

Halleck and Meade telegrams on Lee "bullying" Meade.

Lincoln's telegram to Meade congratulating him on breaching Lee's Rappahannock line.

Gettysburg Address.

Meade's testimony before the Committee on the Conduct of the War.

Historicus article in the *New York Herald* that falsely claimed that Meade ordered a retreat from Gettysburg.

Meade's letter requesting court of inquiry to investigate whether Sickles authorized the Historicus article.

Lincoln's letter to Meade denying his request for a court of inquiry.

Edward Cropsey's *Philadelphia Inquirer* article that falsely claimed Meade wanted to retreat after the Battle of the Wilderness.

Grant's dispatch to Stanton requesting the promotions of Meade and Sherman.

Meade/Burnside telegrams during the Battle of the Crater.

New York Independent article blaming Meade for Grant not being more successful.

Grant's dispatch to Meade commenting on the Battle of the Crater report from the Committee on the Conduct of the War.

Grant and Lee surrender correspondence.

Stanton's telegram advising of Lincoln's assassination.

Meade's letter to the Army of the Potomac informing the soldiers of President Lincoln's assassination.

The following documents are quoted in full in the book:

Antietam pencil notes

Lincoln's letters to Hooker and Meade

Meade's June 30, 1863, circular wherein he authorizes commanders to order the instant death of soldiers who fail to do their duty

Meade's June 28, 1863, letter to Halleck

Meade's June 28, 1863, General Order

Meade's July 2, 1863, 3:00 p.m. letter to Halleck

The October 18, 1863, 8:30 p.m. telegram from Meade to Halleck about Lee's escape

The Gettysburg Address

Grant's dispatch to Meade February 9, 1865, regarding the Battle of the Crater report

Grant/Lee surrender correspondence.

Meade's letter to the Army of the Potomac informing the soldiers of President Lincoln's assassination.

The remaining materials were edited for brevity.

BIBLIOGRAPHY

In doing research for this book, I had the pleasure to read numerous insightful historical works on the Civil War. The following is a list in alphabetical order of authors whose works I read to get background for this novel.

Agassiz, George R., ed. *Meade's Headquarters 1863–1865, Letters of Theodore Lyman.* Atlantic Monthly Press, 1921.

Ambrose, Stephen E. *Halleck: Lincoln's Chief of Staff.* Louisiana State University Press, 1990.

Anders, Curt. *Henry's Halleck's War.* Guild of Indiana Press, 1999.

Bache, Richard Meade. *Life of General George Gordon Meade, Commander of the Army of the Potomac.* Henry T. Coates, 1897. Reprinted by Forgotten Books.

Brown, Kent Masterton. *Retreat from Gettysburg.* University of North Carolina Press, 2005.

Byrne, Frank L. and Weaver, Andrew T., eds. *Haskell of Gettysburg.* Kent State University Press, 1989.

Carmen, Ezra A. Edited and annotated by Thomas G. Clemens. *The Maryland Campaign of September 1862, Vol. II: Antietam.* Savas Beatie, 2012.

Calkins, Chris M. *The Appomattox Campaign.* Schroeder Publications, 2015.

Catton, Bruce. *The Army of the Potomac: Mr. Lincoln's Army*. Doubleday, 1951.

Catton, Bruce. *The Army of the Potomac: Glory Road*. Doubleday, 1952.

Catton, Bruce. *The Army of the Potomac: A Stillness at Appomattox*. Doubleday, 1953.

Chernow, Ron. *Grant*. Penguin Press, 2017.

Cleaves, Freeman. *Meade of Gettysburg*. University of Oklahoma Press, 1960.

Coddington, Edwin. *The Gettysburg Campaign*. Simon & Schuster, 1997.

Conroy, James B. *Lincoln's White House*. Roman & Littlefield, 2017.

Crenshaw, Douglas. *The Battle of Glendale: Robert E. Lee's Lost Opportunity*. History Press, 2017.

Donald, David Herbert. *Lincoln*. Simon & Schuster, 1995.

Dugard, Martin. *The Training Ground: Grant, Lee, Sherman, and Davis in the Mexican War, 1846–1848*. Bison Books, 2009.

Ent, Uzal A. *The Pennsylvania Reserves in the Civil War*. McFarland, 2014.

Fishel, Edwin C. *The Secret War for the Union*. Houghton Mifflin, 1996.

Goodwin, Doris Kearns. *Team of Rivals*. Simon & Schuster, 2005.

Gottfried, Bradley. *The Maps of Gettysburg*. Savas Beatie, 2007.

Gottfried, Bradley. *The Maps of Antietam*. Savas Beatie, 2012.

Gottfried, Bradley. *The Maps of The Bristoe Station and Mine Run Campaigns*. Savas Beatie, 2013.

Grant, Ulysses S. *Personal Memoirs of U. S. Grant*. Charles L. Webster, 1885.

Hennessy, John J. *Return to Bull Run*. University of Oklahoma Press, 1993.

Hess, Earl J. *Into the Crater: The Mine Attack at Petersburg*. University of South Carolina Press, 2010.

Hassler, James A. *Sickles at Gettysburg*. Savas Beatie, 2009.

Herbert, Walter H. *Fighting Joe Hooker*. University of Nebraska Press, 1999.

Hoptak, John David. *The Battle of South Mountain*. History Press, 2011.

Humphreys, Andrew A. *The Virginia Campaign 1864 and 1865*. Da Capo Press, 1995.

Huntington, Tom. *Searching for George Gordon Meade.* Stackpole Books, 2103.

Holtzer, Harold. *Lincoln As I Knew Him.* Algonquin Books of Chapel Hill, 1999.

Hyde, Bill. *The Union Generals Speak: The Meade Hearings on the Battle of Gettysburg.* Louisiana State University Press, 2003.

Jordan, David M. *Winfield Scott Hancock.* Indiana University Press, 1988.

Jordan, David M. *Happiness Is Not My Companion: The Life of General G. K. Warren.* Indiana University Press, 2001.

Korda, Michael. *Clouds of Glory: The Life and Legend of Robert E. Lee.* HarperCollins, 2014.

Longacre, Edward G. *The Man Behind the Guns: A Biography of General Henry J. Hunt, Commander of Artillery, Army of the Potomac.* Da Capo Press, 2003.

Laino, Phillip. *Gettysburg Campaign Atlas.* Gettysburg Publishing, 2009.

Lowe, George B., ed. *Meade's Army: The Private Notebooks of Lt. Col. Theodore Lyman.* Kent State University Press, 2007.

Marvel, William. *Burnside.* University of North Carolina Press, 1991.

Marvel, William. *Lincoln's Autocrat: The Life of Edwin Stanton.* University of North Carolina Press, 1991.

Meade, George and Meade, George Gordon. *The Life and Letters of George Gordon Meade.* Charles Scribner's Sons, 1913.

McClure, Alexander K. *Lincoln's Yarns and Stories.* John C. Winston, 1900.

Nasby, Petroleum V. *Nasby.* R. W. Carroll & Company, 1866. Reprinted by Forgotten Books, 2015.

Nichols, Edward J. *Toward Gettysburg: A Biography of General John F. Reynolds.* Pennsylvania State University Press, 1958.

O'Harrow Jr., Robert. *The Quartermaster.* Simon & Schuster, 2016.

O'Reily, Francis Augustin. *The Fredericksburg Campaign.* Louisiana State University Press, 2003.

Pennypacker, Isaac Rusling. *General Meade.* D. Appleton, 1901.

Pfanz, Harry W. *Gettysburg: The Second Day.* University of North Carolina Press, 1987.

Porter, Horace. *Campaigning with Grant.* Century, 1897.

Rafuse, Ethan S. *George Gordon Meade and the War in the East.* McWhitney Foundation Press, 2003.

Rhea, Gordon C. *The Battle of the Wilderness.* Louisiana State University Press, 1994.

Rhea, Gordon C. *The Battles for Spotsylvania Court House and the Road to Yellow Tavern.* Louisiana State University Press, 1997.

Rhea, Gordon C. *To the North Anna River.* Louisiana State University Press, 2000.

Rhea, Gordon C. *Cold Harbor.* Louisiana State University Press, 2007.

Rhea, Gordon C. *On to Petersburg.* Louisiana State University Press, 2017.

Sauers, Richard A. *Meade.* Brassey's. 2003.

Sandburg, Carl. *Abraham Lincoln: The Prairie Years and the War Years.* Harcourt, Brace, 1954.

Sauers, Richard A. *Gettysburg: The Meade-Sickles Controversy.* Brassey's. 2003.

Sears, Stephen W. *Landscape Turned Red: The Battle of Antietam.* A Mariner Book. Houghton Mifflin, 1983.

Sears, Stephen W. *To the Gates of Richmond.* Ticknor & Fields, 1992.

Sears, Stephen W. *Chancellorsville.* Houghton Mifflin, 1996.

Sears, Stephen W. *George McClellan: The Young Napoleon.* Da Capo Press, 1999.

Sears, Stephen W. *Gettysburg.* Houghton Mifflin, 2004.

Sears, Stephen W. *Lincoln's Lieutenants.* Houghton Mifflin, 1996.

Selby, John G. *Meade: The Price of Command, 1863–1865.* Kent State Press, 2018.

Smith, Jean Edward. *Grant.* Simon & Schuster, 2002.

Stahr, Walter. *Stanton.* Simon & Schuster, 2017.

Stackpole, Edward J. *They Met at Gettysburg.* Stackpole Books. 1956.

Stackpole, Edward J. *The Fredericksburg Campaign.* Bonanza Books, 1957.

Stackpole Books Editors. *Gettysburg: The Story of the Battle with Maps.* Stackpole Books, 2013.

Stewart, George R. *Pickett's Charge.* Houghton Mifflin, 1991.

Sypher, J. R. *History of the Pennsylvania Reserves.* Heritage Books, 2012.

Thompson, O. R. Howard and Rauch, William H. *History of the Bucktails.* Morning House, 1988.

Tap, Bruce. *Over Lincoln's Shoulder.* University Press of Kansas, 1998.

Trudeau, Noah Andre. *The Last Citadel.* Little, Brown, 1991.

Trudeau, Noah Andre. *Out of the Storm.* Little, Brown, 1994.

Trudeau, Noah Andre. *Gettysburg: A Testing of Courage.* Perennial. An Imprint of HarperCollins Publishers, 2001.

Trudeau, Noah Andre. *Lincoln's Greatest Journey.* Savas Beatie, 2016.

Wert, Jeffery G. *Gettysburg: Day Three.* Simon & Schuster, 2001.

Wert, Jeffery G. *The Sword of Lincoln.* Simon & Schuster, 2005.

Wittenberg, Eric J. *Little Phil.* Brassey's Inc., 2002.

Wittenberg, Eric J., Petruzzi, J. David, and Nugent, Michael F. *One Continuous Fight.* Savas Beatie, 2013.

ACKNOWLEDGMENTS

The inspiration for writing a historical novel set during the Civil War comes from my lifelong fascination with the Battle of Gettysburg, which my parents introduced me to at a young age. I read Michael Sharra's *Killer Angels* with awe at how he brought the great battle to life (although he didn't think much of Meade). That novel and ones written by Sharra's son Jeff Sharra and Ralph Peters showed me that Civil War history can be powerfully conveyed in a novel.

I want to thank the following for their tremendous help and assistance.

Professor Andy Waskie, President of the General Meade Society, for providing invaluable background information on Meade. Andy gave me a private tour of the Grand Army of the Republic Museum and Library in Philadelphia, where I came face-to-face with Old Baldy.

Hal Jespersen for his wonderfully detailed maps.

The National Park Service and its dedicated staff of Park Rangers. I made many visits to Meade's battlefields. The Park Rangers bring history to life with their very informative battlefield tours.

My editors, Clete Smith, Michelle Horn, Sharon Turner Mulvihill, and Alexander Rigby. As a first-time author, I had a lot to learn. I was fortunate to have such skilled professionals to work with. Their efforts greatly enhanced the quality of the book.

Paul Barrett, the Art Director at Girl Friday Productions, for the layout of the book and his ingenious placement of a map of Gettysburg in the top and bottom of the book cover.

My extraordinary wife, Rosa, for her editorial insights and her understanding with how much time and effort is needed to research and write a historical novel.

Grateful acknowledgment is made to the Pennsylvania Capitol Preservation Committee for permission to use the painting *General Meade and the Pennsylvania Troops in Camp Before Gettysburg*, by Violet Oakley for the book cover. The painting is part of a mural in the Pennsylvania capitol building in Harrisburg.

ABOUT THE AUTHOR

Robert Kofman is a retired labor and employment law attorney who grew up in State College, Pennsylvania. After obtaining degrees in history and political science from Penn State University, he graduated from Duke University Law School.

During his forty years of practicing law, Robert first worked for the National Labor Relations Board in Washington DC and Philadelphia and then entered private practice in Miami, Florida. Prior to his retirement, Robert was rated among the best lawyers in his legal specialty—labor and employment law—by a number of legal publications, including *The Best Lawyers in America* and *Chambers USA*.

A dedicated runner of thirty-eight years, Robert ran six marathons before injury forced him to the sidelines. Happily married, Robert and his wife, Rosa, live together in Miami, Florida, where they enjoy spending time with their four daughters and four grandchildren.

Fascinated with the Civil War ever since his parents took him to the Gettysburg battlefield at the age of nine, Robert's first novel, *General Meade: A Novel of the Civil War*, focuses on the subject.

Made in the USA
Coppell, TX
20 October 2022

85003816R00312